The Dastard's Progress

● ● ●

*What need had I of Knights, bishops and rooks? I played
the pawn, and thus I took the King*

The journals of H. Sykes Esq; Member of Parliament for Towcester
and Weedon

To Benjamin and Jemima, with much love.

James Anstice

ISBN: 1494969521
ISBN 13: 9781494969523

May 1661: The Tower of London

I shall not trouble my readers with repeated references to my regrets and lamentations over my dissolute and misspent life. While I have time I will tell this extraordinary tale from my eyes as they beheld events unfolding. To do otherwise would underplay – rather than overstate – my repentance. Cum finis est licitus, etiam media sunt licita: this is an evil maxim. Read the following; I shall explain...

I

Sabbath Unrest.

My name, I will tell you immediately, is He-died–for-our-sins Sykes. The giving of long, drawn-out references to Jesus' suffering - or instructions on how to live a godly life - as Christian names was, by the time of my birth, high fashion in Puritan society. It was a custom that began in the reign of Queen Elizabeth, but which by the time of my birth had become something of a competition between people who were willing to use the naming of their children as a means of outdoing one another in outward forms of holiness. My father clearly believed he would be regarded as the godliest man in Northamptonshire for naming me thus. The effect upon my life of being thus baptised cannot be over-stated, and I will therefore, with my readers' permission, return to the matter shortly.

I was born in the Year of our Lord 1617, and raised at Caldecote Grange, near the market town of Northampton by my father, who was a farmer as well as a self-appointed man of God, and my mother's elder sister. My mother died in my infancy, and my memories of her kind eyes and her warm, loving voice have therefore faded with the passing seasons. In worldly terms I am of gentle birth, my ancestors having arrived in England with the Duke of Normandy in 1066. But it was only during the reign of King James I, in the year of our Lord, 1620, that my father's elder brother was granted the newly created Baronetcy of Caldecote Manor.

Much of my childhood was spent trying to avoid my father, of whom I was terrified. He was unpredictable: normally stern, occasionally ferocious, but also capable of sudden displays of affection. When this last sort of mood took him he would become even more fearsome than when he was angry, as he believed that I, whilst a young child, would enjoy such games as being gripped by the ankles and carried upside down into the garden, where he would swing me around his head before throwing me into a gorse bush or into the pond that separated our garden from the meadows beyond, whilst laughing uproariously. But at some point during each of these un-sought for (and highly abusive) playtimes, his expression would suddenly darken, and he would find cause to rebuke me for being a 'tomfool,' even while I was screaming in the middle of the gorse bush, or crying out for his assistance as I attempted to disentangle myself from the reeds in our filthy duck pond.

My aunt (whose original name was 'Eve,' but who had been renamed 'Meekness' - against her will - by my father when my mother and she first became members of his spiritual flock) atoned for my father's ferocity by granting me everything I wished for, or in fact demanded from her. She was a weak and pious soul and I remember her with fondness, even though, as a young child, I used to bite and scratch her if I could not get my way in some matter, or was denied something that I wanted.

My story begins in my sixteenth year, by which time I had been forced to the conclusion that, at least in the most apparent sense, I am almost, but *not quite*, handsome. My nose, which is rather large and bends somewhat to the left, is the most noticeable cause of this. Moreover, my eyes betray, I have been told by many, a furtive and deceitful expression, (although others – the more discerning of my acquaintances - have occasionally been so kind as to describe them as intelligent). I have a sturdy and attractive chin, but will make no other defence of my appearance, as its effect would, I believe, have been ruined by shallow good looks. It is one of dark, mysterious and even sinister menace. I have light brown hair, but this has never diminished that shadowy and foreboding air I here write of (possibly, at least in part, because I was forced as a child and a young man to wear a high-steepled puritan hat whenever I appeared in public, or in fact even stepped outside of my house). It was largely due to the disadvantages here mentioned that my attempts to woo Gwendolyn Smith - a buxom, black-haired serving girl of my uncle's – were rejected as often as I made them.

I confided (whilst omitting to mention the cause) the pique I had felt at one such rejection to my loving and worthy aunt.

"Nay son," she hastily replied, "Fret thee not that Gwendolyn Smith has rejected thee for thine ungainly appearance. What does she know of the hidden treasures that God has planted within thee? Did not our Lord say, when instructing Samuel to choose David as King of Israel, that we creatures are capable only of discerning the outward man, while God discerns the heart?"

She sought to bring me comfort by these words, but unfortunately chose to say them in the garden of our house, and at a time when my cousin Richard, whom I detested, happened to be passing on the road to Northampton. "Aye, but wasn't King David supposed to be good looking?" he asked with a smirk, "I don't think that scripture's going to explain away *that* face very easily."

I cast aside the humiliation I felt at this mockery and took my loving aunt's words to heart. Nevertheless, my childhood and early adulthood were much marred by persecutions from this cousin of mine. From an early age he had delighted in ridiculing me for my drab puritan attire and for the ostensibly pious ways of my father.

He was, however, merely aping his seniors. His father, Sir Richard Sykes Bt., my father's elder brother by about five years, was in a position - being the owner of the nearby manor house and estate - to spread the Gospel and influence the vulgar people for the better, as was his duty. Instead of this he used to encourage the yokels under his charge to make free with their Sunday afternoons after the fashion of pagans and heathens, and to mock our godly ways.

• • •

My memoirs begin in the spring of 1633, the eighth year of the hapless reign of King Charles I. Soon after I attained the age of sixteen, on a bright and warm Sunday afternoon, my father for the first time ordered me to accompany him to the meadow next to the small village of Tiffield, which lay about two miles from the Grange, in order to witness with my own eyes the evil prevalent in our community, which, he said, manifested itself particularly upon the Sabbath day. My father, I knew, had many times sallied forth to, as he termed it, 'evangelise the masses' at these gatherings, but I had never been allowed to accompany him.

As we walked together he explained our purpose.

"Know ye son that the instruction of the Lord is to remember the Sabbath day and to keep it holy?"

"Of course I do, father," I replied in a manner of meekness and in the attitude of one who awaited religious instruction. (When my father spoke in this sort of exaggerated Old Testament language I knew that he was in a particularly pious mood, and would therefore brook no questioning or contradiction).

"And dost thou remember that all thy life I have protected thee, whilst thou wert a suckling babe and a child, from the snares of the wicked one?"

"Yes father" I replied, meekly.

"Well son, you are about to witness the evil from which I have protected thee. Needs must ye know that the so-called King of this country, who could order his people to spend their Sabbath days as the Bible instructs us, encourages them instead to spend their time after morning worship in gathering to frolic upon such places as Tiffield Meadow; that these frolicsome activities consist of idle pursuits such as wrestling and maypole dancing; that, moreover, the young men and womenfolk sing songs after the habit of heathens; and worse, the women raise lascivious eyes - suggestive of an enticement to even more evil - to the young men?"

"How troubling, Father," I replied.

"Know ye also that your uncle, who is my brother after the flesh, encourages and funds these activities, not least in the subsidising of wine and ale to the unruly masses, causing no doubt, through the intoxication of the senses, the common people to fall into the ways of fornication?"

"I, er…"

"Well the time has come for you to share my burden: that being to warn these heathen of the wrath to come."

"What do you wish me to do, Father?" I asked nervously.

"For the moment son, I desire you to stand by my side: to watch and learn; and to do as I do, unless otherwise instructed. You will find that not so much has changed since the days of the holy prophets, and like unto them we must call forth the vengeance of the Lord upon those who hear and yet reject His word…not to mention the fact that His vengeance will be required against those who will, without a doubt, mock thee for thy physiognomy."

These words (yes, even my father's unnecessary reference to my face) proved prophetic to a degree I could not have expected. As we approached the edge of the village, the sounds that reached my ears were those of a musical incantation and revelry that I had been raised to believe were a stink in the nostrils and a piercing in the ears of the Almighty. We met at the same time, and travelling in the same direction as ourselves, my father's friend Joseph 'Trustworthy' Fairweather (hereafter referred to as Trustworthy), with his son Praise God. With them also were a small group of faithful brethren from the congregation, mostly of the Yeoman class.

"Good morrow, Trustworthy" my father said, condescendingly.

"Good Morrow to thee, Elder William."

My father and Trustworthy Fairweather spent a short time in private conference and then, having instructed the other members of the congregation to pray and sing psalms as they followed, began to make their way to Tiffield Meadow. As my father and Trustworthy led the way, both of them with a familiar expression of authority and purpose, I could not help feeling a certain pride when I was beckoned forward to walk beside them, whilst the rest of the congregation were left to follow in our wake.

As we arrived we beheld, ahead of us to our right, a set of targets being fired upon with bows and arrows by an unseemly rabble of the peasant class. Standing upon a grass mound, and apparently judging the proceedings, was my uncle Richard. He was laughing merrily at the jests of those around him and loudly encouraging the participants. He had a tankard of ale in his hand and appeared to be drinking from it freely. Ahead of us to the left, my cousin and some of his young 'gentlemen' friends were playing a game upon horseback in which they charged forth and attempted to shoot from its shoulders the head of a man made from straw, which was being moved along a pulley device by one of my uncle's farm hands. But what shocked me more than any of this was the sight I beheld ahead of us: the common people of the village, of both sexes, conversing, laughing and cavorting around a makeshift tent, apparently resting after a jaunt around the village may-pole.

My father turned and addressed us thus: "Let it never be said that we were unwilling to shout forth the name of the Lord from the rooftops. Even though the hearts of the people are hardened to the point of irretrievable damnation, we shall speak: 'Until the cities be wasted without inhabitant, and the houses without man, and the land be utterly desolate.'"

He then cried with a loud voice, "Be bold and follow me!"

As we made our way towards the throng, chanting the Twenty Third Psalm as we went, I noticed that the people became aware of our presence, and as they did so they started to groan and mutter amongst themselves. My cousin, who was galloping forward to fire at the target as we approached, missed and appeared to curse, although I could not make out his words above the sound of our singing. We made our way through the bulk of the rabble, and as we did so I became aware that I was being glared at by Gwendolyn Smith, who had been serving food from the tent. Her tight bodice gave the impression that her breasts were fighting to break free from the shift she was wearing. I averted my eyes, afraid that my desire for her would become apparent to my father. But as this happened I could not help but notice her smirking and talking to one of the hussies in her company, whilst nodding in my direction. At first I coloured deeply. But then I thought that possibly, just possibly, they were not mocking me, but rather remarking that a *real* man had at last come among them.

My father and Trustworthy led us into the middle of the crowd. They then began to preach boldly: "Turn, ye. Turn, ye from the ways of wickedness; make straight the path of the Lord; the day of the Lord approacheth like a thief in the night. Be thou ready; be thou prepared!"

Some of the crowd, at these words, seemed ashamed of their actions, and any who had tried to ignore us soon stopped what they were doing also. He, realising that his words were having their desired effect, began to preach all the more fervently. "Think ye that ye may say on the great day of judgement that thou wert led into such wickedness by thy betters? Know ye not that God sees into thy hearts and will account thee blameworthy for thy own doings?" He then glanced up at my uncle and, still addressing the crowd said, "Know ye not also that God may be willing to use repentant sinners to bring down those who hold a devilish authority upon this earth, from their high places?"

At these last words my uncle waxed wroth, and began to make his way through the crowd; the people, by now silent, made way for him. I noticed that my cousin and two or three of his friends, who by now had dismounted, were also heading towards us. I remained close to my father as the assembled people began to press in upon us.

"And just what," my uncle exclaimed loudly, "is happening here which is contrary to Holy Scripture? How dare you incite these people?"

My father ignored him, and continued addressing the crowd. "Know ye that it is the intention of the Lord that the Sabbath should be kept apart for the purposes of prayer and religious instruction. That which ye do which is contrary to this commandment is an abomination in His eyes."

The people, I noticed at this point, began to murmur and whisper to one another, I believed in approbation of my father's words. He evidently agreed, for he turned triumphantly to his brother, "Thou see'est: there's fear in these faces; these people are not so far down the road to perdition as I had believed, and thou hast delighted to lead them. Return ye and repent!" he shouted, again addressing the crowd.

At this point my cousin Richard, with his two friends, joined his father. "Oh very good Uncle, bravo," he said with a sneer. "Would it not be a wonderful thing for these people to have to spend their lives as miserably as you pretend to do? You could hold sway over them whilst you, shall we say, dip into the flesh and into the spirit as the mood takes you."

"What mean you, Sir?" asked my father, menacingly.

My uncle however, laid his hand upon his son's arm and said to him, "Peace Richard," He then leant forward and whispered something into his ear. Whatever he said appeared to calm him.

Moderating his tone somewhat, my cousin said "I will tell you what these people are saying. They are saying that, having spent six days of the week working hard at their business, or pulling a plough and praying before every meal; and having spent two hours in church every Sunday morning, they see no harm in enjoying themselves after a harmless fashion for one afternoon of the week. Besides which, archery practice is required by law."

"Aye and we're also saying that we'd like you all to bugger off!" shouted some ignorant and rustic farmer from the back of the crowd.

At this point the crowd, scum that they were, began to laugh; whilst my cousin merely raised an eyebrow, as if in subtle victory. My uncle, who I could see was trying not to laugh also, quieted the crowd: "Peace, friends," he shouted above the din, "And you, Josiah, shame upon you for such language in the presence of women and children." He turned again to my father, who by this time was turning scarlet with rage. He was about to speak when my father shouted "Know ye that those who mock the messengers of the Lord mock the Lord himself!"

"Well there lies the question, brother, does it not? Are we, by addressing you, really addressing a messenger of the Lord? But what say you? If you can answer this question I will not only disperse this crowd, but I will command them never to hold such a gathering forthwith: why, and for what purpose, did our Lord turn water into wine?"

"I will only discuss scripture with those who are worthy," returned my father. So saying, and exclaiming the words "Brethren, follow!" he proceeded to retreat towards the edge of the lawn.

I nudged Praise God, who all this time had been kneeling next to me, praying fervently, and we began to follow. But as we began to make our way to where my father and the others were stood, one of my cousin's friends, a certain Matthew Spencer, stood in our path.

"I have a certain question for you *He-died-for-our-sins*. Your mother was, by the report of everyone, a comely woman, before your father killed her; and he, for all his mental ailments, is a fairly normal looking fellow. How came they to produce someone with a face such as yours? Rumour has it that - perchance on one of her less holy nights - and through understandable desperation - she committed the sin of adultery with a pig."

Now this Matthew Spencer was the youngest son of a local small landowner and distantly related to a noble family, but despite his wealthy connections he was the sort of near-penniless profligate who was most dangerous to a man of godly disposition, for, as is often the way with members of the less-advantaged gentry, he was forever seeking ways of proving that he was a gentleman; and for gentlemen of this time the sport of the chase was willingly substituted at every opportunity for the sport of the persecution of the righteous.

He was, in short, a bully. I, however, was unwilling to cower before him like his other victims. As soon as Spencer spoke these words, blind with rage, I flew at him, clasping my fingers tightly round his neck. We fell to the ground and I started to choke him. He, taken completely taken by surprise, could do nothing other than try to prise my fingers from his throat. The crowd began to press in upon us and, although their amusement was plain from the sound of laughing and cheering, I was aware only of my desire to kill him, until my cousin and another fellow began dragging me away. My cousin and his accomplice, who turned out to be the one who had been pulling the straw man, eventually succeeded in separating us. I tried again to attack Spencer, who was attempting to raise himself, but my uncle stood firmly in my path.

"Press back, press back!" he shouted to the crowd, which did so. He then turned to me, "Come now, nephew" he said, placing his hand firmly upon my shoulder, "be calm, offer the other cheek lad, offer the other cheek." He then turned around to face Matthew Spencer, "You must apologise this instant, Matthew, or you will never enter my house again."

There was a moment of silence before Spencer made his way towards me and, colouring deeply, reached out his hand to shake mine. "That were a poor jest, Sykes, I am truly sorry and beg for your forgiveness."

I looked at him in disgust. "When the devil speaks to me, whether his words be sweet like syrup, or bitter like nutmeg, I'll give him the answer he deserves." So saying I spat in his face and turned on my heel.

I made my way rapidly through the throng, with Praise God following. My cousin however, walked as quickly behind me and, taking hold of my arm, managed to say into my ear, "I suppose, cousin, that was a fair, if somewhat ill-bred response, but why does your father not leave us be and stop provoking us, and now you too?"

I shook his hand off without answering and we made our way to where my father and Trustworthy were waiting for us at the edge of the lawn. I knew as I did so, whether I liked to admit it at the time or not, that our enemies had got the better of us, but only, I told myself, because the devil had given them inspiration.

II

Transformation

I awoke early on the morning after the events just described with the realisation that, however much I dreaded doing so, I would need to speak to my father of some of the words that had been spoken by Spencer and my cousin Richard the day preceding. I deemed it imprudent to address these matters too directly, for I knew from experience that my father's anger could wax unpredictably and without warning. I therefore decided to broach the subject carefully whilst we were breaking our fast.

"Father," I began…"a tush and a fie I place upon all the mocking words of my cousin and his friends…but…Father…"

"Speak plainly, my son."

"What did my cousin mean when he spake to you of the flesh and the spirit?"

He looked at me, and as he did so his eyes narrowed and darkened, piercing, it seemed, the depths of my innermost thoughts (he had always had the ability to do this).

"The time is now past in which I should speak to thee as father to child, the time is upon us for me to address thee man to man…a walk in the woods after your chores."

And with that my father turned his attention back to his food, a tacit indication that for the present our conversation was over.

• • •

After an uneventful morning, my father at last called me, and we walked in silence to the edge of the wood that separated my father's land from my uncle's estate. He instructed me to sit upon the stump of a sawed ash tree, and proceeded to pace the ground before me, his hands clasped behind his back. As he did so, and as I watched him, I decided not to brook the question of my mother's death until I had heard his explanation of Richard's words, which, I decided, was the least controversial of the matters that concerned me.

My father decided to begin his answer to my earlier question with a seemingly irrelevant ramble. "Knowest thou how thine uncle and those like him, from the King down to the meanest peasant, hope to obtain the blessing of God by genuflecting, and repeating often, vain prayers of repentance and supplication?"

"I do Father, and long ere this moment I have scorned them for their folly."

"Thou art correct to scorn them my lad, and yet, in their ignorant way, like a piglet runt searching in vain for its mother's teat, there is some instinctive function here for which we must pity them. But think deeply upon it. Hast thou thought upon the ways in which God intended His blessings to be enjoyed by His Elect?" Art thou aware that we were chosen by God to enjoy the fruits of the earth and the fullness thereof? These are not teachings for babes and sucklings, but for men. I talk here of things that wisdom hath hitherto kept secret. I must speak of these things before your cousin doth fill your heart and mind with distorted and slanderous tales."

I dared not believe, but could not refrain from hoping, that my father was alluding to some mystery which heralded a release from a fear I had always carried in my heart: a fear no less, of the ultimate consequences of a sinful nature. I was confused however, as it was none other than *he* who had instilled this fear into me from my early childhood.

I made as if to speak, but he placed his fore-finger upon my lips.

"It is not for us," he continued, "who are called to be counted among God's true elect, to fear the consequences of sin. The law was instigated by God to control and put down that which is wicked upon this earth. The law is a useful tool and, yea it must be used to beat down the sons of evil. But those who have been truly redeemed are free from the law; to us all things are lawful. Few however are counted among us."

Now my readers will doubtless understand that, as a lad of sixteen years, raised in a strict religious household, my desire for Gwendolyn Smith had sorely vexed me; and the thoughts and feelings it created within me had filled me with no small degree of fear concerning the final day of judgement. A wary excitement began to take root within me when I perceived that henceforth I might be able to live free of such restraints of conscience. At the same time, as must surely be expected, I was beginning to see my father in an *entirely* new light.

"Dost thou understand me, my lad?"

"I, I believe so father, but... does this mean that you are not a puritan, father?"

"'Tis a convenient label…"

I had rarely seen my father in so good a humour. I therefore decided to approach him directly, at least about the first of my concerns. "Begging your pardon, Father, I wondered why my cousin's words had vexed you so."

He laughed uproariously. "Out upon thee lad, I was not vexed at all!"

I became yet more confused, and my father doubtless recognised it, for he went on.

"Needs must I explain to thee first. These are the latter days. Evil waxeth strong upon the earth. The king of this country presides over a wicked court, and his papist harlot of a wife will stop at nothing to turn his heart, and the hearts of this people, back to the authority of the Roman anti-Christ. And yet there is a movement, my son - a stirring among the righteous: not only among the true elect, but even among those who, with a lesser understanding, pertain to a form of godliness. "The time is soon, nay, almost upon us, in which the Lord will smite the Amalekites once more."

This sort of thing my father had told me often. He had successfully instilled in me a hatred of the King and all that he stood for from the time of my infancy. But I did not wish to hear of this now.

"But…"

"In the meantime," my father went on, ignoring my interruption, "it beseems us to keep our purpose from the knowledge of the wicked. It beseems us also to hide even from those who have a semblance of righteousness the true extent and nature of the blessings I speak of. This, lad, is the purpose for which I had to give pretence of indignation at the accusatory words of thy hapless cousin."

"But what meant he by them, father?"

He paused, and then said, "Richard Sykes, the younger, having one summer since found me in one of his father's barns in an act of copulation with a brace of their serving wenches, was instructed by his father not to reveal this information in order to save the family honour. It is imperative for now that we let his worldly reasoning do us service."

I was, for a moment, speechless. You will doubtless appreciate that for my opinion of my father's character to be so transformed in a matter of a few moments was, for me, deeply disturbing. I could not help remembering how he, when I was a youth, had beaten me every day for the smallest acts of wickedness. Moreover, even if I had committed no misdemeanour at all, I would not infrequently be beaten for the thoughts which he alleged 'must oft contaminate my soul.' But, as I have stated, the words he spoke came to me, in part, as a pleasing balm; and I wondered whether his purpose and reasoning could overcome my disquietude at this sudden revelation of his true character.

There was one thing I needed to know however, and could not prevent myself from asking: whether Gwendolyn Smith had been one of the serving wenches.

"Nay lad," he answered with a chuckle, "although I'll have her writhing beneath my steady rhythm before many moons have passed, I'll warrant!"

This filled me with relief on the one hand, and a high sense of panic and indignation on the other. He must have sensed my confusion, although he did not understand its cause, for he placed his hand upon my shoulder and said, "Remember lad, no man having put his hand to the plough and looking back is fit for the kingdom of God."

Although exceedingly perplexed, and with a mounting sense of anger at his patronising hypocrisy, I felt an urgent need, when my father said these last words, to respond with alacrity. "Good Father," I said, "my only concern is the part I may play in bringing to fruition The Lord's judgement against the ungodly."

"Good lad," he said, his eyes twinkling once more. He pushed my chin playfully with his fist; "You see it's all about being dogmatic in doctrine, whilst being pragmatic in practice." So saying, he gave me a playful punch in the ribs and began to stroll back towards the Grange.

But I had yet to ask him the most important question of all. Although terrified of his response, I had to have an answer regarding the words spoken by Matthew Spencer.

"Sir," I said, masking my fear as best I could.

He stopped.

"What now, my lad?"

"Sir, just after you left...having convicted the rabble, yesterday, of their sinful activities, something was said to me...in regard to you... concerning my mother."

I thought I had been prepared for any response to this, including the possibility that he might attack me, but was surprised when he spoke to me extremely quietly, his voice shaking slightly as he walked back towards me.

"By whom?"

"Matthew Spencer, Sir."

"He said...what?"

"He said...that you killed her, Sir."

He attempted to answer, but found it difficult to do so without stuttering. My father had never been confounded by anything said to him by anyone, according to my memory, before.

When he at last spoke, he spoke evenly, and extremely quietly, his face inches from mine. "Thou knowest I have many enemies, my lad, wherefore art thou giving ear to their evil words?"

"I am not, father, I am just..."

"I have many enemies," he repeated, "and mine enemies have spread many calumnies concerning me. It was predictable that they would accuse me thus."

"But of what, Sir, expressly, were you suspected?"

"Of doing away with your mother by means of violence. She was careless when carrying a pewter jug full of hot water…she fell down the stairs. That is how she died; you know that is how she died"

"But father…"

"You believe me, my son."

"Of course, father."

"Then we shall broach this subject no more."

"But…"

"No more, my son," and with those words he left me.

My heart burned towards him, not least because he took my acceptance of the true revelation of his character so much for granted after having raised me like a whipping boy for his evil temper. I thought of the way he had responded with such confusion and hesitation when directly questioned about my mother's death. I believed that I would never know or be able to discover the truth of this matter, but as I thought of my father's evil temper, and his ability to change his mood so violently and so suddenly, I knew that I did not believe him. I began to resent more deeply than I ever had the authority he held over me. And why, I asked, if (according to *his* words) all things were lawful for me, should I remain under his control?

III

Desperation

My hatred of my father, however, was not limited merely to the treatment I had received throughout my life at his hands, nor to my new-found suspicion that he had killed my mother, nor to the considerable fear that Gwendolyn Smith would indeed, as he termed it, 'writhe beneath his steady rhythm before many moons were passed.' There was another cause of my vexation: I wished to attend Cambridge as an undergraduate, as I deemed myself to be of a high intellect despite my shortcomings in the field of academia. To enter Cambridge, however, was not an end in itself; nay, my ambition was to follow my uncle and enter Parliament, as it was only with the sort of power I would thus attain that the Lord's plans for my life could come to fruition.

The Lord's plans I here refer to? I was certain that He intended nothing less than to use me to overthrow the rulers and principalities that for years had been binding the Kingdoms of our Isle in a stranglehold of evil. Many people, I believe I hear you thinking, are touched by similar delusions. But I write these words with the benefit of hindsight, and could easily and conveniently forget my youthful aspirations if Destiny had not become such a witness to their justification.

My father, who himself had benefited from such an education, and who himself had ambitions to 'represent the Lord at Parliament' (as if God and the county of Northamptonshire were synonymous) had always mocked any such proposal whenever I raised it. I had attempted to persuade my tutor, Dr Hair, to recommend me for a scholarship. But this gentleman and I had never seen eye-to-eye. He was moreover, in his own words, 'deeply unimpressed with my academic abilities.'

It was on the morning following the conversation hitherto described, as I was collecting eggs from the chicken shed, that I became aware that my strong desire to enter Cambridge had turned to desperation. This realisation gave rise to a resolution and purpose that had previously been unknown to me; and alongside that resolution an idea which I believed at the time to be foolproof. I left the house after breakfast and, having bribed one of the more senior farmhands with a shilling to delegate the rest of my chores at his discretion, I made my way to the Fairweather homestead. I found Praise God in his father's study, practising calligraphy and letter-writing with the aid of a newly-published book entitled *A Precedent for Young Pen-Men*.

"Look, He-died-for-our-sins," he said with enthusiasm as I entered the room, "it says here that for a young man of lowly origin to have a chance with a maiden of noble birth then it is most expedient to drop words such as 'thee' and 'thou' from his speech, and to take up the use of expressions such as 'gadzooks!' and 'oddsfish!'"

I looked at him coldly. "This is an instruction book in 'courtly manners,'" I replied, picking the book up and casting it down again with a show of disgust, "I understood that you and I had set our faces against such frippery and vanity."

Praise God looked slightly abashed at my response and closed the book.

I sat on the chair opposite to his father's desk and, placing my feet upon it, addressed him thus: "Praise God, it is an accepted fact that you are a man of words and reading."

He listened without responding.

"I, however, although not very bookish, am known for my artful mind. I have the wit to read and write, and yet reading and writing holds little in the way of charm for me. It is also the case, is it not, that as with the Apostle Paul, I can boast both of my worldly status - hailing from the gentlemanly classes, as I do - and of my godly disposition also?"

"He looked at me with a somewhat blank expression. I continued.

"What, Praise God, do you expect to accomplish with your much learning?"

"Well," he responded, "our teacher, Dr Hair, has recommended me to the University of Cambridge."

"This I know," I said, "and afterward"?

"Well," he said slowly, "I intend to become a teacher myself."

"Yes," I said, whilst looking up at the ceiling thoughtfully, "Yes."

He waited, obviously expecting more.

I swung my legs off the desk and looked at him intently. "What Praise God, do you suppose that *I* could do with a degree from Cambridge?"

"Why, er much - a great deal - but you know that Dr Hair will never recommend you. He has always had a propensity to dislike you, both for your misbehaviour and for your poor academic accomplishments."

I chose to ignore the remark about Dr Hair for the present. "You are correct, I could attain much. You know that my uncle was the Member for the locality of Towcester and Weedon when parliament last sat, four years ago; and that he will almost certainly be too old should the King, as surely he *must* eventually, call another. My cousin Richard is unworthy and ill-suited to take up this particular mantle. It is likely, especially as this county contains such a strong puritan influence in places of authority, that my father will be chosen in the place of his brother as the next member. The obstacles therefore to prevent me from entering parliament myself are easily surmountable"

"But all this avails you nothing," replied Praise God, "*We* may agree that your cousin Richard is an unsuitable candidate for parliament, but our disapproval cannot prevent him from becoming so. And if he were somehow prevented, why should your father not go? He is fifty, it is true; but he is of good health, and he is respected throughout the locality as a man of sound virtue, free from worldly vice. But as I said, Dr Hair will not recommend you."

I resisted the temptation to shock Praise God by destroying my father's ill-deserved reputation and chose instead to concentrate on the matter in hand. "It was revealed to me last night in a dream," I lied, "as clearly as the angel Gabriel spoke to Mary concerning the imminent arrival of our Lord and Saviour, that I must take up the burden of the persecuted Christian people of this country; the blood of whom cries out to the Lord for vengeance against this wicked king and his forbears."

I paused in order to study Praise God's reaction, and was satisfied to note that he appeared to be somewhat awestruck.

"But in what manner was this information revealed to you?" he asked after a moment of silence.

"As I said, in a dream, the details of which my angelic messenger prohibited me from revealing to anyone."

Now Praise God's mind had always been a peculiar mixture of high intelligence and extraordinary naivety, especially regarding matters spiritual and supernatural. Nonetheless, I realised as I spoke that I had better push on past the dream as quickly as possible. I would not be able to maintain the deception if he asked for too much detail. The expression on Praise God's face, however, remained void of any hint of cynicism as he continued to question me.

"I still understand you not, He-died-for-our-sins. How do you propose to enter into Cambridge and thereafter into Parliament? I say to you again, notwithstanding all the other obstacles, Dr Hair will not recommend you."

"Surely with your much learning Praise God, you must have read this maxim, *Cum finis est licitus, etiam media sunt licita.*" As he looked at me in silence I translated on his behalf, "Or, 'The end justifies the means.'"

"I know what it means" he said, somewhat peevishly, "I merely wondered what *you* meant by it."

"I intend to take the place Doctor Hair has arranged for you at Cambridge. With the Lord on our side, and whilst we endeavour to do His bidding, all things are within our capability, and all things are legitimate. The first thing with which we need to concern ourselves, and the only thing with which you need to concern *yourself* for the present, is the persuasion of Dr Hair."

"But...."

"...But what, Praise God?"

"But I *want* to go to Cambridge. I have studied very hard whilst you have shown little interest in learning at all. I intended not just to teach children, but to use my education as a means of furthering the cause of the church."

"'Oh faithless generation,'" I quoted "'how long am I to be with thee? How long am I to bear with thee?'... Are you really saying - having placed your hand upon the plough, that in this faithless and wicked epoch you would place the vanity and foolishness of a worldly education above the will and purposes of God?

"In that case," Praise God replied, "why would it avail *you* any more to go to Cambridge than myself?"

"I have already explained to you that my entering Cambridge is merely a means by which I may bring about the purposes of the Lord. But (I stood up and picked up my high-steepled hat and cloak for effect, and made as if to leave the room) where the Lord wills something, the means by which it must come to pass will manifest itself. Perchance the Lord will show me another, more willing to do his bidding."

"Nay He-died-for-our-sins, stay, I never meant that I would not do the bidding of the Lord, but surely you must see that for me, if this *is* the will of God, not to attend university will be a sore disappointment."

"Do you think that any of the prophets or servants of the Lord, when giving ear to their flesh, would not have found their own chosen path preferable? The Lord has chosen you, Praise God, as an instrument to bring about His purpose upon this earth, through your service to me. Be thou grateful and rejoice. Yea, that I do repeat with a willing heart, be thou grateful and rejoice."

"I shall rejoice, I really shall, if you can show me for certain that this is God's will. It has always been my desire to serve the Lord in any way that I can. If you speak God's true purpose then I am sure He will make your path straight in the matter. If there is a means by which you may persuade Dr Hair then I will know that your words truly reflect the will of the Lord."

Praise God was clearly refusing, on this occasion, to respond quite as I had hoped. I could hardly dispute this perfectly reasonable condition. I therefore responded thus: "You speak well, Praise God. As for the means by which this will be accomplished, do not concern yourself. The Lord will grant me the words, should we do his bidding. I intend that we should visit the house of Dr Hair this very evening. Be at the village gate at seven of the clock. Let God's will be done."

So saying, I gathered again my hat and cloak and made my way out of his house, and back to Caldecote Grange.

• • •

That evening, having successfully avoided the society of both my father and my aunt throughout the day, I met Praise God at our appointed time and place, and was pleased to find him punctual also. He wished me good e'en and, as Dr Hair's house was but a stone's throw from the edge of the village, I gave him his instructions before we walked the short way there.

"Now, Praise God, you are to do nought but what I tell you. Your purpose in this visit is merely to acquiesce, silently, when I raise the issue of your intention to relinquish in favour of me the place reserved for you at Cambridge. Trust me completely, and remain stubborn and wilful against any attempt by the Doctor to weaken our resolve. Come, let us go hence."

Dr Ezekiel Hair, schoolmaster and doctor of medicine, was a man with a reputation for simplicity of living, as well as great learning. He owned a house, built during the reign of Queen Elizabeth, on the better side of the village which, although modest enough to befit a puritan gentleman of humility, was large enough to contain a schoolroom in which were educated several of the boys from the vicinity; including, of course, Praise God and myself. He was a widower whose wife had born him several children, but who had only two surviving daughters. These daughters: Abigail, the eldest, who was about twenty-five, and Esther, who was twenty-two, acted as his constant company, as well as his cook and housekeeper. You might be less surprised that they had not been married, worthy Reader, had you met them. Abigail, in her youth, had suffered from Scarlet fever, which had left marks on her face comparable to the surface of a gnarled tree. Her younger sister

Esther, although somewhat more comely in her facial appearance, had suffered as a child so badly from some ghastly, nameless disease, that she walked with the stoop of an old woman. Despite these misfortunes they were devoted to their father, and he to them. They had also suffered my taunts for years (and the taunts of any other schoolboy I could get to join me) with irritating patience and patronising charity.

As we approached the house we spied Abigail removing various items of clothing from a drying line. I realised that this presented me with a perfect opportunity to put the first part of my plan into action. I instructed Praise God to wait at the garden gate, and approached her in a respectful fashion, my hat in my hands.

"Good e'en to you, Sister Abigail," I said.

"Good e'en to you He-died-for-our-sins; and to you Praise God. Have you come to greet my father?"

"Verily we have, good sister, but also, if I might be so bold, to ask a small boon of you."

"Ask, and if it is within my power to grant it, I will do so."

"I know that it is in your power. It is merely this: Praise God and I have been studying the art of letter-writing. We have asked several learned people their opinion as how best to end an epistle. They all give advice so different. Pray, tell me, what is your view?"

She appeared to be pleased to be asked. "Why, if the letter is addressed to someone with a close tie of love and affection, then I believe it is most appropriate to end with the words 'with love,' or indeed 'with affection.' If the letter is of a formal nature, it is best to finish it with words such as 'I remain, Sir – or Madam – your most respectful, humble and obedient servant...'"

"Yes, it is that of a business nature we are most concerned with. Would it be possible, do you suppose, to end merely with the words 'sincerely yours', thus avoiding some of that flowery language?"

"Yes indeed, somewhat curt, but, maybe in the line of business curtness would be your intention?"

"I know it *could* be my intention, my father has to deal with many a surly trader, and needs must I lift some of the burden from him. I know I will forget, could you write on this sheet of paper these words, with your signature as well? If you recall my wanton school days, then you will know that knowledge escapes from my mind like water from a sieve. If you sign the paper as you normally would, it will remind me."

"Why, of course He-died-for-our-sins, let us repair to the house as you wish to see my father anyway.'"

Really, for all the impression of learning she exuded, Abigail Hair was a simpleton. I beckoned for Praise God to follow, and we entered the house.

We made our way into the schoolroom, and as she reached from a shelf a quill and pot of ink, I produced from my pocket a piece of paper upon which I had already written the following words:

We, Abigail and Esther, daughters of Dr Ezekiel Hair, hereby confess to that which is both a crime and a sin: witchcraft.

We have deliberately spurned the Church, as well as God, in the hope that the devil will improve our looks or, if not, at least cast some spell over a couple of young men in order to fool them into believing that we are attractive.

We did this deliberately because our father told us that we would never be able to leave his service, and because we have reluctantly concluded that the only way we could possibly get husbands was to sell our souls to the devil.

I had made sure, when writing this, that my words were large enough to cover the whole page, and that it would not seem strange therefore that Abigail should sign her 'confession' on the other side, and therefore never realise the extent to which, by doing so, she was incriminating herself. In reality however, when it came to accusations of things like witchcraft, everyone at that time was so frantic that they forgot everything about the due process of law. (In some particularly puritanical towns, for someone even to point out that the sisters' 'confession' was not in either Abigail's or Esther's hand-writing, or that Esther had not signed it, might lead to *themselves* being accused of witchcraft).

"I shall write 'sincerely, Abigail Hair,'" she said with pathetic enthusiasm.

She signed it thus, and gave it back to me with a smile. I then called Praise God to my side and she led us to her father's study.

Though I hate to confess it, as I had previously only entered this room to receive physical chastisement, I could not prevent myself from feeling a small degree of fear as we walked in on this occasion. Praise God, who had rarely, if ever, been beaten by the Doctor, also seemed fearful; but that, I surmised, was due to the nature of the information we were about to pass to him.

Dr Hair appeared to be pleased, and yet somewhat surprised (doubtless due to the unusual hour) to see Praise God, who preceded me into the room. His countenance appeared momentarily to change upon my entrance, although not to the point of a scowl or any hint of incivility.

"Praise God!" he exclaimed whilst rising from his chair, "how pleasant for my evening vigil to be broken, for once, by the company of men; and He-died-for-our-sins, how pleasant, how pleasant indeed. Take ye both a chair from the back of the room and sit down before me." When we had done so he added, "I will call back Abigail to bring refreshments for us all."

"Not so, Sir," I said in a voice which indicated there had been a clear exchange of authority between us, "Our business is of a serious nature and concerns the work of the Lord. Needs must we be brief."

His expression darkened. "How now Sirrah, what is this? I called you men as a token of respect befitting those who are about to enter into the world. Do not think to address me as an equal or I will take my stick to your head!"

I chose, as best I could, to ignore this in my response, as well as my expression. I stood to my feet and, placing my hands upon my hips in an authoritative manner said, "The reason we are here, Sir, is that Praise God wishes to relinquish, in favour of me, his place at Cambridge."

"What did you say?" This was the Doctor's initial response, but before I could answer he began to shout. "To take *your* place, at Cambridge, *him*, do not jest with me boy, he (pointing at me) is fit for nothing better, academically, than to be a counting clerk."

"We are in earnest, Sir," I responded, my voice rising also.

Praise God, who had been completely silent during this whole exchange, merely raised his eyebrows momentarily before turning his face to the floor.

"Well," answered the Doctor, his expression changing to that of a sneer, "I have bad tidings for you both, He-died-for-our-sins Sykes cannot go to Cambridge whether you are both in earnest or not. I can prevent *you* going (he leant over the desk and jabbed Praise God on the top of his head) but I have no power to make it possible for *him* to go. Cambridge did not become the world's greatest university by suffering fools to darken its corridors."

I kicked my chair in my anger. "I am no fool, Sir, as you are about to discover to your cost. Praise God, leave the room!"

At this the Doctor strode around his desk towards me, having clearly lost control of his temper. "How dare you give orders in my house?" he shouted, "you sanctimonious little bastard!" He then began to slap and punch us both repeatedly. Praise God covered his head with his hands and darted around us, escaping from the room.

As the blows continued to reign down upon my head, I felt for a moment like a schoolboy once more, and cowered beneath them. I soon regained my composure, however, and realised that the Doctor, being somewhat elderly, was easy to fend off and shove onto the chair I had just vacated. Having done so, I stood over him menacingly and said, "Now give me ear carefully, Doctor, I could threaten you personally, but I know that you are a man unlikely to be swayed by personal threats. You *will* however recommend me for Cambridge."

"This… is…outrageous," he said, shocked and out of breath, "you are a devil!"

"A devil you may think me, I know and care not. What I care for is this." So saying, I removed from my pocket the piece of paper so recently signed by the Doctor's daughter. "It is because of this piece of paper that I will go to Cambridge, see - your daughter's signature?" Having waved the paper in front of him, I placed it back in my pocket.

I backed away from him, hastily picking up an iron poker from the fire hearth. "Strike me again Doctor, and I will use this to break your skull open; listen carefully to what I have to say."

The Doctor, whilst struggling to regain his composure, began to mutter, "Never in all my years...you are a devil, a devil."

"And your daughter, nay both your daughters, according to the confession of Abigail, are in league with *the* devil."

"My daughter has confessed to no such wickedness. You are a liar!"

"Now stop your shouting, old man. This piece of paper, with this signature, is a confession of devilry and witchcraft...behold! (I allowed him a moment to look at the 'confession' on the other side) I intend to keep this in order to prevent you from becoming troublesome to me in the future, and to force you to do my bidding at the present."

"No one will believe you, no one," the doctor muttered in reply.

"Do you really think," I said, "that were I to report that whilst walking in the woods at night I had chanced upon your daughters dancing around a blue flame, naked - or limping in Esther's case - whilst singing incantations to the devil and casting spells, that I would not be believed? Why, I would be believed even without evidence; everybody knows that your daughters are too repulsive to tempt a man without the aid of magic. And I have the very proof here as a safeguard: a confession from the witch herself!"

The old man again made a lunge forward, with the clear intention of attacking me, but I deftly side-stepped him and gave him a sharp swipe on the right arm with the poker.

"Enough of this foolery, Doctor, you have no choice in this matter. You shall visit my father and tell him that - let us make this likely - although Praise God shone more at school academically, it is I, due to my sharp wittedness and potential in life, as well as my being by birth a gentleman, who would benefit the most from a university education, and that you have changed your mind concerning the candidate for your recommendation."

The Doctor sat upon the chair once more, rubbing his arm and glowering with the air of a man defeated. "It is well known that I have fought to give poorer students the opportunity to enter Cambridge, wherefore should people believe I have suddenly changed my principles on this matter?"

"What care I if you should come to be known as a backslider? People often change their principles."

"I tell you again, He-died-for-our-sins Sykes," said the doctor, "the Lord will bring you to a reckoning for this day, if perchance not in this world, then in the world to come. You are committing a terrible sin, that of bearing false witness against your neighbour."

"If you do as you are told, then there will be no need for me to commit such a sin, will there? As for God's reckoning, I will look to that myself."

"And just how do you intend to maintain this pretence, or even last at the university for one month before you are discovered to be a simpleton?"

"As you very well know" I said, gritting my teeth in the effort to maintain my temper, "I am no simpleton; I have got the better of you this day. The answer to your question is straight and easy, Praise God will come with me to advise, instruct and, if needs be, do my written work for me. It is befitting that I should take with me a manservant. My cousin Richard will take a manservant and cooking and cleaning wenches to boot. In this guise Praise God will accompany me. My advice to you, Doctor, is to ask few questions, the fewer the better for your own peace of mind. I know that St Gabriel's College expects you to send thither only the best of students. Fret not, I will not disappoint you."

I was now satisfied that he could be in no doubt as to my determination to carry out my threats should he not comply with my wishes. I turned to him as I was leaving the room, "I will expect you to call on my father in a space of time above that of a week and before that of a fortnight; I will tell him of your coming." As he made no attempt to reply I left him staring despondently at the wall in front of him, still rubbing his arm.

There was no sign of either of the Hair sisters as I left the house, but Praise God was waiting for me in the garden. I walked past him, nodding silently in the direction of the gate in order to communicate my desire for our quick departure. I was in extremely high spirits, having, as I believed, achieved that which I had intended with a degree of ease that even I had deemed unlikely; and so, as Praise God had played his small part in helping me to achieve my aim, I chose not to rebuke him for his cowardice. We walked, at first in silence, back towards the edge of the village.

He could plainly see from the lightness of my countenance that my purpose had been accomplished. "How," he eventually asked, "did you convince the Doctor?"

"Know you not, Praise God, that when you set about the work of the Lord, it is not enough to rely upon your own strength, but upon the Lord who speaks through you?"

We walked on in silence once more, and I knew, although I chose not to say so, that he was dismayed at my success.

"Methinks, Praise God, all things considered, that you *should* come with me to Cambridge…in order to be the servant of the Lord's servant. If you do this with a willing heart you may be counted among the greatest in the Kingdom of Heaven."

I let him ponder this in silence. Indeed, according to the workings of his mind, I believed he had no choice in the matter.

As we reached the place where the roads to our houses parted, I instructed Praise God not to inform his father, or anyone else, of our intentions until I had given him the word. I was just about to depart from him when I heard an unwelcome sound behind me: "Stop there you two!" It was the Doctor. "Stop there!"

I turned and beheld Dr Hair striding towards us, brandishing in his right hand the poker I had recently been holding. "I had," he said, "merely thought to tell your father of today's unseemly events, and I still shall, but I think that there is a certain matter that needs dealing with immediately." So saying he struck me extremely hard on my left cheek bone with the poker, causing me to fall on my back, "as for your witchcraft accusations: just you try them, you arsehole!" Having rifled through my pockets until he found the incriminating sheet of paper, he turned abruptly round and walked back to his house.

So much then, for that little plan, I had been bluffing all along and the Doctor knew it. I began to walk despondently home with my hand covering my cheek, which was bleeding profusely. Praise God walked with me for a while. "We do have the strangest dreams at times," he said, "They don't *all* reflect the will of God, do they?"

I had not the heart or will to respond.

"It is, peradventure, God's will that you should attain your destiny by another means…"

I knew not whether he was mocking me or whether he was in earnest, but I was in too much pain to care. I stumbled home in agony; my shirt a mess of tears and blood.

IV

The consequences.

The reason I gave my father and my aunt for my gashed cheek-bone was that I had fallen from a horse. But two days after my altercation with Doctor Hair my father awoke me at six of the clock by dragging me out of bed by my left ear. Without a word he pulled me to the floor and proceeded to beat me with a birch rod as I cowered beneath him, screaming and begging for mercy. He thrashed me repeatedly for about three minutes, during which time he uttered not a word.

I lay still, curled into a ball, for a long while after he stopped, waiting for him to speak; but all I heard was the sound of his heavy breathing, as well as my own involuntary whimpering.

A mixture of curiosity and fear eventually overcame me, and I dared to raise my arm, slightly, in order to perceive him.

But he was merely waiting, with the rod poised above his head, for our eyes to meet. As soon as they did so he started to thrash me again. This time, however, he spoke.

"You have humiliated me, lad. Understand this: you will not go to Cambridge. You will care for this farm. And when the godly people of this county elect me to parliament, you will care for it in my absence!" He then struck my prostrate form twice more and strode out of the room, leaving my aunt Meekness to rush in and dress my wounds.

I had been beaten so badly that for several days after this incident I was unable to rise from my bed. My father, seeming a little guilty, visited me once; and sought to bring me comfort by reminding me that 'the Grange as well as the farm would be mine when he went to sup with the Lord.'

But with my respect for him gone, and with my new-found rage burning and growing within me, I now despised him in my heart.

• • •

During those solitary days, as my wounds recovered and my bitterness festered, I brooded over the fact that I would need to become a man of property in order to enter Cambridge, as I had been forced to the conclusion that the scholarship route had become closed to me. My father, despite being the junior benefactor of my grandfather's estate, held a substantial acreage and was one of the wealthiest men in the county, but he showed no signs whatsoever of dying at any time in the near future.

Therefore, having tried and failed in every other way possible, it seemed that there was left to me only one solution.

Hemlock.

I would test the true worth of my father's holiness. If I administered to him a substantial dose of hemlock and he did not die or suffer from any of the usual effects of toxic poisoning, then I would know that he was a man, as he claimed to be, chosen by the Lord for great works. If not, then I would rid the world of someone who did nought but stand in the way of God's divine purposes.

• • •

There was a problem which I thought through intensely as I fed the horses the following morning.

Hemlock, or 'Fool's Parsley' as my aunt termed it, grew in prolific quantities by the pond near to my father's house. The means of obtaining it were therefore simple. The means of administering a sufficient quantity of it to my father would require a little more thought. It was, as I knew from times I had been made to consume a small quantity for medicinal purposes, highly pungent, both in smell and in taste. My father, despite the fact that he preached often on the values of 'simple living' was fond of highly flavoured and spicy food. I therefore envisaged no problem administering a small dosage to his food without him noticing. Enough, peradventure, to make him ill, even seriously ill, but probably not enough to kill him.

As I walked again into the sunshine from the dark stable, I realised just how simple the solution was. My aunt, who would have no suspicion (provided I was sufficiently careful) of the true cause of my father's illness, and who had always sworn by the healing properties of hemlock, would almost certainly administer it to him as a medicine (she never actually, like many old countrywomen, administered anything else as a medicine other than dock leafs to skin). This extra dose, when he had already consumed a considerable quantity, could prove to be lethal. Much of the work, therefore, could be left to my unwitting aunt. If all went to plan, *she* would kill him without even knowing it, and therefore with a clear conscience. I would be merely helping him on his way. Moreover, if, as I believed, anyone found the circumstances of my father's death suspicious, and was inclined to cut up his body or something in order to attempt to find the cause, then the result of such an examination would almost certainly be something like 'Death caused by overdose of hemlock administered for medicinal purposes; initial cause of illness unknown.' They were hardly likely to hang my old aunt for a well intentioned accident (I persuaded myself, somewhat, of the truth of this last point for the purposes of self-justification. I knew perfectly well in my heart that they almost certainly *would* hang my aunt if anyone suspected her of anything. But that was a risk I would just have to take).

I then walked to the house in order to break my fast, with a euphoric sense of the adventure and purpose that lay before me. I would henceforth live either an unpredictable and adventurous life; a contrast in the completest sense from the existence I had hitherto endured, or, if my father somehow did not die, I would be able to serve him henceforth with a more willing heart, maybe even, at some point in the future, confessing to him my doubt in his true piety.

A few days after I made this decision I arose early in order to shoot a pigeon and gather, discreetly, a large handful of fresh hemlock.

Both of these tasks proved easy, so, having prepared and cooked the pigeon over a fire in the woods, with a large amount of the hemlock stuffed down its throat and up its backside, there remained only one task before me: that of getting it into my father's food. With this problem I expected no difficulty, mainly because, in the manner of many Puritan households, my aunt ate separately from my father and myself. There was no reason therefore, as she needed not to be a witness to anything, to fear any suspicion on her part.

In order to address another part of my plan, I would need an unwitting accomplice. We fortunately hired as one of our farmhands an extremely unintelligent but hard working man of about thirty years of age, called Brickett. Brickett, I decided, would provide me with the opportunity to add the meat cut from the poisoned pigeon to my father's food.

The following day – a day upon which I knew my aunt was intending to serve game stew - after hours of nervous tension on my part, my father and I finally sat down to dine at seven of the clock. As we gave thanks and praise for the food before us I realised from his manner that my father was in one of his good humours - for the first time, in fact, since the beating I'd received at his hands. This put me out slightly, for my task would have been an easier one had I not needed to indulge him in futile conversation.

"Hast thou thought hard upon our talk of the other day, He-died-for-our-sins?" he asked as he ladled out for himself a generous helping of game stew.

"Verily I have, worthy father. I have sought for guidance as to the path I should follow in the light of your revelations, and I believe God has answered my prayers."

"How so, Lad?"

"I will speak to you on the matter shortly," I said, somewhat testily, "there is a knocking at the back door and I hear your name being called."

By the way that my father looked at me as he left the room, I could tell that he had reacted with disfavour to my tone. He was, after all, accustomed to being addressed by me as a subordinate to a superior. I realised a need to speak with care until my task was done, as he was more likely to eat all his food if his passions were not raised prematurely.

I heard my father open the back door and Brickett, in his usual cringing manner (I could imagine him twisting his straw hat in his hands), saying "Er....beggin' your Honour's pardon, I have come to see you as you required....about the chickens."

I sped into action. Disposing of some of the larger pieces of meat from my father's stew into the flower bed outside the lattice window, I quickly added to his bowl the flesh of the bird I had prepared (which I had previously secreted in an inner pocket). I then, for the sake of appearance, added a thin layer of gravy from my aunt's stew to the top of the bowl and mixed the substance together.

This task was completed in a moment, and all the while I could hear my father's raised voice, sarcastic in its anger, coming from the scullery: "I...required *thee*...to see *me*...on a matter of urgency about...the *chickens*! And wherefore should I require thee to speak to me directly about *anything*?"

"Er, beggin' your Honour's pardon, but Master He-died-for-our-sins...."

"...Told *you*, Brickett," I interrupted as I joined them, "to see *me* about the chickens in the morning. Only an ass such as yourself could have interpreted that as 'see my father during the evening repast,' now get thee hence!"

So saying, I shoved the hapless churl away from the door and slammed it behind him. My father, seemingly satisfied, allowed me to lead him back to the dining room. "Please forgive me for my abrupt mode of speech," I said apologetically, "I was eager to hear more nuggets of your wisdom and was annoyed by the untimely interruption."

I realised whilst saying this that despite my initial reluctance to talk with him, to do so would be a better course to follow, as the more his mind was distracted, the less likely it would be that he should notice anything unusual in the taste of his food.

We both sat down again. He began to eat.

"I find it a matter of high chagrin," he said through a mouthful of stew, "that all the peasants in the vicinity think that they can address me directly because I am a man of God. I tell thee lad, remember this: thou shalt accomplish nought in this life if thou allowest the descendants of serfs to converse with thee on equal terms."

He masticated on his stew, a somewhat curious expression on his face, just the sort of look someone might have if they were trying to work out whether their food tasted slightly different from normal. I watched, with an irresistible fascination, his large chin's rapid rotational movements. He appeared to have difficulty in swallowing the first mouthful, although he did so eventually. He called my aunt through from the kitchen.

I was stupefied with apprehension.

She bustled through and upon her arrival, curtsied reverentially, "Elder William?"

"This stew, pigeon is it not?"

"Mainly venison, Elder William, with a little pigeon and hare."

"Ah, well you've done your self proud, good sister. Pass the salt from the dresser."

She did so, and after waiting momentarily for any further instructions, curtsied again and left the room.

My father began to chew again.

"If truth be told, Son, this stew is somewhat tough on the teeth - eat lad. Now, what was I saying? Ah yes, the peasantry... I mind not that ye know that the unwashed classes must play an important part in the struggle to come. Doubtless I'll be their champion, but by buggery I won't be addressed by them like I was one of their equals."

He then lapsed into a thoughtful silence and continued eating, although more slowly. After a few moments however, he began muttering to himself.

"Something ails you Father?"

"Nay, nothing lad, my feet are feeling a certain numbness, that is all."

He continued to mutter to himself, and eventually put down his fork, although I could see that he had eaten nearly everything in his bowl. He stared at the wall in front of him.

"Something surely ails you, Father."

"I feel a heaviness in my head, and the numb feeling: it is spreading through my legs, as well as starting in my fingers."

"Are you ill, good Father?"

"Nay Lad, nay - nonetheless, I shall retire early to my chamber." So saying, he stood up and walked, somewhat shakily, out of the room. I heard him climbing the stairs slowly and heavily.

• • •

There was no question of my being able to sleep that evening. I told my aunt of my father's illness and then sat fully dressed upon my bed reading, or trying to read, Praise God's copy of *A Precedent for Young Pen Men,* and listening for any noises from my father's bedchamber, which was next to mine. I heard nothing except when my aunt entered his room for a minute, hopefully to give him a medicinal dose of hemlock.

After about two hours I heard him groaning. This at first came as just a solitary noise. After a few minutes however, I heard him call my name, at first just once and quietly, then more loudly and persistently. I got up and went to his chamber.

He was sprawled on his bed, red in the face and drenched in sweat. "Help me to my feet lad," he wheezed, "I am going to vomit." I turned my face away from him, as the effort to maintain a concerned and serious expression and not laugh in an inappropriate and hysterical manner was proving to be almost overwhelming. He may have noticed this however, as when I had helped him from the bed and onto his feet he immediately shook my hand away from his arm. He took one step towards the door, then collapsed, striking his head heavily on the floor. I watched, for a moment dumbfounded, until he turned his head slowly towards me, his head covered in blood. "Call for help, you fool" he said weakly. He then lost consciousness.

I ran to my aunt's bedchamber and rapped loudly on the door, "Aunt Meekness!" I cried, "my father has swooned and gashed his head, come quickly!"

She arose hastily and followed me to where my father lay. Looking upon him, she shrieked, then knelt beside him. "Fetch thee some help, get Brickett or somebody to help carry him."

I ran outside and found Brickett in one of the barns, whither he sallied forth every eventide to sleep with the cattle. I grabbed him by the collar and dragged him towards the house.

"What's gwonaan? What's gwonaan?" He asked repeatedly, although he offered only a token resistance.

"My father has had a seizure," I replied. We ran into the house and up the stairs, where we found my aunt dabbing the blood from his forehead. "Help me to lay him down."

Together, Brickett and I managed to hoist him up, and, with my aunt holding a candle aloft, carried him to his bed.

She took charge. Having ordered Brickett to run for Dr Hair, she checked my father's pulse to see whether he was still alive. He was - just. She then washed his head and, as it was still bleeding heavily, bandaged it.

She then ushered me out of the room. "We will have to wait for the Doctor to arrive," she said in a hushed voice, and then, "What caused your father to fall? Did he trip? "

"In truth I know not the cause," I replied.

I let Aunt Meekness return to my father, and waited by myself in the kitchen.

After about two minutes I heard the gate at the end of the garden open, and looking out, saw Dr Hair striding purposefully towards the house. There was still just a shade of daylight.

Running to the door, I opened it just as Dr Hair was about to knock. Without waiting for him to speak, I said, "My father is being tended by my aunt. Please make haste - this way." I then ran up the stairs with Dr Hair following.

My aunt stood aside from the bed as the Doctor entered. He crossed the room in a moment, then leant over and opened one of my father's eyes with his fingers.

"What caused him to fall?" he asked.

"He merely stated a wish to retire early," I replied, "then having done so rose from his bed and fell over. I know not the cause."

"And neither do I," said the Doctor whilst he checked his pulse, (I noticed he addressed my aunt and avoided speaking to me directly at all) "he seems to be suffering from no identifiable ailment other than the wound to his head. He possibly fainted."

He then stood up. "I can ascertain no cause of Mr Sykes's illness. I have noticed however, that although he may be running a temperature, there is an unusual coldness in his hands. Keep him warm and watch out for any change in his condition for the worse. If there is any need, send Brickett for me." So saying, the Doctor scowled at me and left the room. Aunt Meekness followed him.

"Is there nothing we can do for him, Doctor?" she asked, ringing her hands helplessly.

"There is nothing I can recommend when I know not the ailment, just keep him comfortable. Good e'en to thee, call for me if I am needed."

I had hoped that the doctor would order my father to be given a further dose of 'medicinal' hemlock.

"There is one thing that you *can* do," I said to my Aunt when she had re-entered the room. I placed my right hand in a caring fashion upon her shoulder, "it is more powerful than any medicine a doctor can provide."

She looked at me enquiringly for a moment; her eyes then lit up. "Of course!" she exclaimed, "let us kneel on each side of his bed and take his hands in ours; we shall lift him up together in prayer."

"Not so, good Aunt. You go and gather together your faithful sisters; they will not mind being awoken in such circumstances." I turned to my Father, "I will keep a prayerful vigil by his bedside."

"Thou wert ever a good lad, He-died-for-our-sins." So saying, my Aunt hastily left the chamber, sobbing as she went.

I knew I had no time to waste. I quickly ran outside and, making sure that there was no one to observe me, picked up the pieces of stew outside of the dining room window and hurled them into the field next to the house. I then returned to my Father's bedchamber and sat down beside him.

As I watched him lying there with his mouth open, breathing heavily, I became momentarily stricken with guilt. I tried to keep the certainty that he had killed my mother at the forefront of my mind; to remember his incessant thrashings, and his intention to have Gwendolyn Smith, in order to nullify these feelings.

It was while I was thus struggling within my mind that he woke up.

"What ails me?" he suddenly rasped, staring madly at nothing in particular, "I feel a burning in my head, and my legs and arms are dead as stone! What ails me?"

"I know not, Father, you spoke of strange feelings, and then fell and gashed your head. The Doctor has said that there is naught to explain it."

"Nay, something is wrong with me," he said. He then suddenly turned and fixed his eyes upon mine.

I know not, to this day, whether he somehow knew that I had a hand in his affliction, or whether he was suspicious and therefore sought to test me, or whether indeed there was any such thought in his mind. But I do know that all of my new found confidence and resolution disappeared that moment, as he fixed me with that stare.

"Wherefore are you giving me that look boy?" he wheezed, "Thou hast a guilty look about you, such as a lad discovered performing an act of wickedness."

"I have no such look, Father," I spluttered.

"Thou hast the look of someone who has a guilty secret...the look that Judas gave unto Jesus...at the Last Supper!"

I sat frozen to my chair, paralysed with horror.

"Thou hast never been able to run any wicked thing past me. Thy silence speaks to me more audibly than any words...thou hast poisoned me! You evil, ungrateful little arsehole! I am going to kill thee!"

He attempted to rise from his bed, but found himself unable to move.

I jumped up and ran to my aunt's medicine cabinet, from which I took her bottle of hemlock based medicine.

I knew that if anyone came to the house at that moment, then I would need to suffocate my father quickly; I hoped however, to avoid an action so violent. Unable to help myself from pausing outside his door, I steeled myself, and entered.

My Father stared at me as I approached him, and I recognised, for the first time ever, fear in his eyes. My hand shook as I opened the bottle, and I could not keep myself from weeping uncontrollably as I did so.

"Have mercy on me," he said weakly.

I found myself able to reply, despite the shaking, and despite my tears. "I am not able to do so. If you were truly a righteous man, then you would have nothing to fear from this." So saying, I pushed his head back and proceeded to pour the contents of the bottle down his throat. He gagged, and some of the liquid escaped from the side of his mouth, which I quickly wiped before it stained the pillow. Most of it, however, he swallowed. I then sat back down upon my chair and watched to see what would happen.

His mouth moved silently for a moment, but then he murmured something. I placed my ear close to his mouth. "Have mercy upon me," he repeated weakly.

"I will not trouble your spirit by praying for you myself," I said to him gently, Aunt Meekness is at this moment praying for your recovery. I am sure that the Lord, in His wisdom, will count those prayers as prayers for your salvation."

I could see - even at this time - that his pride was battling with his fear. "*You*...question...*my* salvation?" he croaked.

This question brought back to me some of my resolve. I whispered into his ear, as his breath became feeble and irregular..."I sense that you find the idea of me questioning your status in God's Kingdom deeply vexing, Father, but did you not preach to us often on matters contradictory to your own lifestyle? And have not you, yourself, killed? My mother...did you not kill my mother? Doubtless she got in the way of your whore-mongering..."

My father, however, whilst I spoke, merely stared at the ceiling; and at some point during, or just after my speech, gave up the ghost.

V

Cambridge

A s it transpired, after a fruitless inquiry into the cause of his death, which concluded that he died 'from unknown causes exacerbated by a severe wound to the head,' my father was interred in the yard of St Lawrence's Church, Towcester. All who spoke to me did so with kindness and compassion. Even Doctor Hair, it seemed, did not suspect me.

All obstacles which had stood in the way of my entry into Cambridge were therefore suddenly, and completely, removed. I had to deal with all the usual cares that arise when a man of property dies, and is succeeded, by the next generation. These details I will not trouble you with. Let it be sufficient for me to state that I took care to ensure that my aunt was established more comfortably at the Grange than had been her lot under my father's care. I then rode to the university a few weeks after my father's death – after a decent period of mourning - and sought out the Chancellor of St Gabriel's College, Dr Arbuthnot Harding. I had heard report of him previously as a man with radical opinions, who had fallen foul on various occasions of the churchmen and academics who maintained authority over the university on behalf of the King.

I arrived at St Gabriel's, a gracious and antiquated college that had been founded (I could not help but perceive a certain irony here) during the reign of King Henry II for the benefit of aristocratic orphans. I found Doctor Harding seated behind a large desk in a study, which was lined from the floor to the ceiling with religious books, as well as volumes of legal precedents. He was what I imagine future generations might regard as a typical scholastic puritan gentleman. He was bald headed, with a hooked nose. He also had a very red face, although he gave no impression that this was caused by an excess of drinking. What hair he did have fell from the back of his head over his neck in an unruly manner, as I have since discovered is the fashion of academics from age to age. He was also extremely fat.

He looked up from his desk as I entered, having knocked quietly upon the open door.

"Doctor Harding?" I asked.

"Yes."

"My name is Sykes."

"Yes?"

"I wish to enquire about the possibility of taking up the study of Classics and Divinity at the University."

"Good, good," he replied, and then, "Have you a Christian name, lad?"

"It is He-died-for-our-sins."

"What?"

"I said He-died-for-our-sins."

There then followed a somewhat awkward and embarrassing silence, as often happened when I introduced myself, so I changed the topic to the subject of my father's untimely death, and told Dr Harding that he had become interested in the latter part of his life in advancing the cause of religious knowledge at this most prestigious and worthy college. I also told him of my father's wish that I should enter Cambridge in order to pursue my studies with a view to entering Parliament, when it was next called, as the representative for Towcester and Weedon in Northamptonshire.

I knew that the offer of an endowment of thirty guineas per year (with a promise of ten more for every year of my life after I had graduated) would be impossible for the master of any college to turn down, especially as I put my case in such a way as to convince

Dr Harding that to grant me entrance to the University would be tantamount to doing God a service. This was an easier task than it may seem, for I pointed out to him that my cousin Richard was due to begin his studies at Pembroke college; that he was the only other possible candidate for parliament in my home constituency, and that he was a profligate winebibber and womaniser, with little or no sympathy for the advancement of true religion and the purposes of God.

The Doctor responded exactly as I had hoped: saying little, but showing his acquiescence with a smile when I spoke of the endowment. He was much more forthcoming on the matter of my cousin.

"I count it not as a fulfilment of pride," he said, "but as a fulfilment of duty, that this college has been at the vanguard of the nation's struggle against licentious behaviour on the one hand, and popery on the other. If things are just as you say then I will count it as a blessing from the Lord if we at St Gabriel's are able to place you on the path to a parliamentary career; yea, a joy indeed. Why, forsooth, should worldly people and unbelievers have all the power?"

After this conversation the Doctor invited me to walk with him around the confines of the college grounds. He told me that in the days of papist rule it had been easier for colleges such as St Gabriel's to survive financially, for they only had to offer an assurance of salvation by dint of a few candles and beads pointed in the direction of the Virgin Mary on behalf of some naïve earl, for the said earl to grant them vast fractions of his riches.

"Nowadays," said the Doctor, as the dappled sunshine danced on his shiny bald head, "in the light of divine revelation, it is harder for godly institutions to flourish, but the fruits of righteousness were always harder to attain than the fruits of evil."

"Although, as you have hinted," I responded, "the Lord is raising up for Himself a people fit to do Him service; and the consciences of many wealthy people are being touched. It is, perchance, right to ask, not only: 'why should worldly people have all the power?' but also: 'why should worldly people have all the money?'"

The Doctor seemed to find this highly amusing. He laughed heartily and slapped me on the back, "You've a pretty wit lad, a pretty wit. Needs must we'll have to teach *thee* to contain thy mirth."

I knew however, that the Doctor had said these last words in jest, and that I had in fact impressed him greatly.

• • •

Before leaving home to take up my place at Cambridge I corresponded regularly with the Doctor concerning the endowment, as well as sundry matters such as the reservation of lodgings. I also had to address the issue of the poor report I had received from Doctor Hair. But it soon became apparent that Dr Hair and Dr Harding were already acquainted, and did not get on well due to the moderate views of the former, and the radical views of the latter; and Dr Harding was willing on this score to give me the benefit of the doubt - even concerning the means by which I had attempted to force Dr Hair's hand. I merely told him that I *did* suspect Dr Hair's daughters of witchcraft, and that the tale he had heard concerning my alleged violence to Dr Hair had been greatly exaggerated. He was by this seemingly satisfied.

I left my home for Cambridge with Praise God (who had prostrated himself in a most pathetic manner before Dr Hair in a successful attempt to obtain his forgiveness) in time for the beginning of the Michaelmas term, and we set up lodgings together in a couple of first floor rooms overlooking the main quadrangle of St Gabriel's College. I could not help but feel a certain irritation towards Praise God for the enthusiastic way he almost immediately set about his studies, as well as the fact that he had entered the college as a scholarship student in the first place, instead of entering in the fashion I had intended for him: that of my slave. I soon realised however, that on this score I need not have worried. As I obtained my place by means of my generosity, and he by means of a poor man's scholarship, it was only by my allowing him to live with me that he was saved from a life of extreme discomfort and hardship. Our relationship fell easily therefore into the natural order of things: that of master and unpaid servant.

Notwithstanding this, I was also annoyed with him for a reason connected to my cousin. Richard, because of his father's great influence, and because of the influence that still resonated from the huge endowments granted to Pembroke College by our ancestors, was allowed to live outside the precincts of his college, about half a mile from my quarters at St Gabriel's; and thus enjoyed (despite the strict disciplines that were meant to be imposed upon *all* students) a style of living vastly superior to ours.

In order to understand my vexation it is important for you to know that my cousin arrived in town with several servants, including Gwendolyn Smith and her brother Simon. Upon his arrival he very quickly became known among the aristocratic society of students, and moved freely in their company. It came to pass that the lifestyles of these so-called *gentlemen* became debauched in the extreme, and many a night the sounds of revelry and mirth could be heard from within the walls of his house, disturbing the peaceful harmony of the godly people of Cambridge.

As for my student life: Dr Harding and his wife had both decided that I was an example for all students to follow of good, clean puritan living. They expected me to pray constantly, and meet with them for praise and worship for six hours in chapel on a Sunday, as well as two hours on most weekday evenings.

What really annoyed me, however, was that Praise God, despite past events at home, seemed to be regarded as anything but an enemy to Richard Sykes and his friends; and although he never went out with them in the evening or anything like that, my cousin would talk to him if he passed him in the road or met him in a library, and he was once even invited to his house to drink coffee - and discuss *divinity*.

One evening, having suffered this behaviour for about the space of a month, I spied Praise God through the window of my bedchamber talking with my cousin at the porter's gate. I decided to tackle him about his disloyalty immediately. As I saw him approach the house I ran to his room and quickly picked up a copy of the bible. I sat on a chair next to the window.

"Praise God," I said, looking over the book as he entered the room, in the manner of one disturbed from deep reflection, "Thou art a varlet."

"Why, He-died-for-our-sins?"

"A varlet," I repeated.

I went on reading.

"What have I done?"

I placed the bible down carefully.

"Do you really think that it is acceptable in the eyes of the Lord to show friendship to a reprobate such as Richard Sykes? I tell you Praise God, you are a disloyal friend to do so, a disloyal friend indeed." So saying, I again picked up the bible and pretended to continue reading.

"But He-died-for-our-sins, Richard Sykes has merely been questioning me about puritan beliefs. He asked me to his house to discuss them in the company of other theologians. He really is very open about such matters. I feel, nay I am sure, that he desires to know more of God."

"So, you are a theologian now, are you? Fie upon you Praise God. Do you think that you know my cousin better than I? Have you noticed the devilish goings on in that house? But let me hazard a guess as to his real motive. Have you ever discussed the King, and the matter of whether he should be the head of the Church of England?"

"Only in so much as we have agreed that Christ is the true head of the church, and that the King is his representative."

I exploded with wrath. "You fool! What sort of representative for Christ is Charles Stuart? It is under his authority that this country is going to the devil. I tell you, Praise God, Richard Sykes will use your words against you. You will have your ears cropped for saying anything in his company that smells of sedition."

"But I haven't."

"Exactly Praise God. You haven't. You are, instead of standing for that which is righteous by condemning the king and all that he stands for, consorting with profligate sinners. The worldly snares that abound in this place are causing you to backslide."

"You are confusing me."

"You would not be confused if you took care not to displease the Lord and to keep your steps on the straight and narrow path, would you? Who is the author of confusion but the very devil we speak of?"

"But I don't understand how my behaviour is displeasing to the Lord."

"That, Praise God, is because you have insufficiently studied the scriptures. Look at the very first psalm." I picked up the bible and read to him: "'Blessed is the man that walketh not in the counsel of the ungodly, nor standeth in the way of sinners, nor sitteth in the seat of the scornful.'"

"But," he protested, "If anybody has been walking in another's counsel, it is Richard Sykes who has been walking in *mine*. Did not Jesus eat and drink with tax collectors and sinners?"

"That, Praise God, you vain and proud man, is the argument of the devil. Need I point out to you, in case it has escaped your attention, that you are not Jesus? Look here: one of the requirements for those who wish to 'abide in the tabernacle of the Lord,' is that in their eyes 'a vile person should be condemned.' I tell you Praise God, you are in danger of traversing this road to a place well beyond the reaches of God's grace and mercy."

I could see that these last words had had the effect I desired upon him. There entered into his eyes a look which displayed the greatest fear that can confront any of us, that of a man who believes that he faces the danger of eternal and all-consuming fire.

He responded as I had intended, although I suspected that incredulity might be vying with the fear I had just planted in him. "I do not know what to do" he said, "your cousin Richard, just moments ago, invited me to his house again."

"Pah! The only way you will impress or convince someone like Richard Sykes is by the power of demonstration - as I will show you before many days have passed." I then realised that the time had come to soften my tone. "Fear not, brother Praise God, I will lift you up to the Lord in prayer; and I warrant that He will hear me and turn His wrath from you. As for Richard Sykes, you are to shun his company. When he offers you overtures of friendship, you shall turn away from him as Moses turned his back on the Pharaoh of Egypt. "

So saying, I left Praise God to reflect on my words.

VI

The Young Puritans

I decided, after a few weeks of dining in every evening at St Gabriel's Hall, and thus dividing the whole of my free time between this mundane activity (meals at St Gabriel's were eaten in silent meditation) and prayer time with the Hardings, to begin attending the meetings of the *Young Puritans*, a well-subscribed society which met on Tuesday and Thursday evenings in a hall annexing Sydney Sussex College. Praise God had been attending their gatherings since our arrival.

But my purpose was wider than I have described here; and wider also than a desire for advancement in matters spiritual and temporal. My thoughts were partly directed at my cousin Richard, who had, within a few weeks of going up to the university, become a predominant and popular member of a group known as *The Honourable Protectors of the Divine Right*. This was a gathering of gentlemen students, given to sport and drinking for pleasure; and which actively supported the King in matters religious and political. It was thus made up of a small, but powerful, minority faction within the university. Their members always wore about their person at least one item of blue clothing, or a blue ribbon, to demonstrate their loyalty to the monarch. Certain of them were known to have taken lately to harassing students they deemed to be of too extreme a puritan leaning. This harassment had taken the form of abusive name calling on the street for example, as well as random minor acts of violence.

But they were seemingly invincible due to the wealth and influence of their members, and this I could not help but see as a challenge. It was reported that their only antagonists were individuals and small groups that, despite being affiliated with the *Young Puritans*, in no way typified their membership, as this was a society which owned a reputation for being entirely ineffectual in its opposition to the *Honourable Protectors*. The destruction of this latter group, therefore, became for me a compelling ambition.

But I was aware that it might be foolish to take any action too militant before I had gauged the opinion of Dr Harding. If he had the same attitude as many others (namely, that we should not go out of our way to root out evil – but, rather, merely seek to be a beacon of righteousness in a heathen land) then I would need to tread carefully. I stopped him on our way out of church the next Sunday, and voiced my concerns about the activities of the *Honourable Protectors*. He invited me to walk with him back to his lodgings, and his response was exactly as I had hoped.

"The Puritan students and Fellows of Cambridge," he said, "have too long been willing to tolerate the existence of such stains upon the reputation and spiritual well-being of the university. When I was an undergraduate the whole world was caught up in rumours of gunpowder, treason and plot; and thus half my time was spent suppressing such things. As with then, so should'st be now. If there is one worthy diversion from a life of study and prayer, it is the pursuit and stamping out of wickedness, and the use of necessary force to do so."

This was all I wanted to hear. I merely required assurance that any actions I might take would meet with the approval (albeit that their approval might need to be of the tacit kind) of at least some of the senior puritan element within the university. Having made my excuses as soon as I could, I bowed, and made my way to my lodgings.

• • •

I arrived alone for my first meeting of the *Young Puritans* on the first Tuesday after my conversation with the Doctor. As I entered the hall

I noticed that it was very bare, with nothing but plain benches, upon which the *Young Puritans* were sat in about twelve rows separated by an aisle in the middle. The hall was filled with drably dressed men who in most cases, following the example set by their fathers (or certainly the example set by my father) sat with their hats low over their eyes, their legs stretched out in front of them, chins upon their chests and arms folded. Facing the benches on a small raised platform were eight chairs, seven of which were occupied by similar looking gentlemen. The other chair belonged to a man who was on his feet addressing the crowd. I found a vacant seat and adopted the same posture as my neighbours.

The speaker was a tall angular man of about nineteen years, with sideburns and a dreamy, idealistic expression. He gestured elaborately with his arms as he spoke.

"I tell thee brethren," he was saying, "we must not let pride play any part in our response to these provocations. The Lord would have us demonstrate the essence of his holiness by showing ourselves to be above that which draws unregenerate men to defend their worldly honour."

He paused in the manner of a speaker expecting applause. Receiving none, he went on.

"I will grant unto thee, brethren, there is something in the argument that one must display vigour in masculinity in defending ourselves. But in truth this is surely the way of our opponents, who wish, merely by doing so, to impress their womenfolk. But are not our sisters made of a more blessed substance altogether? Why, I know of some women who, rather than say 'Fight for your honour if thou would'st have me,' are more likely to say: 'To be a true man you must be a man of words but not action...'

But the speaker was at this point interrupted.

"You're rambling again, Geoffrey," said one of the brethren sat behind him.

"Yes, that's enough now," said another.

Despite the accumulation of various cat calls such as 'Boo!' and, 'Get him off!' he continued: "I merely wish to address that which we know to be a reality in all our lives – namely: how to draw a balance between our spiritual calling and the inflaming of our passions."

The heckling got louder, and someone at the front of the crowd began trying to pull him off the stage by the ankle of his britches.

He tried again to speak, but managed to deliver no more of his address before the surly gentleman behind him began to shove him violently forward with his staff. Realising he was about to lose his footing, Geoffrey stepped deftly to one side and jumped off the stage. He departed the hall, angry and red faced amid the raucous jeering of his many brethren.

Amid the loud, continuing babble that followed this incident, several people on the floor rose to address the crowd. The man with the staff, who appeared to be running the proceedings, selected another speaker from the stage. The noise died away as he began to speak.

"That," said my neighbour, "is Lord Clune: heir to the Earl of Clunehaven, and the leader of the *Young Puritans*. He is something of a moderate, and attracts a fair amount of opposition."

"Mr Westmacott," Lord Clune began, "has a bent for excessive self-expression. However, there is wisdom in some of his words. The best way thing for us to do in the light of these attacks is to remember Jesus' instruction and 'resist not evil.' Is not the fact that the actions of these members of the *Honourable Protectors* are so provocative enough of a sign that the devil is trying to draw us out of the peace we have found in the Lord's salvation?"

He paused, and then said "I tell you all that the Lord has changed my heart, but how can I say that he has *really* changed me, or that I have allowed the Lord to do so, if when once I would have drawn my sword to defend my honour, my actions now would be no different?"

Someone near the back stood up and started shouting in a strong Norfolk accent. "Thou speakest a load of *shite…Viscount*; perchance ye're in the wrong place and should be attending a meeting of the *Divine Protectors of the Right*, or whatever their bloody name is!"

The heckler, realising he had taken the meeting by surprise, gathered confidence from the cheering and laughter that met his words from some of the men assembled. "The only reason you are even given an ear is because you're the son of an earl. You talk like one who loves his life in this world; the possession of riches and status no less. But it's hard for a man of noble birth to enter the kingdom of heaven." He then, addressing the crowd, added "This society is all too willing to follow the pattern of this world; I tell you all: the Lord is the great Leveller. The poor shall rise up!"

There was a mixture of responses to this interruption. The people surrounding the heckler shouted "Hear him, hear him!" and slapped him upon the back. Many others shouted "Get thee hence!" or "Get him out!" or "Hold your tongue!" One or two tried to push him, as well as his followers, towards the door.

This clamour went on a while, and looked like it might boil over into a riot, until my neighbour stood up on the bench next to me and, by shouting very loudly the words 'Peace, brethren...peace!' managed to quiet the crowd.

Having caught everyone's attention he turned to the heckler and addressed him thus: "Mr Jenkins, I do – I am sure we all do, really – sympathise with your position, and I for one know that I'd feel exactly the same if God had allocated *me* to a position at the bottom of the pile.'

The effect of this, as you might expect, was that Jenkins jumped onto the bench behind him and attempted to leap across the room in order to attack my neighbour. He was restrained by those around him, and sat down again, glowering with indignation.

When peace was finally restored, Lord Clune continued: "Far be it from me to defend myself against your accusation. If I am to be excluded from the Kingdom of Heaven by reason of my birth, what shall I do? Eat drink and be merry? But nay, I cannot let your words touch me; I will continue to thank the Lord for the assurance of forgiveness and salvation he has given me."

There was something about this man's mode of expression that made me want to thrash his face with a birch rod.

"Concerning," he continued, "the issue already under discussion: Some of you believe that the Lord's cause is best served by means of violence, but there are baser errors, still, than this one: there are others of you who believe yourselves justified in using your so-called religiosity as an excuse for the basest forms of sexual licentiousness. In one instance of which I heard, a woman was held up to a wall and told to 'spread her legs in order that her offspring should be born of righteousness!' According to my informer the speaker of this insult, who sits here in this room now, is fortunate to be alive. There is little point in squealing that you cannot fight your opponents because you are a man of God, when it is your profane way of speaking that has got you into such a tight spot in the first place."

"So there we have it," shouted Jenkins from the back, "consorting with the enemy; finding common ground with the devil's spawn on the grounds of mutual class appreciation! I ask thee brethren (again addressing the crowd) do we need to hear any more of this compromised claptrap?"

There then followed a brief period of further uproar during which the sparring parties were content merely to shake their fists and shout at one another. Lord Clune, who I could see was trying to calm the crowd, could no longer be heard above the sound of raised voices. My neighbour tugged at my sleeve.

"We'd better leave now, unless you want to stay for a beating." I noticed all of the occupants of the chairs on the stage departing quickly out of a side door.

We then left hurriedly, and I could not help thinking as we did so that I was delighted with my first meeting of the *Young Puritans*. Having believed that the Puritan movement on the whole was of one mind on matters of religion, I realised that there were so many divisions and differences of opinion within their ranks that only a fool of the highest order would be unable to use them to his advantage.

"So," I asked him, once we had managed to fight our way through the crowd pouring out of the main entrance, "do these meetings usually end like this?"

"It depends on who is speaking and of what they are saying. The meeting tonight, based as it was on such a controversial matter, was always likely to end in a fight. But some gatherings will concern matters that cannot be disputed, particularly if someone like Geoffrey

Westmacott is speaking, and is in the mood for simple biblical exposition."

The moment I always dreaded then arrived: he offered me his hand. "I am Robert Heron, by the way."

"He-died-for-our-sins Sykes" I replied.

I looked at the crowd still spilling out of the hall, while he shuffled the gravel uncomfortably with his left foot. I was pleased to notice Praise God sauntering in our direction from one of the side entrances of the hall.

"This is Praise God Fairweather" I said, glad of the opportunity to introduce someone with a name that was at least the same *type* as mine.

"Robert Heron of Corpus Christi," he replied. He then, after another awkward pause, pointed at some people walking away from the meeting hall. "They look as if they're going to the inn, shall we join them?"

"I thought," said I, "that one of the things that sets us apart from our opponents is that they meet in ale houses whilst we meet in prayer rooms."

"It depends, surely, upon the reputation of the ale house," said Praise God, pompously.

"True," said Robert Heron, "and the reputation of this one is such that our opponents never cross its threshold." We then followed the group of people to a dark tavern called the *Steepled Hat* about two stone throws from where we were standing.

The *Steepled Hat* was both dark and gloomy. It was dark because coming out of the daylight it took a while for our eyes to adjust, but it would be much more appropriate to refer to the place as gloomy in terms of its atmosphere. It was very crowded and, but for one sour faced woman of about fifty whose job it was to refill the patrons' mugs, the place was entirely occupied by men. All of these were puritans, but the mood in that large and low-ceilinged room seemed to be one of mistrust and suspicion instead of godly fellowship. There were various groups huddled around the tables, apparently in secret conference. Having been refused permission to share the table of one such group, we stood around the unlit fire hearth.

"Part of the problem," began Robert Heron when the sour faced woman had filled our mugs, "is that these people see themselves - so deep are their regional differences - as being from different countries when they hail, in reality, merely from different counties. If you take this problem along with the diversity of religious opinions, you will agree, I am sure, that we hardly have a recipe for spiritual harmony."

"I must admit it has been a disappointment," said Praise God.

"What has?" I asked.

"This dearth of spiritual unity."

"Well that just goes to show, Praise God, how much you lack in spiritual insight. It is pre-requisite, is it not, that for a people to be gathered together, they must first be scattered?"

"I must confess," said Praise God, "that thou dost speak with a certain wisdom. I had not before seen it that way."

"No, neither had I," added Robert Heron, somewhat irritably I thought. "As you could see at that meeting, and as you can see from this crowd in here, there are many problems facing anyone who tries to draw these people together."

"The greater the difficulty, the greater the challenge," I answered and, then, addressing Praise God, added, "And can you stop speaking as if you were trying to impersonate the Prophet Elijah?"

We then fell into a conversation about more mundane matters. Robert Heron, it turned out, was at the university and living at Corpus Christi merely because it was expected that he would - his father being a puritan magnate of the county of Derbyshire. He was, I surmised from our conversation, somewhat phlegmatic about the controversies that were besetting the nation.

"To be honest," he said, "I am rarely impressed by any of the speakers at those meetings. Take Lord Clune. He is all very well; I am sure that he would give his last biscuit to his worst enemy and thereby starve to death; but he is *so* intense. And that other man: you know, Jenkins, the one shouting at him from the back: the very definition of a lowlife. Where do we get them from? And to be honest, I don't wish to be rude, but do you not think that the country has gone a little mad when people start calling their children *Praise God*, and *He-died-for-our-sins?*"

"Well why do you go there then?" I retorted, ignoring his last question.

"That's the trouble. I have to write to my father regularly and inform him of what I am doing, as he puts it, 'for the cause of the true Church,' by which, of course, he means the puritan strain; and the moment I choose to start dressing like a proper gentleman, by which means the young women of this town might start to see me as someone worth paying a bit of attention to, instead of a religious fanatic to be avoided at all costs, my tutor will write to my father; and he will respond, at best by rushing down here and forcing me back to Derbyshire, where I can be watched closely, or, at worse, by cutting me off from my inheritance altogether."

"So," I said to him, "your religiosity is all a pretence."

"No."

"How so?"

"Because I believe in God."

"As do the demons – and tremble," quoted Praise God.

I scowled at him (although I was, truth be told, somewhat grateful for his interjection).

"It is all very well talking to me about demons," said Robert Heron, "I merely mean this: I have been brought up all my life to respect people who seemed in many instances, incredibly dull and, moreover, to be their own worst enemies, as everything about the way they conducted themselves put people off wanting to have anything to do with them. At the same time I have been brought up to view people who seem, in most cases, to be perfectly normal with suspicion and mistrust. I am fed up to my back teeth with it."

"Needs must that those who follow the Lord must be set apart from the world," I replied.

"Well Jesus may have been 'set apart from the world' in one sense, but if he'd been as aloof as my father and his friends, and most of these clowns in here, we'd have never heard of Him, would we?"

"He does have a point, does he not, He-died-for-our-sins?" asked Praise God.

I ignored him.

"Let us say," Heron continued," that all the men in this place profess to be devout Christians; that they profess this is, I think, a certainty. But most of these people would be unwilling to piss on their enemies to save them from dying of thirst. How is *that* Christianity in anything but name?"

Neither of us answered, so he continued.

"I am by no means condemning everyone. The people I can't stand, and I have met too many of them, are the people who love to be seen to be holy, whilst their lives are, in reality, no better lived than the people they enjoy condemning. You speak to me of demons, but when I meet righteous men, unless I see something to prove otherwise I can no longer help assuming that this righteousness is just a mask for their selfish ambition. I keep believing I have witnessed the depths to which people are willing to sink, and then I see something worse, and it is almost always cloaked with the sort of apparel we see gracing these religious gentlemen."

I will gladly confess at this juncture that these words were getting a little too close to the knuckle. Of all the people I could have acquainted myself with at my first meeting of the *Young Puritans* I had to pick this one. I decided that the best means of defence, in this instance, was attack.

"Do you have a reputation?" I asked him, very loudly.

He looked at me blankly.

"Allow me to explain my meaning. I notice that no one in this place seems eager to brook our company. With me they appear unwilling to make acquaintance; Praise God is too insignificant a fellow to have incurred anyone's abject displeasure easily (I ignored his audible gasp), so again I ask you, do you have a reputation?"

"I do not know."

"I think you do know, Sir." (I continued to speak deliberately loudly, and indeed the voices of those in our hearing had become hushed, with several heads turned in our direction).

Fortunately Heron started, at this point, to become emotional, his voice rising. "You're just another pig-headed oaf...whatever made me think you'd be any different from any of these other fools?"

The consequence of this was that several of the men nearest us began to rise from their chairs, or advance towards us, with a clearly menacing intention. He, realising that he was in a hopeless situation, quickly put down the tankard from which he had been drinking, gathered up his hat and departed from the building, shooting me a look of contempt and despair as he went.

I looked around with a bold face as I ordered Praise God to fetch another quart of ale. Those who had stood up slowly sat down again, some looking at the door from which Robert Heron had just departed, others looking at me whilst whispering to one another. The expression on their faces was unmistakeable: that of surprise and indignation directed at Robert Heron, mingled with a stern respect for someone they recognised as no ordinary new-comer.

VII

Gwendolyn

I had always suspected that Gwendolyn Smith was merely following the way of so many others by allowing my cousin Richard to
seduce her.

Allow me to explain. I am writing these memoirs in the year of our
Lord 1661, and I will therefore use the present King, Charles II, as an
illustration. He is about as ugly as a cow with long black hair and yet, as
report has it, women of both high birth and low yearn for his attention
and the opportunity to share his bed. Can there be any doubt at all that
it is the King with whom those women wish to copulate, rather than
the man? I think not.

So I believed it was with Gwendolyn Smith and Richard Sykes:
the same attraction, that of servant and master. I saw no reason therefore why she should not be tempted away from him by a proposi-
tion more alluring. It is true, as I have mentioned earlier, that she had
often rejected my advances, but this was a long time before I went to
Cambridge; and she had had the chance to see me playing the man
on more than one occasion since. I know that when a woman looks
at a man with an expression of contempt, it is as often as not a thin
disguise for sexual desire and admiration.

I also, I believed, had another advantage over my cousin. If there is
one thing that has always appealed to a woman, apart from manliness,
it is power and wealth. Now, Richard Sykes may have been the heir to a
fortune greater than mine, but that was as far as it went, he was merely

an *heir*. I was, since my father's death, the master of my own fortune and destiny.

I had kept a close eye on the comings and goings from my cousin's house ever since our arrival at Cambridge, and I thus knew that every morning around half past eight of the clock, except on Sundays, Gwendolyn Smith would leave the house by the cellar door and walk to the market to buy fruit, meat and whatever types of food were required for that day.

I found it difficult to approach her on these occasions, despite the fact that I had often contrived to be at the market square at the same hour. There was something about the way she walked with such confidence that made me afraid to do so. But it was not just her confidence that deterred me. She had, the first time I had passed her at the market place, wished me good morrow, and I had used the opportunity to ask after her brother Simon, as well as her own general well-being. Upon this occasion, as upon former occasions at home, my desire for her made it impossible for me to avert my eyes from her breasts; and at this she had demonstrated offence by tossing her head contemptuously and turning away, despite my having done nothing but compliment her with my gaze. As if, good Reader, she had not arranged her apparel for the benefit of admirers such as I.

From that moment forward she had walked passed me with her nose in the air as if I were the servant and she were gentry; and as you will doubtless understand, this inappropriate haughtiness stirred my desire all the more.

But it was not until I saw her walking out with my cousin Elizabeth one morning, that I discovered a pretext for approaching her once again.

Elizabeth, like my cousin Richard, had never been a friend. But unlike Richard she had never made it her purpose to antagonise me or ridicule me on matters such as my Christian name or religion. Her own faith was, if anything, even more of a high Anglican leaning than her father and brother. Her strong beliefs had made her into a very serious young woman, and she was celebrated throughout the county of Northamptonshire, and at the Court, as a renowned beauty. She was also a particular favourite of the Queen, to whom she was an occasional Lady in Waiting. Her beauty, which was particularly exemplified by her sylphlike form and her long golden hair, had caused her to be the object of desire for many young suitors, but it seemed that only someone as serious and religious as the king himself would have done for her, as she had apparently refused all of their advances, and her father had been reluctant to choose anyone for her against her will.

Please forgive the digression. It had, as I said, become my custom to hide in wait for Gwendolyn Smith to leave the house of my cousin in the morning. I would sometimes wait purely in order to watch her. Occasionally, if time allowed, I would follow her to the market. But one pleasant November morning Gwendolyn sallied forth with Elizabeth from Richard Sykes's house and, it being my natural duty to give good day to my cousin, I therein had an excuse to approach Gwendolyn also.

I knew that they would be heading to the market, as Gwendolyn Smith, following her usual custom, held her basket in her right hand. Waiting therefore until a time when my arrival would not appear too contrived, I began to follow them and, by walking at a more rapid pace, catch up with them.

I had all but done so, and was just about to make my presence known, when I realised that their conversation was of such a nature as to be of interest to me, and therefore worth my attention. They first mentioned a ball that Richard would be holding two weeks hence, and then the conversation became more interesting still, touching, as it did, upon my cousin Elizabeth's love life.

"I think, dear Gwendolyn," said my cousin, "that you speak with a certain insight, and yet your wisdom can reach only a certain way. It is one thing for you to say that I should marry because I love him, it is quite another thing for me to do so."

"But Miss Elizabeth…" Gwendolyn answered, or attempted to.

"Oh yes, *love will conquer all* is your steadfast belief," interrupted my cousin, laughing, "And has been since you were ten. Methinks you were altogether too smitten with old Josiah's tales of knights of old, and fair maidens who would rather plunge a dagger into their hearts than marry for aught but love."

Gwendolyn laughed. "I cannot deny it, Miss Elizabeth, but does your love for Lord Clune being alike to a storybook romance mean that it must be dismissed as an idle fairytale? Nay, for you to do thus minds me more of the teachings of John Calvin than King Solomon."

Elizabeth's answer was spoken in the manner of a retort. "Whilst I cannot but acknowledge your words as born of your love for me, needs must I check your wit, Gwendolyn, and your propensity to express it so boldly."

"Oh," answered Gwendolyn, "I have been told often that I am altogether too bold for my position. If you wish me to speak to you as a serving wench should address Elizabeth Sykes, daughter of Sir Richard Sykes, Baronet, then I will humbly ask your opinion as to whether I should purchase venison or mutton. If, though, I may speak to you as Gwendolyn to Elizabeth, as you have always allowed and encouraged, then I will not be silent; not when I perceive that your happiness is so much at stake."

At these words, Elizabeth turned and faced her friend (for such was their relationship in reality), causing for me the necessity of ducking into a nearby doorway.

"I must say that I am sorry to you Gwendolyn. You are a good and true friend, and I love you dearly. It is just (she paused and they walked on - I followed once more) that he is so far from me in matters of spiritual doctrine as to make me think our match a sin."

"But the very thing you say makes him so different is the very thing that makes him so similar. You are both..."

But the conversation got no further. At the moment they reached the market place, the sudden shout of "What do ye lack, what do ye lack?" from a stall holder next to me, caused Gwendolyn to turn round sharply, and the look of recognition as her eyes caught mine caused my cousin to look round also.

"Good morning to you He-died-for-our-sins," said my cousin, after recovering from her initial surprise, "My brother told me that you had come up to Cambridge also, how do you fare?"

The suddenness with which I found myself discovered in the act of eavesdropping their conversation caused me to hesitate guiltily before responding. My cousin Elizabeth looked somewhat perplexed as she waited for my answer. Gwendolyn Smith looked at me with the same expression of scorn that I had experienced from her on previous occasions.

Gravitas, I decided as I found my voice, was the best mode of response, and certainly the most impressive.

"Good morrow to thee, Cousin Elizabeth (I nodded gravely in her direction); "Gwendolyn," I nodded to her also, and then said to Elizabeth "what bringeth thee to our city of culture and learning?"

"Gwendolyn smirked whilst muttering something which sounded like "Patronising arse."

My cousin turned to her and said "Gwendolyn, I think it excessive to say - just because I expressed a desire to see some collections whilst in Cambridge - that I have come hither to 'patronise the arts.'" Then, turning to me, "I am, of course, visiting your cousin Richard."

"Ah, Richard...yes."

"Yes...Richard."

"Ah."

My cousin Elizabeth, at this irksome exchange, began to look embarrassed, whilst Gwendolyn glared at the nearest market stall.

"May I walk with you for a short while? I asked Elizabeth."

"Er, if you wish."

We walked in silence for a minute or two while I tried to think of something to say. Gwendolyn walked a few steps behind us.

I began to panic within myself.

"I wonder, good cousin," I finally said in desperation as we traversed the market holdings, "If you would find it within your heart to pass on to your brother the warnings I feel it necessary to bring to his attention."

"What warnings?"

"Er, that there are those within this city who seek his destruction."

"What nonsense!" she exclaimed (not the response I had been hoping for), "Who would seek my Brother Richard's destruction?"

"I cannot say - I am not at liberty to do so."

"Well, are you not at liberty to address Richard directly about these fears of yours? Possibly not: he tells me that your manner toward him, not merely unfriendly, is openly hostile."

This was not going the way I had expected. Far from being impressed, both girls were showing signs of marked impatience. I looked about me as if to suggest an atmosphere of general subterfuge. "We cannot all be moderate in our religious leanings, there are those - I tell you - who would do your brother harm. With his late night revelry and his ostentatious mode of apparel, he has brought unto himself unwelcome attention."

She appeared to find this extremely irritating. I had dug myself into a hole and I was finding it hard to extricate myself.

"Again I ask you," she said, "why you do not speak to him of these concerns yourself?"

"I do not believe that your brother would wish to speak to me on any matter."

My cousin Elizabeth (with whom, as I have explained, I was not very well acquainted) suddenly, and completely unexpectedly, waxed wroth. She stopped walking and turned to face me.

"How dare you suggest to me that you are moderate in matters of religion...?"

"I – er."

"...When you and your friends at home have persecuted God-fearing people Sunday after Sunday for so long? Do you know; do you have any idea at all, how my father and brother have suffered whilst you *moderates* have disrupted their lives so? If there is anybody in this place who has threatened my brother's destruction it is you, but I do not believe that there is any such person."

"But…"

"Have you been following us? Gwendolyn has told me before of her discomfort caused by you doing this often."

This threw me. I found myself unable to answer.

"My brother has told Gwendolyn that if ever your strange propensity for doing so develops into anything more sinister, then she is to inform him. *Then*, peradventure, you will speak to his face."

This was more than I could bear. "So," I replied with a sneer, "the bitch goes whining to its master; doubtless it gets a nice bone for its reward."

At that, Elizabeth, whose frame was small, struck me with a stunning blow to the jaw, causing me to stagger backwards, something which brought immense amusement to the market stall holders gathered around us. She then seemed ashamed at her sudden loss of temper, doubtless because she remembered she was supposed to maintain a position of dignity. Despite this, she was impervious to the small crowd that had gathered to enjoy the proceedings.

Leaning towards me so that our faces nearly touched she said, "You would do well to remember this proverb: 'Many a fool despises what he cannot get.' Come on Gwen."

With that she grabbed Gwendolyn by the hand and led her quickly away up the road, leaving me to the amused looks of the swinish multitude; which, realising that the fun was over began to go about its business.

While a sense of mortification over being caught out in such a manner may have crippled some, I immediately gave my mind to ways I might gain revenge for the humiliation Elizabeth and Gwendolyn had bestowed upon me. I would give Elizabeth reason to regret not heeding my (admittedly somewhat lame) warning concerning her brother. I would, moreover, have satisfaction with Gwendolyn Smith; and as for my cousin's love affair with Lord Clune: well that was very promising news, very promising indeed.

VIII

Compromise-not-at-all

I was determined not to be late for my next meeting of the *Young Puritans*, although I wanted to avoid the society of Robert Heron and (for this meeting at least) Praise God; I therefore found a seat at the back of the hall in the vicinity of Lord Clune's heckler of the previous meeting. As I had expected, people being such creatures of habit, the participants were seated in about the same positions as at my first meeting; and almost all had adopted the same low–hatted and slouching posture.

Now this heckler, Jenkins: I needed to be wary of him. He was the sort of person who cared too much for his cause to care anything at all about his own reputation; and with whom a secret friendship might well be useful, but who was best avoided on any other terms.

As I sat down I could feel the looks of both him and his sycophantic friends burning into me, doubtless trying to work out whether or not I should be counted as friend or foe.

This meeting was a lot less contentious than the last, the reason being that the issue in question was the much more serious problem of the opposition to the imposition of the Book of Common Prayer, as approved by Laud, the Archbishop of Canterbury, and the King. There was therefore a natural sense of unity, as well as an air of caution. The authority of both the King and the Archbishop were still at this time supreme at the University and, although there were several college masters who might, within the confines of their own council, voice radical opinions, when it came to a direct verbal attack on the King or the State almost all still advocated and practised caution.

I had hoped that this meeting would end in a similar fashion to the last one, and was looking for an opportunity to enliven things, but was prepared to be disappointed, when Lord Clune decided to bring proceedings to a close.

"Let us join together as one body," he said, "for only by doing so might we persuade his Majesty not to let the voices of earthly advisers interfere with the designs of the Almighty."

The group behind me were beginning to mutter amongst themselves, possibly preparing themselves for another confrontation. I decided, however, to steal their thunder. Standing up, I said: "I think, Lord Clune, if you will excuse me, that we must be careful to avoid patronising these people here."

I could hear the voices of those behind me..."aye, patronising – that's the word," and, "You tell him brother."

Lord Clune, somewhat startled by the intervention, said that he failed to comprehend me.

"I mean," I said, "that you should be careful to avoid talking to us like you were our teacher. That qualification, if you have it, has been earned by no other means than that you own a superior title after the fashion of this world. No *spiritual* qualification at all in fact."

"I am sorry," answered Lord Clune, "but I do not know you. I think I would remember you if we had met, which means that, unless there is something which has escaped my knowledge, you do not know me either. How can you possibly know whether I am or am not fit to teach or instruct? I made no claims to be a teacher, but I am regularly requested to speak. I think, judging by the way in which I am constantly assailed in this place, that there are too many here, by far, who are eager to remove the speck from my eye whilst unable to see for the plank blinding their own eyes. You are the ones obsessed with status and rank, not I.

The men behind me started whistling and calling out remarks such as "You've got his temper up there;" and "Ahoy, hark at his Lordship!"

"If it comes," I said, "to class, I can, alike to the Apostle Paul, boast of my worldly status, whilst my spiritual humility is plain for all to see; and I have no reason therefore, *your Lordship*, to stoop down to unbuckle *your* shoes."

"My shoes," answered Lord Clune, "you are required neither to buckle *nor* unbuckle. As touching the Apostle Paul: the difference in your case is - whoever you are - that he repented from his earlier evil life. I would suggest that unless you are willing to do the same, the fruit of which might be for you to turn from your apparent propensity for rabble rousing, you should keep your silence."

These words caused many men in various other parts of the hall to laugh, and a stony silence from behind me. "I would that you know," I retorted, "that in mocking me you are mocking a man with his hands to the plough. As for my identity: my name is Sykes."

I did see Lord Clune start slightly when I stated my name, but he did not react in the disturbed manner that I had hoped for, even though I was sure that he must have been trying to work out whether I was related to his lover.` Even if the mention of my name did cause in him some consternation, the effect was doubtless taken away by someone shouting from the body of the crowd (I could not see clearly for the atmosphere was thick with tobacco smoke, but it sounded like Robert Heron) "Come now, Mr Sykes, we are all friends here; no need for such formalities, your Christian name if you will."

I realised that there was no point in hiding my light under a bushel on this occasion. "My name," I said as boldly as I could manage, "is He-died-for-our-sins Sykes."

Although one or two of the men present laughed at the revelation of my Christian name, most did not (so a hot stick in the eye for Robert Heron). But the person whose reaction I was most keen to gauge was Lord Clune.

His attitude towards me however, changed not an iota. It would appear that my cousin had not told him of me. "Well, He-died-for-our-sins Sykes…" And then, as if in afterthought, "did your father not give you a normal Christian name to prefix your lengthier one with?"

"No he did not," I stated defiantly, "and I think that you would be ashamed to carry a name such a name as mine through this world - with all its snares and temptations."

At this point Lord Clune just muttered "Somewhat embarrassed, possibly," and sat down with a deflated air; and so, for the time-being, our dispute ended.

• • •

As it transpired, my altercation with Lord Clune was the most controversial part of the meeting, which ended soon after without further ado. The heckler from the first meeting was, however, apparently impressed by my words, for when I sat down he tapped me on the shoulder.

"We," he said, "like your style and the cut of your jib. Let us depart from this place and together sup upon God's ample bounty."

Compromise-not-at-all Jenkins, for such was his name, led me with his companions to an extremely run down house in the most run down part of Cambridge. It stank so badly that I had to hold my nose as I entered; and I was grateful that I had received this invitation in the fading months of autumn instead of the hot months of summer. I could not refrain from thinking, at that time, that I was taking the biblical injunction to associate with people of a lowly estate a step too far, for I discovered from our conversation along the way that they were not even university students. They were, in fact, hangers-on; local villagers who had naturally migrated to Cambridge - it being, in the words of Jenkins: "The only place in this part of the country where there's any action!" They all now intended (or at least Jenkins intended – and the rest intended to follow) to go and 'seek their fortunes in the City of London.' Despite this, and despite their living in conditions I had hitherto thought suitable only for swine, they thought that they were something, and this was reflected in their attitude of self-importance.

'God's ample bounty,' it turned out, was in this instance a pottage of stale bread with greeny-grey mould growing on it, mashed up with warm goat's milk. This revolting concoction was served by their landlord - a disgusting fellow of the basest description - in a gratuitously rude fashion. Not only did this man's long greasy hair hang down into the muck he was serving, but he appeared to take delight in slopping the 'food' out of a filthy cauldron into our bowls with such force that considerable quantities of it splattered over us. When Compromise-not-at-all complained about this he merely responded in an accent so thick as to be virtually unintelligible, with words that sounded like: "Be thou grateful and pay thy rent."

"You know that we said the rent would be paid by Friday," responded Compromise-not-at-all, "it is the excess of food dripping down my clothes I am complaining of, not your sumptuous fare, although you did promise us roast beef today."

"Piss off," said the landlord graciously, and disappeared into his private section of the hovel.

"People like him," said Compromise-not-at-all, "will suffer greatly for their taxing of the righteous when the wheat is sorted from the chaff. Now, let us introduce ourselves."

They were then presented to me one by one. All of them nodded gravely and silently as their names were mentioned. The brothers Flee sin and Flee fornication Miller came first. These were the only ones other than Compromise-not-at-all with virtuous names: thereafter came John Ballinger, James Taylor, Edward Oates and William Lambert.

After we had eaten all that we could of the slop, we put down our spoons and, although I have always detested the smell of tobacco smoke, I allowed them to light their pipes without complaint, as it at least did something to mask the stink. A moment or two of meditative silence followed during which Compromise-not-at-all gazed thoughtfully into the clouds of blue smoke drifting across the room, and the others, who were clearly used to being led by him in all matters, waited for him to speak.

"I sense in you," he began, "a man after our own heart; a man who is unwilling to let the values of this world snare him and cloud his way. We are persuaded that the way of the Lord has been compromised at this university, not only by reprobates, from whom sinful behaviour can only be expected, but by people willing to fraternise with them, such as Clune, the one you so articulately ribbed at the meeting just past."

"Your views on how to deal with such backslidings seem to differ from many other puritans," I replied.

"Aye, that they do," he said, "and as I just hinted, many of the most damaging backslidings are counted among the *Young Puritans* themselves. Did not the Lord say that we should be hot or cold, but that the lukewarm he would spew out of His mouth?"

I had already decided, even before I came among these people, that as far as my association with them was concerned it was limited to their value to me. There was something about the way Jenkins' followers kept on aping him by repeating his words that I found intensely annoying. He, admittedly, had a certain semblance of natural leadership, but I could tell that Jenkins was destined to spend the rest of his life shepherding toadies such as this lot.

For the time being however, I talked and answered their questions as if they were my equals.

I found out, just as Lord Clune had hinted at the last meeting of the Young Puritans, that it was they, and Compromise-not-at-all in particular, who were responsible for the insults to the female relatives, lovers and servants of the *Honourable Protectors*. I also found out that this was as far as they had dared to go. Their actions had been entirely limited to this and the sort of scuffles I had witnessed at the last meeting. They were, in short, almost entirely talk and no action. I also realised that with the exception of Jenkins, they were all stupid, and certainly had no grasp whatsoever of the potential that the times we were living in afforded them.

"Do you mean to say," I said, "that you have allowed these profligates to go about their corrupting business all but unchallenged, whilst we, who are required to carry the Lord's torch in the darkness, do nothing; except by some accounts I have heard, get beaten and kicked into the dirt?"

They all looked ashamed at these words, so I continued.

"Know you not that we have a duty to halt the devil's activities? Back home in Northamptonshire we would regularly attack these fops and demon's minions as they cavorted on the village green."

"Well," asked Compromise-not-at-all, "what do you suppose we should do?"

"Aye, what do you suppose we should do?" echoed the others.

"'Tis simple," I replied, "start off with a small target, then, as you gather confidence, step up from a walk to a trot; eventually you may find yourself galloping as I have been wont to do."

Apart from Compromise-not-at-all, who looked at me with an air of feigned understanding, they gazed at one another with expressions of gormless incomprehension.

"What we need to do," I explained, "is to show these bullies and jackanapes that they are not the only ones who can wield the fist around this place. I have a proposal: next week on Friday night, my cousin, Richard Sykes, who is heir to the baronetcy of Caldecote Manor, is holding a masked ball. It is my intention to spoil this occasion for reasons both personal and godly. I know what you are all thinking; that there is a marked difference between me and the way I am able to spit upon my noble background, and the likes of Lord Clune and my cousin, who hang onto their love of this present world with such desperation, well I will not contradict you."

"Aye," one or two of them said, whilst the others nodded in agreement, "much to be admired," added another.

"As I was saying," I continued, "this ball gives us a chance to show both these pleasure seekers, and the compromisers within our own ranks, that we are no longer willing to lie down while the devil rides roughshod."

"How do you propose to do that?" asked Compromise-not-at-all.

"By attending in the guise of one of these popinjays, I shall disrupt the ball from within."

They looked at one another in a manner which displayed both admiration and wonder.

"What shall our task be?" asked Flee fornication.

I stood up and began to put on my hat and cloak. "If you would all be willing to meet me at the bell tower near the entrance to King's College at nine of the clock on Friday evening, I will tell you. One thing I will say now though: by following my proposal to the letter you will all be able to work out much of your frustration and, at the same time, make a name for yourselves.

I then took my departure, leaving them to wonder at this strange and gifted man who had come among them. I myself had a problem to solve: how to get into the ball in the first place. I would, I realised, be far from welcome. I mused on this problem as I traversed the road home. The rub was that despite the fact that the ball was masked, however heavily I disguised myself my nose would be a dead giveaway. On the other hand, once I was in the house itself, I knew that my cousin would be loath to create a scene by attempting to eject me.

But it was not my sole intention just to disrupt the ball; I also needed an opportunity to get into Richard Sykes' house in order to find the whereabouts of Gwendolyn Smith's sleeping quarters. I was convinced that, were she to meet me at close quarters, for want of another expression...*ready for action*, she would not be able to resist me.

• • •

The next day, whilst still mulling over the problems and opportunities afforded by life and this ball in particular, I walked straight into Praise God whilst passing the porter's lodge of St. Gabriel's College. He, as usual, had his nose buried in some old book. "You, Praise God," I said with some irritation, "have your head so far up in the heavens as to be of no earthly use to anyone. Get out of my way!"

"I am sorry, He-died-for-our-sins," he mumbled pathetically.

I scowled at him and moved on, but just as he was about to walk out of sight, I realised a change of heart.

"Praise God, Praise God! I shouted, running after him, "it has been so long since we spoke together as man to man. I never know what you are doing these days, or how your studies are going. Come: I will purchase for us both a jug of ale at the *Steepled Hat*."

He, taken aback, muttered something about being late for a lecture, but offered no real resistance.

We walked arm in arm to the tavern, which, at this time of morning, was all but empty. Having had our tankards filled by the sour faced woman I wasted a little time on small talk, but soon brought Praise God to the point.

"Praise God," I asked, what have you been doing of late to spread the word of the Lord?"

"Well I..."

"I merely ask because it seems to me that in pursuing your studies you have been neglecting the weightier matter of the gospel, and its promulgation."

"But I..."

"I have a task for you Praise God, the accomplishment of which will demonstrate your appreciation and gratitude, both to me, for my easing your path in these halls of learning, and to the Lord for His wonderful and limitless mercies."

"What do you wish me to do, He-died-for-our-sins?"

"Merely to preach."

"You wish me to preach? When? Where? Have the *Young Puritans* called upon me?" Praise God asked, with pitiable enthusiasm.

"No, although I am sure that they will after you have performed this task."

He waited in silence for me to explain, so I continued.

"My cousin Richard Sykes is holding a masked ball at his house on the Friday of next week. Your task is to preach to the guests as they arrive, to exhort them to turn away from their evil ways, and to warn them of the wrath to come."

His expression changed to one of alarm. "But I cannot do this," he spluttered.

"And wherefore not," I responded with feigned anger.

"Because this is not the most fitting way for me to spread the word of God. I have already told you that Richard Sykes asks me questions willingly about the gospel."

"And I have told you that such conversations are a waste of time."

"But I cannot preach to these people as they arrive at a ball!"

"What foolishness you speak, are we not required by the Lord to 'shout His name from the rooftops?'"

"Then why are you not doing it?"

"To each, as you know, his own gifting; to some evangelism, to others teaching. Did you think that I intended to do nothing? Nay, it is my purpose to enter the ball in my own person and exhort the dancers and merry-makers therein. Let them look to the left, let them look to the right; they shall find themselves unable to escape the convicting Sword of Truth."

Praise God still looked doubtful, but I knew that he would submit to my will. Really, his spiritual intensity was of such a high level that that he had no choice in the matter. I only needed to hint that he was being disobedient to the Lord in order for him to do what I said. It was so easy as to make the task facile in the extreme.

• • •

The following week I had to spend in preparation for the masked ball. I took the stagecoach to London, only the second visit of my life, and enjoyed the journey in the company of some Calvinists of a genteel disposition. We did not communicate with one another much upon the way, but rather gave one another the benefit of an occasional gesture of mutual appreciation, such as a nod or a polite smile.

I made my way, upon my arrival in the City, to a tailor and costume fitter in Chancery Lane, where I was measured for a suit of elaborate Elizabethan clothes described as 'fit for a fine actor in any Shakespearian presentation.' I took the opportunity whilst there also, at his recommendation, to try on some very expensive underwear on the grounds that – as he said -'surely even puritan women like a man who cares about the little details.' I have to say that despite his foolishness, and despite my wearing (at least the outer clothing) entirely for reasons of necessity and subterfuge, the feeling of soft silk caressing my skin after year upon year of wearing course puritan horsehair clothing, was both thrilling and sensual in the extreme.

Notwithstanding this new sensation, and the stirrings it raised within me, I had no desire whatsoever to change my mode of outward apparel. To do so would be tantamount to a change of religion, and outward appearances are, after all, extremely important. I had to remind myself therefore, that I had come to London merely for the costume, although I did allow myself to be persuaded that there was no reason at all why my outward attire should not continue to demonstrate my piety and humility, whilst my inner should give me the sensation and comfort I so earnestly craved. It was a marvellous feeling to attract, because of my puritan clothing, the respectful glances of passers-by, whilst underneath enjoying that secret sensuality.

I will not spend too long describing the two days and one night I spent in the capital. Suffice it to say that I traversed the streets, taking in the sights and sounds; enjoying as I went the secret sensation of my new undergarments. I will mention, however, that I spent a short time gazing in awe at the Palace of Westminster, and I was delighted to be granted admission to Westminster Hall, wherein the great affairs of state had been conducted in days of yore. Although the great hall was all but empty when I went in, and had been used only for judicial functions for upwards of nine years, I knew, as I stood in that place, that therein lay my destiny.

IX

The Ball

T he day of the ball arrived.

I was pleased (it being late November) that the days had become short and the nights long, as I was eager for darkness to fully fall. As soon as it was twilight I pulled out from under my bed the costume I had bought in London, and which I had secreted in my rooms upon my return.

Standing in front of my full length looking-glass, I slowly peeled off my plain puritan adornments, and, when nothing except my tight silk underwear remained, I gradually began to dress again.

I first adorned a white linen shirt with lace to keep the starchy corset from scratching my skin; a codpiece to enhance (nay highlight) my manhood, and then the corset itself. I realised however, when trying to put this on, that I had a problem. When I had tried on these clothes in the shop, the tailor had tied my corset from behind. It had not crossed my mind that the people who wore these clothes in the reign of Queen Elizabeth would have had servants to help them dress, and the fool had not reminded me of this obvious point. It had not been my intention to let anyone see me half dressed in this elaborate costume, especially Praise God, who I was sure, upon spying my codpiece, would accuse me of genital arousal. I fortunately had an idea which, at the same time as solving my immediate problem, would also keep me from being seen by Praise God in this attire altogether, at least without my mask on.

Jumping into bed I called upon him loudly.

"Praise God," I said as he entered, "I need you to fetch the porter's running boy."

"Are you ill, He-died-for-our-sins?" he asked.

"Nay, I am a resting, that is all, and I would like you to fetch the lad to run for me an errand."

Praise God went away to do my bidding, and five minutes later I heard a knock upon my door.

"Enter."

In walked a grubby boy of about ten years, whom I had often seen loitering around the porter's lodge.

"Young lad," I asked from my bed, "would you prefer threepence, a thrashing, or death?"

"Why, um, threepence Sir!"

"Very well, listen to me carefully. I am about to rise from my bed and give you a small task to perform, if you perform this task as I instruct you, you shall receive a threepenny bit, if you laugh when I rise from my bed, then you shall receive a thrashing, if you tell anyone what you see, then I shall kill you. Do you understand?

"I do Sir."

"Good." I flung the sheets back.

I watched his face very carefully as his eyes involuntarily rested upon my codpiece and tights. I have to confess: he did well not to laugh, as I could see that the temptation to do so was likely to over-power him.

"Help me to fasten the hooks on the back of this corset."

He did so without a word.

"Well done lad." I threw him a shilling and reminded him that death would most certainly follow should he betray me; I then opened the door, gave him a playful kick up the arse and slammed it behind him.

I then set about putting on the rest of the costume: a beautiful doublet of bright scarlet with gold embroidered loops, black panta-loon breeches, and a very wide, somewhat uncomfortable, white ruff. I then put upon my feet a pair of shiny black buckled shoes, and the beautiful scarlet cloak that went over the doublet.

Finally, I put on the gold embroidered mask. I had been careful to choose one that would cover the whole of the top half of my face. It also had a long bird's beak, sufficient to disguise my nose.

I then waited for the sound of Praise God leaving his room. He had complained to me often during the past week about the task I had set for him, but at around half past eight of the clock I heard his slow and heavy footsteps traversing the passage, and I knew that he was on his way to Richard Sykes' house to create for me an unwitting diversion. I followed him moments later, and, once out in the dark, I felt relatively safe from the critical scrutiny of the puritanical element within the college.

I managed to steal past the porter's gate unnoticed. Once in Trumpington Street I shook off my fear of discovery and, as I got closer to King's College, to actually enjoy mingling with the Friday night revellers. So outrageous in their behaviour and appearance were some of the Cambridge undergraduates at that time (despite the Puritan influences I have written of) that the sight of a man dressed in Elizabethan garb wearing a gold mask made me if anything, even less conspicuous.

My first task was to meet and give instructions to Compromise-not-at-all and his rabble. I could see them as I approached King's College, about ten yards or so from the porter's lodge, looking furtive and mysterious. For this reason I decided to address them with an air of subterfuge.

I kept to the shadows, and when I was close enough to hear their hushed voices, dived into the doorway of a shop on the opposite side of the road.

"Pssst."

"Who goes there?" asked Flee sin.

"It is I, Sykes. Do not approach me, listen with care."

"Speak on brother," replied Compromise-not-at-all quietly.

"You must follow my instructions to the letter," I whispered in response, "at midnight you must make yourselves present in the road outside my cousin's house next to the Corn Exchange - the sounds of mirth and mayhem will draw you to the correct address. At this time you will see a man leave the house and walk purposefully in the direction of Queen's College. The ball will be going on late into the night, so the man you see leaving at this time will certainly be the one you are seeking. This man is a notorious disrupter of the true Church, a thorn in the side of the gospel; and a persecutor of true Puritan brethren. At best you must despatch him; at the least you must show him that the Gospel has a heavy fist. I shall be watching out for you: the moment you attack this man I shall begin to preach to the heathen within."

During this time I could see Compromise-not-at-all and his followers staring at me out of the darkness, but they made no comment, other than that this man sounded like 'a legitimate target for the righteous.'

"The time has come for me to go now," I continued. "You have just less than three hours. I think that, such is the burden of the task before you, the Lord would understand should you wish to partake in a little wine and spirit before the deed. Such things are never pleasant. Let it be said of our enemies that they love violence; but that we are men of peace who only take up the sword in defence of God's church...here!"

So saying I threw them a guinea: more than enough for them all to get truly smashed.

"Be gone now," I said, "and Godspeed."

"Thank you He-died-for-our-sins, we shall do as thou asketh," one of them answered

They turned and disappeared into the darkness.

• • •

As I arrived at Richard Sykes' house Praise God was preaching loudly, and standing, not as I expected, on the other side of the road, but right amongst the crowd of ball-goers. They, as I anticipated, had gathered outside to behold the spectacle. I slipped in amongst them.

"I tell thee all," he shouted, "that the time has come for ye to put away this vanity and foolishness. Did not the Lord promise to the Children of Israel that He would smite the Philistines and Amalekites from the land? Be thou not counted among them, turn ye and repent before the wrath of the Lord consumes thee."

The reaction of those present varied. Some laughed, some muttered, while others stood in silence.

"I think someone ought to fetch Richard Sykes," I said quietly to a man standing next to me, "I am sure he knows this fellow."

"Aye, good idea," he said, and disappeared into the house.

A few moments later Richard Sykes appeared wearing the costume of a Byzantine prince with a mask that only partially disguise his face. He stood on the doorstep near to me for a moment watching and listening to Praise God. He then uttered a deep sigh and moved across to where he was standing.

"Come on Praise God," he said, "what are you doing this for?"

"I am sorry Richard," he responded, "but I am compelled by the gospel to seek and save the lost."

"And you don't think this method is somewhat unproductive?"

Praise God looked at him silently.

"Please do not leave me with no choice but to remove you." Richard then changed his tone: "Has someone told you to do this?"

Praise God still said nothing.

"This is not the way you normally go about things," continued Richard.

As Praise God still didn't answer but looked, if anything, somewhat tearful, Richard Sykes said "You know that you are welcome here whenever you wish to talk to us about…anything, why not join us on Sunday afternoon?"

At this, Praise God muttered something semi-incoherent about 'having done enough,' and disappeared into the darkness. I took the opportunity to slip into the hall, where I was immediately offered a large goblet of strong mulled wine fortified with brandy.

I had to confess to myself, when walking into Richard's lavishly decorated withdrawing room, that these degenerates certainly knew how to enjoy themselves in style. I could not keep myself from a twinge of envy when I thought of Richard and Elizabeth being brought up in an atmosphere in which such pleasure was allowed and encouraged, whilst I had been trained to consider that the ultimate joy in life was to break off prayer for a period of bible study; especially when the chief architect of my upbringing, my father, had all along been playing fast and loose with half the willing slatterns of Northamptonshire.

The men were dressed in costumes which marked every era: Roman noblemen, Saxon princes, Shakespearian heroes; they all were there. The women were enough to get any holy man's blood up, despite their masks. They wore the costumes of wood nymphs, Roman and Greek goddesses, and again, some of the more comely heroines from Shakespeare. Most striking of all however: they almost all displayed the most alluring quantities of flesh at the bosom.

Looking more beautiful than any of them, however, was Gwendolyn Smith, who was moving about the room from guest to guest with a steaming jug of mulled wine. She was, as usual, wearing a plain blue gown with an apron; but her figure was no less tantalising for that. She would occasionally stop long enough to answer a question or laugh at a joke with one of the guests, but on the whole they would merely hold out their cups for her to fill.

Speaking of which, this spicy wine was going straight to my head. I joined a group of men in a part of the room she had yet to visit. It was a most peculiar experience to stand there like that. The men were having just the sort of conversation I would have expected, but it was strange nonetheless to hear someone dressed like Nero discussing hunters with a Greek god. I pretended to listen to their conversation, and even threw in the occasional "Oh quite, quite," for good measure. My attention however, was really taken up with Gwendolyn, who was moving ever closer in our direction.

"Yours good?" one of the young men suddenly asked me.

"Oh yes…er…splendid!" I replied.

"Where do you hunt when you're not in Cambridge?"

"Oh, you know, around the brothels, aha ha ha!"

I thought that they would find this amusing; believing as I did that this would be their sort of humour. I could tell however, even despite their masks, that their response to my joke was to regard me with the utmost disdain. The man who had asked me the question, after staring at me in silence for a few moments, and then looking briefly, and contemptuously, at my codpiece, turned his back and continued the conversation with his friends as though I had entirely ceased to exist.

At that moment Richard Sykes joined the group, and slapped the shoulder of the man who had just snubbed me. "Broderick old fellow," he said, "how's the horses?"

"What was happening outside?" Broderick answered, ignoring the question.

"Just a bit of trouble from the Puritan brigade - nothing to worry about."

"You should've called us; we could have given them a kicking."

"Well actually, there was just one, and he's really quite different from most of them. I'm sure he was put up to it."

"Oh?"

"Well my cousin leads him around by the nose, and he's a true stirrer. Prithee, enough of this, the dancing will shortly begin and I haven't even had a drink yet."

This reference to my trouble stirring bothered me not, but I was still crimson and sweating with embarrassment under my mask due to the slight I had received over my brothel joke, when Gwendolyn arrived with the jug of wine. She first of all served the group I had been with, who were by now standing a few yards away from me. Broderick paid her some compliment, or made a joke, to which she smiled, gave a small curtsey and replied, "My Lord," in the expected obsequious fashion, before moving in my direction.

When she reached me she smiled, but said nothing; I realised that she was unlikely to speak unless spoken to first, so I lowered my voice to a hoarse whisper, and said "Well, serving wench you may be, but you could certainly win belle of the ball here, I'll warrant."

She blushed a little, and said "Fie upon you Sir," but I could tell that she had enjoyed the compliment. Now, after years of the treatment I had received from this woman, to just talk to her at such close quarters aroused me incredibly. She made as if to move on, but I stopped her by the arm.

"And for how long must you serve tonight?" I whispered.

"Until about one of the clock."

"I would know where you live."

"Why…here Sir."

"In the capacity of serving wench only? I imagine you sleep then, somewhere downstairs?"

"Of course Sir, what is it to you Sir?"

"Well," I said, looking her up and down, "Methinks I could offer you a better position."

"For what reason, Sir? As far as I can tell, I pour wine as well and as badly as any other *serving wench* with her faculties intact."

"I had a different position in mind from the one you speak of; but I can't disagree with you about your faculties."

"I think that you are drunk already, Sir."

"Drunk I may be, but this I do know, a kiss on the cheek from you would be worth more than a whole night in the sack with any of *these* noble beauties."

At these words her cheeks reddened, and she made for a moment to hit me with her wine jug, but managed to check herself. Instead, she turned on her heels and left the room.

"I will deal with you later" I thought. I then turned my attention back to the party. I worried for a moment that I would be expected to participate in the dances, none of which I knew, so I made my way into a corner as they began and was pleased to see that I was not the only one sitting out. In fact I could see a girl who, despite her disguise, I recognised as my cousin Elizabeth. She was surrounded by a clutch of young gallants, but looked miserable nonetheless, doubtless because of the absence of her puritan lover.

To a tune which I can only describe as pagan and woodland in its tone, the men and women formed two ranks according to their sex and, with the top couple having first bowed to one another, started to jaunt up and down, twisting and turning with the other couples in the most complicated fashion, the other couples form-ing arches which they passed under, as well as obstacles for them to manoeuvre around. No sooner had the first couple repeated this exercise a few times, and thus made their way to the bottom, the next would begin, and the performance would be repeated until everyone had a turn.

As I could not dance, and the provision of intoxicating drink (to which I was not accustomed except in the form of the occasional ale at breakfast) was abundant, I began to quaff more and more of it. Having stood there for some time while watching the female dancers, I realised when I looked at a candle clock at the end of the room that the time was approaching midnight.

I had anticipated sending an anonymous ball-goer out to meet his fate, but realised that without knowing who most of the people were, it would be too risky to just approach someone and tell them: 'You are wanted urgently at Queen's College,' in case they asked, 'Why, who wants me?' or 'Who are you?' or some such difficult question. Lord Broderick however, whose identity I had already ascertained, seemed to me an ideal candidate.

I looked out of a window to check that Compromise-not-at-all and his company had gathered, and managed - despite the darkness outside the building - and the light within - to see their huddled forms under a dim lamp on the other side of the street.

I left the room and, finding a servant, ordered him to take me to a place I would have access to paper and quill. Once I had obtained these I wrote the following:

Lord Broderick.

It is of the most extreme importance that you repair to Queen's College instantly, as I have news concerning a most grave danger to the King and Queen, the knowledge of which will enable you to be of the utmost assistance to their Majesties. Please forgive the lack of formality with which this message has been written; but as it pertains to such a matter of national importance, and as time is of the essence, my respects you must, as you should, take for granted. Please make haste.

Robert Heron of Corpus Christi.

I then made my way up to one of the first floor bedrooms facing out onto the street and, having removed my mask, signalled for one of

Jenkin's gang to come over. Edward Oates stole over silently, keeping to the shadows.

"Take this letter to the door," I whispered, throwing the note at him. "Give it to one of the servants then run away."

He nodded, then picked up the note from the ground and took it over to where a group of menials were gossiping by the front door. I waited to check that he had done his task as instructed then ran back down to the party to see my work unfold.

I had no sooner entered the withdrawing room than from another door on the same side of the room a servant walked in with the note and walked straight towards Lord Broderick, who had just finished a dance.

Although I could not hear his exact words I could see that my plan had worked perfectly, or nearly perfectly. Lord Broderick made a rush to get to the door, but was stopped by one of his friends. They spoke for a moment and then left together. I should, I realised, have added to the note that the matter was to be kept secret.

I quickly ran back up the stairs to the room I had just vacated and managed to attract the attention of the group over the road again. One of them started to come over but I waved him back. I then held up two fingers at them and pointed towards the door. I repeated this action more than once, but then disappeared back into the room as soon as the front door opened, hoping that they had understood my meaning. Lord Broderick and his friend walked hurriedly down the front steps and started making their way up the road passed the gang in the direction of Queen's College. Jenkins and his friends followed and caught up with them as they reached the road below my window. They surrounded Lord Broderick and his companion.

Compromise-not-at-all was the first to speak: "Hold there Sir's, whither are ye going in such a hurry?"

"I *beg* your pardon?" replied Broderick.

"You heard the question, answer it."

"Who the hell are you? Mind your own business."

"We are they who have a care for the spiritual well-being of this nation. We have been watching you lot through the window. Whilst good people are suffering persecution in the name of the Lord, you jaunt around like a hoard of sexual deviants."

"Get out of our way!" Lord Broderick and his companion tried to push their way through, to no avail.

"We have some friendly advice for you, *brother*: when in future you wish to make merry, sing psalms of praise and thanksgiving." So saying, Jenkins landed a hefty punch to Lord Broderick's jaw, which immediately caused him to fall to the ground. As soon as the first blow had been struck, Lord Broderick's companion was wrestled to the ground also and the group surrounded their prostrate figures, kicking and stamping on them repeatedly.

I ran back downstairs again and into the withdrawing room.

"Lord Broderick is being attacked outside by a bunch of puritans!" This I shouted at the top of my voice, and the effect was delightful: the music stopped; there was a moment's confusion, and then all the young men rushed out of the room whilst the women crowded around the window. I slipped back upstairs.

As I again made it to the window, Richard Sykes and his friends piled out of the front door in a confused huddle; one of them shouted "There!" and they rushed over to enter the affray. I have to confess that I could not help being amused as I beheld the comedy of violence and confusion below me. And violence it was: the original attackers, who became the defenders, were given a resounding beating. One of them had his head smashed against the wall opposite the house.

I did not wait for the outcome of the fight, as I had other business to attend to. Having again made my way downstairs, I easily found the door to the cellar and, with the attention of everyone drawn by events outside, managed to enter unnoticed.

The rooms were apparently deserted. I therefore explored the place at leisure and found a wine cellar, a scullery, a storeroom full of gardening equipment and, at the end of a short passage, two bedrooms. I assumed they were bedrooms because behind one of these doors, as I approached, I could hear the sound of heavy snoring. I could hardly believe that such a sound could emanate from the lungs of Gwendolyn Smith but, just to make sure, I turned the handle and quietly crept in.

I was correct in my assumption. On the bed, her face turned upwards with her mouth wide open, was a huge woman whom I recognised instantly as Molly Sheep, second cook of Caldecote Manor. I left her to her dreams, satisfied (especially as the sounds of the fight were quite audible, even in the cellar) that only the noisiest of disturbances could interrupt her slumber.

I tried the other door and, upon entering, realised that I had found Gwendolyn's sleeping quarters. That it was her room was clear, as one of her dresses was hanging from the back of a chair. Even if there had been no such evidence, the very room was suffused with her unmistakeable scent. Such was the effect of that beautiful aroma that I was tempted to take my clothes off and wait for her in the bed there and then, as I was sure that when actually confronted with my manhood flesh to flesh, she would find me irresistible. But this would only have a chance of working if she walked into her bedchamber and undressed in the dark. She would, in fact, almost certainly enter her bedroom equipped with a candle or lantern, and I had a feeling that the sight of me waiting, naked, in her bed, might cause her to scream loudly enough to wake even that cook up.

Nay: for the purposes of seduction I knew I needed to be cautious - and patient also. I therefore left her room and looked for a place to hide myself whilst I waited for her arrival. I then only needed to leave her a little time to settle down before I went in to her.

I decided that the best place to lie in wait was the room full of gardening equipment, as I could not be sure that someone would not come down to the cellar in order to fetch wine.

I hid behind the door, leaving it slightly open; and a short while later the sound of fighting and mayhem ceased, and the mirthful noises of the ball began again. No one came down to the cellar at all, and after a space of about an hour I began to think that boredom would get the better of me. I was in fact prepared to give up waiting altogether, when I heard the door at the top of the stairs opening and shutting, then the sound of descending footsteps and, through the opening of the door, I could see her, looking all the more radiant for the air of hard work and grime she carried about her. She walked straight to her room and shut the door behind her.

I knew then that a period of further waiting was required, as to give her a reasonable amount of time to fall asleep seemed imperative.

After about another half hour I could bear it no longer. I removed my doublet, and then found amongst the garden equipment a pair of shears with which I managed to cut away the top and bottom laces of my corset. I then tore it off. I made my way along the short passage to her door and opened it slowly, relatively safe in the knowledge that if she saw me she would recognise me only as that rude fellow from the ball and throw a shoe or something.

She was however, fast-asleep, or so it appeared. I shut the door quietly and stood next to her bed, listening to her soft breathing as I grew accustomed to the darkness. She lay with one arm over her head; her blankets covering her only to the waste. Her breasts were clearly visible through her thin nightdress.

The moment I had waited for, for so long, had arrived. Removing my mask first, and then my clothes, I gazed at her for a moment longer and then slipped into the bed. She murmured and, as she did so, writhed in the manner of one unconsciously awaiting sexual gratification.

But at that moment, in her warm bed, the place I had so often dreamed of being, I suddenly froze. What foolishness had my longing for this woman led me into? I had imagined her waking and, with the presence of my nakedness close beside her, becoming overcome with desire. It now dawned upon me that she, when she woke, would scream and probably attack me like a wildcat.

I tried, very quietly, to get out of the bed, with the intention of dressing quietly and leaving the room.

"Richard?" she murmured, apparently in her sleep.

I stopped suddenly, as I was still upon the bed, and sat motionless.

"Richard?" she repeated, and I could see through the gloom that her eyes were open.

"Mmmm."

Her voice rose a little: "Have you left your mask on?"

"Mmmm?"

Suddenly the tone of her voice changed completely, and her body went rigid. "Your nose! What is wrong with your nose?"

I could tell, as she jumped from the bed, that she knew what was wrong with my nose: nothing, except that it belonged to me and not my cousin Richard. Before I could do anything to stop her she ran out of the room and grabbed the candle that had been left burning in the passage, returning with it quickly.

She rushed over to me and held the candle to my face. I was now kneeling on the floor trying frantically to retrieve my clothes. I could see her bosoms heaving with panic and vexation. "You bastard!" she screamed, slapping me on the face; "you ugly bastard!" slapping me again.

This got my temper up, but I knew that despite my rage I must at all costs get out of that room and out of the house. For this reason I rose quickly and shoved her onto the bed, hoping she would stay there and just glare at me as I gathered my clothes and fled. Unfortunately, however, she still held the lit candle in her hand, the hot end of which she shoved violently into my left eye.

Now that pain was like nothing I have ever experienced, and distracted me completely from my purpose. Had she burned instead my cheek or forehead, then it would not have been enough to divert me from my intention. But the agony of that hot wax in my eye incapacitated me completely; and she, far from being sympathetic, then kicked me in the groin.

So excruciating was the pain, both to my eye and my balls, that I was able to do nought else but roll on the floor screaming with agony. I was dimly aware of Gwendolyn pulling on a gown and running out of the room; I then heard her climbing the cellar steps. There was still no sign of life from Molly Sheep.

As I became accustomed to the pain, I also became very aware that Gwendolyn was likely to fetch Richard and, quite possibly, a bunch of hot-headed ball guests, who after the fight out in the street were probably still in a vengeful mood. I again started to scramble around in the dark to get my clothes back on, but only managed to find my tights and the codpiece before I heard the sound of the door opening at the top of the stairs.

Panic took over. I pulled on my tights and shoved the codpiece down my front; then, abandoning the rest of my clothes, I made a rush for the window, which was far too small for me to escape through. I then dashed for the door, hoping to force my way past Gwendolyn's rescuers.

But once out of the room I found the passage blocked by my cousin and about six of the male dancers from upstairs, as well as Gwendolyn and her brother Simon. I tried to get past them, but was thwarted in my purpose by Simon and Richard, who between them forced me to the floor.

I have now come to a part of my story that, were I a less frank and honest man, I would have left out, and you will soon discover why. The humiliation I suffered that night is something that I have taken great pains to strike from my memory, with little success. Despite the glorious times that I have experienced since, my mind has often been assailed with a sudden and unwanted memory of the laughter, the taunts, the wrath and the pain I received at the hands of my enemies on that terrible occasion.

"Right, He-died-for-our-sins," said Richard, "I always suspected that you were capable of this sort of wickedness, come with us." So saying, they dragged me from the floor and forced me to climb the cellar stairs.

"I would like," said Richard when we reached the hall, "to give you a good thrashing. However, as you have behaved in a manner unworthy of the basest churl, there is no reason why your rank should protect you from being punished by one who is clearly your moral superior, as well as your victim's brother." As he was saying this he took a cane from a stand next to the door and gave it to Simon Smith. He then opened the door to the withdrawing room and dragged me in by the ear.

"But Richard…." I protested, "Think of the family honour!"

But he, ignoring my words completely, made me stand in front of the guests - about one hundred and fifty in number - and shouted for the musicians to stop playing.

The music ceased, and the dancers, recovering from their initial confusion, looked in our direction. They all reacted in exactly the same way: a shocked silence followed by a crescendo of uncontrollable laughter. I had to stand in front of those people for about five minutes as they humiliated me. Some of the men pointed at my codpiece, others sat on the floor, so overcome with mirth they were unable to remain standing; whilst the women pretended to avert their eyes - the hypocritical bitches. As you will doubtless expect, I swore revenge under my breath against these godless people.

Richard then said that they were not to be shocked by what was about to happen, as I had attempted to rape one of his servants in the cellar. I was taken out onto the street, forced to bend over and caned by Simon Smith in front of all those people.

I was then, after being beaten about a dozen times, made to undergo the further humiliation of walking back to Gabriel College in nothing but my tights and codpiece. This took some explaining to the college porter, whom I had to wake from his slumber; and his errand boy (the one who had earlier helped me on with the corset) did not bother this time to resist the temptation to laugh, doubtless because he had already received his threepence.

Through all of this, moreover, I nearly froze to death.

X

Vexing Richard

The next day I woke up with a very sore eye (although I could at least still see through both of them) and an extremely sore backside. The eye at least, which was swollen and streaming constantly, gave me a convenient appearance of having been attacked (useful for any explanations I was likely to have to give) and my backside, I realised, could well prove useful if needed. I intended, despite these agonies, to go about my normal daily business.

Praise God, up early as usual, had left me some ale and crumpets, and I had just sat down to partake thereof, when I received a message from Dr Harding requesting me to call on him and explain why I had been seen by more than one person walking through the streets of Cambridge the night before wearing nought but a pair of tights and a codpiece.

Having prepared my excuses I made to leave my rooms, but found my way barred by Richard Sykes, who pushed me back inside and shut the door. He held up a blood spattered piece of paper, which I immediately recognised as the note I had written from 'Robert Heron.'

"Who, pray," he asked menacingly, "is Robert Heron?"

"I know not. What is this soiled piece of paper thou art holding?"

He shoved me onto a chair. "Do not play the pious puritan with me, you wrote this note, did you not?"

"I did not, and I know not to what you are referring."

He ignored my denial, and began pacing the room in a most frustrated manner. "Before your perverse actions were discovered last night, this note was delivered to Lord Broderick. I need not tell you what happened, as it is clear that you were the architect of this business. But this I will tell you: having dealt with your friends as they deserved, some of my guests went in search of the said Robert Heron, and I know not whether this gentleman is dead or alive as a result. I have, moreover, two friends of my own who would have been killed but for our timely intervention."

To this I could not resist a little smirk. It is hard not to be self-satisfied when one's plans are carried through so well. But for my unrequited passion and degradation, the events of last night had gone rather well.

My expression irked Richard somewhat. He picked me up and pinned me against the wall by the lapel of my coat. I met his eye boldly, so he glared at me silently for a few moments then dropped me to the floor.

His frustration then began to show, as he proceeded to walk rapidly around the room kicking the furniture with the most extreme vexation. "How can you believe you're right?" he shouted. "What possible motivation or justification can there be for this sort of behaviour? Your self-righteousness might be almost acceptable if you were at least a holy man in other ways...but you are aggressive, lustful, pernicious..."

"I am a holy man in a way that your sort could never comprehend," I answered, still lying on the floor.

"Oh you...idiot!" he shouted, and aimed a kick at my arm.

"That's right, kick a man when he's down."

"You fool!" he shouted, kicking my leg. "You're worse than your father was."

"I suppose you think you're the only one who has a right to have his way with the serving wenches."

"That," he shouted, grabbing my nose and shaking my head with it, "is my whole point. I find your father copulating with two half-wit females at once, both of them barely old enough to bleed; and you, probably because you're so damn ugly (this he said banging my head against the floor) are willing to trick your way into a maiden's bed, and yet you somehow think that God thinks you're better than everyone else. Well I think I understand God better than you do, because I think you make us both sick!" (He banged my head on the floor again to emphasise these last words also).

"I think you and I both know, Richard, that Gwendolyn Smith is anything but a maiden."

At this he raised his fist to punch me full on the face, but after a moment thought better of it. He got up to leave the room, giving me a final cuff on the scalp as he did so. On his way out he met Praise God, who was returning from a prayer meeting.

"Do not ever do that again!" Richard shouted at him, but then in a calmer voice: "just get away from that…fool!" As he said these last words he picked up a book, flung it at me, and stormed out the room, slamming the door.

I got up, dusted myself down, and brushed past Praise God, who stood there gawping at me in his usual irritating fashion.

• • •

I told Dr Harding that I had been attacked by a group of effeminate young men who had beaten me and stolen my clothes, replacing them with the unseemly apparel he had heard about; that I had wanted to remove these disgusting garments altogether, and would have done so were it not for the fact that outright nakedness would have been even more of an offence to public decency.

The Doctor seemed willing to give me the benefit of the doubt and even consoled me for my misfortunes. He then asked me about the *Young Puritans*, and seemed particularly interested in the internal struggles between the peaceful and more militant factions within.

I told him about Lord Clune; how I regarded him as a compromiser, and I lamented the fact that the only people who were willing to adopt a stance more militant seemed to hail from the lower classes of society.

The Doctor invited me for what had now become our customary walk around the grounds of the college. He walked with his hands behind his back and his head bowed after the fashion of many spiritual worthies before him. "It has come to our attention," he began, "that there are too few among the student fraternity (I am talking here of *real* students, to wit, young men of property) who are willing to take up the cudgel in God's cause."

He stopped momentarily and looked up at the sky. "What we need is a galvaniser; someone of your age and class willing to take up the sword for the Lord's cause; someone with a will to stand at the vanguard of the struggle against evil. There is a danger that if such work is left to characters such as Clune, the ranks of the militant righteous will have their mission and purpose diluted, and will be tempted to compromise with the ways of the world."

We walked on. "Frankly, Son, I am fed up with waiting for the *Young Puritans* to show their metal. All they ever do is pontificate about whether they should do this or that, and usually end their meetings brawling with one another. Whenever any of them *do* do anything, they end up being beaten by their adversaries because they go about the Lord's business in such a foolish manner, as I heard report of last night outside a heathenish gathering held by your cousin."

Naturally, I declined to comment at this point.

"There is trouble brewing for the King," he continued. "That he will, at some stage, need to call another parliament is all but inevitable. It may be the King's purpose to use Parliament as an extension of his own wallet, but we need men such as you to teach him that parliament is there to be a righter of wrongs, a light in the darkness and an avenger of evil."

He paused, and then said, "I have had a care to look into your circumstances, lad. There is, I perceive, nought you can do as long as your cousin is able to step before you, do you understand me?"

"I do Sir."

The Doctor then added something I certainly had not expected of him, and which had resonances of the strange doctrines I had lately discovered from my father. "When it comes to the issue of furthering the cause of true righteousness, I hope you are aware that the saints need not overly trouble themselves with vanities such as worldly honour. If occasionally truth must be sacrificed for the Kingdom, then let it be so. Dost thou fully understand me?"

"I do, Doctor."

"Then go and do as thou hast to."

I bowed to the Doctor and walked away from him with an air of solemnity. I was aware of him looking after me, nodding with pride and approval as he beheld my departing form. Doubtless he looked upon me as the son he had tried, but failed, to conceive.

• • •

After leaving the Doctor I went to Compromise-not-at-all's hovel. Flee sin was tending to his wounded brethren, because he merely had a broken nose and a couple of cracked ribs. The rest of them were lying around in a state of shock; all of them had broken bones. James Tailor and Flee fornication Miller were practically dead.

I decided that they needed some encouragement. "Troth," I said, "you showed those popinjays a thing or two yester'een; talk is around that there are certain puritans about town not to be trifled with: puritans with muscle!"

"Oh that'sh wonderful," said Compromise-not-at-all in a muffled, toothless voice, "anth what were you doing to further the cauth of righteoushneth while we were having our heads smashedth?"

"Why, if I understand your question correctly, as soon as I heard the tumult created outside by you brave fellows, I threw off my mask and proceeded to preach to the Heathen within. I was sorely beaten for my troubles. Are not my wounds worthy of one who has suffered for the Lord's cause? Behold my eye as it runneth with puss! Must I show you the stripes on my backside?"

Compromise-not-at-all appeared somewhat mollified by these words. "Yeth He-died-for-our-thins, thou hath suffered too - forgith me."

"I do forgive you, with a true and willing heart. Now there is much work before us, but methinks I had better give you a day or two to recover before we embark upon our next enterprise."

"Yeth, a day or too would be welcome."

I wished them well in their recovery, and slipped Flee sin a shilling for medical expenses.

• • •

My next purpose was to visit Robert Heron in order to see if he were dead, and to deal with any accusations against me if he were not. I arrived at the porter's lodge of Corpus Christi and asked for directions to his rooms.

"Another visitor for the poor gentleman?" the porter responded, "and I had always thought him such a solitary individual." He then directed me to a set of rooms opposite, on the first floor.

The news of Robert Heron's prior visitation gave me cause (as you will understand in the light of the visit I had received from my cousin that morning) to be wary. Having climbed the stairs I knocked quietly on his door and, upon receiving no answer, crept in. His study was empty. But through an open door, which, I surmised, led to his bedchamber, I could hear the sound of voices. I peeped round, but quickly retreated back into the study, from whence I would be able to make my full escape should the necessity arise. For what I beheld was not just the bloody, bandaged head of Robert Heron protruding from his bed sheets, but standing around him my cousin Richard, as well as Matthew Spencer. Included in their company moreover, was none other than Lord Clune.

I could hear their voices easily from my hiding place, as they were spoken in the sort of tone adopted by those visiting a critically ill friend or relative, who wish to keep quiet for the sake of the patient, but who are unable to do so due to the intensity of their emotions.

"I had thought when my guests were attacked (this was my cousin Richard to Lord Clune), that this was another instance of unprovoked puritan violence, and that this fellow was the cause, but I have since discovered reason to believe that my cousin was the culprit, albeit that he is a *puritan* also."

"I will not argue with you, Richard, over your use of the word *puritan*, except to say that a true purity of the church would exclude such violence as much as any other vice. How do you know that this deed was done by your cousin?"

"This note, which appears to be signed by Robert Heron, was, in truth, written by He-died-for-our-sins Sykes. What I wish to know is this: is my cousin one of your party?"

"He has taken to attending our meetings recently, and I saw him leaving the last one with Compromise-not-at-all Jenkins and his mob."

"Who," asked Richard with an audible sneer "is Compromise-not-at-all Jenkins?"

"It is he," answered Clune, "who makes your use of the phrase *your party*, as well as the term *puritan*, so inappropriate. He and his fawning followers have been responsible, not only for the strife betwixt the followers of different spiritual and political leanings in this university, but even among those whom you so loosely label puritans."

"And it was doubtless he and his friends who were the perpetrators of the attack on my two guests last night?"

"Doubtless."

"What then, is to be done? I have coaxed, entreated, admonished and pleaded with my cousin all my life to no avail; last night I even had cause to have him flogged, and yet he will not turn from this pernicious and aggressive way of forcing his false religion upon others."

"We should have the coxcomb publicly flogged until he kisses the Book of Common Prayer and swears allegiance to the King. As for the others: kill them and fling them into a pit." (This was Matthew Spencer).

"Well here, Richard," rejoined Lord Clune, "is the real rub: at least, while they may appear to be of my church and persuasion, I keep people like Jenkins at a distance, and am willing to challenge their behaviour; you seem bent on keeping their mirrored opposites at your very elbow."

"Are you comparing me," asked Matthew Spencer, his voice rising, "to those malevolent half wits?"

"In the tone of your words Matthew," said Richard, "there is some likeness, pray be silent."

"I will not be spoken to thus by – a – *puritan*, be he a viscount or a serf."

"Quiet Matthew, if you please," repeated Richard, "and remember that we are here for the sake of *this* person."

After these words there was a moment of silence. I then heard the sound of someone striding out of the room in my direction. I had just time to retreat into the passage and pretend to tie my bootlace, thus hiding my face with my hat, before Matthew Spencer stormed out of the door of Robert Heron's study. Upon entering the passage, he muttered the words "Out of my way," as he shoved me out of his path with his booted left foot. He then marched down the passage, threw on his plumed felt hat in a careless fashion, and slammed the door as he left the building.

You may well think, worthy Reader, that I should have run after Matthew Spencer and challenged him for his insolence; and you would be correct. I was in fact just about to do so, when from my position in the passage I heard the sound of my cousin and Lord Clune preparing to leave also. I therefore considered it more expedient to hide myself in a conveniently situated broom cupboard.

They talked in the study for a while before leaving, and as the door had been left open by Spencer I could still hear their words clearly from my hiding place. I will not bore you with the slanderous version of events my cousin related to Lord Clune concerning the previous evening, you already have my full confession; but it took all of my strength of resolve not to respond when he attempted to malign me by saying that I tried to take Gwendolyn Smith by force.

"My suggestion," said Clune after professing his shock and horror, "is that we speak to those who have authority over these people, particularly your cousin's tutor. He has no interest in using the university, apparently, for anything other than trouble stirring and sexual licence. Perchance a report of his actions will stir Dr Harding and his colleagues to send him down."

They rambled on about my wickedness for a while (alarming me not in the slightest with their intentions), and then Richard changed the subject. "I am somewhat glad that Matthew has left us," he said, "as his temper is easily raised and easily assuaged; and the destruction of extremism is not my only concern: how fares your secret love for my sister? She almost ruined the dancing last night with her pining, until it was ruined anyway by those fools. There was not a man there who did not take it upon himself to be the source of her consolation; and who did not have his nose put out of joint in consequence. Tell me straightly: are you going to do the honourable thing, or is God unwilling to stand for such a rival for His affection?"

"You are making sport of me."

"Somewhat, but not in earnest."

"My affection for your sister waxes each day. I believe that it can grow no stronger; and then it does, and my heart is full to bursting."

"Oh Alan-a-Dale, lack-a-day Alan-a-Dale!" mocked Richard in a sing-song voice, and then added dryly: "and where, forsooth, are you going to spend your Sunday mornings?"

"I understand you not."

"Well you must have thought, surely? My sister's mode of worship is so high as to make her almost Catholic. She will embarrass you in church by crossing herself at every mention of The Father, The Son and The Holy Ghost."

"Do you not think that I have spent every morning, noon and night thinking of - and lamenting - the very obstacle to our happiness you speak of?"

"This very answer shows me how foolish you both are; for I know that it is the very answer she would give me. As surely as God created Man you are made for one another. If the King and Queen can worship in separate chapels what makes it so difficult for you?"

"Methinks that there is a very narrow gulf between the religion of the King and the Queen, despite their different allegiances."

"There is nothing false about the King's commitment to the Church of England," replied Richard, somewhat tartly. "He tolerates the Queen's Catholicism rather than approves of it. But you two both worship in the Anglican Church…"

And so they droned on *ad nauseam* until they were out of my hearing. I found this conversation repugnant in the extreme, particularly in respect of Clune who, whilst purporting to be a man of God, spoke - when he believed he was out of the earshot of his holy brethren - as if he had warm syrup pouring out of his mouth.

On the other hand I had all the ammunition I needed to bring about the downfall of both of them. Clune, as a renegade, had suddenly become a much easier target. As for my cousin, he would most certainly, along with his sister, be harmed by Clune's downfall.

XI

Clune's Downfall

With the exception of James Tailor and Flee fornication Miller, Jenkins and his friends were all present at the next meeting of the *Young Puritans*, which took place on the following Thursday evening. I again arrived late, and could feel upon my entry that the atmosphere was bristling with an intensity of expectation, as if the members could sense that in one way or another, something, although they knew not what, was going to happen. Doubtless this atmosphere was caused by the rumours and counter-rumours that recent events had given voice to.

Lord Clune was addressing the crowd in his usual fairylike fashion, albeit that he did resemble, in truth, a somewhat angry fairy. He noticed me as I sat down, and his tirade took on an even more personal and wrathful aspect.

"How" he was shouting, "can thorns and briars produce fruit fit for the Kingdom of God?"

I knew that the crowd were expecting me to lead the counter attack, and I had no intention of disappointing them, but I decided to let Clune rant on a while for better effect.

"…You think you will bring about the Kingdom of God in this backslidden nation. You think that God has a particular purpose for you…"

His voice began to reach a pitch which denoted an apoplectic rage of which, I must confess, I had hitherto thought him incapable.

"...Do you think that you will produce anything other than the fruits of evil? Do you think that the Lord requires His servants to propagate the Gospel by the means of rape and violence? Do you think that those for whom we seek salvation will be drawn into God's Kingdom by your example of license and wickedness?"

Clune paused, then added "I must move that there are certain of our company who, as they have made themselves into God's enemies, should be removed from this society and, if any attention is paid to what I say, removed from this university altogether!"

The people had what they wanted; the meeting erupted. Amid the shouting I could hear "Name them, name them!" and "Shame, shame!" Whether the shame was meant to be upon Lord Clune or myself and others I could not tell; perhaps both, for - as was usual - the participants were divided into at least two opposing factions.

At that point I decided to enter the affray, but was thwarted in my attempt by Clune, who managed to raise his voice more effectively above the tumult. "I will name them!" he shouted, "they are the usual rabble rousers who are sitting at the back of this meeting here: Compromise-not-at-all Jenkins and his sequacious sycophants, and worse still, that *gentleman* who sits there, He-died-for-our-sins Sykes!"

At the mention of my name the noise immediately abated, and a tense silence fell upon the spectators. All eyes were immediately turned to me. I knew then that my moment had come: I would, by the success or failure of my response, rise like a star - or sink to the ignominy of homestead farming for the rest of my years. However much the likes of Dr Harding placed their hopes in me, I knew that my future depended upon the outcome of this battle.

I stood, and, fixing Clune with my gaze, began my response thus, at first calmly: "Who, asked the Lord, will go and warn this people? Thus will I, I responded, and the Lord was gracious in using me, the lowliest of his servants.'"

I looked around the crowd boldly and I knew that they were already enthralled. Lord Clune sat down and looked at me stonily.

I continued: "Who do you think that the Lord will use to muster His army against the legions of Gog and Magog? Who will the Lord use to throw the Dragon back to the sea whence it came? Compromisers? Those who are willing to accept hush money from the devil?"

By now I had the audience completely under my spell.

"Oh Lord," I mocked, "I will serve you, only please do not make me stand apart from the world...cast out not my demons – they are my succour and comfort – take not my title from me. In Your Kingdom I must be an ordinary man, but in the world I am fated and honoured. Let me be Your friend and a friend to the world also."

Up until this point I had kept my voice fairly low, allowing the command of my words rather than their volume to captivate my audience. I knew then that the time had come to exert my authority.

"Do you think," I continued, raising my voice all the while, "that the Lord has need of those whose desire to walk the broad road results in the diluting of His message? Has not the Kingdom of God always been thus stifled? I tell you all that I have suffered for the Lord and I have the marks to prove it. While this man has been consorting with the enemies of the Lord I have been persecuted for preaching God's word. He attacks me, but I tell you all: the worst enemies of the Church in this place are my natural relations; my cousins after the flesh. While I go to the House of Sin, braving the Hall of Vanity and the very Parlour of Iniquity; and attempt to turn those people from the ways of wickedness, receiving in return base accusations, as well as *this* for my trouble (I turned around and, dropping my breeches, showed them the marks on my backside, to which they all gasped), as well as this (I pointed to my streaming eye), he (pointing at Lord Clune) is intending to marry the worst of them, the Laudian slattern and servant of the Queen, whom I have the misfortune to know as my cousin: Elizabeth Sykes! (Further gasps from the crowd there were, at that point, aplenty). Well Clune, what have you to say to this? Dare you deny the truth of my words?"

The crowd turned silently, as one, to face Clune, as if not daring to believe my words, and yet convinced that there must be truth in them for me to have said them with such explicitness.

He, meanwhile, had gone very red in the face and sat there in a sort of stunned silence. "Go on," I shouted, "answer the question!"

"Aye," the people began to shout, "answer him; answer the question! Are you betrothed to his cousin?"

Lord Clune began to splutter like a boy caught raiding his mother's larder, "I, er, am – but he..."

But he got no further. The response to his admission was better than I could possibly have anticipated. There were howls of derision from all around, phrases such as "Oust him!' and 'Get him out!' while the supporters of Lord Clune merely sat in an attitude of shocked silence, unable to defend their champion. Lord Clune was given no opportunity to retain his dignity by speaking further, or even by walking out. He was grabbed by the hair and collar by several of the men around him, and forcefully dragged down the aisle separating the benches, being kicked and spat upon as he went. Our eyes met for a moment: a look of utter defeat from him exchanged for a look of triumph from me, before he was ejected from the door.

My moment of glory had arrived. The immediate clamour was silenced by Compromise-not-at-all Jenkins who climbed onto a chair and, raising his hand to the air, shouted "Gentlemen, gentlemen, silence if you will!" Having quieted the din enough to be heard, he said "Brothers we have need of a new leader; need we look any further than this brave member? I give you He-died-for-our-sins Sykes!"

These words were greeted by a deafening roar of enthusiasm, raised by almost all of the members. To be sure Geoffrey Westmacott tried to protest, but he was struck hard upon the face for his trouble, and ran from the hall with blood spraying from his nose. Meanwhile I was hoisted up and carried around the room on the shoulders of my brethren, to shouts of adulation and praise.

• • •

There was, I came to realise, one great disadvantage to my new influential position of head of the *Young Puritans*: I had to, as it were, keep my nose clean. It was one thing to refute the allegations of Richard Sykes concerning the night of his ball, this I did with ease; but as I achieved greater prominence it became very important that I should not be caught again with my breeches down.

This was the downside, but there now followed what to me can only be referred to as a golden age at Cambridge University. The *Young Puritans*, caught up with my holy zeal, and free from the pacifism of characters such as Lord Clune, set about putting things to rights. Under my direction parties and balls were raided, dancers were beaten and scattered into the night; tennis matches were wrecked; golf tournaments were ruined. And not only did the unbelievers come to fear us, for we also served the Lord by searching out items of luxury and recreation from the homes of those who purported to be godly, but who had allowed the snares of pleasure-seeking to make their straight path crooked. Soon, despite the resistance of characters such as my cousin Richard, the atmosphere at the university became so thick with godly fear and religious trepidation, that the very idea of sport or recreation taking place in public began to receive a social condemnation in a way that my father had never accomplished in years of trying. Yea I am talking here of a reign of fear. Moreover, so pleased were the likes of Dr Arbuthnot Harding with the progress of true religion at the university that I was soon elevated, even whilst an undergraduate, to the company of some of its most illustrious dons and masters. I can safely say that it was my own influence which gave these men the courage to stand up to Archbishop Laud and his prayer book; and in standing up to him, they were of course standing up to the King also. And it was the influence of my association with them that gave me the ability finally to crush the activities of the *Honourable Protectors of the Divine Right*.

My role in the crushing of pleasure-seeking at the university soon became so renowned that it began to be imitated, at first in the counties of Cambridgeshire and Norfolk, and thereafter around the country as a whole. In my home county of Northamptonshire my fame was all the more influential in causing godliness and righteousness to take a firm and deep root. It was inevitable that the landowners would be caught up in this new found zeal; that, despite there being no talk of conflict in the land at this time, they were already taking sides in their support for, or antagonism towards, the King and all he stood for. As it was these people who had the power to select and de-select their county's members for Parliament, and as my reputation travelled as fast before me as the Word of the Lord which accompanied it, it also became inevitable that, after many of them became aware of my rise to power (as well as my cousin's fall from grace) at the university, I would oust him as the prospective Member for the area of Towcester and Weedon in the next parliament.

• • •

But we cannot leave Cambridge behind us before I give a short history of my friends and enemies.

Lord Clune sunk into relative obscurity after the events just described. His time at the university was in any case short, because during the first period of Lent after his last meeting of the *Young Puritans*, his father, the fourth Earl of Clunehaven, died, and the new Earl went up to Northumberland. He somehow sorted out his religious differences with my cousin Elizabeth; they married, and disappeared for a time from my life. I found it a matter of some chagrin that as the head of my branch of the Sykes family I was not invited to this wedding, which was apparently attended by the King and Queen. I would not have gone of course, but I should have been invited.

My cousin Richard remained at the University and did his utmost to stifle and oppose the great works of the Lord hitherto described. It became apparent, moreover, that during his time at Cambridge he gained very close links with the Royal Court. But despite his powerful connections – the most notable of whom was the detested puritan turncoat Lord Strafford, who had become the King's closest adviser, it was the cause of godliness, under my auspices, which had the ascendancy at the university at that time; and there was little that Richard could do other than offer feeble resistance and, as was almost certainly the case, spy for the King.

Gwendolyn Smith remained at Cambridge throughout this time pretending to be one of the Sykes' ordinary servants, but living, as I believed, as Richard's live-in harlot. If there was one thing that gave me trouble more than any other during my time at university, it was my eye: the eye that she had stabbed with a burning candle. In the first place the mockery I received on account of this wound, which manifested itself in the form of puffiness and running puss, was a weapon that could be used by any who had such a desire to accuse me and re-accuse me of trying to take the said serving girl by trickery or force. Even apart from this, my eye gave me much trouble. It was always sore and it would stream constantly; especially in the summer. I therefore had to get used to people, especially women, looking at me with a degree of repugnance I had not previously experienced. It was also particularly prone to giving off the puss when I became angry, agitated or exited; just the sort of emotions I would tend to feel when preaching to the occupants of a house as their belongings were being ransacked by the Jenkins mob. I often suspected that these hapless victims were caught between dismay at the destruction of their property, and the desire to laugh and puke simultaneously.

As I have just stated, my eye wound also gave Gwendolyn Smith's serving friends a license to ignore their station - while relying upon the protection of their powerful masters - and mock me openly. As for the girl herself, *she* did not mock me (or even look at me if she could avoid it) but she did not discourage her friends from doing so. I am a patient man; and when it comes to revenge I know how to bide my time.

Another great thorn in my side during the rest of my time at Cambridge was the constant reminder of the letter I had written to Lord Broderick signed by 'Robert Heron.' He, upon recovery, proceeded to assail me with words of mockery and accusation at every possible opportunity. This thorn was thankfully removed by the discovery of Robert Heron's insufficiently holy way of living by his father, whose rage caused him almost simultaneously to threaten his son with disinheritance, and to have a fatal heart attack. He also left Cambridge prematurely, although our paths were to cross again before long.

Praise God tried to keep his head low during the rest of his time at the University. The only act of strength I am willing to recognise from that man is that he stubbornly refused to perform any more exploits on my behalf such as he had done on the night of Richard Sykes' ball. Had he any sort of real strength or authority, however, he would probably have taken up Lord Clune's mantle and formed some sort of woolly alternative puritan party to mine, as it was this sort of insipid, weak Christianity he really favoured. But I, on the whole, allowed him to continue his studies uninterrupted, as I had plenty of others to help me further God's cause without his assistance. During his time at Cambridge his apparently vast intellect was 'discovered' by the legal fraternity, who persuaded him to continue his studies at the Middle Temple in London with a view to being called to the Bar. So much for *his* pious intentions.

Flee fornication Miller did die in that hovel; but his death was not entirely in vain, for his body was sold for medical research in order to pay off some of his, and his friends,' overdue rent. The others, however, all recovered; and revenge there was aplenty for Flee fornication's death.

PART TWO

XII

Short Parliament

Oh how I love the Scots!

You may say to me, worthy Reader, that they are miserly; you may say that they speak with a dialect which betokes ignorance and ill-breeding; that they begin hypocritical in the south, and exchange their hypocrisy for savagery in the north (which land yields nought but tartan-clad peat bog monsters), but I tell you that I love them.

For eleven years the King ruled over England with the authority of nothing but his imagined anointing from God. He forced a prayer book upon us, a few protests there were, but he had his way. He forced us, even we who live as far from the sea as is possible in our small country, to pay a ship money tax for the upkeep of the navy; again, a few protests there were, but he had his way. Worse still, by his very presence our ability to stifle wickedness was capped because he sanctioned evil with such a strong hand. Oh we had righteousness, but he had the law.

But the Scots, oh the Scots; he could do nothing with them. He tried to force the Prayer Book upon them; they threw it in his face. He remonstrated with them, they remonstrated with him. He tried to browbeat them, they attacked his representatives: first his bishops, and then his army.

And then we, having called upon the King to no avail to recall parliament for so many reasons, were summoned to Westminster because the King needed money in the form of subsidies from parliament, to tame these traitorous rebels - so say what you will to me; I say that I love the Scots!

And who was behind the King's policies? Thomas Wentworth, first Earl of Strafford, and William Laud, Archbishop of Canterbury. And who was Strafford's little minion in my part of the Midlands? None other than my cousin Richard Sykes.

The task of being elected for parliament was easy, due to the circumstances mentioned at the end of the last chapter. Richard Sykes would have been the natural representative for Towcester and Weedon. He was the latest of a long line of Sykes's who had represented our part of the county of Northamptonshire both at Parliament and at Court. But such was the strength of the rise of puritan power that he had become all but excluded from the possibility. He had the support of a few local noblemen - he also had the patronage of Lord Strafford. But *I* now had the support of many more of the most powerful of the local landowners, who had heard of my great works at Cambridge. This soon outweighed Richard's former advantage.

To put it simply therefore, while the prospect of Parliament and the high affairs of state lay before me, Richard had to content himself with the important business of shooting ducks and drakes and looking after the welfare of his estate tenants.

But I must mention – before I resume this account of my adventures – that upon my entry into Parliament I soon became aware that even those considered the most radical of members were loth to attack the King directly for his misdoings. Instead they sought to excuse him by blaming his advisers, most notably Strafford and Laud, for their antagonism of the Scots, as well as their misrule of the English and Irish, as if they could have acted without his royal sanction. The most daring of the parliamentarians, such as those of John Pym's party, were willing to hint at the evil influence wrought upon the country by the

Queen, but certainly not the King himself; and even she they dared not attack openly.

But to return to my story: it was announced on the 12th of February 1640 that the State Opening of Parliament would take place on the thirteenth day of April. Thus it was that I found myself, having 'contested' the election, heading towards London via Buckingham with Brickett on a sunny morning on the 1st day of April. I had on my person a petition from the landowners of Northamptonshire by which I intended to make my presence known in the Commons.

I had already arranged my living quarters: a large house in Chelsea overlooking the River Thames. This furnished house I had rented by previous arrangement from Dr Arbuthnot Harding who, in addition to his small stipend from Cambridge, owned a considerable fortune in the form of real estate, both in London and in the country.

I will not regale you with tales of unpacking and the incompetence of Brickett. Suffice it to say that I had to beat him on many occasions for his stupidity. Having been born and raised with the cattle on my farm, he would frequently, both when we passed through the country and when we arrived in London, stop to gawp at any sight or sound unusual to him. As every slight occurrence was to him a novelty, this constant interruption to our progress became most irksome. I noticed moreover, upon our arrival in the capital, that other gentleman and ladies of quality travelled with well-dressed and washed servants. I therefore proposed, when I was settled into my new accommodation, to find for myself a manservant worthy of a gentleman. As soon as my chattels were unloaded and arranged in my house, therefore, I tossed Brickett a shilling and set him on the walk back to Northamptonshire (I would, of course, need his horse for my new servant).

With him gone, I hired myself a presentable young man by the name of John Brown as a valet and general dog's body.

I will here confess to you that a sensation of awe and apprehension beset me upon my arrival in London in that balmy spring, and this was despite the fact that a letter of introduction had already been sent from Dr Harding to John Pym, a prominent and virulently anti-Catholic veteran of the last parliament. But I imagined that this man would have little interest in anything other than the great matters of state before him, and certainly little time to waste instructing a new member.

I had however, become something of a master at disguising fear of any sort (nought was ever achieved by timidity) and therefore determined upon the third day of my arrival, which was nine days before the State Opening of Parliament, to go down to Westminster to seek out the celebrated veteran in order to offer my allegiance and loyalty, and to show him the petition I had brought with me which would, I believed, stand out from any similar documents brought by other members.

However, upon this morning, and just as I was sitting down to a hearty breakfast of sausages and ale, I heard a knock upon the front door of my house. I sent John Brown to answer and could see, as my chair was in sight of the hall, that he opened the door to a man of about five and fifty years, somewhat stout and grey in appearance. He walked straight passed John into the hall whilst throwing him his hat and cloak without a glance. He then strode into the parlour.

As he stood before me, I could tell immediately that he was used to wielding authority; the sort of person who would try to rule you, but would treat you with the utmost contempt if he succeeded in doing so. I made to stand up but he waved me back to my seat. He stood before me for a moment looking keenly upon my face with an air of thorough scrutiny, making me wish I had had time to prepare for this moment, in which case I would most certainly have avoided having my mouth stuffed with sausage. His expression showed neither pleasure nor contempt.

"You are, I presume, He-died-for-our-sins Sykes? Your face unmistakably aligns with the description I have been given."

"I am, pray tell me…"

"My name is John Pym. There is much business for us to attend to before the opening of the House; please come with me if you will." Having said this he turned and immediately walked out of the room. He then snatched his hat and cloak from a peg in the hall as he made his way to the door. I left my breakfast unfinished.

He walked, for a man of his age and stature, with astonishing pace and purpose, acknowledging the many greetings he received along the way with a mere nod of the head or a touch of his hat.

"We have managed to gather together," he said, as we walked beside the river, "many petitions, but yours - I understand from Dr Harding - is comprehensive, in that it mentions - as well as the ship money tax, grievances against the King in matters of religious interference."

"Yes, I had expected to…"

"Oh fear not Lad, I know what you were about to say: you were hoping to use your petition to - as it were - make your presence known in the House, and so you shall - far be it from me to steal the thunder of a young up-and-coming. Nay, you shall have your moment, but we need some semblance of order here; we need, as it were, to gather ourselves. The King will try us and test our resolve to see if he can avoid addressing our grievances. He will tell us that in the best interests of the nation (by which he means *his* best interests) we should set aside everything until we have granted him money to fight the Scots. We must be organised in our resistance to this: if we let the King bully us in this matter he will collect his money, dissolve Parliament and never call another while any of us are living."

Despite my previous point, that I recognised the importance of appearing strong in the company of Pym, it was very difficult not to fawn and cringe just a little.

"I am of course, completely at your service," I responded, somewhat lamely.

"I believe that you are, my lad, your reputation from Cambridge has gone before you, and my old friend Dr Harding has given unto me a very favourable report. That which you will experience here in London however will be a greater challenge for you than Cambridge. It is imperative that we know that you are one of our number; that you are not likely to, shall we say, 'play the King as well as the Knave?'"

"I assure you Sir, that I not only understand your meaning, but that I can be completely relied upon in this matter."

"Aye, I believe that that is your heart, lad, but there are many before you who have, upon attaining a degree of power, fallen in love with the magic which surrounds the King and his court; and make no mistake about it - whatever your intentions - the King does carry about him a certain magic by which many men with previous good intentions have been ensnared, so be careful."

I realised from his response that unlike Dr Harding, who was easy to persuade and impress - particularly by flattery - John Pym was the sort of man who would be distracted or diverted from a held opinion or purpose by nothing. If he had decided that I and all people needed to be proved before they could gain his good favour, then no amount of talk on its own would be likely to change that. He also struck me as the sort of person for whom small talk was neither given, nor was welcome; and as he offered no further conversation we walked in silence until we came to the Palace of Westminster.

Upon our arrival my companion led me past the main entrance of Westminster Hall to a large stone building on the other side of Palace Yard. We entered this house through a small side door and walked along a close and dark passage to a small flight of stairs, at the top of which was another short passage with doors on either side. The second of these John Pym opened. Inside what turned out to be a sizable room there were several gentlemen standing or seated around a large desk upon which was scattered many documents. As we entered, all these men became silent, and those who were seated made as if to stand up. They were all waved back by John Pym, who addressed them thus: "Gentlemen, may I present to you the new member (by the grace of God) for Towcester and Weedon: He-died-for-our-sins Sykes. He has about his person a more comprehensive petition than all those that lie before you."

Pym then introduced me to about ten Members, most of whom were to become insignificant participants in my story, and who therefore do not merit a particular mention in these pages. But I will tell you (for these names were to become important to me) that I was presented among them to two members, who went by the names of William Strode and John Hampden.

All of these men nodded to me gravely as their names were mentioned, except for John Hampden (he who had already achieved renown for his resistance to the ship money tax), who just stared at me, and not, I thought, in a very friendly manner. I expected them to continue their conference, but the room fell into silence. I began to wonder if they were expecting me to speak, but was somewhat afraid to do so without a specific invitation.

Realising my dilemma, Pym said "Peradventure, Mr Sykes, you would care to tell us what you hope for from this parliament."

I had prepared myself for a moment such as this, and so after a moment of rapid gathering of thoughts I began thus: "Gentlemen, I find myself catapulted into the society of men who can only be regarded as the light of Israel; men who have fought the good fight and not been found wanting. Some might say that it is the machinations of the Scots that have brought us to this position, but I say that if it had not been for your constancy in serving the Lord; for your refusal to turn back when your hands had taken up the Sword of Truth - then this parliament would have been full of nothing but the King's poodles and lapdogs. While I have yet to prove myself as your equal, brethren; and while also the past eleven years have been an unhappy time for all those who seek after righteousness, yet I must also tell you that the Lord, as he did in the darkest days of Israel, has caused this time to be the catalyst for a swelling of holy indignation in this land; and only as a fellow witness of this surge can I look you steadfastly in the eye."

I, at that point, did look steadfastly at all of them in turn, and then continued.

"I have here upon my person a paper upon which the godly landowners of Northamptonshire have written a score of righteous complaints against the effects of unholy tyranny in our country. Specifically I may mention the ship money tax, but Northamptonshire can be seen also as typical of all the woes that have beset our English Israel. We have struggled and received the wounds of Christ in our efforts to suppress the lewdness and licentiousness to which the King refers as innocent pleasure. This paper (I said, drawing the petition out of my pocket) is direct and it is bold: this paper accuses and it condemns: this paper calls for the impeachment of the King's advisers. I am talking to you, brethren, of none other than Charles Wentworth, Earl of Strafford; and William Laud, the Archbishop of Canterbury!"

Now as you may have guessed, the bit about Strafford and Laud I had added to the wording of the petition after it had been signed, between all that stuff about tax and religion and the signatures at the bottom (no one would have *dared* to sign it otherwise). The effect however was marvellous, and just as I had anticipated. The first reaction was that of a stunned silence, which was almost immediately superseded by an eruption of cheering and applause, from all, I noticed, except Hampden and Pym. The former merely looked at me with an unmistakably cynical expression, whilst the latter became extremely alarmed. "You cannot read that petition in the House!" he exclaimed.

This I had expected, but I responded nevertheless by saying "Wherefore not, Brother Pym?"

"Oh do not mistake me, brother, 'tis bold; 'tis daring; 'tis indeed the direction I should like us to take should the opportunity present itself, but it is also premature. We need something specific with which to charge both of them. It would be foolhardy for us to take so antagonistic a stance against the King at the outset of this parliament. It would also be foolhardy for you to risk such displeasure from the King when he has the power of the Star Chamber at his disposal. Nonetheless, 'tis a wise notion to beset the King by means of his counsellors, your bravery and initiative has been noted, lad."

To which all, except again for John Hampden, responded with expressions such as 'Aye",' and 'Good man.'

"Place your petition back in your pocket," continued John Pym, "but keep it safe, we will have need of it yet."

I already knew of course, that John Pym would think it too early to present such a petition before the House, but I was convinced that following the extremity of the advice hitherto given to the King by the likes of Strafford and Laud, they would be likely, when the Commons proved obstinate to the King's demands, to advise a course of action to the King for which they could indeed be accused before Parliament; and accused, possibly, of a crime no less serious than treason – if the meaning of the word could be stretched a little beyond its normal usage. But in producing the petition at this early stage I had nought else in my mind but to be noticed by the men there present as a man of boldness and foresight, and, as would turn out to be most correct and appropriate, a man of prophetic gifting.

The company went back to the business of poring over the various documents before them concerning the ship money tax, the religious persecutions and the activities of the Star Chamber. I was very much included in these conversations, and my advice was sought on a variety of matters.

• • •

I was, to all intents and purposes, left to follow my own devices until the State opening of Parliament on the 13th day of April. I used my time as would be expected, improving my wardrobe and getting to know my fellow parliamentarians. I also visited the City of London in order to re-acquaint myself with some old friends from Cambridge.

Praise God proved to be so elusive that I began to suspect, having made many inquiries around the Inns of Court, that he was trying to avoid me. I gave up looking for him after a day or two, and left a note for him at Middle Temple, upon which I had written down my address in Chelsea.

But Compromise-not-at-all Jenkins and his friends were much easier to find, for having left Cambridgeshire to seek their fortunes in London they had all found work as apprentices to various tradesmen in the City of London. I located them after a few inquiries in the vicinity of St Pauls. I decided, as they were clearly no less poor than when last I had seen them, to invite them to dine with me at the Black Bear in Fleet Street. As I expected, their enthusiasm at the mention of a proper meal, especially a free one, was pitiable.

As we sat down to eat and drink I discovered that although my former colleagues were impressed by my progress to Parliament, they seemed completely unable to grasp the significance of this preferment. They immediately, upon their first sip of ale, started referring to 'The good old days' at Cambridge, and boasted that they had continued, unabated, what they referred to as their 'chastisement of the godless' since arriving at the capital. They even expected me to join them in their endeavours. It is not always an easy task to explain to people of an inferior wit that there are reasons above their understanding for which a person cannot continue with such pursuits. My days at Cambridge, I explained to them, had been but mere preparation for the work before us. I encouraged them to continue their 'chastisement' as best they could, but to understand also that the work of the Lord needed to be fought in the high offices of State as well as on the streets; that should I confine myself to the sort of things we had done at Cambridge, then the brewing weather would never break forth into a storm; and that if we truly wished for the advent of the new Jerusalem, we must not altogether confine ourselves to the waylaying of fops and dandies.

This riled them, and Flee sin reminded me that he had lost his brother in furthering the cause of righteousness at Cambridge. "I hope," added Compromise-not-at-all, "that it is not love of this present world which has caused you to make a decision to turn your back upon the godly persecution of - as you put it - 'fops and dandies.'"

I was tempted to tell them to go kill a fop or dandy and hang for it. Nonetheless, they had been extremely useful to my purposes at Cambridge, and I knew it would be foolish to risk their displeasure now when it was very likely that they could be as useful to me again.

"Brethren, I merely refer to our thus far striking at the body. The Lord would have us strike at the head also. The time will come, and soon, when having desolated the works of the devil and the high places he inhabits, the Lord will have much reason to say, "Well done thou good and faithful servants; sit ye down here whilst I make your enemies into a stool for thy feet."

Now this did the trick - particularly the bit about striking at the head. "There speaks the He-died-for-our-sins we know and love" said Compromise-not-at-all, and Edward Oates slapped me on the back, causing me to spill my ale. They then wanted to know what great works I had in mind, but I held back for several reasons: in the first place the sense of mystery my words had created only increased the mastery I held over them; secondly, if there was one thing I had never been willing to do with any of these men it was trust them. Finally, and most important of all, these people, as I have already mentioned, had no understanding whatsoever of the great affairs of state in which I was fast becoming embroiled, and could prove to be most irksome to me should I involve them in more than wisdom dictated. They honestly thought that I might be willing to throw in all I had accomplished in order to pursue the same hair brained fanatical dreams of a 'levelled' society that so obsessed them. Nay, I had risked a great deal to attain my present position, a position that would hardly amount to much should those scapegraces got their way.

Despite these reflections I spent the better part of an evening with them. I told them that I would have much need of their knowledge of the City, and their ability to rouse the anger of the low-born masses (although I did not put it quite like that) should the King prove stubborn in the face of pressure from parliament.

With this they seemed to be content.

XIII

Vexing the Archbishop

The day of the State opening of Parliament arrived.

A hot Spring day, but I dressed for this auspicious occasion as befitted a gentleman of the puritan persuasion. It was of the utmost importance, I reflected as John Brown helped me on with my boots, that as I was now rapidly ascending the ranks of society I should be adorned with the humility expected of one of my political and religious allegiances, whilst at the same time showing that I was no upstart from the ranks of obscurity. I had therefore, having visited the same tailor as on my previous visit to London, made sure that those who had cause to remark upon my appearance would note that my apparel betokened both godliness and refinement.

I arrived at the Palace of Westminster as instructed by John Pym, well before the King was expected, and was pleased to find my new friends waiting in the Great Hall. There were many groups of people standing around, talking to each other in hushed voices; members, it seemed, of both the Lords and the Commons. The majority were dressed plainly, although some much more decoratively. I noticed, from the exchange of caustic remarks and jibes between some of the groups, that they had no mind to conceal their contempt for one another.

I had been expecting (and indeed my arrival in the hall begun thus) to enjoy this sense of grandeur and discovery. My enjoyment was curtailed however, by an unpleasant surprise that greeted me a minute or so after my arrival. Having met my new colleagues I tried to listen to the instructions being given by John Pym in advance of the King's address (which would be delivered by the Lord Keeper). It was doubtless the case that Pym, with his many contacts, had knowledge both of what this speech was going to contain, and how best to respond to it. But I, standing for the first time in the presence of so many important individuals, found it very difficult to give all of my attention to his advice and instruction, not least because after a minute or so two gentlemen of my former acquaintance appeared at the top of the stairs at the south end of the hall, and stood conversing together.. The first of these I recognised as Robert Heron, and I realised immediately that his father's death, like mine, must have eased his passage to parliament. It was plain to see from his attire that he had taken advantage of his father's demise by planting himself firmly in the King's party. His hair was long and crowned by a Spanish velvet hat; he wore a deep blue coat and doublet, somewhat lighter blue hose and cloth boots laced to his knees. He scanned the Hall with an expression of contrived aristocratic haughtiness. Having then bowed in the direction of his companion, he made his way down the stairs and disappeared into the crowd below.

But the arrival of his companion had an equally disturbing effect upon me. It was none other than my previously vanquished enemy, Lord Clune, or, more accurately, the new Earl of Clunehaven. My disquietude was increased moreover, by the fact that he, having made his way to the company of some of his peers near the entrance, almost immediately sighted me (and rest assured good Reader, the start of recognition on his face did not betoke the sort of happy surprise one would normally expect in such a situation from a close relation by marriage). I cursed myself for a fool for not realising that which was so obvious. Lord Clunehaven was certain to attend parliament as a member of the House of Peers, and this small detail had completely escaped my memory. It had been one thing to get the better of him in the heated atmosphere of discontent that was undergraduate Cambridge. It was quite another to come up against him in this place, where, due to his very rank he would hold an ascendancy over me from the outset.

Fortunately Clunehaven's attention was diverted by the entrance of an elderly man who appeared at the top of the stairs he had just descended. This man was dressed elaborately in colourful robes of state, and held in his right hand a long staff. He had long grey hair which escaped in an ill-kempt fashion from beneath his skull cap to his shoulders; he also had a hawk-like expression with which he measured the occupants of the hall for a few moments before knocking loudly on the stone floor with his staff. All became silent, except for Pym, whom I heard mutter the single word "Finch," before he too became quiet as the new arrival began to speak.

"My Lords and gentlemen of the Lower House," he began, "the hour is ten of the clock. His Majesty commands the attendance of the Members of Commons at the Abbey within the space of one hour and a half; he commands the immediate attendance of your Lordships at the Palace of Whitehall. Make haste therefore, for the King himself will be present at the Abbey at noon."

With those words Lord Keeper Finch made his way out, and the crowd began to disperse also. I feared that Lord Clunehaven would take the opportunity there and then to accost me, but the Lords, in a hurry to form the procession to Whitehall, made their departure quickly from the hall, while the members of the Commons loitered for a while before following at a more leisurely pace.

Upon our arrival at the Abbey an hour or so later, I found space at the front between William Strode and John Pym; and in a like manner to my new friends I adopted the stance of my *Young Puritan* days...that of discontent: arms folded in defiance; my legs stretched out across the floor in front of me.

But there was still time to wait, and as I did so I noticed, bustling around the churchmen and courtiers whilst giving orders, a short, fat man with a red face, who looked like a somewhat old and dilapidated curate. There was nothing surprising about that I grant, except that he struck me as the sort of person from whom it would be most absurd to receive, let alone obey, any order. He, however, appeared to have no such doubt as to his authority, and was in the process of commanding "More incense, more incense," to some young man who clearly *was* a curate, when his eye alighted upon the three of us. He puffed over in our direction and spoke very quickly: "Mr Pym, Mr Strode, Sir, you cannot sit here."

"Why not?" asked Pym.

"Because," he answered, "these places are reserved for the ladies and gentlemen of the court, and this place in particular is reserved for Lord Sussex and his family. If you look around you, you will see that you have occupied a place half a dozen rows in front of any of your colleagues and equals."

"I would have thought," said John Pym as he stood up, "that this should be one place where worldly rank has no bearing."

"I could say something," the short, fat man retorted as we started to move away, "about those who take for themselves the highest seat being sent down lower, but I shall let it pass as I am sure that your presumption was in error, and you have seen fit to remedy it."

"I do not really see that it is fitting," I said out loud to my companions as we started to walk to the back of the Abbey, "that we, elected representatives of the people as we are, should take orders from a *curate*."

This remark caused John Pym to laugh out loud in spite of the gravity of our surroundings. I thought his amusement was caused by the expression on the 'curate's' face, which was that of high indignation manifested by a deep hue of crimson. His real reason became apparent as we sat down: - "That *curate* is called William Laud," Pym said.

The name I recollected, its owner I at first did not.

"The Archbishop of Canterbury," he reminded me.

"Rather you than me," muttered Strode.

By these words he meant, I believe, that he was glad that it was me and not him who had upset the Archbishop; which is an attitude (I tried to tell myself in order to combat the feeling of terror welling up inside me) all well and good for those who wish to stay in the background; who wish to live a life for which they can congratulate themselves before settling into obscurity. But I was extremely fortunate at the time (I continued to persuade myself) for having so unwittingly crossed the pride of the Archbishop in this fashion; the accumulation of enemies in matters political is, after all, as essential to progress as the accumulation of friends.

William Laud, having issued all of his orders, disappeared into a room at the side of the Abbey, and after about two minutes reappeared in the vestments expected of an Archbishop. He then stood with his back to the congregation and bowed in the direction of the altar (which was draped, as you will imagine, in all the trappings of popery). This done, he turned around and nodded in the direction of the back of the church. There immediately followed a fanfare of cornets behind us and then, preceded by two page boys, I saw, for the first time as they entered the Abbey, the King and Queen, as well as a boy of about ten years of age whom I presumed to be the Prince of Wales.

It would be tempting at this point to give a scathing account of the King's appearance, and to do so would be easy, as he was dwarfed by almost everyone in the Abbey (even his son nearly reached his height), I shall, however, resist the temptation. He *was* very short, but he also had something about him which no man could deny was majestic. Although his hair and beard were grown and cut in the fashion of the time, and his attire was as gratuitously decorative as would be expected, there was nothing gay about his demeanour; he was, in fact, the most naturally solemn person my eyes had ever beheld.

The Queen however, despite her serious expression, gave a very different impression. She was dressed in a long black and purple dress after the style of the detested Spanish, her hair was adorned in ringlets, and she wore a most ostentatious silver crucifix about her neck. She displayed, in short, her Catholic religion in a manner designed to antagonise her husband's subjects, who were terrified of a return to papist rule. Her whole demeanour in fact, seemed to exude superiority and contempt for a nation she regarded as bound by the snares of heresy.

The Prince of Wales showed no sign at that time of the ugliness that would later compel him to rely on his kingship for fulfilment in matters *de la chambre*. He stood a step behind his father, and took advantage of his parents' attention to other matters to gaze unflinchingly at the breasts of a girl of about sixteen in one of the back rows.

Unflinching that is, until an elderly courtier standing behind him gave him a flick on the side of his nose with his fore-finger. The muted, but audible cry he gave in response to this stinging rebuke caused the King to glance round sharply. He looked at his son with disapproval before turning again to face the front.

The Royal Party stood for a moment at the back of the Abbey and, as the music again started, began to make their way slowly forward. After about two paces the King stopped and, smiling momentarily, tapped one of the pages on the arm with his cane, which he then used to point at the altar. The page boys, who had been walking backwards, turned around and led the rest of the way down the aisle with their backs to the King and Queen who, followed by their son and the elderly courtier, led about forty nobles to the front of the Abbey, where they took their seats.

I will not trouble you too much with a detailed account of that service of dedication. I will tell you however, that it was all, and worse, than I could have expected. It was led in the main by the Bishop of Ely, a man who clearly made his living from servility. He used his sermon to compare Charles Stuart to (of all people) King Solomon. He spoke of how Charles, like Solomon, had been blessed with the wisdom to rule his country as God had intended - with absolute authority; but that the rebellion of a Pharisaic element in Scotland had made it necessary for the King to call together what he referred to as 'a Council of War.' He then went on to warn certain elements within the Abbey that to obstruct 'King Solomon' would be accounted by the Lord as treason and rebellion, which was 'alike in its severity to the sin of witchcraft.'

After the Bishop had prayed and sermonised for about an hour, a fanfare of cornets heralded an end to our agony, and the King's party got up to lead the procession out of the Abbey. We then started to make our way over to the House of Lords to hear the speeches of the King and the Lord Keeper. We were nearly the last to leave, and as we did so I took a position at the back of a long train of my fellow Members of Parliament, who were again preceded by the Lords. But I had not walked more than ten paces from the main door of the Abbey when I was grabbed suddenly, and unexpectedly, by the back of my collar, and pulled so violently backwards that I lost my footing and fell onto the ground, gashing my elbow on a paving slab as I did so. I looked up, and although my view was somewhat curtailed by the bright sun, I could make out someone who appeared to be an officer of the King's Guard standing above me. I could also see the departing backs of my colleagues, although one, who I did not recognise, had clearly seen the incident and had decided to pretend he had not noticed. The officer then placed his foot on my throat, the silent but unmistakable intonation being that if I moved a muscle he would crush my neck. Despite the fear and discomfort, feelings of humiliation welled inside me as we started to attract the attention of his colleagues, who formed a circle around us, jeering.

"Now, *Member of Parliament*, he began: what is your name?"

"Sykes."

"Well, Sykes," said the captain "you have insulted the Archbishop of Canterbury, and for that you are going to apologise. Should you fail to do so I will personally hang you by your balls from the Tower clock."

He then pulled me to my feet and dragged me back into the Abbey, to the same room into which I had seen Laud disappearing to change for the service. The Archbishop was sitting on a stool as we entered, drinking from a cup of wine and reading a tattered copy of the New Testament.

"Here he is, your Grace."

Laud looked up. He glared at me for several moments, causing me to shift uneasily on my feet. I wondered if he would speak first, but the soldier poked me in the back.

"I would like to apologise," I said (somewhat pathetically – I cannot deny it).

The soldier again poked me in the back, harder.

"Your Grace," I added.

The Archbishop looked at me stonily: "For what?"

"Um….for mistaking you for a curate."

"There is nothing wrong in mistaking me for a curate; I am not given to ostentatious modes of dressing…either inwardly or outwardly."

Now I was confused, particularly as his words seemed to imply some sort of prophetic insight into my newly acquired expensive taste in underwear. So I smiled, made a quick bow and attempted to depart from the room. The officer, for the second time, grabbed my collar and dragged me backwards. Laud continued.

"Where the sorrow should lie, if you really have any, is in your scornful disregard for the Church."

He paused again, deliberately, I believe, to increase my discomfort.

"I know your type," he continued, "The Lord, you believe, has revealed Himself to you personally; therefore as God has given you such a particular and specific revelation, everything that seems contrary to your beliefs must be wrong; and you need not stoop so low as to give even a cursory respect to anyone, or anything, if it does not win your approval."

He paused, glaring at me. I could see the anger waxing within him. When he addressed me again he was shouting. "Well you and your friends may treat Parliament as if you own it, but when you enter God's House I will see respect from you, or Member of Parliament or not I'll order the Captain here to crop your ears! You will take off your hat (he knocked it off my head); you will bow towards the altar; you will pray - or at least pretend to pray - and kneel while doing so. And whether I am a curate or an archbishop you will show respect for this cloth! Do you understand me, Sir?"

"Yes your Grace, I am truly sorry."

His temper calmed down as quickly as it had flared. "That is all, you are forgiven." He then sat down again, picked up his New Testament and took a drink from his cup as if nothing had happened. The captain then led me out of the room and towards the main entrance, gripping me most painfully on the back of the neck as he did so.

"I cannot understand you – you lot – had the Archbishop been dressed in cloth of gold you would have despised him for it and accused him of being the Pope's minion…. but because he dresses plainly you mock him for that."

There was no easy answer to his words; and indeed he had not actually asked me a question. He led me more and more quickly to the entrance, gripping the back of my neck even tighter as he did so. He then looked up and said the words "Are we out?" twice. When we had crossed the threshold he finally said "Yes, we're out." He then placed his foot upon my back and shoved me down the stone steps, causing me for the second time to lose my footing.

"I wouldn't have wanted to do anything sacrilegious in God's house – you understand," he said to my prostrate form, before re-entering the Abbey.

That, I reflected as I started to walk towards the Houses of Parliament, was an entirely ignominious start to my parliamentary career – humiliating in the extreme – and I burned with resentment as I thought of Laud's rebuke, as if *he* tolerated the idea of anything that was contrary to *his* idea of what amounted to divine inspiration.

So I entered the Houses of Parliament for my first time as a member, muttering the word 'bastards' over and over again - not the dignified frame of mind I had intended for such an auspicious occasion. But I had to calm myself quickly as I had no desire to relate this deeply humiliating incident to anyone. I was not as late as I had feared, and managed to join Pym and the others in the Painted Chamber.

XIV

In the tavern

The Lords were the first to enter their own chamber, and assembled themselves before the throne at the east wall. We then followed and dispersed ourselves to the right and left. I stood with John Pym at the entrance. Finally, the King arrived with the Prince of Wales at his right hand, followed by Lord Keeper Finch. As the King passed us he stopped and looked about him. He settled his gaze icily upon Pym for a moment before moving on.

He sat upon the throne with his son at his right side, and in a faltering voice, began thus: "My Lords and Gentlemen of the Commons, as you will soon discover, there was never a King who had a more great and weighty cause to call his people together than myself. I pray you all, in the cause of the peace for which we all strive, to let that which is past remain past, and to give ear to the Lord keeper." He then nodded to Finch, and he in turn begun to speak.

Finch made a speech which, were it possible, would have made me long to exchange it even for one of my Father's sermons. It was so drawn out and dull that even the King seemed to find it a struggle to stay awake. The Prince of Wales, although his expression showed an eager interest at the beginning, gradually began to look dismayed, and eventually as if he was about to cry with boredom. As well as calling us to elect a speaker, Finch droned on about the right of the King to collect unpaid taxes retrospectively from the beginning of his reign.

He also repeatedly implied that it was only the war with Scotland that had moved the King to call the Parliament at all.

"Never has a king," he wheezed, "since the reign of Edward II, been so provoked and denied the means of maintaining a steadfast guardianship of his domain by those whose interests he holds in his bosom."

With these words the verbose Lord Keeper bowed to the king; and everyone present breathed a sigh of relief that the ordeal was over. But it was not over. Finch had only turned to the King in order to receive something from him. The King, with an air of contrived nonchalance, handed him a letter, and then looked about him in the manner of someone about to play his trump card.

"I have, here in my hand," Finch continued smugly, "a letter written by the leaders of the Scotch rebels to none other than the King of France, asking for military assistance against the army of our Sovereign Majesty. My Lords and Gentlemen, the rebels have traitorously called for foreign help against His Majesty, and you, his subjects, alike. The King is aware of your grievances; deeply does he feel the troubles and burdens of all his people. We must all however put aside the detail of government whilst our very borders are under threat. Therefore, I would say to you all, that when you think of that which you believe to be the reason you are here, say to yourselves, and repeat often, the words: 'money before grievances - money before grievances,' then, having vanquished the rebel Scots with your loyal help, his gracious Majesty will turn a kindly eye upon your local troubles."

I felt the atmosphere around me bristle with indignation, and indeed I had not even found Lord Clune to be as patronising as that. All however managed to hold their tongues for the present.

With those words Finch turned again to the King, this time bowing extremely low. The King himself stood up, smiled at Finch in a condescending manner, nodded (or rather inclined his head) cursorily to the members of both houses, and walked out in the same grave and dignified manner that he had entered.

The crowd then broke up into various groups, which gradually made their way to the House of Commons or stayed in the Lords, depending upon their business. I had started to move away with Pym and his company when I felt a tug at my right arm. I looked around and beheld Clunehaven.

"A word with you, if I may, Sykes."

"Ah, my noble cousin, Lord Clunehaven, you have the look of a man adorned with the Sword of Truth and the Breastplate of Righteousness, well equipped, methinks, for the struggle before us."

"Until I am given any reason to think otherwise, Sykes, I will presume that your words are as false as your life has been. I have yet to discern, moreover, whether you and I would be on the same side in a struggle of any description."

"You speak unfairly of our heady days at Cambridge, and thus mistake me."

"I am speaking of my fair suspicion that your very presence here speaks of skulduggery and villainy. Your flattering words may beguile some..."

(I was somewhat fortunate in that the sound of many voices around us rendered our conversation private).

"Now you force me to defend myself," I replied, "listen to me but a moment...unlike my cousin, your wife, I was raised in a household in which religion took an outward form alone. I was but sixteen when I discovered that my father, whom I had always accounted the very model of holiness, was in fact the model of cruelty and licentiousness. It pains me too much to recall the circumstances which led to this discovery. As this man had been the very pillar of my childhood faith, that faith crumbled away with my opinion of him. I then spent many months in the spiritual desert: bitter and resentful against God, growing all the more hardened and cynical. But when I had spent some time at Cambridge I began regularly to attend the sermons of worthy divines; men in whom I could see no hypocrisy. I began to see that it was I who had been in error and not the Lord, but I then made the further error that has beset the lives of so many enthusiastic young Christians: I neglected to seek the continued guidance and wisdom of my elders. And there, Lord Clunehaven, we have the reason - although not the excuse - for my over-zealousness at Cambridge: the first love of new salvation mixed with a heady zeal to serve the Lord by purifying His church. I now know (I bowed my head at this point) that the Lord has use only of constant and steady servants such as yourself. I have first and foremost sought forgiveness from the Lord for my past misdeeds; my salvation shall be complete if I obtain your forgiveness also."

His expression remained steely, although his eyes betrayed an inward softening. "You do not need my forgiveness for your salvation, but insomuch as your repentance is sincere, you shall have it. I will, nonetheless, keep an eye on you. As you will discover yourself if you are truly of God's flock, we must be wary at all times of wolves in sheep's clothing."

With that, he touched his hat and disappeared into the crowd.

And that, I suppose, was the best I could have expected. I congratulated myself for my artful use of truths and half-truths in persuading Clunehaven to give me the benefit of the doubt. I was irritated nonetheless by his superior tone, and the fact that I had to crawl to him at all placed me in a bad humour.

After this conversation I walked to Saint Stephen's chapel, wherein sat the members of the Commons. I was one of the last to arrive so I stood along with the other late members around the entrance to the chamber opposite the Speaker's chair, unto which a gentleman (Sir John Glanville) was being half dragged and half led, after the pretend-reluctant fashion adopted by almost all who, throughout history, have been appointed to the high offices of state, particularly this one. He made a semblance of protest about 'not being worthy of the office of Speaker,' but it was easy to see that this was but a thin mask for his pleasure.

Once this excitement was over the members sat around for a while looking at one another, clearly confused as to who should begin proceedings and how. John Glanville did nothing to introduce a debate, but sat instead on his chair talking privately to John Pym and Sir Ralph Hopton, one of the leaders of the King's party. Suddenly Harbottle Grimston, an old member from Essex with a face like gravel, stood up without seeking permission from the Speaker and started shouting.

"So, the King would postpone the address of our 'local troubles' till he has crushed the Scots, whom, I may say, have been sorely provoked. Well, Gentlemen, I have in my hand here a petition from the worthy people of Colchester…"

But he got no further. Many of the members, realising that Grimston had stolen the moment, started waving their own petitions, each clamouring to be heard above the others.

Then the Speaker stood up. "Order, gentlemen…order!" he shouted, with some effect, "this House is not formally sitting, as I am not yet formally sitting. This House is adjourned until Wednesday 15th at two of the clock." With that, he abruptly stood up and left. The members then began to disperse also, until they were called to stand fast by the Earl Marshall, who made us all swear an oath of allegiance to the King before we were ultimately dismissed.

It was towards the end of these proceedings that I found myself unable to shake off the piercing glare of Robert Heron, and when I stood up to leave he did so at the same time, and followed me as I walked out of the palace and towards the City.

I had arranged a meeting with Compromise-not-at-all Jenkins at a prophetically named establishment called the King's Head, to discuss the discontent with the King's policies which was evidently fermenting in the City, and the likelihood of this breaking out into violence. Our meeting had not been arranged for a specific hour, as I could not have known what time the business of Parliament would conclude. Nevertheless, I did not wish to risk meeting Jenkins while in the company of Heron. I therefore started to walk rapidly along the path by the wall that separated the road from the river in an attempt to shake him off, as he followed me at a pace of about ten yards, calling me, amongst other things, a coward and a self-righteous fanatic. These things he said while commanding me by name to stand still and face him like a man.

By the time we reached the King's Head I was left with no choice but to stop. "Be silent, Sir, unless you wish to face me in court over an allegation of slander!"

"Oh how terrifying! We still have that letter you know Sykes, are you sure you want me to 'face you in court?'"

"That letter? That letter? I am fed up with hearing these accusations about that letter. My cause is a godly one; I need not stoop to devilish means to do God's divine will…and even if I did write it, you could never prove it."

Heron said nothing, but glowered at me, looking like he would at any moment strike me.

I softened my tone somewhat: "Robert, you are thinking of violence, but you are now a member of Parliament, as am I also…it is not for ones such as us to resolve our disputes thus.

Despite this admonition his threatening expression remained unchanged. I therefore, in the rash hope that Jenkins would miss him altogether, invited Heron to partake with me in a little wine and refreshment at the tavern. I realised that trouble might well ensue if Jenkins and his gang encountered Heron, but to get him off the street seemed at the time a better option than to risk coming to blows with him in public.

Heron assented to my offer by means of a curt nod. We entered the inn, and he ordered roast venison and a quart of claret from the innkeeper's daughter, saying as he did so that "The ugly one's paying," whilst pointing in my direction with his thumb. He got the flirtatious laugh and blush he was hoping for in reply, but I determined to make him regret making a fool of a fellow Member of Parliament in front of a serving wench. I would also make him regret ordering an expensive meal when he knew I had intended for him to have only a little wine and a hunk of bread.

The tavern was all but empty when we arrived, but by the time we ordered our food several men had drifted in, so we chose a corner with a view of the river, where Robert Heron began quaffing the claret with impunity.

"I have a choice here, Sykes," he began. "For you to have written that letter was totally in keeping with your character: you are a bastard. Should I believe you that you didn't write that letter? It would surprise me, because you are, as I said, a bastard; and if it turns out that you did write it in spite of your denial, you are clearly even more of a bastard. If, on the other hand, you did not write the letter then I have sorely misjudged you, for which I suppose I should apologise. Nevertheless, you were, as my memory serves me, a bastard at Cambridge in many other ways. Therefore I shall withhold my apology, and instead forgive you if I find my food, as well as this wine, to be of satisfaction."

Having said that, he took a slug of his wine and wiped his mouth with his sleeve, smirking at me in the most irritatingly affected manner as he did so.

I chose to make no reply in regard to the letter, as I had already denied any knowledge of it, but I had to say something.

"People will doubtless wonder," I began, "why two people such as you and I should sup together in this place. I, myself, might be reluctant to eat with you, as you are clearly a man of the King, whilst I am clearly a man of God. But I say to you that it is of the utmost importance that those elected to the high offices of state should converse together with mutual regard. There is more than one advantage in this: that we may serve the country to the best of our abilities is, of course, the primary benefit. But there is also, shall we say, the consolation - nay the perk - of our being able to consolidate and advance our social standing through conversation and association with our fellow Members?"

"Well He-died-for-our-sins Sykes," Heron replied, "you may or may not still be a bastard, but you are clearly still an arsehole."

Having said that, he smirked again, swallowed another mouthful of wine, and pretended to take an interest in a passing barge.

Now this man's impertinence was beginning to get to me, and I will freely admit that I became in danger of losing my temper.

"At least," I retorted, "I am not a hypocrite."

He looked round.

"Yes," I repeated, "a hypocrite: to turn away from the way thou hast been reared - from your Christian upbringing - was...wicked; and yea I say hypocritical!"

"Well I have already discussed my upbringing with you once, but we will let that pass. If I was ever a hypocrite, it was when I dressed as you do now, and attended meetings of the *Young Puritans*. There are those who dress plainly because to do so reflects their dislike of ostentation. But I dressed as I did because I was made to; and I was therefore, to a degree, a hypocrite. But you dress as you do because you like to be seen by men to be holy, whilst truth for you is as important as cow shit. It wouldn't surprise me if underneath all that puritan drabness you were wearing women's silk under-garments stolen from your favourite prostitute."

As you can imagine, good Reader, I became furious with suppressed rage in the face of these insults. At the same time, his insight into my choice of underwear was so disconcerting that I almost blurted out that "I didn't get them from a prostitute!" In the end however, I was so incensed that I could think of no retort at all, except to mutter: "How dare you?"

"Why, you are surely not going to try to persuade me that you could have sex with a woman without paying for it? That - and that you didn't write the letter - all in the same hour? That is too much for me.

I glared at my goblet of wine, stricken with the realisation that Heron could at any moment leave this inn with the knowledge that he had got the better of me. I would have to spend the whole of my time in parliament with the sight of him sneering at me across the chamber and spreading malicious stories.

But as I still could think of no answer I was almost relieved when we were interrupted by a familiar voice at the other side of the room, addressing the innkeeper's daughter. "Look here, serving slut, I know your way of thinking. You suppose that because men of God are under divine instruction to show patience, we are willing to wait here to place an order while you give precedence to court toadies and profligates. Serve us within the space of one minute or I will flog you, you whore!"

Naturally these utterances caused us to look up, and I caught the eye of Compromise-not-at-all Jenkins immediately, as usual in the company of his friends. There were also several other men present who looked as if they were deciding whether or not to respond to these provocations, as was the innkeeper.

Jenkins however, upon seeing us, walked straight over. He was clearly drunk. "So this is what you're about, Sykes, not waylaying fops and dandies because you're eating and drinking with them!"

Now I had to think very clearly and quickly. Did I curse Jenkins for an insolent peasant? To do so would certainly result in him reacting with violence. If, however, I said to Jenkins something like 'I know not who this fellow is, he sat with me uninvited and started provoking me sorely for being a man of God - I was about to thrash him,' then Jenkins, whether or not he recognised Heron from Cambridge, would still become violent; his violence however would be directed at Heron, and therefore a fight would begin on that score. In such an instance as this it would be half a day before it got round parliament that I was willing to take the side of a city apprentice who had assaulted an elected Member in my presence.

Being called a 'fop' or 'dandy,' however, didn't seem to bother Heron, and he unwittingly came to my assistance.

"Jesus ate and drank with tax collectors and sinners," he said to Jenkins as he got up from his seat, "but you…you're…just beyond that… you're….*too* holy!" He then began mock-weeping. "Thank you just for being in my presence…. forgive me! Forgive me!"

Just for a moment a look of messianic fervour passed Jenkins' eye before he realised, colouring deeply, that he was being laughed at by almost everyone present.

Heron then advanced, looming over Jenkins as he backed away. When his passage backwards was prevented by a wall Heron bent towards him, his voice very low but, as everyone had fallen silent, audible: "When you get to hell," he said, "you will be able to comfort yourself with the delusion that God wouldn't let you into heaven because He was so jealous. You and the devil can offer one another consolation for the injustice you've suffered."

Jenkins then began to swing his arms about in a series of uncoordinated and drunken movements, and shout, not just at Heron, who took a step back, but at everyone. Flee sin and the others, deciding that their leader was in need of help, began to shove their way aggressively to his side. A fight became inevitable, but it did not begin as I expected.

Jenkins, half crying and half shouting, suddenly raised his voice so loudly as to stop everyone. He was slurring badly and reeling on his feet. "You all think that you will continue to live *splendidly*; to enjoy yourselves, father children and then die in comfort, surrounded by your families. You think that your children will then follow after you and live the same meaningless lives you did. I tell you that you will all die at the point of my sword and the swords of others like me! Could the Philistines abide in the presence of Israel? I tell thee all...thou shalt be smitten!"

Everyone stopped laughing and stared at Jenkins, except for one man, a courtier of about twenty years of age, who suggested to Flee sin that he should take his friend home.

This got Jenkins going again. "You think yourselves safe because you are under the protection of the King! You might as well say to the Lord on the day of judgement that you are under the protection of the devil! Well I say a curse on all of you, and a curse on Stuart and his Catholic bitch!"

At these words the same man unhooked his riding switch from his belt, and in one movement stepped forward and struck Jenkins sharply with it across his right cheek, causing blood immediately to pour from the wound. He then returned the switch to his belt, muttering under his breath that he was "Sure to feel the protection of the King for any consequences to *that*." There was a momentary stunned silence before Flee sin jumped on him, knocking him to the floor as he did so. In a moment everyone had joined in the affray, except for Jenkins himself, whom I saw escaping out of the door clasping his bloodied cheek.

Now by the time this fight started the inn had become fairly full, and most of the people there were the King's sympathisers, at least in so much as could be identified by their mode of dress. It was clear that the puritans and apprentices were outnumbered by more than two to one. I therefore took it upon myself to attempt an exit by moving around the perimeter of the room, hugging the wall. I made it to the door and was just about to break for freedom when I was forced back by about thirty people trying to push their way in. These new arrivals, all City apprentices, had apparently been mustered by Jenkins, as he entered among them, still holding his cheek with one hand, but this time wildly chopping the air with a wooden stave he held in his other.

It was now impossible for me to make my escape by avoiding the confusion. I was pushed to the floor by someone, and used this as an opportunity to make a battering ram with my feet, with which I kicked the genitals of all those who stood between me and the way out. I thus quickly managed to make my escape to an advantageous position on the other side of the road, from whence I could watch the unfolding of events in safety.

I thought until this moment that I had seen real violence up at Cambridge, but in truth the confrontations I witnessed there were nothing compared to this. The shouts and screams I heard from within the building showed that the altercation had become desperate, and had turned from what might have begun as a 'playful brawl' into a potentially mortal conflict. I saw one of the apprentices being thrown through a closed window and landing unconscious, covered with blood, on the road outside. The jagged window frame then became blocked with screaming and shouting people, trying desperately to get out. The situation was further confused by the fact that although there were some, such as the innkeeper's daughter, who managed to escape (and in her case run up the road screaming for help), a much greater number of passers-by, realising there was a good scrap going on, attempted to make their way inside to join in. Among these people were a party of drunken cavaliers led by someone who shouted "Come on boys!" which, having given up trying to get in by the door, went round to the recently broken window and started shoving those trying to escape back inside. This accomplished, they began to scramble in after them.

Before long a number of people began to gather round me in the hope that they had also found a position of safety. It soon began to feel less so however, as by now, through sheer force of numbers, the fight was spilling out onto the street, both from the door and the window.

After a few more moments of screaming and smashing glass, a trained band of the King's Guard, four horse and about eighteen foot, came charging towards the inn, swords drawn; the captain shouting repeatedly, "Stop in the name of the King!" These words had no effect upon the assailants at all; neither did the prospect of imminent arrest.

It was only to be expected that the soldiers would assume that the puritans and apprentices were in the wrong, or that they would oppose them anyway. Despite their being heavily outnumbered, they proceeded to single them out and beat them with the flats of their swords, their boots and their heavily-gloved fists. In one instance I saw one of the guards using his spurred heel to crush the hand of an apprentice who, having already been knocked down, was attempting to reach for a dagger previously dropped by another assailant.

Through sheer force of numbers the King's Guard, along with the other cavaliers, began to beat the apprentices down, and all of those not rendered incapable began to flee as best they could into the streets, chased by some of the soldiers. One tried to escape by running down the bank into the river, but was dragged out by the hair and arrested. Realising that our cause was lost, and that there was no more for me to do in this place, I also made my way from the carnage, and managed after an uneventful journey to arrive safely back at my house in Chelsea.

This was the first I witnessed of the many skirmishes, riots and mass-brawls which took place in London in the weeks and months prior to the Civil War. This time Fortune favoured the Cavaliers. It would not always be thus.

XV

In the Commons

Parliament reconvened on the second day after the events just described.

I took my seat at about fifteen minutes before two of the clock at the back of the chamber, as the House was already nearly full. Despite the fact that the Speaker was not due to start proceedings for quarter of an hour, members from both sides of the house were already shouting at one another. Those amongst whom I had sat were noisily accusing an elderly cavalier of unlawfully profiting from the collection of ship money. One of them, standing on his feet, shouted to him that as far as he was concerned he was no better than a market stall swindler.

"How dare you, Sir?" shouted back the old gentleman, his white moustache quivering with indignation, "I shall see you in court, you damn cad!"

"Oh you would have done, corrupt magistrates thrive in corrupt times; but see here: this is parliament, and for me to accuse you of corruption is my privilege as an elected Member of this house."

At which all the members surrounding him shouted "Privilege, privilege!" until the old man went red in the face and gave up trying to shout back.

Similarly disordered but entertaining altercations continued until the doors were thrown open and the Speaker walked into the chamber along with the Lord Keeper.

After a prayer the new Speaker began an obsequious eulogy with relish, as if he had been waiting in a queue to pay homage to the powers above him; and by the way he crawled to the King in the person of his Lord Keeper, it must have seemed to the veterans of the last parliament that nothing had changed since they had sat eleven years previously.

But after another dull sermon from Finch given in answer, which took up most of the afternoon, things at last began to get going. Certain members began to argue that the desires of the King, however urgent, could not and would not be satisfied until the people's grievances were addressed. After about six of these contributions the Speaker scanned the room desperately for someone who might come to the King's defence. The elderly cavalier with the white moustache stood up.

The Speaker nodded to him: "Sir Thomas Witherington."

The old knight glared around the chamber, waiting for the House to fall silent. "We would be hard pressed to meet as we are now, under the gracious protection of his Majesty," he began, "should various members here present get their way. Who ever heard of a household arranging its domestic affairs when its very walls are under attack? My family's home in Somerset has been the centre of many a bloody conflict in the past few centuries, both national and local. Let me tell you all: if I were stricken with a malady, and had to leave it to my son to look after the welfare of my family, then I would not expect him to bother me with the details of our poorly stocked larder, or news of bickering servants, if there were a gang of cut-throats waiting to storm the ramparts. I'd call him mad....." (He stopped, and settled his gaze upon my neighbour - the one who had compared him to a market stall swindler) "...and if I knew that he was happy for those cut-throats to break into the house, rape the women and plunder our goods, I'd call him a bloody traitor!"

At these last words the House erupted into a deafening barrage of cheers from the King's party, and shouts of anger and derision from the other members, most of whom stood up to try to attract the

Speaker's attention. The ones around me were the most vocal, shouting repeatedly "Withdraw, withdraw!" and "Shame, shame!"

They somewhat played into Witherington's hands here, for he stood up and, gleefully pointing to his chest with his thumb, shouted "Privilege, privilege!" before sitting down and folding his arms in a manner of deep self-satisfaction.

Even at this early stage it seemed likely that this parliament might end as the last had done. Co-operation, let alone compromise, seemed impossible. But there was one card we held up our sleeves: the King needed this money in a hurry. It was impossible, with the Scottish army on his borders, for him to wait around in London and address everyone's problems. Nay, he *desperately* needed the money.

Notwithstanding this, it was clear that there was little that I could accomplish at this stage on a major scale, although there was much in the way of amusement to be gleaned from these early exchanges in the Commons. I had been able to tell even from the short time we had been in session on the Monday, that proceedings in the Commons as well as the Lords were conducted on an almost entirely hierarchical basis. I had therefore been unsurprised when one of the members informed me that my maiden speech would have to wait for at least a week, as the first new members to speak were to be those of the highest rank by birth. In my chagrin I decided to put it about that the best thing for a young nobleman to say in his first speech was that he wished to be treated the same as everyone else while in parliament, and by no means should anyone think that he wanted any special favours due to his rank and privilege.'

This trap could only work once, so I was somewhat honoured that it was a certain George Digby, the heir to the Earldom of Bristol, who fell into it. The expression on his face when, as soon as he finished thus making a public spectacle of himself, the booing and hissing started, was comic to behold. You may think that this was an insignificant achievement; but I would say that to do so much harm to the parliamentary career of one of those golden spoon members in my very first week there showed remarkable early signs of political ability.

But the exchange of speeches, urgings, remonstrations, pleadings and abuse went on with no sign of any intervention or event that might speed us to a conclusion. John Pym gave the boldest speech on the Friday, and so frank and explicit was he in expressing the demands of the puritan members that the King and his advisers could have been left in no doubt that they were highly unlikely to obtain what they had hoped for from this parliament.

With the turn of events so unpredictable it became imperative that I chose my actions carefully. I had always known that it would be difficult to make my name on the floor of the Commons while people like Pym were there to take the vanguard. But he was beginning to see in me a man he could trust, of that I was certain, and this was a reputation I needed to protect and nourish. In my case the way to maintain and improve his confidence was to be patient, become useful in the background; and in order to become really useful in this way it was imperative to cultivate contacts on both sides of the political divide. I decided, whilst contemplating this, that Lord Clunehaven's naivety could, if I chose my approach carefully, still become fodder for my career and future glory.

It was for this reason that I stopped him in the Painted Chamber as he was leaving the House of Lords at the close of proceedings on Friday, after Pym had made his speech.

"A word in your ear if I may, Lord Clunehaven."

"Sykes?"

"I wish to talk with you," I said, "because you are one of the few members, either of the Lords or Commons, who is respected without equivocation by all except those who place themselves, due to their manic extremism, beyond the boundaries of sensible political consideration."

He looked at me somewhat blankly. I continued.

"In the short space of time this parliament has been in session, it has become apparent that there is no way for it to go. On the floor of the House it is easy to see that there is no member willing to yield on any small point. Committees have already been set up solely for the purpose of overturning the laws passed and measures taken by the

King during the past eleven years. It would appear also that the King himself is unlikely to concede anything before he is granted the money he needs."

"This is a concern" answered Lord Clunehaven, "but I would have thought that you would revel in this sort of confusion."

"Again, you misjudge me. It would seem strange to you, perchance, that someone who held such an extreme religious position as I once did should seek to find a solution favourable to all sides, but I tell you that my conscience has ordered me to obey the word and instruction of the Lord: 'Blessed are the peacemakers.' For this reason, therefore, if today is indeed the eve of the Lord's final judgement, let it be said that we at least did our best to turn mankind from his folly."

"Well, you appear to be sincere, Sykes, but I do not understand your purpose in singling me out to talk of your concerns."

"It was my purpose when entering Parliament to serve my country. Surely you and I would be doing no more than our duty by attempting together to find a means by which our king - who seeks at least in his conscience to serve the Lord - and our parliament, might reach an agreement?"

"Well, Sykes, as I said, you appear to be sincere, but I still do not understand what it is you believe we can do together."

"I come to you, Lord Clunehaven, with nothing to offer but despair in Man and hope in the Lord. In my own strength of mind I can think of no solution to the unhappy problems we face as a nation. But where the servants of the Lord pit their wits and prayers, surely wisdom will abound."

"Then...if you are suggesting we talk at greater length, I suggest that you come to my house at seven of the clock this evening. My wife and I are giving a dinner, and our guests have all been invited with a view to our solving the very problems you speak of."

This speedily given invitation was more than I had bargained for. An excellent opportunity beckoned (I reminded myself) to find my way into the society I was seeking, but I knew not who I might meet in this place. Suppose Robert Heron was there, sneering at me, and laughingly persuading Lord Clunehaven of his mistake in trusting me; or worse still: Richard Sykes. Nonetheless, I was not so foolish as to decline Lord Clunehaven's invitation. It was its timing alone that alarmed me, and caused me to realise that I would need to make speedy mental preparation.

So I accepted his invitation with thanks, and as befitted a man addressing one to whom he is in debt, but with whom he can converse with the confidence reserved for those of good earthly birth and godly favour.

"And how fares my cousin Elizabeth?" I asked him, following the same train of familiarity.

"She fares well."

In response to those words I smiled and, doffing my hat, bowed. I then made my way to the stables, from whence I collected my horse and rode to Chelsea for a change of clothing.

XVI

The river journey

C lunehaven House, the residence of the Earl and Countess of that ilk, is a palatial residence set in a huge garden by the banks of the River Thames, near the Palace of Hampton Court.

I arrived at seven of the clock as requested and, having entered the hall, I gave my hat and stick to a servant. I was then taken along a passage to a large salon in which sat my cousin Elizabeth and Lord Clunehaven, along with several of my fellow guests. The room was huge, and decorated with deep crimson, visible only in the gaps between the vast tapestries which covered most of the walls. Most of these depicted Clunehaven ancestors in acts of warfare, or chasing stags and wild boar. For a moment after my arrival, had I had my hat with me, I would have stood there, twisting it in my hands and spluttering like Brickett the Simpleton; for the group of people present, who were talking in low tones around the unlit fireplace, looked up upon my arrival, and instantly fell silent. All of them stared at me in a manner that would normally be reserved for an intruder or stranger.

This expression passed, from Elizabeth's face at least, in a moment. She stood up, crossed the room and, smiling, stretched out her hand and took mine.

"Cousin," she said, "it is good to see you here in London. My husband has told me of your meeting. Allow me to introduce you to our other guests."

She then presented me one by one to the others. They were generally a mixture of the Lord Clunehaven type of puritan: spiritual – yet lacking some of the fire of holy fervour, and the more religious type of courtier: soberly attired, but with a care for current fashion. There were a dozen or so of these ladies and gentlemen, all of whose names I forgot as soon as I heard them, for I suddenly beheld, standing amongst them, and glaring at me with an expression of the utmost disdain, none other than my arch-enemy: my cousin Richard Sykes.

Now it was essential that I did not lose mastery over my own senses and reactions. By this I do not merely mean that I needed to keep myself from saying anything foolish; nay, when I first beheld Richard Sykes after so long I nearly screamed with the disconcertion of the moment. But I could not afford for him or anyone else in this place to know or suspect me of anything other than the most genuine motives for seeking the society of the Clunehavens; and an unwonted display of fear would have given just such an impression. To persuade Richard Sykes that there had been a transformation in my character for the good would be harder than with anyone else. I was tempted to spit at him, hit anyone within reach and run from the room. But I could not do this now, not now I was a Member of Parliament.

I remained calm, realising, despite my panic, that it would be very difficult for him to *prove* that I was anything but genuine.

His manner, however, was worse than I could have expected. I believe that the cause of his rudeness was pure jealousy over the directions our lives had taken; but I would have imagined his attitude towards me to be cold, although haughtily polite, for the sake of his sister and brother-in-law. But he made no such attempt to follow the conventions of polite society.

"Had, dear Brother-in-law," he began saying to Clunehaven in a volume and manner designed to draw everyone's attention, "this been a gathering of friends and relations invited merely for dinner, I would have believed that you had merely gone mad for inviting this fellow, but I would have kept my silence. But we have assembled here to discuss matters of importance, and the issues before us are too weighty to discuss before fools. Were this not so then I would give

He-died-for-our-sins here a currant bun and a glass of milk and bid him play in the corner. But he is insidious; he will feign innocence, and then he'll twist our words and use them to destroy anything we might accomplish here."

Throughout the whole of this tirade he refused to look at me, and you can be sure that I was sorely tempted to bruise his self-conceit with a crushing reply. How easy it would have been to pour scorn over his notion that they might accomplish anything there at all, while reminding him that it was I, and not he, who was now in the position of power. But to respond as such would hardly have confirmed Clunehaven in his new found willingness to believe in my humility. It was also tempting to say to them that if they had no evil intentions then they could have nothing to fear from my presence. But I knew that one of the charges they held against me, and which I therefore had to disprove, was self righteousness. I therefore said nothing. I bowed gravely to my cousin, but left my defence in the hands of Lord Clunehaven.

"I do believe," said he, "that when someone expresses contrition for their past misdeeds, they should be given the benefit of the doubt - until and unless they prove themselves to be unworthy of that trust."

"Were we talking here of a stable boy with a penchant for pilfering horse oats, then I would agree with your charitable stance," replied Richard, "but this man is an elected Member of Parliament (I smirked, involuntarily, at this point); he is probably already in with the King's enemies. He could do us much harm…"

"That which is of God…" I tried to respond, but Richard continued speaking without heeding my interruption.

"Moreover, if you would seek a sign from God as to whether this man is trustworthy, then look no further than the toadstool: the ones which *are* the most poisonous almost always *look* the most poisonous….and then look at He-died-for-our-sins's face, and ask yourself whether the God we love and seek to serve would have been so cruel as to give a righteous man a face like *that*."

This scathing mockery was more than I could tolerate. It was nothing short of unseemly that I, with my reputation and status, should have to brook such humiliation from my cousin in front of these people, many of whom laughed at his words. I realised then that I was no longer capable of keeping up this façade. It was possible that, should I restrain myself at this point, I would still retain the respect of Clunehaven despite my cousin's venom. But Richard had pushed me too far. Thoughts of the power that would be at my disposal once we had gained ascendancy over the King, and how I would use this power to destroy him utterly, welled up in my mind and made the ability for me to retain my composure impossible to maintain.

I was about to break forth in an ejaculation of wrathful threats, when the progress of our communication was interrupted by the opening of the door. The same manservant who had led me through the house then entered, and immediately stood aside for none other than that elusive rising star of the Middle Temple, Praise God Fairweather.

It is one of the peculiarities of man that we, more than any other of God's creatures, have risen above the need to function upon basic instinct. It is also peculiar that the sharpest among us can revert to the use of that instinct at the merest whim. Such it was with me the minute that Praise God entered that room. I immediately regained the ability to perform a dignified retreat, which I knew would prove to be the most expeditious and fruitful course of action. Before Praise God could perform his round of fawning greetings, therefore, I turned to Richard Sykes: "I love you Richard, not only as a cousin, but in faith as a brother. I hope one day, when you truly allow the Lord to touch your heart, that we will be able to work together to bring about peace in this country."

As I spoke these words everyone became silent, including the aforementioned Praise God, who out of the corner of my eye I could see gaping at me. This was a facial expression to which he was very partial, and which I had always found incredibly annoying, particularly in light of the fact that other people seemed to find him intelligent. However, on this occasion, his astonished expression, as well as the stunned silence which engulfed the room's other occupants, only served to show me that my words were having the effect I desired.

I allowed no one time to respond. To the majority of the guests, who I did not know, I bowed collectively. I then bowed in turn to Richard, Lord Clunehaven and my cousin Elizabeth, saying to the latter: "If you will forgive me, Lady Clunehaven." I then turned and walked out of the room, giving Praise God a cursory nod as I did so. Not one of those people said a word in response to any of this. Indeed so graceful and noble was my exit that I wonder what any of them *could* have said.

Nonetheless, my plan to develop a contact within the King's party by means of my acquaintance with the Clunehavens had been foiled. I reflected upon this as I left their house. To be a Member of Parliament without access to the *real power*, even if it was my intention to destroy that real power, was comparable to a ticket for a good box at the theatre from which, as well as the play, one could view the Royal party enjoying the spectacle from their *own* box. And although one might scorn the idea of *joining* that Royal party, it was galling to know that one's exclusion was not of one's own making.

But excluded I must be, at least for the time being; and you may be sure that Richard Sykes, whom I had been happy to leave to his country pursuits, had become once again the primary target for my revenge.

But this night was far from over; all it really required was a change of plan. I left the house from the northern side, and located two river boys; one of whom stated that they would 'Do owt for a few pennies,' whilst jerking his head in a similar fashion to a robin. I instructed him to wait at the gate to the river, and his companion to wait on the other side of the road. Their orders were to do nothing but, immediately upon sighting Praise God, whose description I gave them, run to a nearby tavern named the *Golden Fleece*, wherein I intended to sit and eat the meal that I should have received freely from the Clunehavens. I gave them a few pennies between them, with a promise of a further shilling to the first one to reach me with news of Praise God's departure from the Clunehaven residence.

Having repaired to the inn I chose a dish of dressed mutton with potatoes, and a horn of mead to drink, and was really rather grateful for an opportunity to partake of my own company for a while. After about three hours, however, with my meal long since finished, I was relieved to behold a ragged boy running towards the tavern, and from the way he cocked his head in several directions before spotting me, I was easily able to recognise the bird-like features of the urchin I had left guarding the gate leading to the River.

I did not deem it necessary to stop and talk, but threw to the lad the promised shilling, and quickly made my way around the perimeter of Clunehaven House to the gate, from whence I saw Praise God enter a boat, lit by a single torch. I ran down the small jetty and jumped into another boat, ordering the man as I did so to follow Praise God, who, by the time we managed to embark, was disappearing into the night.

But my fear that I would lose Praise God was quickly dispelled, as he and his boatman, both unaware that they were being followed, were drifting down the river at a most casual speed. I was just wondering as we approached their boat whether Praise God, had he known that I was following him, would have ordered his boatman to stand fast or gather momentum, when my question was answered. While we were yet fifty yards apart I called my disloyal friend and he, realising that he had been seen, issued an order to his boatman, which was clearly obeyed by means of the oars being applied at about three times the rate they had been previously.

But it was too late for Praise God's vessel to get up to a speed required to escape, so after a few moments my boat drew alongside his, and I ordered Praise God's boatman to hold fast.

"And wherefore, Praise God," I asked, "are you attempting to escape me? Why do you treat me thus, when all I have ever wished between us was friendship?"

"I…I was not trying to escape from you, He-died-for-our-sins, but when I saw your boat approach I thought that you wished to indulge in a little sporting boat race, aha ha ha."

"'A little sporting boat race?' After months of not speaking, you thought that I would greet you with 'a little sporting boat race!'" Do you think my time in London has softened my wits? Or perhaps you think that your odious new friendships entitle you to address me as a fool?"

Praise God's boatman then asked him whether he would like to continue the journey. The implication clearly being that he should start rowing again without my permission.

"Silence, dog! You are being addressed by an elected member of parliament. Praise God - pay him and get into my boat!"

I think that as well as the natural authority I held over Praise God, the fact that he had made such a feeble excuse for attempting to elude me embarrassed him into obeying my order without protest. I in turn realised that in order to persuade Praise God that there had indeed been a change in me for the better I should refrain from abusing servants in this manner. So, through gritted teeth, I apologised to the boatman, citing a long and stressful day in parliament as an excuse. I handed him tuppence and helped Praise God step into my boat. We continued the journey to Chelsea.

"Now, Praise God," I began as I made myself as comfortable as was possible in the back of the small vessel, "it is a pleasant night and I am in no hurry; we have all the time in the world to catch up on our neglected friendship. I have heard good reports of your doings at the Inns of Court. Tell me, have you still a thought for 'furthering the cause of the Church'?"

"Why of course I have, He-died-for-our-sins, the Lord has need of lawyers as well as teachers."

"Very good Praise God, I am sure the Lord would have need of you whatever your profession. Now needs must I ask a question I have asked you before: how does it avail the Lord for you to associate with the likes of Richard Sykes?"

"I cannot say if it avails the Lord; I can only say it avails the cause of those who seek to serve Him: almost every move the King makes is directed by one of three people: the Queen, The Archbishop of Canterbury and the Lord Strafford. Of these three only the latter is at all willing to listen to the views of the more moderate of the King's opponents. Richard Sykes is closely associated with Strafford, therefore it avails us much to talk to him. Strafford is expected in London tomorrow."

"I, Praise God, have been rejected and vilified by my cousin when my only intention has been to further the cause of the Church."

"There are some in that house," replied Praise God, "who, so far from thinking that you have rejected violence, believe actually that you are 'a lover of evil;' 'a destroyer;' even 'a wolf in sheep's clothing.' "Don't worry: I assured them that you would have worn a much better disguise! Aha ha ha."

"Oh very droll, your training amongst the nobility and gentry really has made you frightfully witty, Praise God. And yet you can see that *my* life and career carries with it the anointing of the Lord. It is not as if *I* gained my present position via the easy passage taken by the likes of Clunehaven; and yet I am here, in as good a position to serve the Lord as anybody, but for the obstacles set by the enemy."

"What are these obstacles you speak of?"

"My chiefest obstacle is that I have to depend upon those who will use my very godliness as a cause to bar my way, and not recognise that my being chosen for parliament itself shows the stamp of God's blessing on my life. I notice that these God-rejecters are far from willing to spurn *your* company."

Praise God ignored my last observation, and chose instead to attack me in a roundabout way; somewhat typical, I thought, of a lawyer: "Is it possible that people like your cousin Richard are unable to recognise a particular sign of God's blessing in your career, as there were only about four people who could have stood for parliament in our part of the country - one of them your dead father, and there are only about twenty men entitled to vote for them anyway?"

"Such sarcasm, Praise God, ill becomes a man of God. Is it upon this level that I must converse with you - as if I were indeed keeping company with Richard Sykes?"

"No He-died-for-our-sins - not at all. I should not have mocked you" answered Praise God in a reassuringly timid manner.

"You say, do you not, that Strafford is willing to listen only to the views of the more moderate of the King's opponents. Surely you can see Praise God, with your great learning, that this approach could turn out to be catastrophically naïve."

"I do not understand you."

"You describe Strafford in contrasting terms to the Queen and the Archbishop, thinking, no doubt, that through his approach some great breakthrough may occur in the unhappy stand-off that is our parliament, but for Strafford to concentrate his efforts on the likes of Clunehaven is all but useless except in so much as it benefits the King."

"Why?"

"Why? Because Clunehaven and his like would suffer any amount of wrong-doing from the King; and always seek and hope that he will back down in some degree in the face of their grievances. But the King will never back down in the face of any amount of pressure from the likes of Clunehaven. Do you know why, Praise God?"

"No."

"Because Clunehaven would never declare war upon his own sovereign; and the King knows that. Because of this he need back down on no point and in no measure."

"Well who *would* declare war upon the King?"

"The Scots."

"Apart from the Scots."

"Half of – more than half of – the elected representatives of the House of Commons."

"I cannot believe that; things could never be so bad."

"You say 'things could never be so bad' in the manner of one who wishes to avoid war - not because he is a lover of peace, but because he has grown to love this present world and its evil; and is reluctant to see the pleasure upon which his life has become founded disturbed in any measure."

"This is not true."

"That is easy for you to say, but I put it to you that your presence in yonder noble house was nought but folly; and I again say to you that for Strafford to address himself solely to the likes of Clunehaven, particularly when both he and Clunehaven are under the influence of Richard Sykes, will prove to be futile. While they in that house discuss pleasantries and play politics over dinner the dividing line between the

King and his true enemies is ever widening. Why were you invited there anyway?"

"It would be strange for me not to see the Clunehavens occasionally; and therefore of course, more occasionally, your cousin Richard. I saw them regularly whilst he was still at Cambridge; I have been a guest at their castle in Northumberland. I was even a guest at their wedding."

At that point, but for the fact that I regarded Praise God as useful, and for the fact that I was unwilling to be executed as a murderer, I would have taken one of the oars from the boatman and smashed his head with it. As it was I was not only unable to vent my spleen in this way, but I also had to mask my anger altogether. Moreover, despite the darkness of the night, and the fact that my ability to see Praise God was diminished all the more by the consuming light of the flickering torch behind him, I could feel his expression of smug self satisfaction as well as if my eyes had the benefit of full day light.

How easy, and yet how difficult it is, to resist the temptation to break a man's spirit with the power of one's wit, or his head with an oar; but Praise God would be no use to me as a broken man, or a dead one. I therefore let the moment pass, and pursued again the matter in question.

"Let us get to the point, Praise God. You may have decided that the best way to serve the Lord is to placate the consciences of the wicked with words of treacle and syrup. You may talk to Richard Sykes, you may talk to Strafford; you may talk to the devil himself, but that will not quell the likes of John Pym. Pym and his followers - of whom there are many - are determined to back down in no measure on any of the grievances so far raised in the House. Any fool can see that the King, when he realises just how futile it is to try to get anything at all from Parliament, will give these already aggrieved members a great deal more to be vexed about. Allow me to be frank with you, Praise God: do you wish to see this country fall into a state of civil war? Because, believe me, that is what will happen if you and the likes of Clunehaven and Richard Sykes are allowed to carry the hopes of the nation with your polite and pleasant *and futile* conversation."

"Well of course I don't want civil war – but you are mistaken anyway if you think that I have any real influence over the course of events; and there was nothing official about our gathering anyway."

"Well that's just it Praise God, your gathering was completely useless, and no doubt left you with a feeling of impotence in the face of the catastrophic events about to befall us all. Is this not the truth?"

"I cannot deny that there was an element of hopelessness in our parting."

"As there will continue to be until you realise that in order to do anything to save this nation you're going to have to use your wits."

"But what should I do?"

And with that simple question I believed that my friendship with Praise God was restored, or, to put it more accurately, that he was again at my beck and call.

"Your task is a relatively simple one," I answered, "it is merely this: it is essential that at least one person who has the ear of the King's opponents has, at the least, a partial knowledge of the King's intentions. By this means, and by this means alone, can both sides be manoeuvred away from the precipitous position they are now holding. Therefore you must make full use of any contact you have with Richard Sykes; and you must inform me of everything you hear, everything you see; and most particularly the movements and intentions of the Earl of Strafford."

I let Praise God digest this for a moment, then added: "It is also essential that you do your very best to combat the influence of Richard Sykes over Clunehaven. I know his ways far better than you: you are swayed by his appearance of righteousness, forgetting – methinks - that the devil himself easily and often disguises himself as an angel of light. I not only know Richard Sykes, but I know his kind: they see war as a glorious improvement to the hunting field. While you and Clunehaven seek to avoid bloodshed, your efforts will be entirely in vain while this man has any influence over Strafford. If Strafford can be persuaded to listen to Clunehaven rather than Richard Sykes; and if Clunehaven can be persuaded to listen to me (and in this you can also play a most vital role) then, and only then, will it be possible at all for us to avoid war."

Having said this I lapsed into silence, letting the sound of the oars provide the sole accompaniment to Praise God's thoughts for a few moments. Then, aware that this thoughtfulness was as likely to lead him to an unfavourable conclusion as otherwise, I added this final persuasive argument: "I am fully aware, Praise God, that you are struggling within yourself to accept the wisdom of my words; and that you are reacting with disfavour to the thought of being what can only be described as a spy. But I tell you that all things are acceptable in the sight of the Lord if they are truly done in His interests, and I tell you also that generations to come will have cause to thank you for laying aside your natural principles for the sake of that which is clearly the will of God in this most needful of times."

We were now approaching Chelsea, so I did indeed leave Praise God to think for a while. I engaged the boatman in conversation, asking him if he had a family and, as he told me he had a wife and two surviving sons, where he lived; as well as some other pleasant questions that only a true man of God would have deigned to ask such a low specimen of humanity. I then instructed him to stop the boat at the Chelsea wharf and, having paid him double the required fare, and having persuaded Praise God to disembark with me and spend the night at my house, climbed out of the boat with him following. We walked a few yards, and then, just as I could see that the boatman was preparing to leave, I told Praise God that I had left my purse behind and ran back.

"Your name, Churl," I demanded whilst pretending to search the boat.

Clearly taken aback by my change in tone he fumbled an answer: "Why – er, beggin' your honour's pardon, it be Sam the boatman."

"Well, *Sam the boatman*, I now know where you live; and if I discover that one word of what has been said in your hearing this night has been spoken of in the wrong place, and by the wrong person, I will have you and your family burned inside your house. Do you comprehend me?"

"I be just an honest worker..." he spluttered in answer, but I held up my purse with a smile and climbed again out of the boat, thanking Sam the boatman loudly as I did so.

• • •

I said many comforting words to Praise God as we sat down for a last cup of sack before retiring. I also gave him some instructions.

"I am not expecting you to work miracles, Praise God; merely to realise that if I know the intentions of Strafford, and Strafford, through Richard Sykes, is able to know the intentions of the King's enemies, then there will be much we can do together to avoid ultimate conflict. The only way this can be achieved at present is by your informing Clunehaven of all that I tell you. It must be hoped that he will pass on these morsels of information to my cousin. It is my strong suggestion that you, if asked from whence you come by your knowledge, refer to me merely as 'a source close to the centre of government.' It is also my strong suggestion that you avoid any reference to your friendship with me and, if asked, deny that you still know me or wish to have anything to do with me. Fear not: we are called to be 'As wise as serpents;' and must therefore be practical in working out our salvation, as well as the salvation of the nation. I will not take any pretended rejection I receive from you personally at all. In the meantime I desire you to wait upon me, weekly - and whenever I specifically call upon you – for further instruction."

From the moment I had first started talking to Sam the boatman, until the moment I drained my last mouthful of sack, Praise God had said very little. But just as I was about to suggest that we retired for the night, he suddenly started to speak in a most animated fashion. "I hope," he began, "that you will forgive me if I appear proud in your eyes, but you referred to my 'much learning,' and yet you appear to take me for a complete fool."

"What?"

"I said you appear to..."

"I heard what you said, explain yourself."

"Well for one thing the Lord did not just require us merely to be 'as wise as serpents,' but also to be 'as harmless as doves.' You should have made sure that I was standing further away from the boat; I heard everything that you said back there. Secondly, even if I hadn't, your sudden propensity for speaking on equal terms with your social inferiors hardly matched up with your referring to my boatman as a 'dog' merely for asking me if I wished to continue my journey, and as for that so-called apology…"

I made to interrupt, but he had the thorough impertinence to *silence me with a wave of his hand.*

"Apart from this little piece of evidence of your persistent degenerate behaviour," he continued, "I could make neither head nor tail of what you wanted me to do anyway: introduce you to Strafford? Destroy your cousin? Introduce your cousin to Strafford? Introduce the King to the Queen? Do you wish me to spy on Pym's cousin for the Queen? Or shall we settle merely for finding the family of Sam the boatman and burning his children at Smithfield? As I said: I cannot make head or tail of it."

"You are mocking me!"

"Most certainly I am…fool."

"How *dare* you?"

"Much more easily now I can see you for what you really are."

"HOW DARE YOU?" I repeated. I then started to call loudly for John Brown.

"Worry not," Praise God said, "I am leaving. I was once willing to believe (and have cursed myself often for my foolishness) that you are despised by so many people because, as Jesus said: 'If they have hated the Master, then they will hate His servants also,' but you are not despised because you are any sort of servant of the Lord. Did you think I wouldn't find out what you tried to do at that ball after I had stood outside making a clown of myself? Why do you suppose I have been avoiding you? Well if you want someone to do your filthy work, ask Compromise-not-at-all Jenkins. I have seen him bullying his way around the City just like you and he used to do at Cambridge.

And with that, and before I could say anymore, Praise God had stood up and left the room.

I am ashamed to say that instead of treating Praise God's words with disdain, as I should have done, I ran after him, shouting and begging for him to come back. I entered the hall in time to see him walk straight passed an extremely confused looking John Brown, whom I shoved out of the way. I managed to catch up with Praise God on the road outside.

I just wrote that I was ashamed to say that I chased after Praise God. The truth is that I regretted it in other ways also; for in trying to persuade him to change his mind and return with me into the house, I said certain things to him that for several years I had kept within the confines of my own council. I will explain thus: you will remember, no doubt, the conversation I had with my father in the woods; how he had revealed to me that the children of righteousness are not bound by the restrictions placed upon the…partially enlightened. But when Praise God suddenly mentioned the incident at the ball the desire to extricate myself from my sense of embarrassment overwhelmed me.

I therefore took hold of Praise God's arm and held him fast. "Praise God," I said, with real urgency, "please do not depart from me thus! You do not understand - how could you? If you had attempted to persuade by such means Gwendolyn Smith, or any maiden, to partake with you in the delights of the bedroom, it would have been a sin indeed; but for certain of us, unto whom the deeper secrets of heaven have been revealed, it is not a sin at all, but rather a fulfilment of the instruction of the Lord: 'enjoy the fruits of the earth and the fulfilment thereof.'"

"What?"

I knew instantly that I had made a mistake. I let go of Praise God's arm and backed away.

"I…er."

"You are mad."

"Praise God – please, step inside with me; I can explain. Perhaps the Lord would wish to reveal these secrets to you also…"

But, as I previously stated, I knew that I had made a mistake; and these last words did nothing but increase my sense of confusion. My sudden lack of confidence must have been strongly reflected in my tone of voice.

"Are you aware," said Praise God, "that the King justifies his authoritarian stance as Head of the Church of England with the need to protect his people from the snares of heresy?"

"So, (I took a step back in a manner of affected disgust) you have decided to throw in your lot with the King!"

But Praise God was entirely undaunted by this accusation. "I see no need to justify myself to you at all, but I will say this: for all the King's faults, he at least stays loyal to his own conscience; to what he believes is right. I think that he is often wrong, but he at least *believes* he is serving the Lord. As for you: be weak and be sorry; be a sinner and then admit your folly, is not the Lord a merciful God? But to take Scripture and twist it as you do....you will find no comfort or mercy on the judgement day. I was speaking in jest before, but you *are* a lover of evil; you are a wolf who has got in amongst the sheep; and as far as I am concerned, you are a reprobate, cast off by God and left to wallow in the mire of his own making!"

With these words Praise God walked away. I tried to take hold of his arm, pleading with him as I did so to stay, but he shook away my hand and disappeared into the night.

I was at first overwhelmed by a sense of darkness and loss, and called out Praise God's name, begging him to return; but all I heard in response was the sound of a baby crying and the distant barking of many dogs. I went back inside the house and, being deeply disturbed and upset by Praise God's words, smacked John Brown twice about the head before sitting down and pouring myself another cup of sack. I am not trying to elicit your sympathy, good Reader, but as I held that cup and stared at the chair Praise God had so recently vacated; and as his words echoed in my ears, I trembled so much that I was barely able to lift the cup to my lips. I have to confess that I was at first deeply fearful that I would indeed be cast away by the Lord on the judgement day.

But as the strong liquid started to warm my throat I began to see things with greater clarity. I remembered my days of leading the *Young Puritans* at Cambridge; how I had served the Lord by enforcing His will onto the lives of so many of His enemies, and how He had honoured me by causing me, and not my cousin, to become the Member of Parliament for Towcester and Weedon. I then thought of Praise God again, and compared his condemnatory words with the approval I had received from the likes of John Pym. I therefore rejected them. Despite this, his words rang in my ears for many hours after he left, and no amount of strong drink would entirely get rid of them.

XVII

Strafford

I awoke the next morning in my chair - having drunk myself to sleep a few hours previously - realising that there was a certain danger hanging over me. I had said a great deal more to Praise God than I should have done, and it was likely that he would repeat my words to Clunehaven. Clunehaven, of course, would be as shocked by my words as Praise God had been, and was highly likely to repeat them to John Pym, with whom he was almost certainly acquainted. I was not so sure of the unstinting spirituality of my parliamentary colleagues, nor in their belief in my own righteousness, that I did not think it highly probable that they would take his word against mine purely on the grounds that he was an earl.

But I knew one man who had always believed in me, whatever the accusations that were thrown in my direction from the likes of Clunehaven and Richard Sykes. I therefore went to my desk and, taking quill and paper began to write:

Sir,

My felicitous salutations.

I know you will remember the troubles and persecutions that you and I encountered at Cambridge during my happy years under your care, during which we set ourselves to combat, on behalf of the Lord, compromise and wickedness, wherever the foot of the Lord, in the person of we His soldiers, was wont to trample. There was one aspect, however, of the service I rendered unto the Lord at university, which still gives me great pain whenever I recollect it, and all the more now that I am faced again with such sorrowful behaviour from those I should be able to count amongst my friends. This was the persecution I received, and now receive, whenever I sought, and now seek, to perform and accomplish the will of the Lord.

Verily I know well the response that you, as an experienced and long-suffering servant of God, will give unto these words, but I have never been able to keep myself from grieving when those who, whilst purporting to be accounted among the godly, seek to hinder the great works the Lord requires of us in His name. You will doubtless say to me that persecution is a sign of God's blessing and, although I would desire to conduct myself with the same boldness as yourself, I find myself now weighed down by the opposition I face as I seek to accomplish God's purposes here in London. If the devil would attack me openly, then this I could easily brook and combat; but the devil (oh how I should have predicted this) has sought to undermine me by sullying my name in the same manner he sought to undermine our great works at Cambridge.

As for the manner in which the enemies of righteousness are maligning me: If I were merely a private gentleman, seeking to bring the light of God to my local community, then I would find the means at my own disposal to dispel false rumours and false witnesses, and all the darts of the enemy. But I find, now that I am a Member of Parliament, that the stakes are too high for me to risk alone the attempt to withstand Satan and his demons. I am afraid that my colleagues in the Commons will find the beguiling words of my enemies (as well as those I should account among my friends) impossible to resist. I pray therefore that you would, as a matter of urgency, make speed to come to London in order to assist me in preserving and protecting the integrity of my reputation. As I have hinted: I count my repute as of importance merely because of the great works the Lord has set before us.

I pray that you will, if possible, return in the company of my courier John Brown. If you are unable to do this I pray that you would send unto Mr Pym a reference on my behalf. I cannot sufficiently stress the need for haste.

I remain, Sir, your humble servant,

He-died-for-our-sins Sykes.

Of course the truth was that when I referred to 'the great works we accomplished at Cambridge,' my intention was to appeal to Dr Harding's somewhat over-inflated sense of self-importance. He really did nothing at all to help our violent struggle, and I cannot really blame him - he was far too old and fat; but I knew that I was soon likely to need a further reference from him as to my good character if I was to avoid being cast aside by John Pym.

I sent Brown away with instructions to deliver the letter safely to Cambridge, giving him a plentiful supply of money to change horses at Bishop's Stortford, as well as hire a horse for Dr Harding should he be willing to return in his company, for, I told him, speed was of the essence (I cannot have been as entirely devoid of conscience as Praise God had suggested, for I gave him two shillings on top of the necessary expenses to atone for the beating he had received at my hands on the preceding evening). I then made my way to my bedchamber; and for the whole of that weekend, and on the Monday following, I made a vain attempt to blot out Praise God's words by sleeping and, when awake, consuming vast quantities of sack.

• • •

On the following Tuesday I finally made my way to the House of Commons: the worst place possible, it turned out, for nursing a hangover. Everyone seemed to be shouting at once; and I began to think that if I heard the word 'grievance' again, then I would throw myself into the river.

Worse still, I had sat at an unoccupied place at the back of the chamber and shut my eyes in an attempt to dispel my pounding headache. But I had been sitting in this position for no more than five minutes when I was suddenly hit on the side of my head by hard object. This, as well as being extremely painful, gave me a very unpleasant shock, and caused me to start to my feet. I looked to my right in time to behold Robert Heron, who was standing behind the Speaker's chair and being encouraged by one of his friends, throwing what turned out to be a small marble ball straight at me. He succeeded in hitting me again, this time on the forehead.

While I was being thus attacked the attention of the members was centred upon Sir Henry Vane, the King's fawning Secretary of State, who, standing about six feet in front of my two assailants, and next to the Speaker's chair, was calling the members to attend the King at one of the clock in the Banqueting House at the Palace of Whitehall.

I at first responded with great restraint by indicating to Heron and his accomplice that I wished to pay attention to the proceedings in the House. Having gestured to them thus, I turned my attention to Vane and raised my face loftily in the manner of one who, although momentarily distracted by the misbehaviour of children, has more important matters pressing and can therefore no longer afford them any attention. Far from heeding my silent adjuration however, Heron took careful aim and hit me with another marble on the side of my nose.

I was as aware as any in that place of the dignity of my surroundings, and can therefore only give account of my reaction to Heron's childish behaviour on the grounds that I believed myself to be a guardian of that dignity; but so incensed was I after being hit for a third time by one of these missiles, that I picked up one of the marbles and threw it back at Heron with the full force of my strength. I failed to hit him, but was compensated for my lack of accuracy by striking his companion on the right eye. At this they started behaving as if I were the attacker and not the defender, and hurled about a handful each of these marbles in my direction in a most aggressive fashion. Heron's pocket appeared to be crammed full of them. For a moment I could only cover my head with my arm and call for them to desist, my voice lost to all but those to whom it was directed by the shouting of the other Members.

But they refused to desist, and as you can imagine this completely unprovoked attack, coupled with my violent headache, caused me eventually to lose control of my temper. But there was so much shouting and waving of papers going on in the Chamber that no one was aware of any such attack at all, until that is, a most unfortunate thing happened: the Speaker had stood up and was calling loudly for silence, and had just succeeded in quieting the Chamber at the same time as I, having managed to retrieve a handful of marbles from the floor, threw them with all of my might in the direction of Heron and his companion. But my aim was not true, or at least not entirely true, for although some of the marbles hit both of them, they had anticipated the counter-attack by turning their backs and covering their heads. Sir Henry Vane, however, had prepared for no such attack, and I saw, to my horror, one of the marbles hit him with full force on his left temple. He (and I am sure to this day that he was exaggerating his injury in order to stir up trouble) fell to the floor in a crumpled heap.

Of course Heron and his friend took advantage of the confusion created by this incident by leaving the Chamber hurriedly through the door behind the Speaker's chair, sniggering like school children. I was forced to follow them, greatly relieved that amid the tumult I could only hear the members exclaiming that someone had thrown a hard object at the Secretary, but no one identifying me as the particular culprit.

And as I am sure you will have realised, under any circumstances an attack on the King's Secretary of State would be regarded with the utmost gravity, but in the atmosphere of London in 1640 the perpetrator of any such attack would, at best, have been sent to the Tower to rot at the King's pleasure; but more likely had his head removed from his body, even if the weapon used was something so insignificant as a child's marble ball.

So I walked as quickly as I could down the main passage away from the chamber of the Commons, which led, as I have previously mentioned, in the direction of the House of Lords. I reached the Painted Chamber in time to see Heron and his companion disappear up a flight of stairs, but I decided against pursuing them on the grounds that were I to antagonise them, they would probably report me to the Sergeant at Arms as the thrower of the wayward missile; and even if they did not, I was sure that they would pelt me with more marbles.

So I ascended a small part of the spiralled staircase until I was out of sight of the members, who I knew would soon come spilling out of the Commons. After about a minute I began to hear the sound of many voices. As soon as I had ascertained that there were a sufficient number of them in the room, I climbed the staircase and lost myself amongst them.

I made my way to the group of members surrounding John Pym who, like all the others, were discussing the event just described, and asking if anyone had seen the perpetrator of the attack. No one had apparently done so, so I joined in with their enquiries, and when I felt entirely safe, even made so bold as to suggest that the missile must have emanated from the general direction of where I had been sitting. But after a few minutes the conversation began to centre again upon the important matters of state being shouted about in the chamber before and after Vane had made his intervention, of which I had no heart on this particular day to take an interest. I therefore began to make my way towards the main door that led out of the Palace. But as I walked out of the Chamber my progress was arrested by two members of the King's Guard who, although not displaying any overt aggression, as their swords were not drawn, barred my way, making it plain by doing so that they intended to let no one pass.

At this point I began to panic, believing as I did that the purpose of this martial intervention could only be the interrogation of the members in order to find out Sir Henry Vane's assailant. Of course no one had so far *said* that they had seen me, but Sir Henry Vane was extremely unpopular amongst the King's opponents and this may have been the only reason. If anyone *had* seen me then it was quite possible that they may give me away when under the pressure of examination, and Heron and his companion would be delighted to drop me in it.

And then, just as I had turned away from the door and was attempting to negotiate for myself another mode of escape, the double doors which led to the House of Lords were thrown open, two more soldiers entered and stood in front of them to prevent them from swinging back, and a most impressive looking gentleman entered the room with a retinue of followers. I will tell you in a moment what it was about this man that makes me use the word impressive. For the moment I will tell you that I knew immediately who he was: none other than Charles Wentworth, Earl of Strafford, the King's deputy in Ireland; and the very bane of the King's opponents.

I knew who he was for several reasons. For one thing the reaction to his appearance among the majority of the members was such as can only be attributed to the arrival of a great enemy. It was much worse, for example, than the way they had previously responded to the reappearance into their lives of the former Speaker Finch. What made his identity so obvious to me however, was the fact that amongst his followers was my beloved cousin Richard Sykes.

And the most remarkable thing about him became apparent when he began to address us. Despite the clear loathing he elicited from most of those present, there was none of the deliberate obstruction usually directed at the King's representatives, which was manifested on the most part by everyone talking while they were trying to speak; and this was despite the fact that Strafford's words were much more offensive than anything I had heard up to this point.

But I was about to describe his appearance. He was about forty-eight years of age, although the ravages of illness gave him the appearance of about fifty five. He was tall and dark, although his hair had now turned quite grey, and his height was compromised by his walking with something of a stoop, the cause of which also required him to lean upon a cane.

You will by now be aware that even when describing my enemies I give nothing but an honest account, for by no other means can the true history of my time be known. I must stress to you therefore that the most remarkable aspect to this man was something not tangible; something which a description of his appearance alone cannot convey. I have mentioned on previous pages that my father had the ability to pierce my innermost thoughts, and that his brother, my uncle, had the authority to sway a crowd. Strafford had both of these attributes and more. I have never, before or since, met or heard of a man whose sheer presence created such consternation in his enemies, or such adoration in his followers and friends. It was impossible not to see why he was so detested - and so loved - from the very first moment I set eyes upon him.

As the conversations of the members began to die away, which they did with no command having been given, he scanned the room with a face which, although essentially devoid of expression, seemed mildly contemptuous. He then began to speak: "I am not even going to ask who has just assaulted the Secretary of State....not, I may add, because I regard such an action as anything short of treasonable..."

"He detests Vane" said a voice quietly into my ear. I looked around and beheld William Strode, one of my aforementioned colleagues. I think that my sigh of relief must have been audible.

"...but because," continued Strafford, "I know that the sort of people who play at politics while their own country is under attack are the sort of people who think that playing at marbles at such a time - or fiddling while Rome burns - is a justifiable occupation. I have the utmost faith in the integrity of your schoolboys' code and know that you would never give up one of your friends, so I will advise the Sergeant at Arms to let the matter drop. I understand that Secretary Vane is up on his feet again."

"Absolutely detests him," repeated Strode.

Strafford's expression then darkened. "The King will address you this afternoon at Whitehall, and I am here to give you some insight into what he intends to say in order that, as time is pressing - something of which you are very well aware - you can prepare a response acceptable to yourselves and to his Majesty...he intends to compromise. Why? Because he understands that despite the unreasonableness of your demands there are greater matters at stake here...the King is therefore willing to abandon the ship money tax in return for twelve subsidies needed desperately to repel the Scots from our border."

At these last words the Members started murmuring, and the murmuring grew louder as they began arguing among themselves. After a few seconds Strafford continued and all fell silent again.

"And now I will address you briefly on a more personal level, and say something that I know the King cannot - or will not - say to you...to you who have been elected to represent the people of this country. Who benefits if this country is protected because there is a tax paid by the rich for the protection of our shores...the people of Dover...Plymouth? Yes the people of Dover and Plymouth; but not just them: all of us...the people of London, Derby and Birmingham...all our cities, and all our counties, and all our little towns, and all our castles. Oh you are so brave Hampden, you shall no doubt become a folk hero...have eulogies and songs composed in your honour for resisting this tax, but what a cause - the protection of your own personal rights; the protection of a little fraction of your property. Your very nature leads you to oppose all that authority ordains for you, and I suppose your popularity drives you on like a spur; but you would be better served, Sir, by someone willing to take the pains to whip you into your right wits. But I thought I had seen the bottom of it; and then you, Pym, have the effrontery to stand in that chamber claiming to be a man of the people, when all you are interested in is protecting the contents of your own purse. You know well it is not the poor who suffer under this tax but the rich...who pretend to suffer, when their real grievance is that the tax was raised by the King without their consent. If, by your leave Sir, your grievances centred merely upon matters of religion and the methods of the Star Chamber, then I for one would gladly give you a listening ear; but you are not a man of the people, you are a man of your own manor house; and you have forced the King to place your own selfish designs before the interests of *his* people. If the common people of this country truly had a voice then I'll warrant they'd have you and your friends out of this place quicker than it takes you to say the words 'sedition' and 'treason'!"

Strafford then paused again, and took in all of the members with a glance. His expression softened. "To the rest of you, I adjure you to accept the King's terms; he has an ear for your grievances, and the very life of our nation depends upon your giving a reasonable response to the olive branch he is about to offer you."

With those words he turned and walked out in the direction he had arrived, followed by my cousin and his other boot-lickers. As soon as they had passed through the door the King's party erupted into spontaneous cheering and applause. I saw Sir Thomas Witherington weeping with the joy of the moment, and then I turned to gauge the reactions of Pym in particular, and Hampden also.

Pym stood for a moment surrounded by his colleagues, his face ashen. When he finally did speak his voice was completely calm: "He believes that he can use the same divide and rule policies he applied in Ireland over here...I am going to bring about the ruin of that man. One day he will slip, and on that day I will ruin him."

He then turned and strode back in the direction of Saint Stephen's Chapel.

By this time, the soldiers having withdrawn, the members were beginning to disperse; but I beheld John Hampden leaning against a wall with his arms folded, and I was struck by the fact that he was *glaring* at me. I might have used this opportunity to speak to him in order to dispel the discomposure I had felt at his apparent dislike of me, but I was entirely put off by his expression, which was nothing short of *venomous*.

So I turned also toward the House of Commons, deciding that my time would be better served in ingratiating myself with Pym ahead of the unwelcome tidings he was soon bound to hear concerning my words to Praise God. But before I had stepped more than two paces Hampden called on me to stop.

He approached me, glowering, and stood facing me in silence for about fifteen seconds as the last of the members passed by. This lack of communication I found entirely disconcerting, so I eventually broke the ice myself. "That was jolly rash of him, was it not, to mention yourself and John by name?"

His response matched his expression. "Be quiet, Sykes, and listen to me. I knew all about you before you even came here. There are some, and I count myself among them, who have spent the last eleven years risking life and limb to change the direction of this country…"

"I have, 'tis true, heard nought about you but that which is complimentary."

"Be *quiet* Sykes" he repeated in a voice even more menacing…. "and there are some, and I count *you* among them, who are just in it for themselves: wreckers and parasites; people responsible for nothing but pushing people too far for their own ends, so that we can't get anywhere because we're all tarred with your filthy brush!"

"I…I do think that's a bit strong."

"Oh do you?" He then looked around to see if there were any stragglers, saw that there were not, grabbed me by the lapels of my coat and *pushed me up against the wall!* "I saw you in there Sykes, throwing marbles while we are trying to conduct the business you should be concerned about..."

"But Heron…"

"Your childish behaviour - and even your former reputation for bullying - I can just about brook….but you are a Ranter; a distorter of scripture…*you*, and people like you, have driven Laud and the King to their extreme position."

I have to confess that at these words I was speechless. I had expected an accusation of this sort; but I had expected it to come from Pym, and not so quickly either. It was also the first time that I had heard my uncommon religious doctrines being described by anyone other than my father, as well as given a title. I could be left in no doubt whatsoever that Praise God had spoken to Clunehaven, and Clunehaven to Hampden, or that Praise God had spoken to Hampden directly.

"What are you going to do?" I asked feebly.

"I will tell you exactly what I am going to do, I am going to meet Pym at six of the clock in the committee room as previously arranged; and you are going to arrive at fifteen minutes past. I will leave it to him to decide what to do with you."

"Which committee room?"

"The one where I first had the misfortune to set eyes on you," and with those unpleasant words he followed the other members into the Commons.

XVIII

Despair and jubilation

My feelings as I walked out of the Palace of Westminster that morning were the closest I have ever felt to sheer despair. Not only did I believe that I would excluded from the House of Commons, but I was also convinced that as word got around about my doctrinal deviations (as *they* would call them), I would be cast out from society altogether. As I strolled down the banks of the Thames I was assailed with visions of myself being henceforth accepted only into the company of the likes of Compromise-not-at-all Jenkins, and dying eventually in a gutter, having spent the winter of my life trying in vain to convince all I met that the sad relic of humanity they beheld before them had once been a man of power; a member of Parliament who had rubbed shoulders with the Great. I must say to you, good Reader, not for the first time, that it is not my purpose to invoke your pity, but as I looked out upon the water, and the midday sun gave forth its dappled reflections, the tears cascaded down my cheeks more freely than I had known since when, as a young child, my father had informed me in his brusque and uncaring way of my mother's unexpected death.

But I could not cry forever. I remembered that I was still, for the time-being, a Member of Parliament; and that as such I was still required to attend the King at the Palace of Whitehall, at one of the clock.

So I spent about an hour loitering in the vicinity of Westminster Palace, until approximately half past twelve, at which time I saw first the members of the House of Lords, and then my fellow Members of the Commons, leaving the Palace and heading in the direction of Whitehall. I hid from view until Pym and Hampden had passed (they were speaking together in an animated fashion, doubtless about me). I then joined the train at the back, making sure as I did so to keep out of their sight.

To describe the Banqueting House at Whitehall would be as pointless as attempting to describe the sky, so well is it known to all of us. The sheer ostentation of its ceiling in particular, then so recently decorated by Inigo Jones, was the source of much chagrin among the more austere of the godly. Indeed in happier times I would have joined in their vocal revulsion with a glad and willing heart. But on that day the beauty of my surroundings served only to highlight for me the belief that I was about to be cast off forever from all that I had worked so hard, through the persecution of God's enemies, to obtain.

But I did not have too much time after my arrival to dwell on thoughts so maudlin. I found a place at the back of the hall among some members unknown to me, and within a minute the King arrived through a door at the far end in the company of Strafford, Vane and a few others I did not recognise.

This time there was none of the ceremony that marked the previous occasions I had encountered the King. He walked quickly and, having arrived at the throne, turned to us, but barely acknowledged the bows with which he was greeted by all present. He sat down, and Strafford and Vane (the latter of whom wore a most superfluous bandage around his head) stood on either side of the throne.

"My Lords…Gentlemen," he began, stuttering more than the last time I had heard him, "it has come to my attention that there are those among you determined to use the aggression of the Scots to further their own ends. There are some who have hinted even that they have sympathy for their…northern brethren, as if this is a just cause for enmity against their king."

His voice then became bolder. "Do not I have sympathy for the Scots? Am I not, by birth and name, myself a Scot? But the governance of the Scots has been usurped by a rebellious faction. They are a people with loyal hearts who have been led astray; and while under such a delusion they must in some measure be chastised – and we, on a practical score, must protect our own border..."

This, good Reader (and I crave your forgiveness) is all I am able to recollect of this speech, which went on for some time. As I stated but a moment ago, my surroundings served only to remind me of my sorrowful state, and the King's speech had the same effect. I may have despised him, but I had believed that I would witness his downfall, and that I may even be its chief architect. But I looked upon him on that afternoon with something almost akin to affection, as I felt that having in a sense known him for such a short time I would behold him no more – except maybe in the company of a grovelling crowd of unwashed peasants.

But I do remember waking from my melancholic reverie as the King stood up to end his speech. He did so by asking us to repair to the House of Commons, where Secretary Vane would place before us the details of his proposals, "And," he added, "I pray that you will suffer him to speak to you unmolested."

The King then stood, bowed to us in a cursory fashion, and walked quickly out of the hall, followed by Strafford and Vane.

The time was two of the clock when the Members made their way back to the Palace of Westminster, and although I still felt reluctant in some part to join them, the fact that my self-inflicted illness was beginning to wear off put me in a slightly more positive frame of mind. I therefore left the Banqueting House quickly and again found a vantage point from which I could ensure that the Members had re-entered the Palace ahead of me. I then followed them inside and sat at the back of the chamber.

As I sat down Secretary Vane was just starting to speak; and here, for your benefit, is a summary of what must have been (and I think the record still stands) the worst speech ever uttered in Parliament. I should put it into some sort of context. As I had followed the other members into the Palace of Whitehall I had heard more than one of them discussing Strafford's recent intervention. Not one, but all of the members I heard speaking, appeared at the very least willing to consider the King's proposals. And these were not the King's men, or even woolly Members of the Clunehaven type, but ardent opponents of the King's government. So, let this be understood: until the moment that Vane stood up to address us, it was highly likely that the King would have dropped the ship money tax, and we would have granted the King, maybe not twelve subsidies, but at least a sufficient number to finance a war with the Scots. This parliament therefore, unlike any of the King's previous parliaments, could have been a success. In one sense it could be said that this speech altered the course of history.

But I digress again: here, for posterity, was the most important part of Secretary Vane's speech as best as I remember it.

"Gentlemen: I see before me many who believe themselves to have been mistreated during the past years of his glorious Majesty's reign. Some among you even have the effrontery to claim that your goods have been molested by our sovereign Lord who, as Defender of the Faith, is the very representative of the risen Christ whilst we await His return from the heavens. Those among us of the higher Patrician Order would as fain question any of the King's doings as we would question the Lord Himself. But it is the King's burden to rule over the common people as well as the noble; and some of the Members of the House of Commons have been responding to the King's kind overtures as only the Common would…or could. You talk of suffering, but *I* know what it is to suffer: this bandage upon my head represents the persecution suffered by all who remain loyal to the King during his afflictions; and yet I stand here in this place laying myself open for further attack."

He then stopped for a moment to look around the chamber, whether to see if anyone was about to throw a marble at him again, or because he expected everyone to burst into applause, I know not; but no one either threw a marble or applauded him, so he continued.

"Concerning the matter before us: the King has been forced, due to your obduracy, to grant you a compromise in order that he may fulfil his duty as your liege sovereign. Of course he knows perfectly well that in asking for twelve subsidies you will resort to your usual stubborn and ungracious ways of responding to his kind proposals, and probably grant him six, but there you have another attribute of his Majesty: wisdom. Were he to ask you for six you would doubtless grant him three, and six is the very least we need from this parliament during this current crisis!"

With those words he took in all of the Members present with a sweeping look of self-satisfaction, shouted, "Accept the King's terms!" and turned to leave the Chamber.

The response to this speech was as you would doubtless expect: stunned and open-mouthed silence, followed quickly by uproar. Vane, realising that the reaction was not as he had hoped, started to quicken his step as he approached the main door, where several members jostled and shoved him as he tried to make his way through.

I then spent the next two hours listening, I believed for the last time, to my colleagues insulting and abusing one another across the floor of the Chamber. I then left, somewhat early, for the committee room in which I had first made acquaintance with my parliamentary colleagues. My anguish was therefore increased by my having to wait outside, listening to, although not able to understand, the muffled but animated voices I could hear from within.

At last, at the appointed time, I knocked upon the door.

"Enter," said a voice from within (this I recognised as Pym's).

The first thing I realised as I walked into the room was that there were not two occupants, as I had expected, but five. Pym and Hampden were there, but with them also were William Strode and an elderly gentleman who, as he had his head bent in conference with Pym, I did not instantly recognise, although his appearance was familiar. The fifth gentleman was a largely built and ill-kempt looking Member of Parliament, whom I had seen and heard in the House, but not met. He had scraggly grey hair, several warts on his face and a somewhat shrewd and intimidating expression. He looked fixedly at me as I entered, and although it was impossible not to find his expression disconcerting, it was not nearly as overtly unfriendly as Hampden's. There was no chair provided for me, so I walked towards the large desk at which they were sitting until Pym, without looking up, held out the palm of his hand as an order for me to stop.

And there I had to wait for at least a minute, during which time Hampden stared at me, unblinking. Strode busied himself by examining, or pretending to examine, some papers in front of him and Pym and the elderly gentleman continued their private conference.

Pym finally stopped talking, and as he did so he looked up, as did the other gentleman. You may be sure that as I beheld Dr Arbuthnot Harding sitting there next to Pym my heart leapt so that I had to contain myself from walking straight around that desk and kissing him. Yes, good Reader, in the shock of the sudden accusation of Hampden I had all but completely forgotten that I had written to him.

Despite my joy I needed to contain myself; and this in particular because Pym started speaking to me with no joyful countenance.

"Hampden here has told me," he began, "that, as well as having witnessed that you were the thrower of that marble ball this morning (something we are all agreed to overlook for the sake of the weightier matter before us), he has heard from a reliable source that you are a holder of dangerous doctrines; that you are in fact a follower of the sect known as 'the Family of Love,' or, as they are more derisorily known (with reason), the Ranters – apostates, as I would call them, from the true doctrines and instructions set out in Holy Scripture. I must tell you that we, as Members of Parliament, are interested in dealing only with the grievances hitherto mentioned in this place, and the suppression of popery. We have no business and no truck with heretics, but hold them in contempt. They are, in my view, worthy only to be ostracised, cast off: - anathema. Heretics in our ranks accomplish nought but to give substance to the arguments of our enemies. Speak, for there are those here willing to defend you, but their defence will be granted no credence if you insufficiently defend yourself. Speak!"

So I spoke, knowing as I did so that the future of my whole life depended upon the success or failure of my words.

"Gentlemen, I found when at Cambridge, that those who should have been in the vanguard of our struggle against wickedness and immorality were all too often too fond themselves of their worldly status and the comforts and snares of this present life. So I pleaded and begged; I exhorted them through the scriptures; I fasted and prayed but all, it seemed, to no avail. Had I had more faith in God I would have realised that there were those as willing as I to serve Him with gladness and self-denial. Soon the Lord brought us together and, through the use of prayer and the exhortation of our fellow men we were able to put some sort of stamp of godliness upon the university.

But then I stumbled by reason of another personal failing: that of naivety, for I had expected that the work of the Lord would attract enmity, but I believed that my enemies would fight me openly and with, at the very least, the honour that the unredeemed world knows as honour. This was naivety indeed, for instead I found myself defamed by the reports of false witnesses. I was stripped and beaten for preaching the word of God; I was cast into the night all but naked except for the undergarments of the sexually perverse, which they forced me to wear. I was accused of sexual depravity; and in this way was my name maligned. My enemies are now here in London seeking to destroy me by the same means. I can only beg you, gentlemen, to let me prove my worth and to give no heed to the lies of the wicked."

"Are you saying," asked Pym, "that there is no truth to these allegations?"

"I am, Sir."

"Then leave us please and wait outside the door, we will call you when we are ready."

And so I waited outside again. I was more confident than I had been before, in the light of my defence as well as the presence of Dr Harding; although I knew not the part Strode, or the other gentleman, to whom I had not been introduced, would play in my fate.

I was relieved when after about ten minutes Pym again called me inside.

As I entered the room he was talking quietly to Dr Harding, but he kept me waiting no longer than a few seconds. "I am bound to say," he began," that were we able to rely upon your testimony alone I would still be inclined to give you the benefit of the doubt. You have impressed me lad, and of that I make no secret; nor do I make any secret of the fact that I was disappointed to the core at the thought that we might have to dismiss someone I see as so promising. What leaves us (Hampden coughed here) - or most of us - in no doubt of the truth of your words, are two witnesses here who have come to speak in your defence. Dr Harding you already know. He has informed us that your account is true; that you were victim to just the sort of persecution you have spoken of at Cambridge" (Dr Harding at this point smiled in my direction, inclining his head slowly as he did so). Pym then turned to the scraggly haired man on his right. "This gentleman informs me that you have not met, and yet he is also here in the capacity of a witness for your defence. Perhaps, Oliver, you would care to speak for yourself?"

"First of all," replied the gentleman as he stood to his feet, "I would ask why we keep our brother in the struggle standing in our presence?" And with those words he came striding round the desk, seized a vacant chair and placed it behind me. "Sit thee down, lad."

As I obeyed this friendly command he stepped back to the desk, turned, and perched himself on the edge, obscuring my view of both Strode and Hampden.

"It is time," he said, "that we made our acquaintance anyway, I am Oliver Cromwell, Member for Cambridge, and it is in this capacity that I have come to speak for thee. Dr Harding and I are of a like mind. We believe that nought will be accomplished by passivity and a good will; and for that reason little *was* accomplished at Cambridge in the 'thirties until your influence became known around its halls and precincts."

He then crossed the room in two strides, and grabbed my hand, shaking it with vigour. "I think that I, in part, must thank thee (if being a Member of Parliament is aught to be grateful for), for without a doubt if the voters of Cambridge had not felt the effects of your influence at the university they would have returned yet another dissolute court fop to parliament."

"'Tis true," Dr Harding interjected, "it was primarily by my prompting and exhortation that Master Cromwell was chosen as one of the Members; and I may add that the wielding of such influence became much easier during and since the time young He-died-for-our-sins took up his studies."

"Well," said Cromwell, returning again to the other side of the desk, "I think that we have spent enough time dousing the fiery darts of the enemy; let us to the matter in hand, pull thy chair up to the desk lad."

"Whoa, whoa – stop there, Cousin!" (This was John Hampden).

"Your cousin I may be John, but that does not give you leave to speak to me as if you were addressing your horse!"

These sort of remarks (not very amusing but clearly meant to be) were, I later discovered, regularly made by Cromwell. I came to see the degree to which people laughed at them as a measuring stick for their sycophancy (his sergeants and corporals all seemed to find them hilarious).

Hampden did not laugh however, nor did he excuse himself for speaking to Cromwell 'as if he were addressing his horse."

"You are surely not going to tell me that you are going to take him at his word? Deceit and trickery are some of the very things he is accused of!"

"But John," said Pym, "it is not just at his word, is it? It is also at the words of Oliver and Arbuthnot."

"Sorry, I should have said deceit, trickery and the ability to pull the wool over people's eyes."

Cromwell's cheeks coloured at this, as did Dr Harding's. I, however, tried to interject before either of them: "If I may make a suggestion…"

"Be silent, Sykes" (Hampden again).

"Now come on, John," said Pym.

"The source of my information is unimpeachable," Hampden argued. "It is much more reliable than the word of this…weasel, and the report he gives of his adventures leading the *Young Puritans* in Cambridge is very different from the accounts I have heard."

"But can those accounts be corroborated by any who are not counted among our enemies? We have more than one witness here to vouch for Sykes' integrity. Should we so readily accept the testimony of those who might wish to destroy him, and who you refuse to produce for our examination?"

"And what of our own God-given ability to discern good from evil, and the fact that my witness is unwilling to appear because he believes Sykes will have him maimed, or killed?"

"Methinks, Cousin," put in Cromwell, "that our ability to discern the good and evil in others may be somewhat overly affected by the good or evil report we hear of them. You know perfectly well that we cannot condemn this man without proof…now, enough of this; let us to the matter in hand. Vane's absurd eulogy has entirely put paid to the King's proposals; it is hard to tell where he can go from here if he still hopes for money for the Scottish war, other than to accept all of our terms."

"I think," I said, "he may be forced to step where he should not in order to finance this war."

"I understand you not" said Pym.

But at that point Hampden stood up and marched out of the room, slamming the door behind him.

There was silence for a moment, then Pym said: "I think it would be best to end the meeting anyway at this point. We cannot act for the moment except in response to the movements of the King, and it is impossible to say at this time what direction he will take."

So we finished there, and I was left in the company of Dr Harding. My feelings were mixed. I was clearly relieved and delighted with the outcome of my 'trial' as far as my fate was concerned, but on the other hand I was somewhat frustrated at Pym and Cromwell's lack of fore-sight, and at my own inability to put my ideas into action. It was clear to me what needed to be done, but without the contact I needed in the King's party my ideas seemed hopeless. I mulled over this problem as I escorted Dr Harding back to my house along the Thames, thanking him as I did so for his kindness in making such haste to London.

Now, as you will have gathered, Dr Harding was an insufferably boring man, and I was sure that half or most of the stories he told me about his radical youth were at best exaggerated, but he had certain qualities. On the one hand I could trust him, and on the other hand he did have a semblance of wisdom. I therefore explained my problem to him when we had reached my house and sat down to a cup of claret.

"I wonder whether the method to use in answer to the situation we face, Dr Harding, is antagonism."

He gestured me to continue with a nod of his red, blubbery face (you doubtless think that I should have written 'head' instead of 'face,' but I can assure you that the movement of his head was barely perceptible, whereas the shaking of the fat hanging from his face caused by that barely perceptible movement was remarkable).

I continued: "The only true purpose of this parliament for now, in my opinion, is to take power from the King, but it seems that even Pym and Cromwell - and of course Hampden - hope or expect that some sort of compromise can be reached. It will never work."

"From what I have seen and heard I cannot help believing that thou art correct my son, but, I surmise, your problem lies in the difficulty of finding an alternative."

"Not so – it is clear to me what should be done, it is how to accomplish it."

He gestured for me to explain with another nod of his face.

"The King must be encouraged to bypass the Commons altogether. The Lords would inevitably vote for him the subsidies he needs, thinking to teach the Commons a lesson. The result of this will be divisive in the extreme. Pym is a true Parliamentarian, I am but a new member; therefore he, unlike me, is unlikely to recognise the wisdom of persuading the King to take such a course of action. Therefore *I*, as the only one who sees the necessity, must convince the King that it is the only course of action to take."

Dr Harding looked at me with a somewhat baffled expression, so I explained.

"We were in full agreement, were we not, that in order for the University of Cambridge to feel the full weight of our godliness, the compromising ways of Lord Clune needed to be dealt with?"

"We were."

"Well it is no less true with the country as a whole. If it is our genuine desire that our land should be ruled by the Saints of Zion, then there is no point at all in trying to obtain this end by bargaining with the devil - or his minion the King; therefore the King must be persuaded to go further in antagonising his enemies. This is the way to go about this."

"Ah," said Dr Harding, "I begin to understand you now, and your sense of logic does not disappoint me; well, the answer to your problem is simple."

"How so?"

"You will accomplish nought by looking too close to home. By home I mean the political arena altogether. Nor will you achieve anything by acting in too overt a manner. What you need is someone who is independent of politics, and yet has a persuasive influence over the King. The candidate for this role seems to me entirely obvious, and has more sway over the King than anyone."

He paused, expecting me, apparently, to guess the person he had in mind, but I could not, so he continued.

"I am talking here of that arch-Catholic bitch, Queen Henrietta Maria."

Now I must confess that I was not a little taken aback by this, not least because I saw no way of influencing *her* to influence the King.

"I know what you are thinking, but the beauty of Henrietta Maria (apart from those somewhat beguiling eyes) is that she despises the King's opponents with such a blind hatred that to persuade her to do our work for us will be a simple feat to accomplish. All you need to persuade her - of this I am sure - is an anonymous letter purporting to come from a Member of Parliament sympathetic to the King and, even more importantly, sympathetic to the Pope, suggesting the course of action you have in mind. Is your cousin Elizabeth still one of her ladies-in-waiting?"

"Yes."

"And do you think that she would be reliable as one who would, if it were in her possession, pass on information to the Queen if she thought it in the Queen's interests for her to do so?"

"Yes but…"

"Yes but nothing. You must write to your cousin, as if from a sympathetic Catholic member of the Commons, asking her to deliver a letter to the Queen as a matter of urgency. You must tell her that you are deeply concerned that there are those in the House seeking to harm the King through this political stand-off, which, you must add, they have created deliberately. You must stress that these Members of Parliament are not just hoping to get their way through this political stalemate, but that they are seeking to harm the King and Queen personally. Your cousin will have no choice in those circumstances but to pass on the letter. I have heard from Pym about the King's latest proposal, and about Secretary Vane's dog's breakfast of a speech, but this will not matter to the Queen. As I said, she is blind in her fury at anyone who dares to question her husband's authority, and she will, believe me, respond to that letter in just the manner you wish."

Now this, in my opinion, was an excellent notion; and if you, worthy Reader, have had any doubt that these memoirs are anything but entirely true then let me assure you that if I was to resort to any sort of falsehood I would have claimed Dr Harding's idea as my own.

"Hast thou a House of Commons Seal here in your house, my lad?"

"I have."

"Then let us to work."

So I wrote to my cousin immediately as Dr Harding had suggested, and I must add that I was astonished at his pragmatism, as what he was doing would have been for many others impossible due to the boundaries of their weak consciences. Dr Harding and I composed this, as well as the letter to the Queen, together; and it was with the aid of his scholarship that I was able to write the Latin text, which we used for the purpose of authenticity. For your benefit I here provide an English translation of the more important of the two letters.

Your Majesty,

As one of the few Catholic Members of the Commons, I must crave your forgiveness for writing this letter anonymously, but I fear that, such is the venomous intent of the arch-heretics who infest the halls of Westminster, my life would most certainly be forfeit should it be intercepted before it reached your Majesty's safe hands.

You know better than most that these are dark days for all adherents to the True Religion; but even I am shocked at the determination of these heretics to stamp out, by any means, all that they perceive to be a vestige of influence wrought in this country by His Holiness, whom they call 'the Bishop of Rome.' Things have come to such a head in Parliament that I can, in no uncertain terms, say that I have become fearful for your Majesty's well-being. We of the True Faith look to you (if I may be so bold) as our very own Queen. We fear the worst for you, for your kind and sympathetic husband, and for your family.

It has been a happy state of affairs for us that his Majesty, in his wisdom, has regarded Your Majesty not only as a loving wife and queen to his people, but as a sage counsellor; and we believe, if again I may be so bold, that it is largely your influence that has kept these enemies of the Faith at bay.

But how they are raising their ugly heads now that the King has been forced to call Parliament by the traitorous Scots. Even today they have impertinently rejected his Majesty's kind and gracious overtures. I fear that no amount of Christian charity on his part will break through their corrupted hearts; nay, I fear that his Majesty, in trying to show these scum reason, is merely casting pearls before swine.

I must therefore exhort your Majesty to plead with the King on behalf of we, his true subjects, who, like him, realise that there is much to be feared from the Scottish heretics; and to realise that his nobleness and kindness will never be recognised by these 'people,' but to ignore them. The Lords, as a whole, will view his predicament with much greater sympathy, and I am sure will grant him the subsidies he so desperately needs.

I must therefore take a liberty to which I feel hardly qualified, and ask you again to urge his Majesty to pass by the elected representatives of the House of Commons altogether, including us - your loyal but helpless supporters within the Lower House, and go straight to the House of Lords for the subsidies his Majesty, and we, his people, so desperately need. The matter, as I know you are aware, is of the utmost urgency.

I will remain, unto the death:-

Your most humble and obedient servant.

Having finished the letter and sealed it; I folded it inside the letter to my cousin, which I also sealed. Dr Harding and I then smiled at one another with mutual appreciation.

I then called John Brown into the room.

"John," I said, "You have served me well by so speedily fetching Dr Harding from Cambridge. Now, in return for delivering this letter safely I am going to give you enough money to buy for yourself a new suit; you'll be the talk of the market wenches I'll warrant."

"Why…thank you, Sir."

"You must wake up much earlier than normal, John, and deliver this letter to Clunehaven House, you know the place?"

"Yes I do, Sir."

"This letter must be delivered before Lady Clunehaven leaves the house in the morning, and on no account must she know - on no account John - from whence it came. I am going to give you two shillings again for yourself, and a further sixpence to give to whichever servant takes your letter in order to ensure that they give it priority and ask you no questions."

"Very well, Sir."

"Now, off to bed with you."

"Thank you, Sir."

And with the letter sent there was no more I could do for the present. Dr Harding and I drank a last cup of claret and retired to bed also. He left in the morning to see John Pym again ("not to divulge our little secret," he added) and to conduct some other business in the City concerning his properties. He told me as he did so that I had given him greater cause for pride than any of his other charges, and asked me to keep him abreast, whenever I could, with developments.

I never did, for soon after, I think at the end of April, his heart decided that it had had enough of supporting his enormous bulk, and gave up without warning as he was saying his morning prayers; which is a more hopeful way to go, it cannot be denied, than dying in the arms of a harlot while your wife's at home faithfully starching your collars.

• • •

The King attempted to obtain his subsidies from the Lords, and the Commons were so incensed that they immediately set about obstructing, through threats and sheer bloody-mindedness, the Lords' efforts to authorise the King's demand. He therefore dissolved parliament on the 5th day of May having failed to obtain the subsidies he had requested with such urgency. We in turn had failed in our attempts to persuade the King to redress the grievances that had accumulated during the eleven years of his personal rule.

He said, in his final lamentable speech to the Lords and Commons together, that it was not in his heart to blame all of the members of the House of Commons for the failure of his parliament, but that its failure was the fault of 'A few cunning and ill-affectioned men.'

But how much closer to the truth that assessment was than even he must have realised! For I knew in my heart that it was the letter so artfully created by Dr Harding and myself to the Queen that was the final catalyst for the King's foolish approach to the Lords. I would soon discover just how completely the King had come to rely on the misguided advice of his beloved wife: she whose very religious dogmatism would play such a major part in hers, and her husband's, downfall.

XIX

The assault on Lambeth Palace

In light of the fact that the King had dissolved parliament, it was evident that my ability to operate in the political arena must be, for a while at least, curtailed. It was also evident that the day of that most reliable aspect of English culture: the Mob - had arrived. Some of the members ejected from Parliament were downcast at its dissolution, but I saw it as a great opportunity.

But it was the King who made it all so easy, or rather the King and his advisers. The day after the dissolution I heard that Pym, Hampden and a couple of others had been placed under arrest, and their houses and belongings searched for evidence of complicity with the rebel Scots. I had thought to join with Pym in order to discuss the way forward. But in the light of these arrests I decided my time would be best served writing an account of the King's shocking duplicity and corruption during the brief parliament he had just ended; and denouncing the Queen, Strafford and Laud. I then had these copied and despatched around the cities of London and Westminster for the benefit of the public.

I am willing to recognise that although the mind steers the movements of the body, there would be little it could do in the way of action without use of the fist and foot. I decided therefore, a few days after I heard of Pym's arrest, to visit Compromise-not-at-all Jenkins in the City of London. I left my house on the morning of the sixth day after the dissolution with this purpose in mind; and had just begun my journey east towards the City, when I met William Strode coming the other way.

"I am leaving London," he said, "but had intended to call at your house in order to tell you of some interesting developments; most notably that in a meeting of the Privy Council, which convened on the evening of the day we were ejected from Parliament..."

Strode produced a piece of paper from his pocket. He read out loud.

"...Strafford would not heed the advice of most of the others present and urged the King to go vigorously on. He suggested to the king that, 'An army in Ireland may could be employed there to reduce this Kingdom,' and said, 'I am as confident as anything under heaven, Scotland shall not hold out five months. One summer well employed shall do it.'"

The curious thing was that Strode seemed depressed by this news. "It appears," he said, placing the paper back in his pocket, "that the King will get his way without Parliament after all if he can subdue Scotland with an Irish army, and we'll be back where we started."

But I was fascinated to know from whence he had obtained his information.

"Vane's son Harry - he told me he heard his father discussing the matter, so stole the minutes of the meeting from his father's safe."

He imparted this information as if he thought its value was of trite importance.

"Um...may I have the paper?" I asked, in as meek and casual a manner as I could muster.

He shrugged his shoulders and retrieved it from his pocket. "It's not the original you know...just a copy." He then, having given it to me, spurred his horse on, "I doubt we shall meet again," he called over his shoulder, "or, if we do, hopefully in happier times."

So I left the shallow fool to wander back to his home and wallow in self-pity. My only hope was that no one got the opportunity to tell Pym of the trap Strafford had fallen into before I did. Frankly I do not think that I could have imagined a better reason for bringing about Strafford's downfall than he had provided out of his own mouth.

But more of that later, that was politics, and I was hardly likely to discuss such issues with people like Compromise-not-at-all and Flee sin.

I was at first apprehensive about meeting them, remembering that the last time we met was at the King's Head, during which time Jenkins may well have decided that I conducted myself with an insufficient degree of loyalty. I need not have concerned myself however, for I found the whole group on the corner of a side street leading off the Strand, distributing my recently distributed pamphlets, which, although written anonymously, were well known through the puritan grapevine to have been written by me. They therefore welcomed me with open arms (somewhat disconcerting as they all stank like a burst pile on a demon's arse) and told me that they had initially had to distribute my pamphlets in secrecy, but such was the strength of feeling in the City since the dissolution of Parliament that they were able now to do so without fear of reprisal.

I invited them again to lunch at my expense. "Now Gentlemen," I began as we settled down to a plate of hot beef, "the time is ripe; our halcyon days of yore are upon us again. The time is come to raise the flag and fight the good fight!"

They all cheered like children who had been thrown a toffee-apple each, and told they can have a day off school. When they had calmed down a little, we placed our heads close together and the mood became earnest.

"What we need to do," I told them, "is to take full advantage of the people's discontent. If we wait any time at all the people will again become complacent. Now, various puritans, such as Pym, and the old sailor Lord Warwick, have been arrested. The dock hands and mariners are already seething with discontent, as most of their ships are being held up under the King's orders. Warwick's arrest will antagonise them further. One of you must go down to the docks. Go and stir them up; tell them that their religious freedom is about to be further curtailed; and remind them that their elected representatives have been ejected from parliament. The King needs to know how angry the people are, and the people need to show him."

"I will go" said Edward Oates.

"Do so now, and quickly, there is no time to lose. Go to Southwark and bring as many of them as you can to the south end of London Bridge. Tell them to come armed. Flee sin, you had better go with him. Oh, and point out to them that the reason their merchant ships aren't allowed to sail is that the King is making underhand deals with Spaniards; who were invited – add - by the Queen."

Edward Oates stuffed a handful of beef into his mouth and departed quickly as instructed, with Flee sin following.

I turned to the others. "The very worst we can expect from all this is that the King will be forced, eventually, to call another parliament, in which case - let me assure you - he will be in much weaker position than he was at the beginning of this last one. But that is the worst we can expect." I leaned even further forward and quieted my voice to a whisper. "Make no mistake about this, boys, if we take full advantage of the moment, it's just possible that we could overthrow the King altogether; but you must keep this always in mind: let your anger and your words be directed at the King's advisers and the Queen. Remind the people constantly that the Pope, and the Queen, his vassal, has designs on their freedom; and that this is why the city is full of Spaniards, and that this is why Catholic priests have been allowed to walk the streets unmolested."

"Why should we not set forth for the purposes of ribaldry and mockery the name of the King himself?" James Taylor asked, stupidly.

"Because the ignorant people aren't yet ready for anything so revolutionary" I said, (pretending I didn't place *them* in this category). "They are convinced; and even most Members of Parliament are convinced, that the King's foolish policies are the fault of everyone *but* him."

"Are they not?" this was Tom Ballinger.

"In part."

"You will not be with us, He-died-for-our-sins?" asked Compromise-not-at-all Jenkins, somewhat suspiciously.

"I will. Lambeth Palace, and the Archbishop of Canterbury, is the target!"

They needed no further encouragement, and I watched with satisfaction as they grabbed their hats and ran out of the inn.

But it was clear that I, with my position in society, must not be recognised among the mob. I decided, therefore, to adopt the disguise of a vagrant. I left the inn a moment or two after the others, and went to a milliner's, where I purchased a high and wide cloth hat; wide enough in fact, to cover the upper part of my face. This I rolled in some dust and kicked until it was in a sufficient state of disrepair. I then found, among the many tramps inhabiting that part of London, the one whose clothes were closest to mine in size, and the least offensive to the nose, and swapped my expensive attire - with some regret - for his, and had to pay him a shilling for the privilege. My last purchase before joining the crowds was a small tin drum, which I bought for tuppence from a small boy.

I idled for about half-an-hour, until dusk, at the north side of the bridge, from whence could be seen a considerable number of people gathering on the south side, and making a remarkable amount of noise whilst doing so. I waited for a further ten minutes and then heard the sounds of many more protesters approaching from the north. I mingled easily with the crowd as we marched towards the south end of the bridge, and I banged my tin drum as we walked to attract as many people as I could to join us. The crowd were numerous, and sufficiently rowdy to be a worry to the authorities, but not enough, as yet, to suit my purposes; in particular because they were shouting things like "Come on your Majesty, bring back parliament" and "Too many Spaniards and Catholics!" I had not envisaged such a tame affair, so I sought out the most unpleasant looking group I could find.

"A pox on the Catholic Bitch!" I shouted. They looked round at me, their expressions a mixture of admiration and wonder.

"Aye….a pox on the Catholic Bitch!" they returned.

"Death to the Pope and William the Fox, his quisling archbishop at Lambeth!"

"Aye…. death to the Pope and William the Fox, his quisling archbishop at Lambeth!"

Now they were beginning to get the idea; I only hoped that they realised we were actually rather close to Lambeth Palace and would therefore take the appropriate action. I moved away from that particular group, as I began to fear, from some of the suspicious looks being cast around, that there were more than one or two spies in the throng. I approached a lad of about nineteen.

"What do you do, lad?"

"City apprentice."

"What is your name?"

"Mark. What do you want?"

He spoke to me with an air of superiority, although I realised this was probably due to my shabby appearance.

"My arms are tired with beating this drum, but it is essential for the rallying of the disaffected. Pray take it from me and use it awhile to gather in our brothers at Southwark, and those in the neighbourhood, who know not that this opportunity has arisen."

He did so, and I stood away from him. This was much better: as well as the drum, which Mark beat with enthusiasm, the group I mentioned but a moment ago had become thoroughly warmed up; and were now shouting slogans such as "kill the Queen and burn her demon children!" and, just as controversially, if a little less explicitly: "Pym for King!"

The two groups, both of them several hundred strong, met at the south bank. By now the anti-Queen and anti-Archbishop of Canterbury slogans, as well as many attacking Strafford, had been taken up by the majority of the crowd, and had, in fact, become quite deafening. The only thing that could now be heard above the noise was the sound of Mark beating my tin drum. My work appeared to be done, so I made my way to the side of the crowd: close enough to affect proceedings if circumstances required it, but far enough out to be counted as a mere onlooker to anyone with hostile intent.

But I was determined that this gathering should leave its mark. I could see Compromise-not-at-all Jenkins standing on a box shouting at people and trying to stir them up, but there was nothing that he was saying that was likely to provoke them any more than they were already; and he, as only such a fool could, was setting himself up as a public ring leader. I started to move surreptitiously around the crowd once more.

"The King's spies are *everywhere*," I whispered to one group urgently.

"The King's spies are *everywhere*," I repeated to another.

"Oh God, no, please: not the *Spanish Inquisition*..." I said to a third.

I repeated these alarming reports and false supplications to the Almighty until the rippling effect of the rumours I had created started to affect the mood of the crowd. The fear soon became almost tangible, and as it did so the drum's rhythm seemed to take on a sinister overtone, as if it had given up its attempt to be a rallying cry for the disaffected, and had instead become a portent of some tragic event that was about to occur, or a summons to the demons that fresh prey would soon be available for collection.

And then, after a minute or so, the tension created by this fear erupted. A fashionably dressed man in the crowd was accused by those around him of being a spy, and was the first to be attacked. His friends then turned on his attackers. This fight quickly spread to other parts of the crowd. Then, when the confusion and tempers were at their height, I stooped down, and shouted at the top of my voice: "The Archbishop is about to hang them! The Archbishop is about to hang them!" I did not think for a moment that they would actually take time to wonder who *them* were, or why they would be hanged by the Archbishop of Canterbury in particular, but the effect upon the majority was nothing short of miraculous. With Mark the drummer at the vanguard, they started shouting "Laud out!" and "kill the Pope's housemaid" (why 'housemaid' I never learnt) and then began charging west towards Lambeth Palace.

Although some tried to restrain the people, it was far too late. The mob arrived at the heavily guarded palace, and the leaders needed no encouragement to attack and disarm an unfortunate group of soldiers who had been unable to make their way to the safety of the outer wall.

This was a high structure, very difficult to penetrate, over which some of the protesters, still shouting abusive slogans, started to hurl stones and various other missiles. I could just make out the voice of someone shouting from within, but the sound was all but drowned out by the noise of the rioters. By now the people, thwarted in their attempt to enter the palace, had become delirious with excitement, rage and frustration. About a dozen of them started to kick and pound the great door with their fists, while about fifty more continued to hurl whatever they could over the wall. Then, just as their attempt to break through the door began to seem futile, a young sailor ran forward with a crowbar. The sound of the crowd was for a moment reduced to near silence as he tried to wedge the crowbar behind the metal surrounding the lock. He succeeded in the third or fourth attempt. There was a splintering sound, followed by a deafening cheer as the door began to give way.

But almost as soon as the crowd started pressing forward, I realised that they were not just moving because of their eagerness to get through. They were also being crushed forward against their will. The cheering then turned to screaming as some of the people at the front were knocked to the ground and trampled upon by their desperate accomplices. The reason for this panic soon became evident as, although I could not at first see the new arrivals, it was clear from the thundering of horses' hooves, and the fact that people had started screaming "The cavalry, the cavalry!" that the cavalry had indeed arrived.

Now there were only two differences between what I then witnessed and some of the battles I was to experience later in my career. The first was that no actual gunshots were fired; the second was that unlike in a battle, where you expect to hear the issue of commands such as 'no quarter!' the officer in charge shouted, "Take as many of them as you can boys!"

The cavalry then set about the protesters, mostly using the flats of their swords to beat them about the head and, occasionally, the blades to cut them about the arms. Where possible two of the soldiers would grab a protester between them, by the hair or whatever came to hand, and drag him away in the direction of Southwark Gaol. The only way, it seemed, to escape, was around the perimeter of the wall; and it was around this wall to the left that I, and about a score or so of the rioters, tried to elude our would-be captors. But our move had been anticipated. The palace was surrounded, and we were thus driven back to the crowd.

By this time the cavalry, about fifteen horse, had been joined by two contingents of trained bands, both about a hundred strong. There was, it would seem, absolutely no alternative but to turn and fight.

And so I fought; and I fought as only someone who is desperate to avoid death or capture at any cost *can* fight. I managed to wrestle from one of the soldiers a mace that he had taken from a protester, and with it I tried to force my way through the crowd. I at first had some success in this, but then something happened that made escape even more urgent. In the confusion I was jostled and pushed to a position very close to the officer in command. I was close enough in fact to hear his words clearly, which consisted on the most part of commands such as, "Get that man with the crowbar!" or "Get that man with the drum!" or, more generally, "Surge forward lads!" But even in the chaos I recognised the officer, it was he who had so mistreated me after I insulted the Archbishop of Canterbury; and as soon as I recognised him he spun his horse round and our eyes met. For one of those moments that seemed like an eternity we stared at one another, then his face gave a start of recognition, and he urged his horse forward in my direction.

Even in the desperation of that moment I knew that I faced three possible outcomes: he would try to kill me if he could, of that I was certain; or if he failed to do so and I escaped – well he had recognised me, and I dreaded to imagine the fate likely to await anyone known to have been involved in this little protest; or, the third option: I must kill him myself - immediately.

My first instinct, despite this, was still to attempt escape. I therefore ran again as fast as I could, swinging the mace wildly in the hope of breaking through the crowd. But I soon realised that this had become impossible, such was the intensity of the fighting. I had no choice therefore but to turn and face him, and did so just in time to see him raise his sabre and swirl it round his head with a cavalier flourish as he prepared to use it to cut my head off, or kill me by some equally dreadful means.

But it was the cavalier flourish that was his undoing. I am sure that if I'd had any time to think about my actions the outcome would have been different; but in that brief moment, just before that sword came crashing down on my head, or neck, I managed to jump up and land a single heavy blow with my mace between his eyes. He fell from his horse with a deep groan, landed heavily on the ground and lay completely still.

I turned again to run, but my chances of getting away were no better than before, as by this time the cavalry and troopers really had got the upper hand. They were now dragging the protesters by the dozen towards Southwark gaol. My sense of urgency therefore became extreme: I had to get away at all costs or doubtless be hanged as a common murderer; it was not as if I hadn't been *seen*. But I knew that to try to escape by myself was futile, so I ran towards where the crowd of protesters was at its thickest.

But they were so confused by that time that they had no idea of what to do or which direction to go, so, thinking quickly, I shouted "Come on, come on: to the gaol – before they hang our brothers!"

And so the remainder of the crowd, about five hundred strong, ran in sheer desperation towards Southwark gaol; and in doing so presented me with my only remaining hope of escape. Even as we ran some of our number were pulled out from the crowd by the soldiers and pinned to the ground. But the majority, with astonishing ease, and with whatever weapons came to hand, smashed through the door. Having then attacked and overcome the guards, they set about releasing the prisoners.

The amount of time that was left to me to avoid capture, I realised, depended entirely upon how long this chaos lasted. As soon as the militia had been able to restore order I would be singled out from the remaining protesters, and summarily executed as the captain's murderer. I had rid myself of the mace at the first opportunity, so now needed to find another weapon. I could hardly have asked someone in all that confusion if he would mind swapping garments, so I picked up a heavy stone, knocked the first person I saw on the back of the head and dragged him into a side alley, where I quickly stripped him of his coat and breeches.

Not that donning these clothes made me safe. Nay, a disguise, even a disguise from my original disguise, was no longer enough: the time had come to get away altogether. I ran into a nearby brothel, up the stairs and into a room in which several people were already crowded around the window. They were so transfixed by the proceedings below that they didn't even notice my appearance in the room.

As I joined them there were only a few protesters still remaining. The rest had either scattered into the night or were fighting desperately, being attacked as they were by both the cavalry and trained bands. Separated from the remaining rioters were a small group of prisoners including, I noticed, my drummer boy. I also recognised Edward Oates among them. He was attempting to rally any who would follow him in a last desperate attempt to free the rest of the prisoners, waving a metal spike about his head as he did so, and shouting "God bless them all, God speed them all!"

He also was arrested, and I am ashamed to say that as he was dragged off by two soldiers, he started screaming, and shouting the words: "I was praying for the King and his ministers! I was, I tell you: I was praying for the King!"

Really rather pathetic in my opinion.

I considered it wise to wait inside for some time after the end of the fight; so when the people at the window asked who I was and how I came to be there, I explained that I had been caught up in a fight of which I knew not the cause, and had managed to break free and escape to this *inn*; and that I considered myself fortunate in the extreme to have survived, so violent had been the actions of the protesters. Any suspicions they may have had were quickly dispelled when I produced a small bag of coins I had secreted about my inner person, and offered to buy drinks all round.

I managed, by means of this generosity, to make the occupants of that house of ill-repute content with the prospect of my continuing company, as I wished to become inconspicuous among them in the event of any of the soldiers calling to search the place. I therefore endured the company of those whoremongers and prostitutes for approximately three hours, during which time the place was entered and searched by two dragoons. They paid me little heed, except to insult and abuse me along with the other men there, for neither I nor anyone else present fitted the description of the person they were searching for, who was of course the vagrant who had killed their captain.

At about one of the clock in the morning I made my way back over the bridge, and arrived back in Chelsea having experienced no further adventures.

XX

Strode's belligerence

T he riots continued unabated for a while, although I, remembering that sickening feeling of the captain's face being crushed by
the mace I was holding, had not the heart to take further part. Various
prisons were attacked, as it became apparent that the main aim of the
protesters (doubtless inspired by *my* riot) was to release prisoners who
had either been incarcerated in earlier insurrections, or had languished
in gaol for any amount of time as a penalty for refusing to pay tax or
adhere to the religious laws.

But the release of prisoners was not the sole purpose of the protesters. The hot weather came early that summer and rumours spread
easily, growing like the stink on the streets. One such rumour was that
the King, as well as the Queen, was attending Catholic Mass; and that
their servants had been forced to pray to the Virgin Mary before they
could enter into their employment. As these tales gathered momentum
they gave rise to much in the way of further violence.

By around the twentieth of May things had calmed somewhat, and
having already relied upon John Brown for all of my information concerning the outside world (as I had at first feared detection) I decided
to venture out with the purpose of seeking for news of Pym and my
other colleagues, the time being right, I decided, to reveal to him the
information I had received from Strode. I also decided that it would be
wise, if possible, to obtain a reference from Pym concerning the accusations of which he, Dr Harding, and Cromwell had recently acquitted

me, in case I was met with the same charge back in Northamptonshire. I rode to the King's Head, having chosen to do so because of its proximity to the Palace of Westminster; for here, I believed, I was most likely to locate some of my colleagues, all of whom must have been wondering what to do with themselves during their enforced idleness.

I left my horse in the charge of the stable lad and, having entered the tavern, I sat in the same place as on my previous visit. The inn-keeper's daughter approached my table, and had just started to tell me that they had a 'fish pie made from freshly caught cod,' when a familiar voice called out the words, "Sykes – over here!"

I looked up and saw Strode standing in the doorway of a small ante-room. He smiled and gestured for me to join him.

"I thought you had gone to the country," I said as I followed him into the small dark chamber.

"I became rather bored, so decided to come back and see what was happening."

"I hear," I said to him as we sat down, "that there has been much in the way of trouble of late, and that Pym and Hampden have been arrested; and yet I have heard so little, laid up as I have been in bed with a malady. Can this be true? What can you tell me of these riots, the sounds of which I have even heard in my bedchamber?"

He registered surprise that I knew less than he did, when he had just returned from the country, but then informed me that the account I had heard of Pym and Hampden was indeed true, but that they had since been released; only, he suspected, because by doing so the king and his ministers hoped the anger of the crowds might be abated. He then gave me his account of the worst of the riots, which had taken place, he told me, at the Palace of Lambeth.

"...Although the riot was in a sense pointless," he said, "because the Archbishop had fled over the river to Whitehall well before the crowds reached the palace walls."

He then told me that a young cavalry officer and three of the riot-ers had been killed, and that as they had been unable to capture the officer's killer, three more of the rioters were being held up as particu-lar examples to the population.

"Apparently," he said, "the rioters were almost all apprentices and dock workers. They have already tortured and publicly maimed some city lad who was beating a drum in order to attract others to the mayhem, and they are going to hang and draw a sailor who tried to break into the palace with a crowbar. There was also some lunatic who's under sentence of death for leading an attempt to release the prisoners."

"Oh."

"As far as the Johns Pym and Hampden are concerned, I suggest we repair to Pym's house; he probably has some sort of plan, and I certainly don't."

So we quaffed what remained of Strode's wine, and bought another flagon for the purpose of celebration. We then rode together to John Pym's town house, which was a few hundred yards back in the direction of Chelsea.

We found the fêted parliamentarian holding court, as it were, in his parlour. I use the phrase 'holding court,' because he was sitting on a high backed chair surrounded by about twenty men, some of whom I recognised as fellow members (or rather, former members) of Parliament. John Hampden, I was pleased to note, was not among them. They were all, however, of the puritan persuasion, and all of them were listening to him as he gave an account of his recent adventures.

He broke off in mid sentence when we entered: "Now the joy of this day is complete!" he exclaimed, "William, He-died-for-our-sins, welcome, welcome – be seated, I will finish here soon!"

So we sat down and listened as he finished his account.

"Now, where was I?"

One of his younger guests prompted his memory. "You were telling us of how you were accused of complicity with…"

"Ah yes, of complicity with the Scots," rejoined Pym, "we were all searched - as I have mentioned - for evidence that we had been in friendly contact with the Scottish Covenanters. They thought that if I was making treasonable overtures to the Scots, I would be stupid enough to keep any evidence of such correspondence about my person, or in my house! Without a hint of conceit I think I can say that a man with half of my intelligence could have seen that this was coming, and that a man of quarter my intelligence would have hidden any such letter....if it existed. What I do know is that they found nothing on any of us."

"And *is* there any such letter?" This was asked by a rather stupid looking lad of about twenty.

"You'll forgive me, Herbert," answered Pym, "considering the current political climate, if I decline to answer; and I think I have had enough of being questioned for now. What I will say is this: I told my persistent interrogator that as Scotland has been used as a testing ground by this King for his oppressive religious laws, I have a perfect right to be sympathetic with them; but if sympathy for some of my fellow subjects now amounts to treason then let us declare the Common Law void; let us abolish *habeas corpus*, for by no other means could such an unjust law stand; and by no other means could they continue to detain me without charge and without so much as a fraction of evidence."

Every one cheered at this, and Strode asked him how they had responded.

"By releasing me" answered Pym. "Now, if you will excuse me gentlemen, I have much to discuss with my two lately arrived colleagues."

And so John Pym's guests left amid much laughing and cheerful conversation, buoyed up as they were by his release and the account of his bold confrontation.

"Thirsty work this popularity," said Pym cheerfully, "I see you've brought a little libation. There are some glasses in the cabinet there. Make free."

When we each had a glass of claret, Strode asked Pym whether he had any suggestions as to how we should employ ourselves over the coming months.

"We must do our utmost to persuade the King, by whatever means, to recall Parliament. It is my intention to spread abroad the news of how and why this last parliament was dissolved. The gentry in particular must know that the King refused to hear their just grievances and silenced us because we wouldn't roll over and act as his poodle. It is up to them now to place pressure on him, and the best way to do this is to raise the issues concerning their grievances when the King - as he will - commands them to provide men to fight the Scots. It is also my purpose to discreetly recommend the withholding of taxes. I would suggest that you join me in this, were it not for two points: in the first place I mean to travel with John Hampden."

He looked at me knowingly as he said this, and I nodded my head discreetly in the manner of someone who is aware that he has been wronged, but whose love of the cause is placed above his own personal feelings.

"Secondly," he went on, "It would be much more expedient for you to follow the same plan, but in your own parts of the country."

I nodded my head again, as did Strode.

"What is also important," he added, "is that by the time the King is forced to recall Parliament I'll make damn sure Strafford and Laud are held in such derision by every right thinking person in this country that the best they'll be able to hope for is perpetual banishment."

I here saw my opening. Despite the regrettable fact that Strode was there to share the glory I knew it was time to produce the piece of paper he had given me earlier. "We have here," I said, "a record of some of Strafford's suggestions from a meeting of the Privy Council that took place immediately after the dissolution."

"Where did you get that?" asked Pym.

Strode answered. "One or two contributions to the meeting were communicated by Sir Harry Vane to his son, who told me what was said. Sir Harry recorded the meeting."

"Alright, what does it say?" Pym's face took on an eager expression.

"When Strafford began addressing the Council the other members were apparently on the edge of despair. But he managed to breathe new confidence and cheer into the party by advising the King to (and I read)…

'Go vigorously on – you have an army in Ireland you may employ there to reduce this Kingdom. I am as confident as anything under heaven, Scotland shall not hold out five months. One summer well employed shall do it.'"

When I had finished reciting these words I returned the paper to my pocket and watched Pym for his reaction. He was speechless.

"Lad," he eventually said, "you are brilliant."

"I'm not sure I understand," Strode interjected.

"Not understand? 'This Kingdom...this Kingdom,'" replied Pym. "We have proof here that Strafford was encouraging the King to bring the Irish over to subdue us by force. This is treason!"

"Yes – er," said Strode irritatingly, "he said 'there.' He was talking about Scotland; clearly he was telling the King that the Irish army could be used to subjugate the Scots."

"Don't be stupid, William - he said 'this Kingdom;' he said it here... at Whitehall. He was clearly referring to England."

"I'm sorry, but I beg to differ, he was clearly talking about the Scots; *this* was clearly a reference to *the* kingdom they were talking of: Scotland."

Suddenly, and unexpectedly, Pym exploded. "Do not bandy words with me, with your 'begs to differ' and your effeminate ways of speaking. I have been trained for the Bar, and I know when someone has made a cock up, and Strafford has made a cock up which, if I have my way, is going to cost him his life!"

"I think," I said, "that we need not speak anymore as if Strafford's downfall depended upon some future misconduct. He has done enough through these words, and his past misdeeds, to deserve any punishment that the Commons thinks right."

"Quite so Sykes," answered Pym, "and no loyal Englishman would see it any different."

"I do not think," said Strode, "that you would believe what you say you believe about Strafford's words if you did not so dearly *want* to believe it."

That was too much for Pym: "Alright Strode, get out! If and when Parliament is recalled, and if and when you are returned again as a member, I will expect more from you in the way of loyalty."

Strode gathered his hat and coat and left with as casual an air as he could muster.

"You see Sykes," said Pym when Strode had shut the door, "I have had to put up with this sort of double-mindedness ever since I first entered Parliament in the reign of King James. It is no wonder that the King was able to dissolve Parliament in 1629, and again three weeks ago for that matter, when this is the sort of feeble resistance he is faced with."

I again asked him how I could best be employed during the summer. In truth I hoped that my producing that document would lead to some sort of work preparing for Strafford's inevitable trial, but Pym did not seem ready for this.

"You must fear nothing and waver not at all," he said, "I am not sure if you are aware of this, but the King is so desperate over the Scottish question that he's been reduced to seizing the gold reserves from the Tower of London,. There are even rumours abroad that he intends to debase the coinage. He will antagonise the City of London, and the people, in order to fight a battle against the Scots that he cannot win. He will have to recall parliament before long, but we clearly cannot do anything against Strafford until he does so."

After we had spoken these words Pym yawned and, begging my forgiveness, said that he needed to retire as the past few days had exhausted him. "And," he added, "we need to rest awhile to gird our loins for the struggle ahead!"

I made as if to leave, but realised I had nearly forgotten to ask Pym for the reference, the lack of which, had I done so, might well have made things very difficult for me in Northamptonshire. I explained the reason for the likelihood of my needing such a letter (I was almost certain that tales of my suspect doctrinal views would have got back to my uncle and cousin through Clunehaven, or at least to Trustworthy Fairweather, through Praise God). Pym, upon hearing this, said that he understood my position completely, and acquiesced readily and willingly with my request.

XXI

Anne Hussey

It has doubtless become apparent from these memoirs that the iron rule with which the King had governed the country since 1629 was loosening at a rapid pace; evidence, if it were needed, that his solitary rule had been built upon foundations of shifting sand. Multitudes of contentious and illegal gatherings, both small and great, which would never have been thought of but a few months earlier, were becoming all but commonplace in the capital. It was therefore no coincidence that I was musing as I made my journey home from John Pym's house, upon the potency of phrases such as 'Popish plot,' and 'Catholic conspiracy,' when my thoughts were interrupted by the sight of a crowd blocking my path. They were listening in silence, and with close attention, to a ranting Irish woman who by first impression appeared to be nothing other than an intoxicated lunatic.

My first instinct was to beat my way through the crowd with my riding crop. I spurred my horse onwards, but before I struck the first blow I became aware of something about the woman and her words that prevented me from doing so.

"I tell you," she was saying, as her wild eyes roved around her captive and trembling audience, "they are here, here in this city. You think you are safe; you think you are among friends, but the papist Irish are everywhere - and they are ready to overthrow the good and God-fearing Protestants of this city. They come in by stealth. They pretend to be potato sellers; horse traders, but they will arise in the night and take you by force unless you prepare yourselves."

She stopped speaking for a moment and looked about her. All was silent except for the fearful crying of two young children.

"And then you know what they will do, oh yes you know: the Inquisition! They will call in the Spaniards to set up the Inquisition; and then your very righteousness will be the reason for the burning of your flesh; the extraction of your eyes; the cutting out of your tongues…"

The crying children started to scream hysterically.

Now, as I have just stated, these sorts of speeches and demonstrations were becoming all too common in London at this time, but, listening to this woman, it dawned on me that if she proved to be compliant (and in my experience a few shillings was usually enough to make anyone so) she might well be of use to me. I therefore decided to disperse the crowd in order to be able to speak with her privately.

"Look," I shouted (the crowd spun round to face me) "behold the wailing of these children! The Irish Catholics will take them away from you and make them slaves of the Pope. The last your sons and daughters will ever see of you is your flesh burning on the side of the road, as they are led into captivity! Do you want your children to be slaves of the Pope?"

"No!" the crowd shouted together.

"Do you want your women to be raped?"

"No!" they shouted again.

"Well then don't stand around here doing nothing. Protect your women! Save your children! Defend the elderly and infirm! Go and find these Irish and throw them into the river!"

"Right!" shouted one, who appeared to be some sort of leader among them, "grab what you can for a weapon. Follow me!"

I watched with satisfaction as they stormed off in an easterly direction, looking like a good old fashioned English lynch mob, leaving me and the Irish woman alone together.

She looked at me resentfully.

"You appeared to me at first," I said as I dismounted, "to be a mad old crone with a penchant for strong drink, most likely port wine. I perceive however, that there is more to you than first appearances suggested. Wherefore are you looking at me with such an evil eye?"

"You are correct in your reassessment, I am neither mad nor drunk, and I resent your use of the word 'crone.' I am an Irish woman of gentle birth: cast away from my family because both my father and husband mistook my prophetic zeal for insanity. I am not partial to having my meetings disrupted and dispersed by strangers."

"I wish to know if there is anything specific and true in the words you have been speaking. If there is then I can offer you a greater audience than that rabble."

"I speak nothing but the truth, Sir."

"What is your name?"

"My name is Anne Hussey, pray tell me yours."

"It is of no import...Sykes. What is important is that I can make sure you get the attention you deserve, and that you are paid well for your information. Do you know of anything specific? The stuff you were passing on to that crowd seemed somewhat...general."

As I said these words I drew out my purse. I produced a shilling, and noted with satisfaction that she beheld it greedily. She made to take it from my hand, but I held it back.

"I ask you again....do you know of anything specific?"

"Why...er yes....of course, I am not in the business of misleading people."

"What do you know?"

"Um....that there's a great many Irishmen hidden in London.... ready to rise up and murder all of the Protestant leaders of this city."

"This I have heard already. What then?"

She began to gather confidence. "As I said, once they have taken over they intend to call in the Spanish Inquisition to force the country back to Catholicism."

I gave her the first of the shillings.

"How many of these Irishmen are there?"

"Er….five thousand."

"Are they armed?"

"Armed to the teeth."

"Peradventure…they have been funded by all this Spanish bullion coming into the country?"

"Yes…that's right; that is just what I was going to say: they've been funded by all this Spanish bullion coming into the country."

"And do you think it likely that such a rebellion could be organised without the help of the Lord Strafford, or someone close to the centre of power? I merely mention Strafford because of the Irish connection."

She looked at me meaningfully, and then answered slowly. "No… no, no - I do not Sir."

I gave her another shilling. "You were not born, 'tis clear, to associate with people of mean birth; nor should such dire warnings be heard by those not educated to understand their significance. There are several noblemen in this city who will know what to do with this information, for if we are to expect an uprising the King himself should be prepared. Follow me. If those to whom I am about to lead you pay heed to your story then the rest of this money is yours to spend at your leisure."

I decided that the best person to approach was the recently incarcerated Earl of Warwick, the Lord High Admiral, who, I guessed, would still be railing after his imprisonment, but who was much more likely to be successful in receiving the attention of the King, or someone close to him, than would John Pym. I was also aware that while Lord Warwick was almost certain to take Anne Hussey seriously, the King, or those close to him, almost certainly would not. But *I* took her words extremely seriously, calculating as I did that if a rumour of this gravity were spread abroad then a decision by the King to allow Strafford to 'bring over an Irish army to subdue the Scots' would suddenly be open to an even more sinister interpretation. Thus, if the King took the threat seriously he would find himself in an impossible situation; but if he did not – but still allowed Strafford to bring the army over – well this could prove catastrophic for him.

So I put her on my horse and led her back to my house, where I fed her a substantial meal of mutton, as well as bread and fruit; and we afterwards made our way on horseback to the Middlesex home of Lord Warwick.

This proved to be a tedious journey, as my companion spent her whole time ranting about a prophet (herself of course) not being recognised among her own kin and people. Her husband and father (apparently) had conspired together – due to her alleged insanity - to send her to the madhouse, the true reason being because men and women of God throughout the ages had always been thus accused, and treated in the same fashion.

"I suppose I should expect to be burned alive or stoned to death really - or even crucified after the way those wicked Jews and Romans killed Jesus. I'm only surprised that this hasn't been my fate already." She went on about this with a sort of maudlin triumph until we finally arrived (and not a moment too soon) at Lord Warwick's large Elizabethan house.

I told Mrs Hussey to wait as I dismounted and ran to the door. This I pounded repeatedly in the manner of someone who desperately needs to convey some news of grave import. I continued to do so for several minutes until it was finally opened, many bolts having been slowly and methodically drawn back, by a creeky old manservant. He looked at me with the air of someone who had witnessed many great events unfolding throughout history, but was frankly fed up with all of them.

"You only need to knock once you know – you can pound on the door a hundred times and I won't get there any faster."

"A curse on your impertinence, old man! I have some urgent tidings for Lord Warwick: I must see him immediately."

"Yes, they all do, and they all must. Well I'll warn you of one thing: the last people who came here with *urgent tidings* for Lord Warwick arrested him and took him to the Tower, and he's still in high dudgeon about it, so if you've come here to waste his time I'd take this opportunity to turn around now....no? Wait here then."

He started to shuffle off, but then turned around. "I suppose I should ask your name."

I told him my name and that I was a colleague of Pym's. He, at least, did not smirk when he heard it.

"Does your mother also want to see his Lordship?"

"If you mean the woman on the horse, she is not my mother: yes she does, her name is Anne Hussey."

"Call her in then." He shuffled off again.

I waited for what seemed an interminable length of time while Anne Hussey muttered to herself about having been denied her birthright, and that she had been 'born to all this' (doubtless referring to our sumptuous surroundings). Finally, however, the creeky old manservant returned and beckoned for us to follow him.

He led us up a long flight of stairs, then along a gallery full of ancestral portraits to a large oak door, which he flung open without ceremony. Behind this door there was a huge library, furnished from floor to ceiling with books; and the far end, sitting by a roaring fire, and surrounded by several wolfhounds, sat the great Earl smoking a long clay pipe, and staring dreamily into the flames as he did so.

Now, judging by the earl's appearance alone, it would not have been beyond the bounds of reason to expect him, as soon as anything like a 'Spanish invasion' was mentioned, to rub his hands in glee and call for a celebratory flagon of Rioja. He had a pointed beard, dark hair and a somewhat Latin appearance; and reminded me of a portrait I had once seen of King Philip II of Spain.

The Earl did not stand up. "I understand you have some urgent tidings for me. I may as well tell you that I am somewhat tired of the affairs of state for the time-being, so, please, let it be worth our whiles. Speak."

"My name is Sykes, my Lord. I was a Member of Parliament until the recent dissolution and am closely affiliated to John Pym. This is Anne Hussey. It is she who has come to speak with you in particular."

For a woman who laid such emphasis upon her good breeding, Anne Hussey approached the earl in an embarrassingly obsequious manner. She wrung her hands together and took it upon herself to walk with an affected stoop, as if she wanted to show him just how much the woes of this present life had beset her.

"Yes my Lord. I *am* Anne Hussey: known throughout the green country of Ireland as a sage and a prophet. I am accounted as like unto the Apostle Paul: born well unto the riches and wealth of this world: of noble birth indeed; but called also like the Apostle Paul to lay all this aside for the better riches of God's Kingdom. Yea it hath pleased the Lord..."

"Stop rambling, wench. State your business or get out!"

"Er, yes my Lord. I, er, have grievous tidings of a plot hatched by a certain Irish priest by the name of William O' Connor. I heard the same speaking, when I was recently in the County of Cork, of a plot to take London by force by means of an uprising from within; and to invite the Spanish Inquisition here with the purpose of forcing this country back to the dark and heathenish days of Catholicism - although he obviously did not use the words 'dark and heathenish' my Lord, those were *my* words, he he. He thought that I would sympathise with his cause, as my family are so firmly rooted in the evil practices of Rome. How could he have known that I had seen the light in the manner of Saul who, when still caught in the bonds of iniquity, was showed mercy by the Lord our God on that momentous journey to Damascus? Furthermore my Lord, when I started to warn sundry people in London of this plot, and my words reached the ears of the enemies of righteousness, I was attacked as I lay asleep in my bed by a band of Irish brigands who, having stripped me naked and tortured me grievously, warned me to stay silent upon pain of death. They told me that there were five thousand of them in London; that they would cut my throat if I breathed a word to anyone, and that the plot had been countenanced by the King's closest advisers. But I would not be intimidated Sir. And it was as I was relating these tidings to the good Protestant people of London that I was found by Mr Sykes here, who recognised immediately the gravity of my warnings, and brought me to your Lordship."

I decided that the Earl had probably heard enough. I asked him if he would mind if we spoke alone for a while.

"By all means," he responded with undisguised relief, and beckoned for Anne Hussey to leave the room.

"My Lord," I said when she had shut the door, "I cannot say whether this woman is speaking the truth for certain or not, but despite this uncertainty, I considered it necessary to take her words seriously. I understand that you have been sorely mistreated by some of those who are closest to the King; and while I know it would be beneath your dignity to hope for any form of petty revenge..."

"It would."

"Yes, while I know that this would be beneath your dignity, I am also aware that you owe the likes of Strafford no favours. It is for this reason, as well as the fact that it would be the wisest choice anyway, that I suggest we take this woman's story seriously. There will be nothing to lose if her words turn out to be false, as we would be doing no more than our duty by reporting her story to the correct authorities; but there would be much to gain if her story turns out to be true. Moreover, it will be upon anyone's heads *but* ours if, in these circumstances, we give a report of what we have heard to whomsoever your Lordship regards as most fitting, and *they* do not take the story seriously."

I could see as I spoke these words that their wisdom was having its desired effect. The Earl's face lit up.

"I have seen you around Parliament in the company of John Pym, and if there is one thing that I know about that man it is that he chooses his companions wisely. You have spoken with wisdom here. I will immediately write a letter to Sir Harry Vane. I suggest that you, in the company of this woman, take my letter immediately to Whitehall. If Vane refuses to take the matter seriously, then let it be upon his own head. Fetch again Mrs Hussey."

When she had entered again, still wringing her hands, the Earl addressed her thus: "I am sending you to Whitehall - to the Secretary of State, in the company of Mr Sykes. I advise you most strongly to do no more, and say no more, than Mr Sykes instructs you. Wait outside again while I write a letter. My manservant will give you refreshments."

When she had left, muttering under her breath, the Earl crossed the room to a large desk, where he sat down and started writing. He read to me as he wrote.

Secretary Vane,

It has come to my attention that the woman you see before you as you read this letter, one Anne Hussey, has witnessed, and has knowledge of, the creation of a certain plot by rebellious Irish subjects, to infiltrate and occupy the City of London in sundry disguises; that it is, according to her testimony, their intention, through the use of subterfuge and artful design, to subvert and overthrow the establishment of true religion in this country. The words I have heard are quite specific. It is the intention of these Catholic renegades to destabilise and disempower the established authority of this Kingdom; and thereafter to cause a foreign power: namely the Spanish Inquisition, to enter into this country and re-establish the heretical doctrines, under which weight, during the reign of certain misled sovereigns in times past, the godly subjects of this Kingdom have laboured beneath a heavy burden.

I pray that you will examine this woman; that you will ascertain the truth, or otherwise, of her report, and take whatever action you deem necessary to protect our country from the snares of papal heresy.

Finally: I pray also that you will bear in mind that in matters of such weight as this, we should not only set aside our differences, but that you should remember also that these differences of opinion concern only our variant views of the best way to serve His Majesty; and that when we are faced with an alien threat, our loyalties should make us as one.

I remain: the King's loyal servant in Christ

Warwick

"My only advice to you now," the Earl said when he had sealed the letter, "is to make haste with Mrs Hussey to Whitehall. Urgency could be the key to the prevention of a catastrophe."

I bowed, although without too much reverence, for I am not, as you know, of low birth, and left the Earl's presence.

Anne Hussey's resentment at having been sent out of the Earl's library made the journey from Middlesex to Whitehall even less bearable than the last. "I suppose *His Lordship* is unaware that I have been used to conversing with the Mighty in the withdrawing rooms of the Great: which goes to show all the more that he is nought but an upstart in comparison to me. Why my family can trace our bloodline back to…" etc., etc., etc. To continue an attempt to record her words would be a needless sharing of my pain; and indeed anything I added to the words I have already recorded would be made up, as I started, as soon as she began to rant again in this fashion, to allow my mind to be diverted by anything and everything I possibly could so as to avoid actually paying her any heed.

We arrived at Whitehall at about seven of the clock, but were at first refused admittance by a guard on the grounds that it was too late to disturb any of the Royal personages, or any member of the Privy Council; and that we should return the following morning. But when I produced the Earl's letter he immediately went to fetch an officer. He, when he arrived, ordered us to be let through, and then lead us towards Vane's study.

It was as we were making our way that I suddenly, and unexpectedly, was gripped with a fearful sense of foreboding.

"Remember not to speak until you are spoken to," I whispered urgently to Anne Hussey as we climbed a set of wooden stairs. "You are a proud woman and I have a strong feeling that your pride could be your downfall."

As I finished saying these words we reached a long gallery, the right hand wall of which was decorated by pictures of various Plantagenet kings with their wives and children. The effect of these portraits upon me was daunting, as it emphasised the fact that I was traversing the halls of a royal palace. But I could tell that our surroundings were having no such effect upon Anne Hussey. As we started to walk towards the far end I could feel her mustering up some sort of indignant response to my instructions, which would doubtless have been in the same vein as her previous ejaculations. But just as she was about to speak a most unexpected thing happened. The door at the far end was thrown open by two guards, who stood to one side, and two gentlemen began to traverse the long passage towards us.

The officer immediately turned to us: "Get to the side quickly. It's the King. Get to the side!"

I obeyed his instructions immediately, for I had realised at the same time as him, to my horror, that walking towards us, but so far seemingly unaware of our presence (as they were deep in conversation) were none other than the King and Lord Strafford. But Anne Hussey remained riveted to the spot, with her mouth wide open; and then, when she had gathered her senses, started patting her hair as if she was preparing herself for an audience.

In vain did we try to urge her to join us, but she steadfastly refused to look in our direction, and the King and Strafford, who were conversing in low voices with both their heads turned downwards, did not notice her presence until they were almost upon her.

They did not become aware of her in fact, until she threw herself at the King's feet, and the officer who had been accompanying us took a step forward and attempted to drag her out of the way.

"Your Majesty," she sobbed, your Majesty, your Majesty!"

The King, entirely startled by this unexpected encounter, took two steps back.

"Your Majesty, long have I desired to see your face. With desire have I desired to see you…"

The King turned to our companion, "Major Fellingham, who is this woman? What is her business here?"

The officer tried to answer, but I realised that I was going to have to rescue this situation. "Your Majesty," I said before the major could answer properly, "I pray that you would forgive this intrusion. My name is Sykes. I was a Member of Parliament for Towcester and Weedon, in Northamptonshire."

For a few moments the King, as well as Strafford, looked at me in silence. The King spoke first.

"There are many Sykes's: I would have your Christian name, Sir."

"It is He-died-for-our-sins, Your Majesty."

The King appeared incredulous. "Your Christian name is…*He-died-for-our-sins?*" He looked at Strafford as if he needed confirmation that I was not mocking him.

I coloured deeply, and was about to answer the King's question in the affirmative, when Strafford intervened: "Do you have a cousin by the name of Richard?"

"I do, my Lord." As I said this I broke out in a cold sweat.

Strafford's expression darkened.

I decided it would be wise to attempt to answer the King's first question. "We have a letter of introduction from the noble Earl of

Warwick to Sir Henry Vane concerning an alleged plot to overthrow your Majesty's government. This woman is called Anne Hussey: it is she who has uncovered this conspiracy."

"Oh Your Majesty," interrupted Anne Hussey, "it is not just for this purpose that I have so longed to behold you. My father and husband have cut me off from that which is rightfully mine. If I was to tell you of my poor circumstances I know that you would write to them and tell them to...."

"Woman," rejoined the King, "One who is greater than I said before me, in answer to a similar petition, that He was no divider and sharer among us. I will, by your leave, follow His example." Then, turning to me, he reached out his hand in silence. I at first thought that he was holding it out for me to kiss. I was about to do so when I realised that he was demanding that I hand over the letter.

"I think," he said, when I had given it to him, "I am justified in opening this, even though I am not its intended recipient." He looked to Strafford as if he somehow needed his approval, and upon receiving his tacit agreement, broke the seal.

When he had read the letter he handed it to Strafford and, having allowed him a moment to read its contents, turned to me and the captain. "As this letter is addressed to Secretary Vane, to Secretary Vane it should go; and as it concerns us it would be appropriate for us to accompany it. I think we will dispense with protocol. Major Fellingham, if you would lead the way we will walk behind. Our *guests* can walk between us." The King gave Strafford the letter.

And so we walked down the long passage in silence, with the eyes of the King and Lord Strafford boring into our backs. I was afforded no opportunity to speak to Anne Hussey. When we had passed through the same door through which the King and Strafford had entered the gallery Major Fellingham stopped at another door immediately on the right. He looked at the King, who nodded to him, and then knocked twice upon the oak panelling.

"Enter," said a voice from within.

The Major turned again to the King, inviting him silently to pre-
cede us, but the King gestured for him to carry on, and we entered the
room in the same order we had approached it.

We found ourselves in a large study, and beheld Sir Henry Vane
sitting behind a desk opposite the door. He stood up as we entered.
"Major Fellingham, the hour is late, who is this puritan and this..."

But he had no time to finish his sentence before we were followed
into the room by the King and Strafford.

"Your Majesty I..."

"Pray forgive this intrusion, Sir Henry," said the King, "you will
understand its purpose in a moment. My Lord Strafford, please hand
to the Secretary of State his letter. I pray you will forgive me, Sir Henry,
for breaking its seal."

Strafford gave the letter to Vane, who despite the fact that the King
was present could not resist the temptation to snatch it rudely out of
his hand. Before opening it he invited the King to sit down.

"I think," said the King, "that we should all do so."

He sat on one of the chairs opposite the desk, and gestured with
his cane for Anne Hussey and me to sit on two hard chairs next to the
wall on the right. Strafford pulled up a chair and sat next to the King,
while Fellingham remained standing, facing the King, with his back to
the door.

The Secretary of State read the letter in silence, and I, feeling more
vulnerable at that moment than I had ever before in my life, began to
wish that I had never involved myself with this mad Irish woman. If
only, I thought, I had chosen a different route home.

He finally placed the letter on his desk. "The Lord Warwick has
requested that I examine this woman. I cannot but - for the moment -
give him the benefit of the doubt concerning his motives. By your
Majesty's leave..."

The King nodded to him in his usual grave fashion, so he turned
to face us, and he spoke to me first.

"What is your name, and what is your involvement in this?"

I told him my name. He turned to the King and Strafford. Strafford
nodded, while Major Fellingham started sniggering into the sleeve of

his buff-coat. The King turned to face him. "Major Fellingham, we require you to be alert and vigilant. Stop laughing this instant."

The King turned again to face Vane, who gestured to me to continue.

"Sir: I have become deeply concerned at the tumults and riots that have so lately beset this city and the country round about. I was riding home this morning from the house of a friend, and found this woman speaking to a crowd of the plot to which the Lord Warwick referred in his letter. I regarded it as my duty, both as a loyal subject and as a former Member of Parliament, to question her in order to ascertain whether there was any truth in what she said. I decided that although her words could not be proved without closer examination, they were of sufficient gravity to show such an examination was warranted."

I hoped (despite a feel of impending doom waxing strongly within me), that following such artful sophistry the Secretary of State and the Lord Strafford would nod their heads gravely while the King turned to me and said "You did well and you did wisely," or something similar. But no one gave any response at all, except for the Secretary, who asked me why I had taken the woman to see the Earl of Warwick.

"Do you not realise that the Lord Warwick has recently been arrested and imprisoned?" he asked. "Why did you think that a letter of introduction from him would give your story more credence? Why did you not bring her straight here?"

"I believed that despite Lord Warwick's recent misfortunes a reference from him would perhaps be viewed with more gravity than from an obscure Member of Parliament."

"And a notorious troublemaker," put in the Lord Strafford.

The Secretary of State turned to Anne Hussey. "Tell me about this plot," he said abruptly.

"Your Honour, I was back home in the County of Cork about two months since. I was praying in the Church of St Peter on a Wednesday morning (for, Your Majesty, when it comes to prayer all the days of the week are the same for me: let everyone do what they will - I say, but let holiness be sought after and maintained constantly and with vigilance...)"

"Get on with it!" said the Secretary of State.

"Yes, well, it was when I was at my prayers of a Wednesday morning that I heard the parish priest, one William O' Connor, plotting with some evil looking fellows to bring over enough men, weapons and explosives to London to overthrow your Majesty's government by force. I asked him what he was about, and what he meant by such demonish (*sic*) words; and he answered me without a hint of shame, but with pride and boldness, that the Spanish Inquisition would know how to deal with the apostate English, and that he had enough funds, thanks to some of the King's closest advisers, to ensure that the plan would run smoothly and without any trouble at all, any trouble at all so he said."

The Secretary smirked when he heard these words. "And who, pray, are these 'close advisers of the King?'"

Anne Hussey turned to me. I looked at the floor but I could feel her eyes staring at me, imploring me, as if she wanted me to give her some sort of stage prompt. I refused to look at her.

"Um…um….Well there's always that Catholic Archbishop and…. Strafford, yes Strafford; the Earl of Strafford – that's the one!"

"Woman – you are deranged!" I shouted, jumping from my chair. Strafford threw back his head and shook laughed out loud. The King laughed also, although somewhat more discreetly. The only one not to do so in fact, was the Secretary of State.

"But you said…." she continued, imploring me to rise to her defence.

"Silence woman! Your Majesty," I said, turning to the King, "I shall have this time waster taken out and flogged! I shall…."

"Be quiet and sit down!" shouted the Secretary.

When I had done so, and the Lord Strafford had recovered his composure, Vane continued. "Let us establish a few facts here. Mrs Hussey, are you a Protestant?"

"I most certainly am, Sir."

"Then why were you praying in a Catholic Church?"

"I, er…"

"Why did this William O Connor speak to you?"

She gave no answer.

"How, and in what way, was the Lord Strafford, whom you see sitting before you, involved in this *plot?*

She gasped at this revelation, and then pointed at me. "He paid me to mention Strafford I tell you; he paid me to."

I rose to my feet. "That is a lie! Your Majesty, by your leave I will escort this woman to the madhouse."

"You will both be silent and you will sit down!" shouted Vane.

But Anne Hussey, as you will have gathered, had no idea when to stop talking. "I...he...I was attacked by some of these Irishmen the other night as I lay asleep in my bed. They poured hot wax on my breasts so they did, you can see...!"

"Silence woman!" repeated the Secretary of State. "Your Majesty, this woman is clearly insane, as for her accomplice..."

The King stood up, and was followed by Strafford and Vane. Major Fellingham prodded me with his sword to make me do likewise.

"We have wasted enough time this evening," said the King. "My Lord Strafford, Sir Henry, I will leave it to you to deal with these two as you see fit. Major Fellingham, we require you to stay here as some sort of punishment doubtless needs to be administered, or indeed to prevent this woman placing a curse on the Royal children, or some such." And with those words he left the room.

Strafford turned to us, while the Secretary of State coolly lit a pipe, picked up a book from his desk and pretended to pay us no further regard.

"For the sake of your uncle, and of your cousin," said Strafford, "I am merely going to have you flogged. I know that they would agree with me that you deserve a greater punishment, but for their sakes nonetheless, I have a mind to be lenient, and besides, this attempt to besmirch my name is too absurd to be taken seriously. Major Fellingham, you will be so kind as to ensure that this punishment is carried out immediately, I think a score of lashes would be sufficient. As for the woman: lock her in the gatehouse. If she shows any signs of sanity you may release her after the space of a fortnight."

He then also left the room.

Major Fellingham could not refrain from mocking us as he led us to our fates. "Really you two, some people spend their whole lives hoping for an audience with the King. I feel almost sorry for you, but you didn't deal with it very well, did you?"

At this point he laughed uproariously, and then when he'd calmed down added "In fact, it was the sorriest thing I have *ever* seen."

We arrived at the gatehouse, where he spoke to a group of guards. "Right, this woman has to be locked up, under direct orders from the First Minister. Now, Mrs Hussey: be good, don't rant, and I'll probably be able to get you out of here after half a dozen days or so. Be quiet see, and it'll be easier for you and pleasanter for us."

To my surprise she was led off as quietly as a lamb, and that was the last I ever saw of her.

"Now then, (he said, turning to another soldier) you're going to have to do this. A dozen lashes will do, and don't make them too heavy - he and his old friend are only half-wits."

And so I suffered the indignity, not for the first time in my life, of receiving a flogging. At least this time there was no audience. I was afterwards let out into the night.

I found it difficult to believe, but I heard that even after this episode, Anne Hussey went round spreading the same story upon her release from the gatehouse; and that she was even believed by some. The Catholic priest at the centre of her tale then had the misfortune to be spotted in London by some zealous puritan soldiers. When confronted with her accusations he contradicted her account by claiming that he had been in the Capital for many months, and that he had once rebuked Anne Hussey for lewdness and drunkenness when she had attempted to expose herself to him. Who was telling the truth is a question that will always remain unanswered.

As for me, it may seem difficult to believe, but apart from the unfortunate way that night ended, I really achieved much by that unexpected episode. I had a tale to tell of an alleged plot, an alleged Catholic plot no less, which had been dismissed summarily and out of hand by the King, his First Minister, and his Secretary of State.

XXII

Shame and glory

Strafford, having urged the King not to dissolve Parliament, encouraged him once he *had* done so to deal with the protests and riots with the heaviest weight of his displeasure. A consequence of the resentment created by these policies was that I had a great deal of success in London and the surrounding counties, both in persuading people to withhold their tax money, and in using Jenkins and others to stir up the public to destroy the interiors of churches that displayed any high church imitations of popery. (Edward Oates was no longer among them, for with the slayer of the cavalry officer remaining unidentified, and with him having been caught wielding a metal spike, he was hanged drawn and quartered after the briefest of trials).

But even the best of summers need ultimately to be relegated to our memories, and when, at the end of August, I heard that the Scots had invaded the north of England and were ravaging the southern side of the border, and that the King was making a final attempt to defeat them without Parliament's aid, I realised that I had better make my way back to Northamptonshire in order to assure my seat in the next Parliament, its recall now being all but inevitable. And so it was that I found myself on the twenty fourth day of August wending my way home in the company of John Brown, my manservant.

Upon my arrival my Aunt Meekness fell upon my neck, weeping as she did so with the joy of beholding me once more. I entered the house, and sat down in the kitchen as she prepared a meal of beef stew with dumplings.

But although she appeared at first happy, she soon began to bustle about in the manner of a woman with a weight upon her mind, and seemed not to be the joyful psalm-singing woman I had known before my departure; so I asked her the cause of her concern.

She was glad of the opportunity to tell me. "Oh He-died-for-our-sins, there have been horrible, unspeakable rumours spread abroad concerning you. Do not ask me what they are - I cannot bear to repeat them. Your uncle Richard has asked me about them, and I have defended you as only someone who truly knows you could. I know that they are wicked lies...and yet..."

"And yet what, Aunt?"

"And yet the rumours started when Praise God came to visit his father."

This I had expected. "My dear Aunt," I said, "I had hoped to save you this, for I know how fond you have been of Praise God in times past. In truth I blame myself, for had I kept a closer watch upon him he would not have fallen so far as he has into the depths of iniquity. I became aware even at Cambridge that the wiles and snares of the Enemy had begun to tempt him from the paths of righteousness; and in the midst of the battles I was fighting against the forces of darkness, I neglected to give him the attention he so clearly needed. By caring better for my poor, sinful brother I could have saved him from perdition, for it is the road to perdition he is surely traversing. I have discovered him committing the most unspeakable acts of evil in places in which no godly person would set his eyes or feet. Even last week I followed him to Whitechapel, pleading with him to return with me to the City so that we could pray together, and for him not to enter the den of sin to which I knew he was traversing; but when I laid my hand upon his arm he shook it off, and told me that he was going to sleep with a prostitute and that nothing and no one was going to stop him (my aunt here gasped with horror). He then told me that he was going to go home to Northamptonshire the following day; that he was going to spread some lies about me, and that by the time he had finished I would not only never again be chosen to enter Parliament, but that if he had his way I would be executed as a heretic."

My aunt's first reaction to this was to place her hands to her mouth in an attitude of shocked horror. But then her face took on a more curious expression, as if she was trying to imagine Praise God actually saying all that. I realised that she might at any time ask me why Praise God would tell such lies about me, and apart from reiterating that he had been led away from the true path I had no answer to this, so I decided that for the time-being I had better change the subject. I began relating to my aunt an account of some of my experiences in Parliament.

But I knew that there was little time to waste, and that I had better meet the inevitable accusations of my enemies head on. So after a few minutes of appeasing my aunt, I gathered my hat and cloak and made my way on foot to Caldecote Manor.

As a member of the family I made bold upon my arrival to walk through the main door into the hall and towards the withdrawing room without, as would be expected, waiting for a servant to announce me. It is true that I had for years been afraid of my uncle, but that was before I had entered Parliament. Yea, my association with Pym and his like had rendered me willing to treat no man as my superior. I was also aware that if my arrival was announced I would almost certainly be refused admittance.

Despite my resolve, as I approached the oak door, which was slightly ajar, my courage began to fail me. I stopped just outside, and because of this was able to hear several voices including those of my uncle and my cousin Richard, who was speaking whilst someone, probably his mother, was playing the harpsichord. There was another voice which seemed familiar, but which I could not at first identify. I listened closely in order to hear their words, and was thus able to catch some of the conversation over the sound of the music.

The voice of the familiar stranger spoke thus: "Had I known, Sir Richard, that our arrival would be so late, I would have stopped for the night at an inn. I fear that I am in reality the worst kind of intruder despite your kind welcome."

"Had we discovered that you had done so, my lord" my uncle replied, "then we would have been truly mortified. Your presence can only serve to cheer us."

"In truth," answered the nobleman, "this gout would render a night in any inn an unpleasant experience, as would the fact that half of the country seems bent on hanging 'wicked Black Tom,' and would doubtless string me up given half of an opportunity."

"Yes, although Towcester remains - and will always remain I trust - loyal to the King despite the puritan influence in the country round about…"

But when I heard the nobleman address himself derisorily as 'Black Tom,' I took a sharp breath and started to retreat from the door. I had taken two steps backward and was just about to turn and flee the house, when a hard shove from behind propelled me forward again. I tried to arrest my forced progress with my hands on the doorframe, but heard Gwendolyn Smith's voice behind me say "You could hear more clearly if you actually went in," before she shoved me for a second time. I therefore entered the room much more rapidly than had been my original intention, but managed, thankfully, to avoid losing my step altogether. I straightened myself and bowed graciously and formally to the assembled personages, who included of course, the notorious 'Black Tom,' more formally known as Lord Strafford.

My uncle and cousin were at first so stupefied by my unexpected entrance that they said nothing at all, neither did the various other people assembled, the only one of whom I recognised was Matthew Spencer, who was looking at me with an expression of the utmost loathing. It was left to Strafford to speak to me first. He looked at my uncle and cousins as if gauging the reason for their reaction to my entrance and, as they communicated nothing to prevent him from doing so, addressed me thus: "Mr Sykes, it cannot be that you have received any pleasure from our short acquaintance, and your relations appear ill disposed towards your arrival. May I be so bold as to inquire as to your purpose in making this visit?"

My uncle then recovered himself. "How dare you enter this house uninvited?" he shouted. He was so incensed that the steam from the sweat on his brow was clearly visible.

Now, as I have stated, my purpose in going to the house of my uncle was to deny the charges that I knew would be brought against me as a result of Praise God's recent report. I had scorned the idea of going to the house of Trustworthy Fairweather first, on the grounds that I considered his opinion, although worthy of my consideration, less a matter of personal pride. I was also aware that it would be easier to combat Praise God's allegations when he was not present: something I could hardly guarantee in his own father's house. I now regretted my decision, for I had not contemplated the fact that in his presence, as opposed to my mere imagination, my uncle's ability to strike awe into me was entirely undiminished. This sense of awe was hardly decreased, moreover, by the unexpected presence of Lord Strafford. I had imagined myself making free with my uncle's hospitality, placing my dirty boots upon his sofa with a nonchalant air of satisfaction as I threw the letter I had received from Pym into his cringing hands. Instead, my response to my uncle's question was an unintelligible, nervous gabbling.

My confusion was increased moreover, by the entrance of Gwendolyn Smith, who had apparently been waiting outside the door. She, with an expression of innocence of which only the truly guilty are capable, walked to the middle of the room, curtsied to Lord Strafford, and then asked my uncle whether 'Mr He-died-for-our-sins Sykes would be joining the household for dinner?'

"No he will not!" he shouted in response, then – "forgive me Gwendolyn, you could not have known: no, Mr *He-died-for-our-sins Sykes* will not be joining us for dinner."

Gwendolyn then curtsied again, first to the Lord Strafford, then to my relations and all the other guests, and then, finally, to me. She did not giggle or smirk, but her eyes betrayed more mockery and contempt than any outward expression could have.

My uncle waited for Gwendolyn to leave the room, then spoke to me once more: "for what purpose have you come here?"

"I, er, have come to refute some false allegations spread abroad concerning me."

"What false allegations, why should you come here to refute them?"

"Allegations concerning a rumour that I espouse the doctrines of the notorious sect known as the 'Family of Love' or…"

"Explain."

"I do not think," I replied, "that to describe the beliefs and actions of such a movement in front of the ladies present would be entirely appropriate."

"Oh, so you have become aware of the sensitivities of women whilst in London; this account of yourself fits ill with the reports I have heard."

"It is these very reports that I have come hither to address."

"The allegations are true. Why add to your sins by coming here to deny them?"

This direct statement of accusation at first threw me into even greater confusion, but I had to respond somehow, and decided that this would be the most apt time to resort to the reference I had received from Pym. I drew it from my pocket. The feel of that letter in my hand, with the words 'To whom it may concern' written at its head by the leader of what was effectively the King's opposition in the Commons, gave me a sense of boldness I had hitherto been lacking.

"I have here in my hand a letter from Mr John Pym, Member of Parliament for Tavistock, in which he says: (I opened the letter with a flourish)

To whom it may concern,

It has come to my notice that He-died-for-our-sins Sykes Esq., Member of Parliament (until the recent dissolution) for Towcester and Weedon, Northamptonshire, has been accused in a manner most malicious, of espousing, and putting into practice, the heretical and rightly condemned Antinomian doctrines of the 'Family of Love,' or, as they are more commonly known: 'the Ranters.'

Let it be known, wherever and whenever Mr Sykes needs it to be known, that we, the Committee for the Examination of Internal Affairs within the House of Commons, have questioned closely the said Mr Sykes; that we have found no cause of guilt within him and that, furthermore, we are satisfied that any such accusations are, and have been, created fictitiously in order to harm the said gentleman in the same way that all who seek to serve the Lord face persecution.

John Pym.

Having read the letter out loud, I offered it to my uncle, but he waved it away.

"Your letter means nothing at all: I know the accusations are true, as do you. Doubtless your note will work well with some of the powers that be in this county, but do not think that we are such fools."

Having expected that Pym's letter would stand as the only guarantee I would need to dispel these accusations, I was deeply perplexed at the prospect of still having to defend myself despite it. Moreover, our conversation had inevitably attracted the attention of everyone in the room. Richard had sat down on an armchair and was sneering at me whilst he cracked nuts with an air of nonchalant menace, and the way he looked at me as he did so seemed to say: "One day cousin, I'll replace these nuts with your balls." The other occupants of the room, most of whom I imagined to be retainers of Strafford, had stopped their various conversations in order to witness this diversion without hindrance.

In truth, I did not know what to say in answer to my uncle's attack. There was clearly no point at all in denying the charge. I therefore determined to leave as quickly as I could in order to salvage what I could of my dignity. I replaced my hat with an air of defiance and turned to leave the room without making any gesture of obeisance.

But my departure was prevented by Strafford. He (as I have already hinted when I earlier provided his description) was not the sort of person one could easily ignore. "Are you not going to defend yourself against these accusations, Mr Sykes?"

"My lord – I"…but I could not carry on speaking. As I turned to face Strafford his dark eyes penetrated my soul. This effect was not the same as with my father, who used to make a deliberate effort to intimidate me with his piercing gaze. The expression on Strafford's face was that of someone merely waiting for an answer to a question, as if there was no contrived intention on his part to have such a disconcerting effect upon the person he was addressing.

But as I have just mentioned, I could not carry on speaking, so Strafford spoke again. "Is your unwillingness to answer my question caused by a noble refusal to defend that which it is beneath your honour to defend, or do you find yourself unable to defend the indefensible?"

I again could not answer, so he spoke yet again, although this time he addressed me as if he had already decided the answer to his previous question. "There is a further question, Mr Sykes, a particular question, which has been troubling me deeply, and for which I have earnestly sought an answer. I will now, by your leave - ask you the same. There are diverse doctrines and opinions that seem to be threatening the teachings of the Church. One of these - a particularly notorious one - you stand accused of espousing. But what I wonder is this: there are those who serve the Lord all of their lives, and there are those who do not do so but wish they had; and it seems that if they approach Him with a knowledge of their own need for His mercy, then He is indeed merciful. So, I must ask you, is the mercy of God not enough for you? Has not God decided, in His wisdom, the means by which we can enter His Kingdom? Can you not accept that we must enter into Heaven the way God ordains it, or by, as it were, the Straight Gate?"

This series of questions was more than I could stomach. I felt myself exposed in every way imaginable. Having stood there for a moment longer, staring at him, I muttered something about there being some in this county who could recognise righteousness, and fled from the room and out of the house into the fading evening light.

I wandered about for a while, avoiding Strafford's soldiers, who were camped at Tiffield. But I could not bear the thought of going home immediately as I knew I would be unable to mask my emotions sufficiently to divert Aunt Meekness's concerned questions. I therefore chose to take a circular route through the woods in order to avoid reaching home until after her hour of retirement.

As I traversed the beech wood that lay between my house and Caldecote Manor, I fought my melancholic reflections with the thought that Strafford was, after all, a man of evil; and that on no account, or in any circumstances, would the Lord ever use a man such as he to rebuke one of His Elect.

But his words, nonetheless, had brought to my soul an element of disquietude, enough to create in me a need to feel the sense of personal reassurance which emanates from appreciation by others. I therefore, despite my original resolution, decided to risk the possibility that Praise God would be present, and repair to the house of Trustworthy Fairweather.

"And what," I asked myself as I wended my way, growing in confidence as I did so, "should I have to fear from Praise God anyway, when I carry in my pocket such a guarantee?

I could see as I approached the Fairweather homestead that Trustworthy was holding some sort of gathering. There were several carts and tethered horses outside the house and, judging by the hats I could see adorning the occupants of his parlour, it looked as if a prayer meeting was taking place.

I decided that as the custom during my father's time was to walk straight into a meeting when late, rather than to knock and disturb the prayerful members, I had better do the same on this occasion. I therefore entered the house and, upon walking into the room, sat upon an unoccupied chair near to the door. The first thing I noticed was that Trustworthy was praying out loud. His eyes were screwed tightly shut and he was speaking with that voice and demeanour of nasal desperation I remembered so well from my childhood. The second thing I noticed was that Praise God was not present.

There were about sixteen men there, of varying ages, most of whom I recognised. All of them had their eyes shut while Trustworthy was speaking, and one or two were rocking backwards and forwards, their lips moving rapidly in the silent motion of prayer as they did so. After about five minutes however, Trustworthy instructed his hearers to spend a few moments contemplating the condition of their souls. I knew from experience that it was during these times of silent meditation that the beady eyes of the more critical members, particularly those of Trustworthy Fairweather and Hezekiah Barker, the fishmonger, would steal around the room in an effort to identify any who were not sufficiently concentrating upon their devotions. This was a habit and custom I had known from my youth. I recalled at that moment the time when, at the age of twelve, I had remarked to Trustworthy that his inspection of others during prayer time must surely render him unable to say his *own* prayers properly, he gave me a sound thrashing in front of my father, who watched in silence whilst eating his Sunday lunch, before beating me himself afterwards. Why, you may ask, was I punished twice over? Because, my father told me, I could not have been concentrating sufficiently on *my* prayers or I would not have noticed *him* not concentrating sufficiently on *his* prayers.

Which is a somewhat long-winded way of informing you that I became aware that my presence was likely at any time to be noticed; and indeed, after about thirty seconds, I saw Hezekiah's eyes open, steal furtively around the room and then settle upon me.

He looked at me quizzically for a moment, before giving an involuntary start - as if it had taken him a few seconds to recognise me. He then glared at me as he leaned sideways to whisper to Trustworthy, who was on his right. Trustworthy's eyes opened, and then looked slowly round at me, his face tilted upwards in order to be better able to peer at me down his nose. This look, twelve years previously, would have had its desired effect on me: terror - but I had no time for that sort of nonsense now. I stood up just as Trustworthy said the words "Praise God has informed us…"

"I," I interrupted in a raised voice while standing to my feet, "have been serving you faithfully at Westminster; I have stayed up all through the night - night after night - in an attempt to bring your grievances before the King. I have risked life and limb on many occasions. Think very carefully brethren; think very carefully before you would speak, for I know what you would say, and I will brook no evil accusations; and I will listen to no evil reports concerning me. Those among you who have given an ear to - nay believed - these vile accusations: you have been listening to the devil; you have been beguiled, bewitched, bedazzled; and I adjure you one and all to repent!" As I finished saying these words I drew the letter out of my pocket and threw it unceremoniously at Trustworthy, adding as I did so the words, "Read it!"

My boldness had exactly the effect I desired: it shocked Trustworthy out of his arrogance and stunned all of the other occupants of the room into silence. Trustworthy fumbled while opening the letter and then began to read it out loud, with a shaky hand. For your benefit, good Reader, I will refrain from repeating its contents.

When he had finished, there was, for a moment, complete silence. Then they all spontaneously cheered and crowded around me, the older men slapping me on the back and rubbing my hair; the younger ones gazing at me in wondrous adoration.

And so I took my rightful place among them, at their head, and listened graciously as they paid me homage. They were all eager to hear my news from Westminster, of which they knew nothing but that Parliament had been dissolved. So, having elicited a promise from Trustworthy that he would force Praise God to undertake a ceremony for the exorcism of the lying spirit that had clearly possessed him, I told them all that they wanted to hear.

The adulation I received made it easy for me both to forget the downcast feelings that had assailed me since Parliament's dissolution, and the feelings of self-doubt invoked in me by Lord Strafford. I did think, for a moment, of informing my audience that Strafford was but fifteen stone's throw away at Caldecote Manor, but I refrained from doing so on the grounds that they would probably form a lynch mob, that they would almost certainly be unsuccessful, and that as it would be apparent that I had informed them of Strafford's whereabouts I would probably end up being hanged with them.

So I employed my time in instructing them in the means by which they could best place pressure upon the King to recall Parliament. "The King," I told them, "will try to persuade his people that it is Parliament's fault, and not his, that we were unable to reach a conclusion in regard to the issues before us. This is a lie; and you must refuse to pay the taxes he attempts to raise by means of his own authority, as well as encourage as many others as you can to do the same. If enough of you tell the King's tax collectors that you can no longer trust any authority but parliament to dispose of your income wisely then the king will be forced into a corner."

Some of them were at first reluctant to do this, until I pointed out to them that they could surely account themselves exempt from the instruction of the Lord to 'Render unto Caesar that which is Caesar's,' when the said Caesar was spoiling their goods to such an degree that they were unable to put into practice the other half of the Lord's injunction: to 'Render unto God that which is God's.' Naturally, as my role in all this was on a much higher plain altogether, I had no intention of making trouble with a refusal to pay my own taxes. A Member of Parliament could not be seen to break the law; and besides, I could afford them.

And so, with a mixture of satisfaction at my accomplishments, and resentment against my relations and their noble guest, I made my way home for a night of well-earned and uninterrupted slumber.

XXIII

The fall of Strafford

I sought, during those weeks of late summer in Northamptonshire, to understand just what it was about my near relations, and about people such as the King and Lord Strafford, that made me detest them with such vitriol; and it was when I was watching through my uncle's withdrawing room window one evening, while my cousins and he were giving a dance, that I realised what it was.

An incident had occurred in September when I was invited to something described as a 'dinner dance' at the home of Lord Yelvertoft, an obsessive Calvinist and public enemy of Lord Strafford, which illustrates this point perfectly. I had imagined that this gathering would consist of a sumptuous dinner in the company of some of the land's more refined puritans; and then a seemly dance, at which I might finally meet a young woman of my own social standing, who would, perchance, help rid my mind of Gwendolyn Smith. Instead of this I was forced to sit for three hours in the company of twelve middle-aged and elderly men, who discussed nothing other than religion and politics while we ate a meal that was so revolting, due to the bitter herbs that had been deliberately mixed into it, that it could have been created by none other than a masochistic, religious fanatic.

Towards the end of this dreadful experience Lord Yelvertoft, a man of studied misery, stood up, coughed loudly, and said in a monotone voice: "I expect ye've all been wondering about the dance part of the evening, especially as dancing is rightly frowned upon by the Holy.

I have been studying the Old Testament, however, and could not help but notice that King David did so as he performed acts of worship. It seems that this was pleasing to the Lord and I have therefore decided that it would be uplifting for us to follow, on occasions, his example... minstrel!"

Lord Yelvertoft clapped his hands as he finished these words and his 'minstrel' came out of a side room, only he wasn't really a minstrel at all, but Horatius Grieg, a local puritan teacher of music, detested for his arduous and painstaking campaigns to rid the Anglican Church of any forms of worship he considered too melodic. With no hint of a smile or introduction he started to drone through some of the weightier psalms without the aid of an instrument. This was bad enough, but then Lord Yelvertoft, dressed as he was in his sombre clothes, and still wearing his steepled hat (which nether he, nor any of the rest of us, had removed during our meal) started to jerk his body about (supposedly in time to the 'singing') in a manner I found deeply embarrassing to behold, and which I imagined would be equally embarrassing for my fellow spectators. I looked about me, knowing, or rather *thinking*, that if I caught someone's eye we would both start laughing, but was horrified to discover that they were all taking him *seriously*! Worse was to follow: they each in turn got up to follow their host's example, and I realised to my horror that I had been left with no choice but to join them. It was plain that nobody actually enjoyed themselves, although one or two of them 'danced' with their faces fixed into the most foolish of grins, their arms flaying about in the air in a vain attempt to pretend otherwise; and I was greatly relieved when the insane baron resumed his seat, enabling the rest of us to do likewise.

This event made me deeply resentful. I could not fathom what it was that made the true enjoyment of my younger years such an elusive dream; and why it was that so much of my life seemed so grey and dull, despite my supposedly emancipating doctrinal views. I could not help but think of this, and of Yelvertoft's 'dinner-dance,' as I watched through the open window my uncle's and cousins' guests enjoying themselves. Was this, I asked myself, why I detested them so? Was it because they always seemed to be enjoying themselves so much more than me? My reflections were violently interrupted when Richard Sykes slammed the window onto my fingers, which had been resting upon the frame.

• • •

Despite the miserable event I have just detailed, in terms of prestige within the Puritan community I had no reason to be anything other than satisfied; and I was pleased to be able to impress my brethren with the regular tidings I received from Pym concerning the affairs of state. The King and Strafford, he informed me in a letter addressed from Nottingham, had met with nothing but humiliation from the Scots, who by now, having routed the English army at Newburn in Northumberland, had gained control of vast swathes of the northern part of the country.

Pym told me that the King had called a Council in which he allowed members from both the lower and the upper houses of the former parliament to remonstrate with him, and even to rebuke him, within the bounds of decorum. He promised to recall parliament, and listened to many attacks upon Strafford (whose threat of an invasion from an Irish army had come to nothing) without rising to his defence.

Pym ended his letter with these words: 'Make thee ready Lad, for our time is surely come. The King's position is weak; Strafford's position is even weaker, for it is he who has borne the brunt of blame for the mess; and we have the means at our disposal to ensure the King can never again by his own authority dissolve Parliament.'

But not all was good news. I was somewhat alarmed to hear that while the King had been allowing Lord Strafford to be berated as the nation's scapegoat, some noblemen, including Strafford and Lord Northampton, had been ensuring that the seats in which the King's supporters were most likely to attain a majority were represented by their friends and followers. This scheme was only partially success-ful, but it was, I discovered, due to these machinations that Strafford found a place for my cousin Richard Sykes, representing the area of Northampton West and the Bramptons. This at first worried me. My own seat in parliament was safe, but I could well imagine that Richard Sykes would organise a team whose main aim was to render my life there entirely miserable. I comforted myself as best I could with the thought that Richard's presence would make the downfall of Strafford all the more satisfactory and enjoyable.

• • •

I arrived in London on the thirtieth day of October and repaired, at the first opportunity, to the lodgings of John Pym; and there again I found a hive of activity. This time, as well as many Members of Parliament I remembered from the former session, there were many who I did not. There were also several gentlemen who, from their strange accents, as well as their peculiar mode of attire, I recognised as preachers of the Covenant from the north side of the border. One of these Scotchmen was ending a sermon as I arrived. John Pym smiled and gestured to a place next to a wall where I stood next to several others as the preacher finished his discourse.

"Kings," the preacher was saying, "were placed among the people of Israel as a just recompense for their ingratitude and hardness of heart. The Children of Israel were granted Saul, and we have been granted Charles. Doubtless a people pleasing unto the Lord would warrant a good King, and thus it appears that the Lord hath shown this nation to be a nation in need of repentance. But look ye, brethren: harm not the Lord's anointed. I say to thee again, for I feel a sense of deep foreboding, harm ye not the person of the Lord's anointed."

At that the preacher sat down, and after partaking of refreshments in the form of buttered buns and milk (they would not touch alcohol) the Covenanters got up to leave. "We look forward to hearing you again in church on Sunday next," said Pym as they departed, "fare thee well."

Pym then turned and embraced me warmly. "Sykes," he said, "the sight of your face brings me nearly as much joy as the reason for seeing it. He then asked me quietly, "Have you still that petition, lad: the one you wanted to produce at the beginning of the last parliament?"

I answered his question with a nod.

"Good, we will have need of it now, and I am going to make sure you get a chance to be heard on the floor of the House at the earliest opportunity. Now gentlemen, it is a time for rejoicing indeed, but it is a time for hard work also. We must set about the serious business of government. All authority is currently held in the name of the King. This, gentlemen, is the parliament that will change this!"

"Brothers in arms," I exclaimed in response, "let us raise our hats and our voices for our illustrious leader...King Pym!" So saying, I lifted my hat aloft and led my fellow parliamentarians in a eulogy of praise: "King Pym! King Pym! King Pym!"

He, embarrassed but clearly pleased, responded with a mere shake of his head." He then turned away from us in order to hide his grin, and the extremity of his emotions.

• • •

The King, it seemed, could do nothing right.

I had hoped that when he travelled to the Palace of Westminster to open Parliament, he would ride in a glorious procession as had been his custom on previous occasions. I was convinced that had he done so the people would have jeered him for his arrogance. As it was, the King attempted to travel by river without being seen, and the people sulked *en masse*, because of the curtailment of their right to a public display of grandeur.

So, with his people sullenly waiting around outside, the king opened Parliament for the second time in one year, on the afternoon of Tuesday 3rd November. He again took his place upon the throne in the House of Lords. Strafford was not present, as, although it was rumoured he had refused several recommendations to flee the country, he was currently journeying to London; and his arrival had only being delayed by a visit to his family in Yorkshire.

"I hope," Pym muttered as we waited for the King to begin speaking, "he is taking care to make a fond farewell."

The King spoke. "My Lords and Gentlemen, I called the last parliament, fully aware of, and willing to address, your grievances; but I called it also as our country faced a great peril. Had I been believed, I sincerely think things would not have fallen out as they have. Now, I cannot pretend to you that matters are better than they were in spring - they are worse...so let us lay aside our differences: I know that the views of many of you are different to mine as to the cause of the failure of the last parliament to achieve a satisfactory conclusion. My foremost concerns are the chasing out of the rebels and the satisfaction of your just grievances. The first of these must be done, and that quickly...but the English army must be paid before it can be used further. I leave it to your consideration what dishonour and mischief it might be if, for want of money, my army is disbanded before the rebels are put out of this kingdom."

"One thing more I desire of you..." the King added, "as one of the greatest means to make this a happy parliament: that you, on your parts, as I, on mine, lay aside all suspicions one of another."

He then stood up and, as was his custom, bowed his head cursorily but gravely to the Commons and Peers. "It shall not be my fault if this is not a happy and good parliament," he added, before leaving for the Palace of Whitehall.

We gathered around Pym before taking our seats.

"Listen carefully," he said, "I have just heard that Strafford arrived last night and is now at Whitehall. Tomorrow I will denounce him on the floor of the House. We must take the vote and carry it to the Lords before anyone can get to Strafford to warn him of what's afoot. If he's warned he'll be able to browbeat many of the lords into supporting him, or even flee abroad. That means it needs to be done quickly. It is of the utmost importance that no one mentions Strafford's name on the floor of this House until I give the signal. Now, there are a few things we must establish. We'll be preparing the trial from the committee room. It must be secure. *We* must each have a key. *Nobody* else must have a key. That means not even a servant to do the cleaning. Someone will have to be in charge of the room. Who?"

"I suppose I could wave a duster around," replied Strode.

"Good," said Pym. "Now remember, tomorrow..."

When the others had dispersed around the chamber I took Pym to one side. "If you will forgive me," I said in a strong but hushed tone, "I do not think that it necessary to enter into this with such a lack of confidence. As you must know, the weaponry that was used to fight the Scots in the north has been stored in the Tower. This is useful to us. If you will allow me to be the one to denounce Strafford, I have news of an incident earlier this summer which, when heard by the Members present, will stir this House and the Lords alike against Strafford to his irretrievable downfall. If you will instruct one of our members to complain, or rather, raise a concern about the weapons and soldiers in the Tower, and then allow me the opportunity to speak thereafter..."

But Pym was at that moment called to the Speaker's chair, and I was left to hope that my words had persuaded him.

• • •

Little had changed it seemed since spring, other than the replacement of Speaker Glanville with a somewhat timid looking man called William Lenthall.

But the number of members who stood in opposition to the policies of the King, which had made up a majority in the spring parliament, was now overwhelming. After the Commons had been in session for about twenty minutes on the morning following, many old members, as well as new, began to produce petitions from around the country. I had found no further opportunity to speak with Pym, so I was forced to watch helplessly and impatiently in the hope that he would cross the floor and address the Speaker, when George Digby, heir of Lord Bristol, whom I have already introduced as the young man who made such a fool of himself when making his maiden speech, stood up.

In the usual way of these things he, as an earl's son, was called by the Speaker the moment he rose to gain his attention. This in itself did not overly worry me, but his words did.

"I," he said to a hushed audience, "have been forced to watch, helpless, as this country has been brought to the brink of ruin. I have seen my friends imprisoned, and in some cases tortured, and why? Because their conscience told them not to pay a wicked and evil tax; or worse, because their hearts led them to a form of worship different from that which has been ordered by the Archbishop of Canterbury. Brethren, I put it to you that it has become our duty to remonstrate with the King directly concerning the cause of the unhappy situation with which we, as this nation's elected representatives, have become concerned. The evil to which I suggest we draw his Majesty's attention is the evil which emanates from his advisers, most notably Laud and Strafford, and by which he is in danger of becoming the nation's inappropriate scapegoat."

Now most of the members of Parliament were delighted to hear the King's advisers being attacked thus. For Digby to mention Strafford and the Archbishop directly, whilst exonerating the King himself, was exactly what they wanted to hear. The danger was that the mention of Strafford and Laud might lead to a mass of denunciations, and that things might spin prematurely, and irretrievably, out of our control.

Digby sat down again with an expression at once serious and self-satisfied, and what I found particularly irksome was that he was surrounded by members eager to slap him on the back or shake his hand.

It immediately became clear that if I did not move quickly this dandy would not only render our hard work fruitless by stealing all the glory, but by creating the pandemonium that inevitably followed his words, he might give Strafford an advanced warning of our intentions.

I leant over to Pym from the second row, and discreetly tugged at his sleeve, while the members shouted around me.

"Digby could have ruined everything then," I whispered, "we'll have to move now. If we wait any longer Strafford will slip through the net. Tell the Speaker that Strafford, following today's business, is likely to be required to answer serious charges brought against him by the Commons. You must persuade the Speaker that this business is of such a nature as to make it likely that certain members will try to reach Strafford in order to warn him. I would suggest that you advise him to prepare the palace guard to lock us in, if necessary, so that our business can be conducted privately and speedily."

He stared at me for a moment. "Very well, Sykes: but be aware that this moment will make or destroy you." He rose and walked to the Speaker's chair, where he and Lenthall spoke briefly. Pym then walked back. He paused to address an Irish Member named Sir John Clotworthy (another renowned for his personal hatred of Strafford) and then sat down directly in front of me.

The Speaker spent a moment looking through some papers, and stood up. "I already have in mind that there are many petitions being brought before the House, and that we shall set this morning aside to hear them. Let all be brought out into the open: the needs of his Majesty, and the needs of his people. Remember: to those who are crooked in their dealings, the Lord will show Himself crooked also. To those who are true and faithful the Lord will show Himself to be true and faithful."

As the Speaker had been talking, news of Strafford's arrival in London began to travel around the chamber. Many members feared that if Strafford had his way then they would be blamed for stirring up the riots, or at the very least not doing their best to quell them. The news that he had returned, therefore, created some consternation among the members, which in turn gave rise to a considerable amount of noise.

"Order, order." called the Speaker.

The House came to a semblance of order.

"Sir John Clotworthy."

Clotworthy stood to his feet. "Gentlemen, it has become a matter for serious concern that, without the assent of Parliament, a huge stockpile, both of weapons and soldiers, has accumulated - with no explanation provided - in the Tower. While it is the duty of this House to condemn, however justified they may have been, the random acts of violence which occurred both in London and in the country round about during the summer, I would say that it is the right of Parliament, nay that it is Parliament's necessity, to be provided with an explanation. Is this army to be used against our own people? Are we to face the same treatment as has been meted out to the Scots? I have heard that the Lord Strafford has recently spoken of subduing the City of

London. Is this the purpose, the true purpose, of the billeting of this army at the Tower?"

Now, whether it was true that Strafford said anything about 'subduing the City of London' I do not know; but what I do know is that the mention of his name this second time, and in this context, had an effect upon the House akin to the explosion of suppressed gunpowder. Almost everyone stood up at once, all were shouting, and the Speaker tried desperately, although unsuccessfully, to call for order.

Somehow, Sir Thomas Witherington, the septuagenarian referred to earlier in these pages, eventually managed to be heard. His authority was carried by his sheer indignation. "That *army*, which is now in the Tower of London, is there ready for its disbandment having been brought down from the North. It is waiting only for a review by the King before its dispersal." He pointed to Clotworthy. "This gentleman knows this to be the case. He is party to this information. Mr Speaker, this gentleman is a liar, a rabble-rouser and a scoundrel! I will not withdraw: I demand that *he* withdraws!"

The House again descended into uproar. Witherington sat down next to my cousin, his arms folded, breathing heavily. His face was purple, and made a startling contrast to his white moustache. Opposite him about fifty members were shouting, but he sat staring in front of him, looking, in fact, as if he were about to have a heart attack.

"Order, this house will come to order or I will close this sitting. Order! Order!"

But every member was by now on his feet, and some of them at the front had started to jostle with one another, violently. Cromwell, as well as two other members, stepped down from the back of the Chamber and started pulling and pushing them back to their own benches.

"The time is now!" I whispered to Pym.

Pym, very discreetly, nodded to the Speaker. He, just as discreetly, nodded to an officer of the Palace Guard, who had been waiting by the door behind him. The officer threw the door open, and a dozen soldiers marched in. The House, astonished, fell silent as they positioned themselves in front of the doors, their orders clearly being to prevent anyone leaving or entering. Lenthall then said, quite calmly (for the presence of the soldiers had had a remarkably subduing effect) "If any member fails again this day to restrain his temper I will ask the Sergeant at Arms to close this House. Now, if we are prepared to conduct ourselves as befits gentlemen..."

I stood to my feet. The House became silent again.

"Mr Sykes."

My eyes met those of my cousin for a moment, and then, having glanced loftily around the Chamber, I began.

"Gentlemen, it is with a heavy heart that I make this, my first speech in this House. For the past seven years, since the death of my father, my only longing has been to serve my country in the way that he always desired that I should: as a Member of Parliament. He even sought my earnest pledge upon his death bed, that I would honour him to the greatest of my ability by attempting to enter into the halls of power, and to undertake the good works that he himself had so longed to accomplish. But how have I wept. How great has become the burden upon my shoulders - and upon your shoulders also, my brethren. I thought when I came here that we would all be of the same heart; that all would have the same will to honour and serve their King and country. I knew that some of us would differ in opinion as to the best means by which we could accomplish this, but I believed that the deepest desire of our hearts would be the same. Think not that there has been nothing to give me cheer, there has been much indeed, but I have also been forced to witness the deeds of those who make a pretence - a blasphemous pretence - of serving the Lord, and a pretence of serving the King also, while their hearts and actions have shown them to be nought but evildoers. Oh that I could believe - that I could know - that Sir Thomas Witherington was correct. How I have wrestled within myself to maintain my trust in the virtue of those who hold so much power in this country. The Lord Strafford told us that we had to fight the Scots because they were a threat to this nation's security. I believed him, for the thought that someone so close to the King would mislead him, as well as us, his loyal servants, was too much for me to bear. But this very summer I received reliable intelligence of a serious plot to overthrow the King's government by a papist army from Ireland. Had this been an open declaration of war, then part of me would have rejoiced, yea I say rejoiced, at the opportunity we faced to meet our enemies in open conflict. But this was never going to be an open declaration of war. I took news of this plot to Sir Henry Vane and the Lord Strafford. I will tell you their response. I will tell you what I, as a Member of Parliament, denied his seat - and the opportunity to serve those whose care I held in my bosom - was forced to bear. They laughed gentlemen, they laughed, and yea I tell you they laughed my words to scorn. They caused me to be flogged, without even making so much as a cursory investigation into the business to which I had attempted to draw their attention."

Now when I had started to speak, the members present (and the House was all but full) had listened to my words with politeness and respect. I could soon tell, however, that they were no longer listening out of mere politeness, but had become entirely spellbound. And when I started to speak of the Anne Hussey plot they started to become restless; and several of them, including my cousin, rose to their feet in an attempt to catch the Speaker's eye. Sir Henry Vane was not in the Chamber.

"I will, with your permission, Mr Speaker, give way in but a moment." I continued: "Gentlemen, it is not merely our duty to serve those who sent us here, it is also our duty to serve our King, as well as the nation as a whole. But not all who claim to serve the King have his, or the country's, interests at heart. Have we not, through the fault of the Archbishop of Canterbury, provoked the Scots, who, as well as being our neighbours, are our spiritual brethren? Has this futile war not been waged in a manner so incompetent as to endanger the very peace and stability of this nation by the King's Commander in Chief, Lord Strafford? Oh how I would love to believe in him, but how can I do so?"'

I then drew from my pocket the list of grievances I had kept in my possession since I came to London for the opening of the first parliament in April. The whole House remained completely silent – enraptured - as I drew the paper from my pocket.

"I have heard the many grievances brought forward by the honourable Members of this House. I also brought with me a list of grievances from my constituency in Northamptonshire. They are, in many ways, similar to those I have heard, but those who elected me demanded something more, and this was even before the catastrophes of this past summer. I, with a lack of foresight, told them that they were too harsh; I told them that the King's advisers surely have the King's, and therefore this country's, interests in their bosoms. Gentlemen, circumstances have forced me to change my mind….I now ask, nay I demand, that this House, this parliament, impeaches the Earl of Strafford and the Archbishop of Canterbury for the crime of High Treason!"

I then sat down and folded my arms, my expression that of the surly Puritan elder statesman. Everyone rose to their feet once again, and no one could be heard above the sound of their colleagues' raised voices, although I could just make out Richard Sykes, having abandoned all of his usual contrived composure, shouting the word 'liar,' at me repeatedly. To see him so disturbed and alarmed at the imminent downfall of his hero and mentor brought me my first taste of that sweet revenge; revenge that was…. almost tangible.

But whatever anyone now said, or however violently they reacted, the die was cast. I noticed that Pym, with a look of sheer gratitude and approval, had turned to face me and was nodding his head slowly, as if to say "Well done, my son."

Several Members, including my cousin, then tried to leave the Chamber, but were thwarted in their attempt by the soldiers. They were then compelled to listen as their champion's character and reputation was repeatedly exposed and destroyed before the House.

Nor was the House in any mood to listen to anyone who had a word to say in Strafford's defence. They were all shouted down until it was agreed, by an overwhelming majority, that the House of Commons intended to accuse Strafford before the Lords of High Treason. As soon as this motion was passed the Speaker ordered the doors once again to be opened. Pym walked straight over to me with about eight followers. "Come on Lad, we haven't to lose" he said as he grabbed me by the arm and yanked me to my feet. So I, as well as the others (who included George Digby – somehow he had just *included* himself) walked with him out of the chamber. As we were departing, Richard Sykes shoved his way past us, doubtless on his way to warn Strafford.

• • •

"Now," said Pym when we had gathered in the Painted Chamber, "if, as I suspect, Strafford is at Whitehall, I would say that we have no longer than ten minutes before someone fetches him back to the Lords. It is vital that he is not there to refute the initial charge, or he may be able to bully the other Lords into rejecting it. Digby, would you be so good as to run to the Lords with all haste and inform them that we wish to wait on them immediately with a most important communication from the Lower House?"

Digby left, muttering something as he did so about being used as a fetching boy. I suspected however, that his feelings were mixed on this matter, as he probably relished the idea of addressing the Peers, and would doubtless have refused to run Pym's errand otherwise.

"Now," said Pym as we were waiting, "before anything happens it is beholden upon us all to express our heartfelt thanks to He-died-for-our-sins Sykes. I am glad as I can be that I listened to you and allowed you to speak back there. I know that you are aware that if Strafford survives this then you will be a marked man, more than any of us; and for this we all owe you our thanks for placing the welfare of this country above your own well-being, as well as our congratulations for such an inspired speech."

The other members all applauded and cheered, and started to ask me questions such as, 'From whence did you receive your inspiration?' when George Digby returned, breathless. "They are expecting you immediately," he said, "may I go back with you?"

"No," said Pym, "but thanks for delivering the message. Sykes, follow me if you will."

So, with a feeling of additional pleasure at Digby's humiliation, I followed Pym to the House of Lords. As we were passing a window I caught a fleeting glimpse of a coach arriving outside the Palace. I thought that I saw my cousin inside along with Strafford, although I could not be certain of this.

We paused briefly outside the door of the House of Lords, removed our hats, and entered.

The Lords, who themselves were in a fairly heated mood when we arrived, were immediately silent when they noticed our entrance. It was plain that they knew why we were there, although the Lord Keeper, who was the only one standing upon our arrival, asked us our business.

Pym was plain and to the point: "We, as representatives of the Commons of England, are here to accuse Thomas Wentworth, Earl of Strafford, Lord Lieutenant of Ireland, of High Treason."

Not one of the peers looked in any way surprised by Pym's statement; some, indeed, looked positively pleased.

"You are sent here by the majority of your peers?" asked Finch.

"We are, Lord Keeper," replied Pym.

"We will consider your charge, but you must withdraw as we do so."

We both bowed and turned to leave. As we did so I heard a voice behind me saying "We will meet here shortly." I realised immediately that my path was blocked by Strafford, who had been speaking to my cousin Richard and who, just too late, was trying to make his way into the Chamber. I immediately determined that *he* should stand aside for *me*, so I stood my ground, and replaced my hat upon my head. Now if he had said something like 'Get out of my way,' or 'Stand aside for your betters,' then maintaining my position would have been easier; but he looked at me in the manner of someone who *knew that I had no choice* but to give way for him. I moved aside, and cursed myself for not having done so in the first place. He walked past me without as much as a glance to one side.

I lingered as long as possible in order to see the outcome of his untimely entrance. Pym had already left.

Strafford walked forward, and made to sit in a vacant space on one of the front benches, but the Earl of Manchester barred his passage. "My Lord Strafford, you must withdraw from this place."

Strafford tried to sidestep him, but a cry went up from about fifty of the peers: "Withdraw! Withdraw!" If he had any supporters there at all at that time they remained silent. He stopped and turned to Finch. "My Lord Keeper, I require an explanation."

Although I could not see Finch, his voice betrayed his unease. "We have received a communication from the other House accusing you, in no uncertain terms, of the crime of High Treason. You must withdraw while we consider this charge."

Strafford looked about him. All were silent, although some of the Peers made no attempt to conceal their delight in his humiliation.

He turned and started to walk slowly back towards me. I slipped through the door and hurried towards the Painted Chamber, where I found that many of the Members of the Commons were milling around waiting to see what was going to happen.

"He's coming, he's coming!" I whispered loudly and urgently. Almost everyone then crowded around the doorway, apart from a group I noticed at the far side who were struggling to prevent Richard Sykes making his way through. He was forced to the floor and then dragged towards the door. During this time Strafford arrived, but on this occasion he was compelled to push open the heavy doors himself and, having walked through, he stood leaning heavily upon his cane.

He looked about him, taking in the sight of so many of his sneering enemies, until his attention was caught by the struggle still taking place at the far end of the Chamber. Strafford noticed Richard Sykes just in time to see him being forced out; and at the sight of his friend being thus removed, his expression, which had been one of contrived indifference to his misfortunes, became one of undisguised loneliness and sorrow.

The members started to walk around him, taking his sadness as a sign of weakness on his part, and victory on theirs. They stared at him and blocked his path both forward and back, so he had no choice but to remain standing where he was. Now, with my friends around me, I knew that I would find it easier to mock him than it had been at any of our previous encounters, but I somehow could not. I left it to some of my colleagues to address him with such questions as 'Are you having a pleasant day *Your Lordship*?' and 'Are you not going to command your army to come to your rescue?' He made no answer any of these questions, and I think, to be truthful, that his refusal to respond made them feel somewhat ashamed.

After a few minutes the door behind Strafford was opened and Maxwell, the Gentleman Usher of the Black Rod, stepped through. "My Lord Strafford, their Lordships require your immediate presence." He said this before stepping back and holding one of the doors open. The crowd immediately made way, and Strafford walked back to hear the Lords' decision. Maxwell slammed the door behind him.

This time I knew that there was no possibility of my getting into the Lords, so I waited with the others. Pym was nowhere to be seen, and I took his absence as confidence in the likely outcome. Some of the members, however, seemed less certain, and I heard one of them asking what would become of us all if the Lords immediately threw out the charge.

I realised they needed some encouragement. "Fear not brethren. You may or may not be aware, that I have just accompanied our leader into the House of Lords. We were followed in by the Lord Strafford himself, and I can assure you all, that while we were met with nothing but respect, Strafford met with nothing but enmity from those peers present. I would be willing, were gambling not a sin, to stake my life on a favourable outcome for our cause."

This cheered them, and as I finished speaking Strafford walked through in the company of Maxwell and two soldiers. It was plain for all to see that he had been placed under arrest, and he, for a moment, looked undecided as to what to do and where to go. As he did not immediately receive any instructions from Maxwell, Strafford started to make his way towards the main entrance.

"Your coach has gone!" someone shouted. He stopped, and looked about him in confusion.

"What's the matter?" shouted another.

He continued to look about him. "A small matter, I warrant you," he muttered in response.

"Aye," someone shouted from the crowd. Startled, Stafford swung round. "'Tis a small matter indeed: High Treason!"

Maxwell stepped forward, as much to rescue his prisoner as to take him into custody. "It is a lie my Lord, your coach is still waiting for you. However I must ask you to order your driver to depart without you, and I must ask you to give me your sword. It is my duty to keep you in custody until the Lords are ready to present to you the articles of impeachment."

Strafford gave Maxwell his sword, which he passed to a servant. They then walked down the stairs, with me at the head of the crowd following. There were two coaches outside, and Strafford, having dismissed the driver of his own coach, got into the other with Maxwell. We watched them in silence as they disappeared into the gloomy November afternoon.

XXIV

The accosting of Praise God

Pym and I urged the committee set up for drawing the charge against Strafford to remain positive and confident before the members of the Commons in general. Even Hampden was able to cast aside his dislike of me for the sake of the important work before us (his attitude towards me changed from overt aggression to a sullen silence). We received encouraging news from Ireland that the Parliament in Dublin, hearing of his troubles in England, had issued a remonstrance against Strafford, accusing him of every type of injustice and corruption; and of being personally responsible for their 'extreme and universal poverty.'

This was encouraging news, although in private Pym was willing to admit to me that he was worried. "There is no doubt in my mind whatsoever," he said one morning as we sat alone in the committee room, "that we are justified, both morally and politically, in taking this action against Strafford. I know that, you know that; and every right thinking subject of the King knows that, but if we fail our cause will be lost. I have seen it happen before, you see, when Parliament failed to impeach the Duke of Buckingham in 1626."

"Fear not," I said, placing my hand comfortingly upon his shoulder, "I will, I am sure, find something that will give us all the reassurance we need. In the meantime, sleep easy in your bed, it is not merely for your own benefit that you need to have a fresh mind to fight the good fight, it is for the benefit of all the true saints who are relying upon you in this time of great need. If you could take steps to ensure that Strafford's supporters are silenced where possible, then allow me to assure you that I can take care of the rest."

Pym, instead of answering, looked at me curiously.

"I have to ask Sykes – have you washed recently?"

"But a fortnight ago" I replied, somewhat insulted.

"It's just that… you cannot deny it…there is an unpleasant smell in here."

The truth was that I *had* smelt something unpleasant, rather like dead animals; but had presumed it was Pym. I, however, had been too polite to accuse *him* of not washing.

We tried to ignore it as we could not find the source. It was however, somewhat overpowering.

"This room needs a little airing," he said.

He then moved towards the window, and as he was opening it, said, "We should be ready four days from now to present the Commons with the articles of impeachment. Make sure you're there to prevent any attempts at errant voting. It will be up to the Lords after that."

I got up to take my leave, and Pym looked at me as I opened the door. The nervous tension was clearly beginning to weigh him down: "He-died-for-our-sins…"

I turned to face him.

"Thanks." The look on his tearful face was that of sheer gratitude, and I realised that if I had not been there to help him he would probably have crumbled under the strain. I shut the door quietly, leaving him to weep in solitude.

● ● ●

Now I knew that Pym was by profession a lawyer, and that it was his knowledge of the law that was making him so worried now, as it was clear that the evidence we had at our disposal was insufficient to convict Strafford in an impartial court, even if that 'impartial' court was the House of Lords. I was certain, however, that there must be something more that could be used to help promote or justify our cause. I thought in particular of the ways in which Kings and Queens of old used to execute people who had fallen from royal favour.

I knew just the man to help me. Praise God, who I will freely admit I had regarded in our youth as, in comparison to me, an oaf, was gathering fame about himself in London and beyond, for his ready wit and legal expertise. He had already won several high profile cases in the defence of people from all estates of life, his clients ranging from lowly born people accused of theft and murder, to puritans of greater means, charged before the courts for their failure or refusal to pay ship money tax, or some equally burdensome and legally questionable charge by the state. I knew, of course, that Praise God would refuse to help me, so before I went to see him, I paid a visit to the home of Compromise-not-at-all Jenkins and his friends in Sweet Lane, a notorious dive in the City inhabited by street urchins, pickpockets and prostitutes.

I knocked upon the door of the first (and most revolting looking) house in the road, expecting it to be answered by some worn out whore from whom I could ascertain their whereabouts, but I was not altogether surprised to discover that I had actually chanced upon the very house inhabited by my wretched acquaintances. Flee sin answered the door upon my summons, and ushered me in. Paper and ink is entirely insufficient a medium to describe the stench that suffused that household, and I discovered the rest of the gang sitting around the floor (for there was no furniture to speak of) like a group of opium addicts or drunkards who had lost all hope of entering real society.

"Troth," I exclaimed to Flee sin as I entered the room, "One might almost think you should spell your name F-l-e-a sin!"

He looked at me with an expression of total incomprehension, as did all the others apart from Compromise-not-at-all, who asked me if I had come to their house to mock their poverty.

"Not a whit," I replied hastily, "not a whit. In fact, I have come hither to offer you a way of doing the nation a great service and of alleviating the very poverty you speak of."

"How?" he asked, his frosty tone thawing a little.

"You will remember Praise God Fairweather. He was a young man in whom I once had much hope. When we arrived at Cambridge his only ambition was to serve the Lord in the humble capacity of a teacher and instructor of the young in the ways of godliness and wisdom; but the snares of this present life have reached into his very soul and led him astray, so that he now traverses with a glad and willing heart the very paths of wickedness."

"We remember him."

"His heart, in fact," I continued, "has become so darkened with evil that he would not think (as is the way of all lawyers) of doing even the cause of righteousness a service were it not for filthy lucre, or unless he were under some sort of coercion. Praise God must be forced to do a certain task I have set out for him. This is where you can be of service."

"How so?" asked Flee sin.

"Simple: you will doubtless have heard that Black Tom is about to go on trial for his life. We need to ensure that if the prosecution fails on the charges, he will not be able to escape the hand of righteous judgement. In order to ensure our success we need the private and discreet advice of a lawyer. Praise God is the man to speak to, and, as I have said, he will need to be coerced into helping us, as well as made to dread the consequences of betraying us. I will give you a guinea between you if you will perform this task satisfactorily. Are you willing?"

"Aye, we're willing," said Compromise-not-at-all.

"Good. We must walk together to the Middle Temple, where we shall doubtless find Praise God ensconced in his chambers and buried in his books. There is really very little you are required to do other than assail him with violence if he proves obstinate. Make sure however, that you allow me to do all the talking unless I signal otherwise"

And so we made our way to the Middle Temple. Once there I entered the building and inquired as to Praise God's whereabouts, while the others loitered outside with the purpose of apprehending him should he arrive in the meantime. I was told by the porter that 'The honourable Mr Fairweather' was in court, and that he would, as was his custom, be soon arriving for the evening repast. I decided that the best plan was to wait for him with the others, but was fortunate that he arrived just as I was leaving the building. His expression as he approached and recognised me was one of unmitigated horror.

But after a moment he composed himself and took on a look of contrived nonchalance as he attempted to walk past me into the Hall.

"Just a moment there, Praise God," I said, grabbing him firmly by the arm. The others, who had not immediately recognised him, quickly surrounded us, and we led him together down one of the many dark alleys that separate the Middle Temple from Fleet Street.

"What do you want? Leave me alone!" he bleated uselessly.

"It is unfortunate for me, Praise God, that I have to treat you thus, but such is the end of all renegades from the true faith."

"I am not a renegade."

"Silence! Know this: you have the chance now to do God and your country a service. As I have clearly been called by the Lord to use you in this great venture, you should count yourself as deeply blessed that He, in His wisdom, has not cast you aside altogether."

"I asked you what you want."

"You are to instruct me. If you fail to instruct me adequately and sufficiently I will instruct my friends here to kill you."

"There was a time," replied Praise God, "that any suggestion on your part that I had displeased the Lord would have filled me with fear and foreboding, but now I see you for what you really are: a liar and a bully who can accomplish nothing but by evil and falsehood; and the company you keep shows only how low you have sunk. I will not help you, and I am quite prepared to stand before the Lord on the day of judgement and explain why. Good day to you."

And with that he tried to push his way through us in order to make his escape. I will freely confess that his words had the effect of making me somewhat embarrassed by the company I had brought to meet him. Nonetheless, I had to set my face like flint against any such feelings and concentrate upon the work in hand. I nodded to Compromise-not-at-all, who dragged him back and punched him in the stomach. Praise God fell to the floor, doubled over, and started to retch.

"You do not understand, Praise God," I said, kneeling next to him, you *will* do as you are told, or you will be killed; and I do not think you will find this task too burdensome, or be opposed to the cause behind it."

"What is it?" he asked with his face still to the ground.

"Walk with us a while down to the river and I will tell you."

"So you can push me in."

"No, Praise God, we will not push you in, nor will we harm you at all if you do our bidding. You may walk with me alone, and our friends here can walk twenty paces behind, enough space between you and them in fact, for you to make your escape should you wish to. But see here, if you do run away then they will hunt you down and kill you, won't you lads?"

"Aye - that we will."

So we walked along the river bank; and as we did so I told Praise God that Strafford, as he knew, had been accused of High Treason, but that we needed to ensure that should the Lords fail to convict him he could not escape with his life.

"Surely if the charges fail," he replied, "it means that he *deserves* to escape with his life. He could never survive politically from this, so why can you not let him retire to his estate and his wife and children? His gout and stones will probably finish him off within a few years anyway."

"Because," I said, recalling Pym's words, "he is the true power behind the throne, and parliament will never obtain its rightful sovereignty and independence from the Crown as long as he lives. It is not many years since that Kings and Queens would execute their opponents at their leisure…which brings me to my question: have such powers really been done away with, or have they merely fallen into disuse? If you do not know I need you to find out."

"Well," answered Praise God, "I have been following these events very closely, fascinated as I am to see whether your case against Strafford will stand up to scrutiny; so you need not have attacked me in the way that you did back there - but I suppose you lack the imagination to think of another method. I have, you are right, concluded that you do need more to be able to destroy Strafford. There is only one way, and it is just as you speak of - but you cannot use it."

"What? What is it?"

"It is the use of an obscure and all but obsolete method of wielding the ultimate power of the Crown, but its use contravenes every moral convention and every established principle of the Common Law. Certain Kings of old, and Queens, would use it when they desperately wished to despatch one of their enemies, but were unable to do so by any legal reasoning."

"What is it?"

"It is known as Attainder, and it was dreamed up during the wars between the Houses of York and Lancaster. Parliament, by enacting a Bill of Attainder, can destroy its - or the King's - victims merely by the passing of the Act, however weak their legal case."

Now this was exactly the sort of thing I had sought out Praise God in order to find out. I stopped and turned to face him, waving to the others to stand fast. "Can it still be done? When was it last used?"

"During the reign of Queen Mary," he answered dryly, "for the burning of Protestants."

I ignored the irony. "But, but – it *could* still be used?"

"Its use has never officially been outlawed by Parliament."

"Then it can still be used?"

"Think upon it. I know, as do many people, that you are a man devoid of principle. But I was under the impression that Parliament's struggle against the King was based upon his arbitrary use of the Royal Prerogative. How can Parliament justify the use of this means when it was used under the command of monarchs such as Henry VIII and Mary, who used Parliament as a mere tool? How would History judge your cause, when you, who wish to transfer the power of the King to Parliament, are willing to use such a barbaric means of wielding power when the King himself has not done so?"

"It is not my business to concern myself about..."

But Praise God would not allow me to finish: "The other reason that you cannot use it is that the King will never sign it. It cannot be passed but by an Act of Parliament, and an Act of Parliament is not legal until it receives the Royal Assent, therefore unless you beat Strafford in open trial you will not beat him at all."

He paused, but only for a moment.

"You once said to me that 'the end justifies the means.' You were wrong. The means might bring about the end but the end does not signify that the means are justified. Go on: produce a Bill of Attainder, you might even be able to force the King to sign it - although I do not see how - but you cannot justify such an action."

I shifted uneasily on my feet.

"Oh, but I was forgetting," he continued, "the earth is yours; you are one of the enlightened. You are specially chosen by the Lord and need not concern yourself with burdensome things such as a conscience."

He looked at me in sheer disgust. "There," he said, "you have your answer, now leave me alone." He then strode off in the direction of the Middle Temple. I started to walk back towards Compromise-not-at-all and his friends, my feelings a peculiar mix of guilt and jubilation, when Praise God suddenly turned and started to retrace his steps. He was shaking.

"And you can tell your hired thugs," he shouted, pointing at my companions while refusing to look at them, "that I do not live or work alone at the Inns of Court; and that if I see them around here again..."

He stopped - tears of anger and belated shock welling up in his eyes, then turned on his heels and walked away again. Flee sin made to follow him, rolling up his sleeves, but I held out my arm and stopped him. I then tossed them their promised guinea and walked off in disgust, while they shouted after me to join them for a tankard of ale. I ignored them and continued towards Westminster.

It is a strange statement to make, when I had just treated him thus, but I detested Jenkins and his friends from my heart at that moment, and wished that I had never lost Praise God's friendship.

XXV

Balfour and the crone

On the fourth day after this unseemly event I travelled to Parliament in order to witness Pym placing the articles of impeachment before the Commons, and it was clear from this performance why he so needed one such as I by his side. He, although previously known for his fine oratorical skills, seemed on this occasion to be entirely lacking in self-confidence. There was a good reason for this. All of the accusations in the articles were ill-prepared, and not one of them on its own could be regarded as in any way treasonable. Pym knew this, and while he should have brought forward the accusations with a stinging blend of aplomb and vitriol, he instead appeared weak and defensive when Strafford's few friends in the House mocked him openly for what they rightly perceived to be an ill-prepared statement.

Pym, towards the end of his speech, looked at me imploringly. He sat down to the sound of half-hearted cheering and cat calling.

Realising his need for my support, I stood up.

"Mr Sykes," said the Speaker.

"Thank you Mr Speaker. Gentlemen, honourable Members: I perceive as I look upon you this day that there are some here that doubt the righteousness of our actions. Well you might think it a small thing, corruption; and that corruption is not High Treason. You might think it a small thing, bullying; and that bullying is not High Treason. You may even think that to threaten our shores with a foreign army does not amount to High Treason. But I say that when the corruption stretches to the impoverishment of this nation by the threatened debasing of its coinage - and the seizure of its bullion - for an ill-advised war against the King's Scottish subjects: this is High Treason. I would say that the threat to hang Englishmen for their opposition to an illegal and immoral tax, which led in turn to the fermentation of unseemly riots and death on our streets: that this is High Treason. Most of all (I took time to look around the chamber and enjoy the tension) I would say that to threaten this good Protestant people with the invasion of a Catholic Irish army: that *this* is High Treason!" (Some members started to cheer at this point - I waved them down). "But even if I am wrong; even if none of these things alone amount to High Treason, I tell you now by all that I hold dear - by peace, godly love and the fear of the Lord - put these crimes together and, yea gentlemen, I give you High Treason!"

This time I did allow them to cheer, and how they cheered. I left the Chamber soon after I had finished speaking, bathed in their manifest adoration. I was fortunate that day, in that I was wearing a large black Swiss cape that I had bought for several guineas a few days previously from my favourite tailor (the one I have mentioned as my costume provider for Richard Sykes' ball, who now dealt exclusively with Puritan gentlemen with an eye for fashion). I had not removed it before entering the Commons due to the cold weather, so I was able to sweep its right side over my left shoulder, giving my exit a touch of finesse, as well as grandeur.

• • •

Strafford was escorted from Black Rod's house to the Lords to hear the charges the following afternoon, and thereafter removed from his comfortable prison under the care of Maxwell, and confined in the Tower. But rumours soon began to circulate that even in the extremity of his misfortunes the King was still obtaining advice from him as to how to conduct the affairs of state. This correspondence was something that Pym and I determined to put a stop to as quickly as possible, for while they were in communication there was no telling what mischief they could hatch together; and it proved Pym's point that until Strafford was removed entirely his influence would remain undiminished. I personally petitioned the Lords to put a stop to his receiving visitors, but for his legal counsel, altogether.

The Lords were unwilling to agree to my requests entirely, but granted me access to Strafford's place of confinement at any hour of my choosing, with the right to search his rooms for incriminating documents, as well as his visitors.

My first meeting with Strafford in prison had not been a satisfactory experience. I ordered his door to be unlocked, then shoved it open with my foot and stood in the doorframe, my frame silhouetted by the light of the torch behind me. I was wearing my Swiss cape and my sword, and my hat was low over my eyes. But Strafford, who was writing at a desk opposite, merely looked up for a few seconds, and then, doubtless due to his custom of affecting superiority, carried on writing without acknowledging my presence.

This placed me in an irritable humour. I walked in, followed by Sir William Balfour, the Lieutenant of the Tower, and proceeded to traverse the large room, picking up books and papers, and casting them down. There was nothing to condemn the prisoner among them. There was, however, something about Strafford's total calmness that made me want to rile him.

"I wonder, Sir William, why it is that the prisoner is allowed so many privileges: know you what he is accused of?"

"Yes," returned the Lieutenant, "that is why he is allowed his books of law and his papers. He has to prepare his case. I believe that there are no restrictions placed upon his accusers. My Lord of Strafford's resources are, in comparison to yours, extremely limited. I have no instructions to withhold these from him. Have you brought any such instructions?"

I declined to answer. Strafford carried on writing.

"How many rooms has the prisoner at his disposal?"

"Three."

"You think this not somewhat excessive? Are you an inn-keeper or a jailer?"

Balfour became impatient, and began to speak to me with what I can only describe as a *nasal Scotch sneer.* "As Parliament has ordered that the prisoner must provide his own food I regard your inn-keeper taunt as *most* inappropriate. Your questions, moreover, appear to me to be somewhat *ultra vires.*"

"Beyond your powers," explained Strafford without looking up from his letter. "Or, in excess of your authority."

"I, *my Lord Strafford,* am a Cambridge graduate and can therefore assure you that I need no help with *my* Latin translation."

"Of course," he said, turning to me with a benign smile, "I have heard much of your university days: *parva leves capiunt animus.*"

I looked at him in silence, terrified that he would say something like 'Go on, what does it mean, then?' But he turned again to continue his letter.

I again addressed Balfour: "As you know I have been granted the right to check the identity, and search the person, of all of the prisoner's visitors, can you assure me that he is receiving no one after twilight, and that *all* his visitors are being searched thoroughly to prevent illicit correspondence."

"I can."

"Except for the crone, Balfour," said Strafford in a sardonic tone, "you must not forget the crone."

"Oh yes, his Lordship receives foodstuffs of an evening from a pox-ridden crone from the market; food that those of us in more fortunate circumstances would not touch for fear of the infection with which it is doubtless ridden. To this you have reduced his circumstances: his Lordship is so detested throughout the length and breadth of London that even a good servant cannot be found to bring him his necessary victuals."

"I would say that if *his Lordship* is detested throughout the length and breadth of London then he has no one to blame but himself."

"Yes indeed," sighed Strafford, "may I get on with writing this letter?"

"I expect *you,* Sir William, to inform me immediately if the terms of the prisoner's incarceration are in any way breached."

"That is somewhat impertinent, Sir," retorted Balfour.

"And in this matter you are under my authority, *Sir*. I have the right to check - without providing notice - that these terms are being adhered to. Rest assured I will not shirk my duty."

And with those words I left the room.

• • •

It appeared that Strafford's only regular contact with the outside world after I began my regular visits was, in fact, the old crone they spoke of; and I found it irresistibly amusing that the Earl was reduced to such desperation. She was, to me, the most revolting specimen of female humanity I had ever set eyes upon. She appeared to be about seventy years of age, although I could never fully see her face as she was bent over double, and supported her frame with a stick. She stank of stale wine, urine and excrement; and scratched her head, as well as her armpits and her backside, repeatedly as she hobbled along. The first time I saw her I was arriving at the Tower at nine of the clock at night on Christmas Eve. She was hobbling towards me over the drawbridge, so I decided to question her.

"Whither goest thou, Crone?" I asked.

Her stench was all but overpowering. "The evil earl," she muttered towards the ground.

"It is not fitting that *he* should receive anything of a special nature to celebrate the yuletide season. Pass me your basket."

She did so, and I nearly heaved on the spot. There was a leg of ham: rotten and infested with maggots; and a piece of fruitcake dumped in the middle of them, which was therefore also infested. There was also a three quarters full bottle of wine that looked like it had mould floating in it.

"Get thee hence, she dog!" I exclaimed with horror, as I shoved the basket back into her arms. "Take the Earl his *Christmas fayre* and be gone with you!"

She limped away, muttering, into the darkness.

• • •

Nota bene: Parva leves capiunt animus is roughly translated into 'Small things occupy small minds,' as I discovered later from a textbook I had kept from my schooldays: *Dr Hair's Amo Latin.*

XXVI

Westminster Palace and the Tower by night

I now had to busy myself constantly with preparations for the trial.
Such was the volume of work that was concerned in preparing state-
ments for our witnesses, that on the third day of Christmas I decided
to remain at Westminster and work into the evening. But my decision
to stay behind after the departure of the other members was not solely
based upon the necessity to work, for the wind and rain were rattling
against the window of the oak panelled room, making the prospect
of a return journey to Chelsea most unwelcome. I therefore placed
several logs upon the fire and prepared myself to work until slumber
overtook me.

But I soon became disconcerted by the ferocity of the storm,
which, having at first distracted me, began severely to affect my peace
of mind. I therefore decided to take a brief stroll around the offices of
my colleagues in the hope that one of them might share my solitude
with a cup of brandy. But I was soon forced to the conclusion that I
alone had chosen not to brave the elements. For as I traversed those
empty halls and passages, accompanied by no sound except the howl-
ing and shrieking of the wind, I saw no sign of activity apart from the
shadows thrown out by my flickering lantern. So unnerved did I then
become by the storm, and my solitude, that I contemplated the idea
of visiting the guards outside the palace. But as it was their duty to
stand outside *whatever* the weather, I decided that they might think it
somewhat strange my *choosing* to join them on a night like this for the

purpose of idle chatter. Besides which, having spent several hours with the rain trickling down the backs of their necks, they might not be in a very good humour.

So I returned disconsolately to the committee room and poured myself a drink. I then sat again behind the desk with the intention of resuming my work. This, however, soon became all but impossible, as the force of the storm, which was coming directly from the north (in which direction my room was facing) began to shake the window with great violence, as well as to blow the outermost branches of a tree against its opaque panes. This began to give me the unfavourable and yet overwhelming impression that a phantom was pounding and scratching at the glass in an attempt to get in. In my growing fear I started to imagine that this phantom was none other than my father who, having bided his time, had now decided to take advantage of my solitude by returning from the dead to mete out his ghastly and ghostly revenge. For this reason I dared not look in the direction of the window, but walked over to an armchair by the fire, into which I began to stare intently as well as recite psalms in an attempt to dispel my fear. But the words I spoke served only to bring me an even greater sense of terror.

And so it was that I found myself, after five minutes, rocking backwards and forwards on the large chair, stupefied by fear. The lightning flashes and thunder by then had the effect of making me moan, rather than scream, with terror; and when after about another ten minutes the window flew open and smashed onto the outer wall, I merely wept with self-pity. I eventually found the strength to get up and cross the room, lamenting my misfortune with bitter tears and chattering teeth; and then, as I leant outside to take hold of the handle of the swinging frame I saw something which did indeed make me scream. I saw the figure of an old woman staring at me from a west-facing window to my right. She was in a part of the building that protruded northwards at a right angle, about ten yards from where I was standing. I felt my heart leap into my mouth. I was struck dumb – unable to make a sound – with sheer terror.

Even then I might have been relieved from my fear if the old woman had done something human, such as wave at me (for she was clearly aware of my presence). But she instead did the very thing that had the power to petrify me the most: in the momentary blindness that followed a flash of white lightening, in which her ghastly features – her sunken eyes and her grinning black teeth – had been plainly visible, she vanished from the window.

Now panic consumed me. I ran to the door, determined to get out of that building as soon as possible. Yes I knew that I might meet the spectre by doing so, but at least by charging forth from the room I would not merely have to wait there for it to come to me on its own terms, in order to kill me with the power of fear, or overcome me with the assistance of demons.

But when I reached the door it would not open. I pulled and pulled but it would not give. It was jammed, or locked, or someone was pulling it fast from the other side. Now there was nothing I could do but let my terror overwhelm me. I started screaming uncontrollably, yanking at the door once more. It suddenly gave, and the force propelled me backwards, causing me to lose my footing and crack my head on the edge of the desk. In the delirium that followed, I thought beheld the ghost walk forward, gather my head in her arms and start stroking my hair – gently - as if to soothe me. I had no fear at that moment. If anything I was comforted, and felt a strange familiarity with my ghoulish companion.

But then I realised that the ghost was not alone. Someone or something had entered the room behind it. Its companion, who I could not see, suddenly knelt on the other side of me, held my nose back and started pouring brandy down my throat. I gagged at first, but the ghost held me fast while its companion forced me to drink until the moment when, just as I slipped away, I noticed a familiar smell of rotting meat.

A few hours later I awoke in a latrine about a hundred yards from the palace of Westminster, tied to the bars of a high window. My clothes were wet, and I was for this reason freezing (it was, you will remember, the end of December). I also had a pounding headache, and could tell by the stink of vomit - as well as brandy - on my clothes, that the last part – nay the whole – of my 'apparition,' had been no apparition at all.

I vomited again, although there was nothing whatsoever for my stomach to give forth apart from the most bitter tasting bile. My head pounded, and as I hung by my wrists from the bars of the window - my knees too weak to support me - I thought that it was just a question of what would kill me first: my illness (which was beyond compare worse than anything I had previously suffered), my raging thirst, or the intense cold.

After a half hour or so however, my strength returned sufficiently to enable me to stand, and as I did so the chime of the palace clock told me it was about four of the clock in the morning.

I started to shout for help. Eventually, as the storm had entirely abated, my voice carried to the guards at the north east gate of the palace.

They at first stood staring at me, confused in their astonishment (to be fair, it was not an everyday occurrence to find a member of Parliament tied fast to the bar of a window in a latrine). I demanded that they release me immediately, and that one of them accompany me back to the Palace.

My first impression as I entered the committee room was that all was well, as nothing seemed to be damaged. There were a number of loose papers on the floor, but the cause of this was just as likely to be the wind blowing through the broken window as any human (or ghostly) activity.

I also noticed that strange and unpleasant smell (the same that Pym had mentioned).

I now began to fear again, despite the evidence of brandy and vomit on my clothing, that the room was indeed haunted; and that the smell was the smell of death, left by the ghosts I had encountered on the preceding evening.

But having checked thoroughly to ensure that all was well, and having ascertained that nothing had been stolen, I began to reflect upon these matters, not least upon the fact that my ghosts were so *physical*. I was inclined not to tell Pym and my colleagues of my experiences. People now, as I write these memoirs in this new age of enlightenment, are much more sceptical when faced with questions of the supernatural.

But in 1640 such things were much more readily believed; and indeed (as you will remember from earlier in these papers) used as a means of destroying, or at least attempting to destroy – other people's lives. Moreover, Pym was a very practical man, and somewhat unpredictable in his reactions. He might decide - whatever the popular beliefs at the time - that I was deranged, and cast me aside in consequence.

So I decided to say nothing to anyone, including the guards who had rescued me from the latrine, and paid them a considerable amount of money to stay silent about what they had seen.

I then stayed away from parliament for a few days, until I had recovered from the blow to my head and the shock of my experience.

• • •

I became increasingly concerned as the day of Strafford's trial approached at his constant cheer in the face of his forthcoming ordeal, despite the fact that I had hindered him as much as was possible in his ability to prepare his defence. I would see him frequently as I visited the Tower, enjoying his daily exercises in the gardens, or writing letters in his cell, and never did I see him looking worried or cast down. I once, when listening outside his cell, heard him loudly asking Richard Lane, his leading counsel: 'How on earth he was supposed to prepare his case when Sykes had so harmed his ability to communicate with the outside world?' But in truth his demeanour never really reflected this concern; and I could not help believing, as I suspected he was aware at the time of my presence outside of the door, that his words, while ostensibly addressed to his lawyer, had really been intended for me.

Not that I was referring to his demeanour in any sense but a spiritual one, for on the thirtieth day of January he was finally brought to the House of Lords to hear the charges read against him, and as I waited among the crowd to see him led up the steps from the river it was impossible not to notice the destructive effect that two months in the Tower had had upon his already poor health. He was worn out, stooping, and both his hair and skin were grey. Unfortunately, I had long since, in expectation of this auspicious day, purchased a large quantity of fruit and vegetables and allowed them to rot in my scullery. I had instructed John Brown to distribute these to the crowd in order that they might use them to vent their hatred upon the Earl as an accompaniment to their shouted insults. The waiting people initially received these free gifts with enthusiasm, but the moment they saw Strafford, in the condition I have described, their resolution died away. As he stepped off the boat and onto Westminster Stairs the people fell silent. They started to drop the missiles I had provided for them, and some of the men even *removed their hats.* The ground soon became littered with discarded rotting fruit and vegetables (all but the ones the more desperate stuffed into their mouths); and they allowed him to walk past, in the company of his guards, without interference.

This in itself was nothing more than a small set back; and indeed I had only planned the hurling of these fruits and vegetables as a minor form of entertainment. I was more concerned with the business in hand. Half an hour after Strafford arrived at Westminster, having joined Pym in the House of Lords, I witnessed the first full reading of the charges. As I arrived there was a general hub of excitement and expectation. We stood around the main entrance with the many others who, although not members of the Lords, were involved in some capacity with the trial. After we had waited about five minutes Strafford was led in, and everyone, whether his friend or his enemy, was struck into silence by the change in his appearance.

The quiet was finally broken by the sound of Strafford's racking cough.

This seemed to awaken the Court, and a clerk immediately sprang to his feet and read the charges, which consisted of three accusations: that Strafford had fomented the war with Scotland, that he had encouraged the despotic stance of the King in order to assume the King's role personally; and that he had usurped parliament's authority in order to misappropriate the nation's revenue with a view to pursuing his evil policies. To the last was added the specific accusation that he had encouraged the King to call Parliament merely in order (by placing unreasonable demands before the Commons) to give the King an excuse to continue the harsh measures of his personal rule unrestrained and unchecked by Parliament in the future. He was also accused of having encouraged the King to dissolve the English Parliament before subsidies could be granted, while his real intention had been to use an Irish Army forcefully to subdue the English people.

Lord Manchester then stood and faced the prisoner. "You have been accused of many individual offences – amounting, it is alleged, to High Treason, what is your answer?"

Richard Lane, Strafford's leading counsel, sprang to his feet. "My Lord Manchester, it is impossible for my client to answer so many charges at once. His accusers have had many months to prepare their case…"

"Surely the prisoner needs no time to know whether he is guilty of that with which he has been accused?" interrupted Lord Yelvertoft from the benches, "a righteous man would need no such favours in order to prepare the answer 'yea', or the answer 'nay', to his accusers. Did I eat bread with my breakfast this morning? Yea. Did I eat mutton? Nay."

Strafford stood and faced Yelvertoft, his expression one of unconcealed contempt. "And did you have mutton or bread for breakfast on the thirteenth of July 1639? Would you like to inform us of what you ate for supper that day…and on April fifteenth, 1635? No? My Lords this is the power of recall that is expected of me. We merely ask for some time to prepare our answers to the charges."

"Oh we're going to have to do better than this," muttered Pym.

Manchester spent a short time in conference with some of the peers around him. He then turned to face Strafford.

"A fortnight," he said abruptly. He then turned to Sir William Balfour. "Sir William, if you would be so good as to escort the prisoner back to the Tower."

"But my Lord" exclaimed Lane, "this could lead to a gross injustice."

"There will be no injustice," interrupted Lord Manchester.

"How can he prepare a defence in such short time, and without fully knowing the details of the charges?"

Lord Manchester ignored him, and demanded again that Balfour return Strafford to the Tower.

Richard Lane again tried to protest, but before he could do so Strafford stood, smiled at him, bowed to the assembled peers, and departed from the Hall.

I left with John Pym, and we made our way to the committee room. Hampden was there along with several others.

"I would like to know," said Pym as he reached up to some documents on a shelf next to the window, "why it is that Strafford is so calm, considering…" He then looked at the papers with a curious expression, turned them over, and sniffed them. "George," he said to Digby, "have you been looking at these while eating your lunch?"

"Why do you ask?"

"Because you've spent the most time in here working; and because they stink of rancid meat, that's why."

"Well I haven't, and if I had they wouldn't smell of rancid meat."

"Does anyone here know about this?"

We all shook our heads.

"Methinks verily," said one of the more stupid members of the committee (doubtless hoping to ingratiate himself with Pym) "that the fact they relate to Strafford may be the cause of some spiritual putrefaction."

"Don't be stupid," answered Pym, "this is no spiritual putrefaction: they stink of rotten meat. Come on, someone must know about this?"

We again shook our heads.

"Digby, do you always lock these doors at night when you're the last to leave?"

"Of course I do."

"And the door is always locked in the morning?"

"Yes."

"Has anyone been in here recently while you were working?"

"No."

"Strode, you have been doing the cleaning – as you said you would?"

"Yes."

"And you haven't found any dead animals or anything… you must have noticed the smell."

"Well I did notice the smell, but I imagined the wind was blowing it from a slaughterhouse or something."

"Well I just want to know why these papers," replied Pym, his voice rising, "which we are going to have to present as the very crux of our case before the King, Lords and Commons, stink of rotten meat. How many keys are there for this room?"

Nobody answered. I could see Pym's temper waxing.

Pym turned to Digby. "Have you been bringing women here, Digby? Your morals are markedly suspect."

"Oh it's my women now. I eat rotten food and I'm attracted to women who smell of dead animals."

Pym started shouting then, and I decided to use the distraction to leave them to row amongst themselves. I was entirely unwilling, for reasons of which you are aware, to be drawn into their conversation.

I rode to the Tower to check upon my prisoner, and arrived there after an uneventful journey at about eight of the clock. I asked the guard at the main gate whether there had been any visitors for the prisoner and, receiving 'no' as an answer, walked across the draw-bridge, passing, as I did so, the old hag who was walking in the same direction.

After I had crossed, I stopped and watched for a moment as she shuffled passed me, bent nearly double to the floor, muttering to herself. After she had passed the guard at the inner gate I walked up to him.

"This great earl they have locked up in here," I said, "have you seen the filth that that old slut brings him to eat? You'd think he would have the sense to get one of his friends to bring the Lieutenant something half-decent for him - there's nothing to stop him. I nearly mingled the contents of my stomach with the stuff in her basket when she showed it to me at Christmas…"

Suddenly, in a moment of time, my mind became flooded with thoughts of horror and deep embarrassment. I somehow knew at that moment that the old hag, with her rotten meat and fruit cake, was the cause of the smell that had inexplicably made its way onto the papers in the committee room.

I sprinted after her, but was unable to catch her before she entered Strafford's cell. I therefore decided, rather than flinging the door open - which was my first instinct - to listen to their conversation from outside. I may after all have been wrong in my suspicions, and I did not wish to be embarrassed in another interview with Strafford.

But my suspicions were confirmed immediately. The 'hag,' believing she was safe, was no longer speaking like a hag. She now spoke in the voice of a young woman, and it took me no more than a few seconds to realise that the voice belonged to none other than Gwendolyn Smith.

"And this," I heard her saying, "is from his Majesty: Richard Sykes instructed me to tell you that despite your ill-treatment the King was much encouraged after hearing the charges against you, as there is clearly nothing in them that amounts to any type of treason. There is a picture there also, painted for you by the Princess Elizabeth to brighten your wall, although I suppose you'd better keep it concealed. The King begs that if possible you will grant him an answer by tomorrow evening in regard to the matter in the sealed letter. There is also another letter from Richard Sykes. There's some decent food hidden in here somewhere...here it is: I'll throw the rest of this stuff in the moat."

I heard nothing at first from Strafford, who I imagine was overcome by the messages of kindness that had clearly been hidden under the maggots and rotten meat, and whatever else had been carried in Gwendolyn Smith's basket. As for me, I started to walk rapidly backwards and forwards along the passage outside of Strafford's cell. I was overcome with shame and rage on several counts: the fact that Gwendolyn had so completely fooled me with her disguise, both here and at Westminster, where I had mistaken her for a ghost; that the smell of rotten meat on the papers in the committee room was clearly due to her having stolen them and passed them right under my nose and, above all, that by making it my personal responsibility to patrol the Tower, I had allowed her to make me into a laughing stock.

But for the moment I was undecided as to what to do. Should I wait there in the passage and confront Gwendolyn as she left Strafford's cell, or confront both of them together? I decided upon a third option: to wait across the drawbridge in order to accost Gwendolyn in the dark. By this means, I believed, I would either be able to claim all the glory for bringing about her arrest, or I would be able to demand any favours she might be willing to bestow upon me in order to avoid an inevitable curtailment of her liberty, or both.

As soon as I had made this decision I heard the sounds of Gwendolyn making ready to leave the cell. I therefore ran as quickly as I could down the stone steps, through the gardens, and out of the main gate on the eastern side of the Tower to the river, from which direction she had always arrived. I then hid on the far side of the draw-bridge in the dark shadow of the gate house.

I noticed, as I watched her five minutes later, hobbling through the gate and over the bridge towards me, that even though she was still affecting the guise of the old hag, Gwendolyn Smith still had an overwhelming power of attraction.

But I determined to wait until she was over the drawbridge and safely into the shadows of the outbuildings and trees opposite before I made any approach towards her. I was not worried about her scream-ing, for it was not my intention to attack her, but rather to persuade her as to the foolishness of *not* yielding to me; and I knew she would be unwilling to draw attention to herself anyway. Nonetheless, I wished to stay close enough to alert the guards if she found an opportunity to escape into the dark streets beyond us.

By the time she had reached the end of the drawbridge she had changed her walk from that of the old woman to her own, and by the time she had reached the shadows where I was standing, she had discarded her wig and stuffed it into her basket.

"Well, *serving wench*," I said, stepping out of the dark and placing my hands upon my hips, "this time you are truly in my power: the righteous arm of the Law hath found thee out!"

She started, and then spun round to face me. For a moment she was speechless.

"Do you know the penalties for transgressing a direct order from Parliament?"

She remained silent.

"I would say a hundred lashes and a night in the stocks would cover it."

"I, I would appeal to the King."

"Oh think not to get anything from *him*. Look how he has to use you to pass his messages back and forth. He is in the very lap of Parliament and will not dare cross its will openly unless Strafford wins his case, which he won't. And even if the King did try to raise some plea in mitigation before your judges, do you not think that such men, commissioned with the noble task of passing judgement upon you, would not set their faces like granite; steadfast as they would be in their determination to mete unto you the justice you so richly deserve?"

She wrung her hands. "Oh why have I been so foolish?" she wept, "I should have known that you would discover me sooner or later, what are you going to *do* to me?"

"I am going to accompany you back to the Tower, where I will keep you in confinement until I can ascertain Parliament's will for you…and until I have obtained from you – by whatever means necessary - the identity of the person who gave you access to the room in which our papers have been hidden."

"Oh I just know I am never going to see home again." said Gwendolyn. "The King and Strafford - and your cousin as well - they only used me because it mattered not to them whether I live or die."

"Think not to move me with your tears, Gwendolyn."

"There must be something I can do for you that would move you to deal with me sparingly, but I know not what." She wrung her hands again, looking at me imploringly.

I looked at her, shaking my head; but as I did so I looked down at the curve of her breasts. My intention was clear, and as our eyes again met, I knew that she understood what she must do to avoid the punishments I had at my disposal.

"There must be *something* I can do," she repeated. This time she was smiling at me coyly, walking slowly in my direction. She then stopped in front of me, her expression suddenly serious. She took my left hand and guided it to her right bosom.

Now, despite the stink I was immediately mesmerised, and started to squeeze her: softly at first, and then more rapidly and with greater urgency. She encouraged me by pressing my hand against her, and then parted her clothing, seemingly in order to allow me the freedom to touch her unhindered. I spoke to her as I touched her naked breast, but realised as I did so that my voice had become monosyllabic and expressionless, so hypnotised was I by the moment.

"The time has come, Gwendolyn," I said, "if you wish to avoid the destroying revenge of a wrathful parliament, to lie on your back in the position ordained for women to be the most expedient in the serving of their masters."

I then leant over and started to kiss her throat, my mouth slowly making its way downwards. As I did so I became so entranced that I failed to notice that she was reaching for something fastened by her belt to the inside of her ragged clothing.

After a few moments Gwendolyn gently placed her right hand under my chin and raised my head. Her mouth opened slightly, and she licked her bottom lip in a most seductive manner before leaning towards me. She then (and this all happened in a moment of time) leant forward, sucked my bottom lip into her mouth, and bit it so hard I thought she would take it off altogether.

Despite my shock I managed to wrench her off by pinching her nipple so painfully that she was unable to keep herself from screaming. I then pushed her over with a view to diving on top of her and pinning her down, but as I landed on the ground she managed to roll to one side, spring to her feet, and produce from her clothing an extremely long, thin and sharp dagger which, having removed from its scabbard, she pressed against the place where all men are most reluctant to sustain an injury.

"If you," she said, breathless and panting, as she rearranged her tattered clothing, "tell anyone…anyone, that you have seen me here, you will be killed. I will go from here and tell those that sent me that you discovered me, so that if I am taken at any time they will know it was you and they will kill you. Do you understand?"

"Yes," I said weakly (and what else, indeed, could I have said, with a knife pointed at my scrotum?)

She then stood up. "Here," she said, picking up the basket and producing the old wig, "you can have this as a keepsake; I shan't need it anymore." She then threw it at me and disappeared into the night.

I decided, as I gathered my horse and started the long journey home, to follow Gwendolyn's advice and tell no one of this evening's events. I realised that her threat had been anything but idle. Moreover, even if it *had* been but an idle threat, for me to tell of our encounter would merely have embarrassed me in several different ways, not least that it would become evident that it was in part due to my negligence that she had been able to convey to Strafford the very papers upon which the prosecution had prepared its case.

XXVII

The trial begins

Relations between the members of the committee set up to manage the prosecution, particularly between John Pym and George Digby, became somewhat strained in the last few weeks before the trial. We were all asked again whether we knew anything about the source of the smell, and I denied that I had spent any time alone in the committee room further than a few seconds after my colleagues left on the night of the storm. I pointed out to Pym that Digby had spent many hours alone in the room, but that we should not really condemn him as he had been working so hard. I suggested that he must have become overtired, and had probably forgotten to take home some meat he had bought from the market, which had rotted in consequence of this.

But I was aware that in reality I had mistaken Gwendolyn Smith for an old hag first, and then a ghost; and that she had been stealing the papers and then returning them, leaving only a stench from the rotten meat in her basket behind her. Our case was already very weak from a legal perspective, but now I realised it was almost certainly lost from the outset. It was some consolation to know that although it was my foolishness that was to lead the cause of this, it was also my wit that was going to save the day with the alternative, and fool-proof means, of using the Attainder.

On the twenty fourth day of February Strafford was brought before the Lords to formally answer the charge of High Treason. The King was present, accompanied by the Prince of Wales. Richard

Lane, as I expected he would, answered each separate charge with confidence, asserting that his client denied some of the charges on the grounds that they consisted of mere fictitious libel, and attempting to justify others on the grounds that he was merely doing his duty. He also pointed out that many prisoners who had been sentenced to death had thereafter had their sentences reduced to a few days imprisonment or a fine under Strafford's personal dictation. "I wonder," he muttered for all to hear as he finished speaking, "whether the Lord Strafford can himself expect such justice and compassion."

"We may be sure," answered Lord Manchester, "that this parliament, which is the envy of the world as well as the guardian of justice and righteousness in this land, will grant the prisoner a fair hearing."

Richard Lane again stood up. "Then with regard to the forthcoming trial...the Commons, we understand, are prepared to call many witnesses in support of their accusations. We also need to produce witnesses on behalf of the defendant, as well as to cross-examine those brought forward by his accusers."

Manchester crossed over to Pym, who was gesturing towards him.

"It would be most inexpedient for us," whispered Pym, "if Strafford were allowed to call his own witnesses. Doubtless they will be corrupt and willing to lie in the hope of gaining favour and preferment from the King."

"Yes, but it will look like a poor display of justice if we allow Strafford none of the advantages granted to *you*."

"If I may be so bold as to make a suggestion," I interjected, "as far as cross-examining our witnesses is concerned I see no harm in it. But several of these people, such as Sir Harry Vane, have said that they fear the spiritual consequences of inadvertently telling a lie due to their imperfect ability to recollect minute details. I would therefore propose that Strafford should be allowed to cross-examine our witnesses, but that they should not be required to answer his questions under oath, thus saving them from the fear of Divine Retribution. As far as Strafford's right to call his own witnesses is concerned, I would request, with the utmost humility, that your Lordships grant us some time to think upon this matter."

Lord Manchester looked at me keenly for a moment. He then glanced at Pym, who also looked in my direction, before nodding to him discreetly. Manchester then crossed the floor to his former position at the far end of the chamber

"We will affirm or deny your requests in due course," he said to Lane.

"But the trial…"

"Shall take place around the twenty second day of March."

"So we need more time…"

"We will affirm or deny your requests in due course," Manchester repeated. He then turned to the King: "By your Majesty's leave…"

But before the King could so much as nod in response, Manchester announced that the hearing was ended, and instructed Sir William Balfour again to 'Escort the prisoner to the place from whence he came.'

"The important thing," I muttered to Pym as we walked through the door and back towards the Commons, "is that we spend a good while – three weeks maybe - pontificating about Strafford's right to call his own witnesses, seeing as he will have to call many of them over from Ireland."

I then stopped him before we entered the chamber. Placing my hand upon his arm in the attitude of a disciple who has much to teach his master, and yet is too humble to reach for so lofty a part of the body as the shoulder, I said "There is one other very important thing that I would advise."

"Speak on."

"The actual piece of paper upon which Secretary Vane wrote his account of the Privy Council meeting: I would strongly advise you not to bring this out as evidence during the trial."

"Why do you say this?"

"I must just ask you to trust me in this matter. I cannot say the reason for now, but I believe that much should be made of Vane and his evidence during the trial, but the actual paper upon which it is written should be withheld. I will know when to produce it, and you will understand at the same time why it was right to do so."

Experience, by now, had taught him to trust me and he therefore asked me no further questions. In accordance with my plan we waited until three days before the commencement of the trial to tell the Lords, that having made up our minds, Strafford should be granted permission to call his own witnesses.

But as I have stated, I knew the trial, as well as our attempt to stifle Strafford's ability to defend himself properly, was now all but futile. But despite the fact that I knew that our only real hope was in the Attainder, as far as Pym still believed, the Attainder would hopefully be unnecessary, as Strafford would be tried and condemned by the court. But in order to really antagonise the King, as was my intention, the *sheer injustice* of the Attainder would be so much more effective.

"So," I said to myself with satisfaction, "by making the trial so much easier for Strafford it appears that Gwendolyn has inadvertently done me a service."

• • •

During this time I was relied upon to put the final touches to the case for the prosecution, as well as to give our witnesses the *non-legal* side to their briefing. Sir Harry Vane, who, despite his ability to show solidarity with Strafford when I was at their mercy at Whitehall, was torn between the desire to drop Strafford in it, and his fear of facing the never-ending displeasure of the King. He therefore proved very difficult; and in the face of this dilemma, to have lost entirely the cold authority I had encountered when I met him in the company of Anne Hussey. Pym and I interviewed him on March the fifteenth, and when we came round to the issue of Strafford's threat to 'Bring an Irish army to subdue this (or that) kingdom,' Vane started to wring his hands and whine that he 'did not know what to do.' This he did so often, and in a manner so irritating, that I eventually resorted to intimidation. I remembered, as I threatened him, the humiliation I had received at his hands in the presence of the King.

"If you do not say what we tell you to say, then I will be forced to spread it round this place that you were ready and willing to bear false witness against Strafford in court, but at the final moment were too afraid to do so. In speaking thus I will not only make you look like a coward and a fool, but I will be able to do so without departing one whit from the truth."

He looked at Pym, then at me, and then turned to Pym again. He finally stood up and walked out of the room muttering the words, "If only we could know what was going to happen, oh if only we knew what was going to happen."

• • •

Strafford, on a bright but icily cold day, was brought along the river from Traitor's Gate to Westminster Hall.

Pym and I were shown to our places about an hour before Strafford was due to arrive. We were accompanied by the official chairman of our committee, a learned Member of Parliament by the name of Bulstrode Whitelocke. George Digby was there also.

Only the few members of Strafford's counsel stood between us and the makeshift dock. We were ushered into a wooden enclosure to the north-east end of the Hall, at the front of about four hundred Members of the Commons; behind which were about fifty Scottish commissioners. Our enclosure was designed to give us exclusive access to an ante-room behind us, which had been placed at our disposal, not only with a view to our comfort, but, conveniently, as a waiting room for our witnesses. Beyond the members and commissioners were a mass of spectators who had managed to force or bribe their way in. Strafford was to take his place at the lower end of a raised platform which, on two levels, spanned half the length of Westminster Hall. Ahead of the dock on either side of the platform sat the peers: their positions allocated from the front according to their rank. Facing out from the platform towards them sat Strafford's judges. On an even higher platform sat the Earl of Arundel, who was to preside over the trial.

Strafford entered at five minutes before eight of the clock, and, as I had come to expect, was greeted by a silence that could almost be described as deferential, despite the number of his enemies who populated the Hall. He was dressed entirely in black, and wore the insignia of the Garter on the left breast of his cloak. Having looked about him he made his way slowly to the bar. The sound of voices, which had abated upon his arrival, then gradually began to rise again as we waited for the King and Queen.

About twenty five minutes later the sounds of voices again began to die away, and our attention was drawn by a movement in the Royal box behind where the peers were sitting. All who were sitting in the Hall stood up, including Lord Arundel, who, when the royal couple had seated themselves, began the proceedings.

"Thomas Wentworth, Earl of Strafford, you are called to this place to answer before your peers a charge of High Treason."

The charge was then read out in detail by the clerk of the Parliament. Strafford's rebuttal was read out in turn by Richard Lane.

Pym then stood, gave a cursory nod in the direction of the Royal box, and launched the first attack for the prosecution.

"It has been brought to our attention," he said as he traversed the length of the Hall, taking hold as he did so of the lapels of his gown, "that the Lord Strafford, in answering the charges brought against him, has referred many times to the *legality* of his actions. Your Majesty, Your Royal Highness, My Lords, Gentlemen: it is an evil thing for a man of power to use that same power to make cruelty a societal norm; to make avarice common place, and the crushing of the Common Man a run-of-the-mill-affair; so that this power usurps the law and wields itself arbitrarily by means, merely, of its own ubiquity; and then for that same man of power to state, when faced with his accusers, that he was *acting in accordance with the law.*"

He turned and pointed at Strafford. "Acting in accordance with the law? Acting in accordance with *his* law maybe, but what *was* the law to this man…this *lord?* Did he not say that the little finger of the King is heavier than the loins of the law? Did he not usurp the Royal Prerogative and use it to his own ends; to increase his barns, and to enrich his fields, and to lay a heavy burden upon the English and Irish people; and then, when such things had become so commonplace that the very judiciary were infected with his love of power, then say that he was *acting in accordance with the law?*"

He paused for a moment in order to give full effect to his words.

"I must warn you, my Lords, not to be lulled by any such argument. My Lord Strafford has taken as much care - has used as much cunning - to set a face and countenance of honesty and justice upon his actions, as he has been negligent to serve the rules of honesty in their performance. Think what the law was before this prisoner was able to distort it through its constant transgression, and then say that he has acted in accordance with the law."

When Pym had finished this speech he asked leave to call the first witnesses for the prosecution. Upon receiving a nod of assent from Lord Arundel he turned to face the gallery. "Sir Piers Crosby..."

Now here was another reason I knew the trial was likely to flounder from the outset. Pym had insisted on calling this old enemy of Strafford's from Ireland to testify. The fact that Crosby had lost a very public civil trial against Strafford previously, and had publicly sworn revenge against him in consequence, would obviously make him a very poor witness, was entirely ignored.

"My Lords," said Strafford, rising from his chair, "I hope that the Prosecution are not going to base their whole case on the testimony of my sworn enemies. This man has been discovered as a willing perjurer; and has since desired my destruction. I think the facts of that case are well known to this court."

"Yes, my Lord Strafford," said Lord Arundel, "they are well known to this court." He then looked to his right and left and, deciding that the peers probably agreed with Strafford on this point, told Pym to skip Crosby and call his second witness.

This was no small victory for Strafford. From then on he raised no more objections to the calling of our witnesses, but as they were all so clearly of the same mould as Crosby, we started to look like we were deliberately calling everyone we could who had a personal reason to desire Strafford's downfall.

Pym finally returned to our enclosure, while one of our lawyers, John Glyn, stood to take over.

"We request the Court's permission to read the remonstrance recently passed by the Parliament in Dublin."

"That is not in the charge!" protested Strafford, rising to his feet, "there was no mention of that in the charge."

"...Which is hardly surprising," John Glyn continued, "seeing as we only received news of this remonstrance after the charge was formulated."

Strafford made a great display of his astonishment at this answer. "I cannot, and would not, accuse my accusers of falsehood," he said, "but I received a request to answer the remonstrance of the Irish Parliament whilst I was in the custody of Black Rod. This was as long ago as...the end of November...I cannot see how this can have escaped you. There is clearly a conspiracy here."

Pym immediately jumped to his feet. "My Lords, these words are not to be suffered. The Commons are not on trial here, and yet the prisoner accuses us of conspiracy. We desire your Lordship's justice in this!"

Strafford replied "My Lords I ask you to forgive my inappropriate outburst. But the honourable Gentleman has mistaken me: I meant nothing worse than that I was surprised that my prosecutors, who *are* the Commons, had not heard about the Irish Remonstrance. An accusation of neglect does not amount to an accusation of conspiracy. In using the word conspiracy I was referring to the Irish, who produced the remonstrance."

Another easy victory for Strafford, I could see the King smirking discreetly.

So the remonstrance from Ireland was read out, but its effect on the trial was questionable. It was meant to have plunged a sharp dagger into the defence, but Strafford had successfully blunted it before it was even read to the court. Our witnesses then continued to support the articles of the remonstrance with accusations, none of which seemed strong enough to stand up to cross-examination, and after a few hours of this their accounts of the violence and general wickedness of Strafford and his henchmen began to sound repetitive and dull. I looked about the Hall, and like many of the spectators my mind began to wander away from the proceedings. Our attention was eventually drawn back when Strafford rose to answer Pym's accusations.

"These *witnesses* have brought evidence against me that cannot easily be checked; and as their testimony cannot easily be checked it cannot easily be proved. And the burden of proof, if we have not decided to dispense altogether with the Common Law, rests upon you, the prosecution."

"As far as the Irish Remonstrance is concerned: the same people who drew up that paper praised me but eleven months ago for applying the very policies to Ireland for which they now hope to see me condemned. They praised me because they hoped, in me, to have a champion for their ruthless corruption. They vilify me now because I would not. They pretend that their policies are one thing, when in truth they have merely modified them for the purposes of this trial. This is a conspiracy. I stand by what I said."

Pym stood once more to make sure that he, and not Strafford, had the last word. He said that Strafford may have been able to defend himself very eloquently against generalities, but the more specific charges to follow would prove his undoing.

Despite this last salvo however, it was easy to see who had won the first day.

XXVIII

Constructive treason

T he next day John Glyn began proceedings.

"Your Majesties, my Lords and Members of the Commons, the Lord Strafford has been partially correct in the defence of his actions. He has asserted that many of the things of which he stands here accused have been perpetrated by his own accusers, and that nothing of which he is accused in itself amounts to treason. But I say to you all: we are here to try him for the whole of his actions, and the effects of his actions upon the nation as a whole. Nay, we are not concerned with trivialities here. We will show that by a series of measures the defendant has undermined the relationship between the King and his Parliament, and by that token the King and his people. We will show that the defendant has placed his own ambition above the peace of this nation, and that he has antagonised the peace-loving Scots into a war against this country, with whom they normally live side by side in harmony and mutual understanding."

This last remark caused a great deal of scornful laughter in the Hall, not least from the contingent of Scottish ministers.

I thought for a moment that apart from his stupid closing remark about the Scots this acidic attack might herald a change in the fortunes of the prosecution. Unfortunately this thought lasted only seconds after his speech, for he then had to start examining the articles of impeachment. The first of these created yet more humiliation. It referred to Strafford's tenure as President of the North. Strafford,

according to Glyn, had persuaded the King to greatly increase his powers, something which should not have been done without the consent
of parliament. "These increased powers," Glyn said, "were used to…"

Strafford was on his feet again. "I must beg the court's pardon, but
I fail to see the relevance of this. I persuaded the King to grant these
powers to the Court in the North *after* my tenure as Lord President,
and at a time that Parliament was not in session."

Now, at this moment, had Glyn been of a slightly quicker wit, he
would have moved hastily on to the next matter. But Strafford's unexpected statement flustered him.

"But it says here that these increased powers were used by you
to…"

"If there are any specific accounts of any action perpetrated by
me, for good or evil, under the increased powers granted to that Court,
then those accounts have been falsified. This I can easily prove. But it
ill serves my purpose to interrupt you. Pray continue…"

Glyn did not continue, but it was obvious from his discomfort that
he did have a number of 'specific' accounts, and it was also obvious to
all those present that the Commons had falsified the contents of the
very first article.

During this altercation I could see that Pym, who was on my left,
was beginning to display signs of tension.

"Who was responsible for the contents of that article?" he asked
in an unnaturally calm voice, as his hands gripped the wooden rail in
front of him.

"George Digby," I lied.

Pym's nails dug deeply into the wood.

"I think we had better get to the meat of this," I said to him quietly.

He looked at me for a moment, then nodded and rose to his feet.

"We would ask the Court to ignore the defendant's attempts to
explain away the accusations in the individual articles, and to view the
charge, as a whole, as an accumulation of wrongdoings, which, therefore, when taken together, amount to one charge…of *constructive, or
constructed, treason.*"

"Oh, *now* I understand," said Strafford as he rose unsteadily to his feet, "*constructive* treason, of course. How could I forget such a long-standing principle of our law? A treason which is made up many lesser faults and crimes; or a felony made up of several misdemeanours. We should put this principle into greater usage. I will write to my wife and tell her to warn the village children that if we find them pilfering our orchards *one more time*....then we will have them charged with murder."

Pym was just about to reply when Lord Yelvertoft's nasal voice resounded from the back of the Hall, "Peradventure," he rasped, "the Lord Strafford would do well to stand before this court with humility and a visage which betokes repentance, rather than resorting to sarcasm, which, as wise men of yore have said on divers occasions, is the wit of the devil."

Yelvertoft paused momentarily. It was plain that he intended to continue speaking, but Pym tried to interrupt his progress.

"If Lord Straff...."

"He would do well also to remember," Yelvertoft butted in, "that where an analogy might serve him, one might also serve his opponents. He speaks, mockingly, of the pilfering of his orchards as amounting in its gravity to murder on the part of the perpetrators of that crime, when repeated, as if that were a suitable comparison to the much weightier crime of constructive High Treason. But I say that in order to understand the crime of constructive High Treason one would be better served in looking at the ingredients of a pie. Individually those ingredients do not make a pie, but together they do make a pie."

Now that (I had to hand it to him) was quite a good argument, even if it did come from a lunatic.

But then Lord Yelvertoft looked around the Hall and, with a twinkle in his eye, added "And as far as Lord Strafford's neighbouring village children are concerned, may I point out to the noble earl that he doesn't have to charge common children with murder to have them hanged, as the children of the village of Yelvertoft discovered to their cost five years ago when I caught *them* pilfering apples. I do not have a problem any longer with apple stealing on *my* land."

Lord Yelvertoft then sat down with the air of somewhat who believed he had shared an amusing anecdote with an appreciative audience.

Pym looked rather deflated at this. Whatever he had been intending to say beforehand was never said. He glared at Yelvertoft, and sat down.

"As I said," said Strafford, addressing the Court as a whole, "a new treason I have never heard of before." He then sank tiredly to his seat.

"I think, as it is now five of the clock, that this would be a suitable time to adjourn until tomorrow morning," said Lord Arundel. He then stood up and bowed to the royal box. The King in turn stood, returned his bow, and left the Hall quickly.

• • •

Over the next few days it became clear that the majority of those who had made no prior decision as to Strafford's guilt or innocence began to be swayed by his arguments, or by the poor performance of his opponents. While the prosecution had begun the trial with the confidence of those who believed that Right was on their side, as time went on we began to start looking desperate.

As far as *my* plans were concerned, things could not be going better. The prosecution had all but exhausted their stock of arguments, and they were now going to have to place much importance upon the 'evidence' of Sir Harry Vane. It had become all but inevitable that the Commons would, in order to avoid ultimate humiliation, have to rely upon the Attainder to bring about Strafford's death. If the King refused to sign the Bill then he would set the people irreversibly against him. On the other hand, if the King were forced to sign the Bill he would never forgive those who were responsible for making him sacrifice the man who had become his strongest supporter, while at the same time infringing upon his 'divine right' to rule without hindrance. I was not so foolish as to think that Strafford's death would lead directly to civil war; but oh how easy it would be to push the King, who had been pushed so far already, just a little further; and how ready and willing would be the Commons, once they had tasted the blood of Strafford, to do the pushing.

Nota bene:

The more sensitive of my readers will be relieved to know that Lord Yelvertoft was arrested the moment he left the chamber of the House of Lords, and placed in the Tower of London pending a multiple charge of infanticide.

XXIX

The trial collapses

O n the fifth day of April the Commons decided to mount what was generally regarded as the centre of their attack. The first nineteen articles had now been covered without us laying a serious blow upon Strafford. The next five dealt with the accusations that Strafford had encouraged the King to wage war against the Scots, and that he had told the King 'to take money from the Treasury as he needed it if Parliament failed him.'

Glyn began to lay these charges before Strafford, and he, unwilling to accuse Glyn directly of falsehood, resorted to sarcastic congratulations upon his witnesses' perfect recall of the precise words of conversations of which he 'could not remember the substance, let alone the detail.'

I watched this exchange from the vantage of our enclosure, where behind me Sir Harry Vane was receiving his final instructions from Pym. At fifteen minutes past eleven the door of the witnesses' room was thrown open, and Pym called me in.

"Help me drag him out!" .

"But the King is present…please," Vane begged.

"Why should you fear to speak the truth in front of the King?" I asked as I approached him.

He answered nothing at all, but folded his arms with a defiant expression, in the manner of someone who, having run out of arguments, has determined to rely on sheer stubbornness as his only means of effective resistance.

But I took a firm hold of his elbow and started to lead him, with some degree of force, towards the door. With Bulstrode Whitelocke preceding us, Pym grabbed his other arm, and by the time we had got him through the door and into the view of those outside, we had managed to take a firm enough hold of him to give us the freedom to disguise our actions as those of the friendly and concerned supporters of a man we wished to support in his performance of a duty he found most painful, but which righteousness rendered necessary. We let him go at the foot of the platform and, as I watched his trembling figure walk up the steps to the witness stand, I made sure my face displayed the sort of reverential expression we reserve only for those we respect and admire most deeply.

As soon as Vane collected himself, Pym started to question him.

"There was a meeting of the Privy Council on the same day as the dissolution of the last Parliament, was there not?"

"There was," answered Vane. His eyes darted around the Hall as he spoke, his hands clenched tightly together in front of him.

"You were present at this meeting?"

"Of course, I am the Secretary." Vane's eyes rested momentarily upon Pym as he said these words, then darted away again.

"And was the Lord Strafford present?"

"He was."

"The Council will have been occupied primarily with the parliament just dissolved, and the continuing problems north of the border?"

A somewhat superfluous question, I thought. Pym paused briefly to allow Vane to nod in answer.

"What was the Lord Strafford's advice to the King and the Council concerning these matters?"

"My Lord of Strafford said…" began Vane. He then fell upon his knees.

"Please believe me, your Majesty, my Lords, I have never in my life loved to tell an untruth. It is for this reason that I am here, to tell the truth as is required of me by…"

"Would you please answer the question? (This was Lord Arundel). Kindly get up off the floor and answer the question."

Vane stood up, composed himself, sat down again, and answered: "Lord Strafford, addressing the King, said: 'Your Majesty, having tried all ways, and being refused, in this case of extreme necessity, and for the safety of the Kingdom, is acquitted before God and man; and you have an army in Ireland which you may employ here to reduce this Kingdom,' or some words to this effect."

Until the moment Vane added the words 'or some words to this effect,' the effect of his account could have been the more harmful for Strafford than anything spoken at the trial thus far. Few people can have realised that he was likely to be accused of something as grievous as a direct threat against England by an army from overseas. This might have been the first real strike against Strafford had Vane not allowed his paralysing self-doubt get the better of him.

He then, momentarily, managed to gain some confidence. "It is true that Lord Strafford said the words 'you may.' What he meant by them I cannot say, but it is true that he said them."

"Sir Henry," continued Pym, "the most important question regarding Lord Strafford's words concerns the word 'here' and the word 'this.' Are you certain that the words the Lord Strafford used were '*here* to reduce *this* Kingdom?'"

"I am."

Richard Lane interrupted. "Are you sure - it has been almost a year - that he might not have said '*Here* to reduce *that* Kingdom,' or even '*There* to reduce *that* Kingdom?' Or, to place the question into context, are you sure that as the country under discussion was Scotland, that the Lord Strafford, even if he did say '*here* to reduce *this* Kingdom,' was not using the word *this* in a sense of *this country under discussion* as opposed to *this country we are in as we speak?*"

"I am certain that the interpretation I have placed upon Lord Strafford's words is the correct one."

"You seemed less certain when you started to give evidence. How can you remember what he said, word for word, after so long, and how can you be so sure that your interpretation of his words is the correct one?

But before Vane could answer, Pym spoke again. "Sir Harry Vane has stated, quite emphatically, that Lord Strafford said '*Here* to reduce *this* Kingdom.' We have no reason to doubt his word. The question is therefore quite simple: whether *this* Kingdom be *this* Kingdom?"

This last remark may have improved matters slightly, but it was easy to see that we were not going to get very far if, on the very rare occasion that something was said to the prosecution's advantage, Strafford and Lane were so easily able to tear it to pieces.

Lane then called Lord Cottington, one of Strafford's few remaining allies on the Privy Council.

"Were you also at the meeting of the Council in question?"

"Yes."

"Did you," asked Lane, "on that or any other occasion, hear the Lord Strafford suggest anything to the King that could be construed as a suggestion that he should import an army from Ireland to subdue England?"

"No."

"What can you remember of Lord Strafford's advice to the King at that meeting?"

"He said that the King, who needed to put down a rebellious and hostile army of Scots, was now entitled to raise money by his own royal authority, as parliament had proved unwilling to do so. I must remind this court that this country *was* invaded by the Scots, and that it was therefore the King and his advisers, not the Commons, who were proved correct in this matter."

Pym was on his feet again.

"History will record, Lord Cottington, that it was not the policies of the Commons that pushed Scotland to war!"

"Then you must be admitting, Mr Pym, that Lord Strafford is now being accused of nothing other than recommending a lawful course of action to the King, unless you would like to suggest openly that he should be a scapegoat for the policies of your political opponents. You say that the war in the north was caused by the bad policies of others, while others believed *your* policies were bad, and, moreover, that your policies prevented the king from effectively performing his duty to suppress unlawful rebellion. Who is right? And why should one man go on trial for his life in order to discover the answer? Are you offering anyone on your side for trial?"

"Do not be so foolish," growled Pym, "it was not our policies…"

"This is the point," returned Cottington, "the prisoner is on trial for opposing your policies."

This argument continued until Lord Arundel announced that the court would adjourn until the morning after the day following, and I decided, with the prospect of the Commons facing an imminent humiliation, that the time had come to complete the details of the Bill of Attainder. I therefore arose early on the morning following and put the final touches to the Bill, ready for its announcement in the Commons. This took all day and most of the evening.

I then wrote to Compromise-not-at-all Jenkins, who was likely to be essential to my plan for the close of the trial.

• • •

By the time I arrived at Westminster Hall the following morning proceedings were already underway.

"We have evidence, irrefutable evidence," Glyn was saying, "that after the dissolution of the last parliament you threatened to hang the aldermen of London for their opposition to the payment of ship money."

"I cannot and would not deny it, Strafford replied, "It is exactly the sort of thing I might have said in a moment of exasperation. I can no more excuse it than I would any foolish, hasty word spoken in a heated moment. Touching the Ship-money itself: I was responsible, it is true, for prosecuting people for withholding Ship-money, but never since the tax became illegal. This cannot, surely, be part of your *constructive treason*, that I enforced a legal tax."

"A legal tax it may have been, but would it have been legal had you not advised that it should be so?"

"So, am I on trial for the advice I have given in council?"

Glyn made no attempt to answer this with anything other than a scowl. He then returned to the enclosure, and, while everyone in the

Hall waited, started to engage in a heated argument with Pym, stating that the time had come for the prosecution to rest its case altogether. Pym, who must have at least suspected that the trial was slipping away from us, was nonetheless desperate to continue. Lord Arundel ordered them to hurry up.

I leaned over to John Glyn. "We must not let Pym or anyone call more witnesses," I whispered, "Strafford is going to win this trial and make public fools of all of us in the process."

Glyn looked at me gravely for a moment. He then nodded resolutely, and stood as soon as he judged it likely he would be heard above the noise. He addressed Lord Arundel.

"We wish to call no more witnesses. We would ask you to instruct the Lord Strafford to say anything he has to say in his defence, now. I will then sum up for the prosecution."

Strafford protested, and Lord Arundel ordered that Strafford should be given three days to prepare, then adjourned the court.

This may have been a welcome reprieve for Strafford, but it also gave me enough time to put into practice my final plan for the end of the trial, of which I had now heard quite enough. Compromise-not-at-all Jenkins arrived at my house as requested, for once without the company of his friends. I knew he would be willing to impart any information to the court of which I chose to instruct him - for a sum. I told him to meet me on a corner of Tuttle Street on the morning of the tenth of April, the day the trial was due to resume. I thought it unlikely, for reasons which will soon become apparent, that he would be called as a witness, but I needed him to be prepared for the possibility.

• • •

On the morning of the tenth of April I arrived early at our designated meeting place and, having greeted Jenkins briefly, I told him that if he was called, to say to the court that he had been instructed to give evidence by Lord George Digby. This 'evidence' being that during the last summer he had seen Lord Strafford conversing with a Jesuit priest, in sinister undertones, in the cloisters of Westminster Abbey, before receiving from him two large sacks of gold coinage. I also told him to say, if he was asked why he had not presented this evidence to Digby or anyone else sooner, to look his questioner boldly in the eye and say 'Verily, I informed Digby of these facts last August!'

I was aware in doing this that a report from as shifty looking a man as Jenkins would serve for nothing but to make us look like we actually *hired* witnesses (or at least Digby did), and doubtless at the cheapest rate going. But whether Jenkins would be called as a witness or not, I needed someone to place at the centre of blame for the inevitable collapse of this trial, and Digby was clearly the man for the moment.

Having instructed Jenkins to wait in the Palace Yard, I arrived in the Hall just as Strafford was making ready to speak. I approached Glyn, and whispered into his ear.

"Digby has told me he has a witness who is able to provide fresh and vital evidence that Strafford has been seen receiving large bribes from a Spanish Jesuit. I have now met this witness myself. He is loitering outside. Digby says this witness has enough to convict him without fail. He says that it vital that you call him to take the stand before Strafford is given the opportunity to speak. Do not fear that Strafford will have anything at his disposal to answer these new allegations. Make haste!"

Glyn looked over to Strafford and, seeing that he was standing up, jumped quickly to his feet.

"My Lord," he shouted, waving at Lord Arundel, "we would seek your permission to call a new witness."

Lord Arundel was momentarily at a loss as to how to respond. "But you said…"

Strafford intervened.

"If they, at this stage of the trial, are allowed to produce new evidence, having told me to prepare my final defence, then surely I must be granted the same liberty."

Arundel considered for a moment. He then adjourned the court for fifteen minutes in order to make a decision.

"Right," said Glyn, turning round, "where is this witness?"

"What witness?" asked Pym.

"The witness Digby spoke to you about, Sykes. Where is Digby?"

"Up there" I replied, pointing to the crowd of members.

Now there are some things in life worth making personal, life-long enemies over, and this was one of them.

Glyn climbed the stairs to where Digby was standing, and began to speak to him. It was plain, even though I could not hear them, what they were saying.

"Where is this witness?"

"What witness?"

"The witness you told Sykes about."

I was torn between amusement at the spectacle, and apprehension at the scene that was about to unfold.

"What witness was Glyn talking about?" Pym asked me.

"Some witness of Digby's knows something about a Jesuit priest paying Strafford, or something."

Glyn and Digby both started to walk down the steps to where we were standing.

"Glyn here says you told him I said something about a new witness."

"Yea brother," I responded, "but twenty minutes since. You spoke of the witness who saw Strafford with the Jesuit. The same witness, you said, as the one now outside awaiting our summons."

"I am not your brother, peasant, and I said no such thing. You are a liar!" He turned to the group gathered round. "He is lying, I know not why, but he is lying."

"I am no peasant, unless, in your opinion, a peasant is someone brought up to love the truth, as was I. I believe you are mischief making, Sir. You spoke to me of this new evidence and this new witness. You then deny that you have done so after my relaying this information to Mr Glyn has had its effect, its detrimental effect, upon this trial."

"He's right, Digby," said Pym, You have been nothing but a thorn in our side since the start of this, and I'm beginning to wonder whose side you *are* on. Do not think we don't hold you responsible for this mess. First there's that stink in the committee room..."

But at that moment Digby, as I knew he would at some point, lunged at me. Fortunately there were enough men around to ensure that he was restrained and forced to the floor.

My voice shook with emotion. "I must ask you, brethren, but one question: who in your opinion has proved to be the most trustworthy before this moment: this gentleman, or me? I have nothing else to say. I know not why he has said this when now he denies it. The witness is outside waiting."

It can only be described as a remarkable example of self-restraint that I managed to keep myself from laughing out loud as Digby was then dragged out of the Hall, cursing me as he went.

But his departure did not solve the prosecution's problem with the fact that although we had called, or nearly called 'Digby's' witness, the value of whose evidence was a mystery to all but me, Glyn's calling him so hastily (as I had prompted him) had prompted Strafford to call his own witnesses also. These witnesses would certainly bring about the final collapse of the trial.

"What are we going to do?" whispered Glyn urgently.

"Sykes, what shall we do?" added Pym.

"We must wait to see what Arundel says."

They had no time to discuss this before Lord Arundel resumed his seat and an usher called for silence.

"If the Commons are allowed to raise new evidence," said Lord Arundel, "the defence should be allowed the same privilege."

"Might I call my own witnesses to defend me on any of the charges, or merely the ones re-opened by the prosecution?" asked Strafford.

"He's bluffing, he hasn't got any new witnesses - he couldn't have," I muttered loudly enough to be heard by my neighbours. "He's banking on the fact that *we* haven't got any more witnesses, or any decent ones."

"Aye, he's bluffing," repeated Pym.

Of course I alone knew that Strafford, at a much earlier stage, had gained access to the prosecution's papers, and that being thus aware of our intentions, he had had much longer than the prosecution believed to bring as many witnesses as he wanted, and from as far away as Ireland. I was almost certain therefore that he was *not* bluffing.

"The Lord Strafford may call witnesses on any of the charges," said Lord Arundel.

Now, really, the outcome of the trial was entirely at my disposal, or rather, the mode of our defeat was at my disposal. We could call this great witness, Compromise-not-at-all Jenkins, and pit him against all of Strafford's witnesses, thereby dragging the trial out further. But as I have stated, I had had enough of it. The time had come, I decided (to use a nautical term) to *abandon ship*.

"He *must* be bluffing," I whispered urgently, "he has no new evidence."

But Strafford was entirely calm, and looked anything but like a man whose life depended upon the success of a single deception.

Glyn considered for a moment. If, as he was thinking, he called 'Digby's' witness, and Strafford could not counter any new allegations or produce any new witnesses, then Strafford's defence would, even at this late stage of the trial, be lost. If, on the other hand, Strafford *could* provide witnesses there was no telling what further damage he could do.

"He must be bluffing," muttered Glyn as he stood. Then, to the Court, he said, "We will proceed immediately to our new evidence. Call…"

But before Glyn could finish his sentence Strafford was on his feet. Then I would like to call Sir Edward Hyde, Lord Powerscourt…"

"He wasn't bluffing," Glyn muttered, his face ashen.

"No he was not" I said. "We must withdraw immediately."

Suddenly, every member of the prosecution's team, as well as its supporters, became aware that our case was about to, publicly – and most humiliatingly - collapse. A murmur rose from the ranks of the Commons: "Withdraw!"

"Withdraw now!" I shouted, and at these words we started to scramble for the door, desperate to get out in case Lord Arundel refused to halt the proceedings. The hall descended into chaos, with dignified Lords and Members of the Commons fighting to get out. As I pushed my way through I saw Strafford and the King exchange glances, it was one of the few times I ever saw the King laugh, and it was probably the last time Strafford laughed at all.

XXX

Cum finis est licitus, etiam media sunt licita

It was one thing, I realised, to have gained my reputation by denouncing Strafford and Laud on the floor of a sympathetic House of Commons, but to become known as the man personally responsible for bringing about Strafford's death would attract an altogether different level of renown. Pym, I decided, could produce Vane's evidence. Just as the spoken evidence had failed because it had been produced by the weak and hesitant words of Sir Harry Vane, the production of written 'evidence' at this stage would justify the Commons in doing away with Strafford by means of the Attainder.

As well as this, however, I also needed to find someone to produce the Bill itself, as I knew that Pym would be unwilling to introduce the evidence as well as the Bill for fear of an accusation of vindictiveness. As soon as Strafford's trial had been abandoned I moved with the crowd from Westminster Hall to the Commons, where the members were assembling. All of them were hotly disputing the events that had just occurred, and most of them were blaming the prosecution for allowing Strafford to get the better of them.

I scanned the room for the most indignant looking member, and settled my eye upon a certain Sir Arthur Hazelrig, who was renowned for his hatred of all those who had advised the King during his personal rule, and who was manifesting this hatred by shouting at a group of about eight puritan members, most of whom were nodding slowly whilst stroking their chins. I tapped him upon the shoulder.

"What do you want?"

"Merely to say to you, Sir Arthur, that were I to produce one more thing against the Lord Strafford, then my mind would accuse me of an absence of Christian charity. The cause against him is a just one, and should not be conducted by bitterness, but by the Sword of Truth."

"What the hell are you talking about?"

"I have done enough against Strafford; I can do no more…"

"I am in no mood for…"

"…And yet Strafford must die, and I have the means here at my disposal by which God intends to wield His judgement."

I produced from my pocket the prepared Bill of Attainder and handed it to him carefully. I let him read for a moment in silence.

"Yea, by this means," I continued, "we need not find Strafford guilty in open court, but merely judge him in accordance with divine inspiration. And yet, I wish to hold back my arm from his destruction, even though to produce this Bill before the Commons would be an honour…an honour indeed."

"You want me to do it."

"Yes I do – Pym is about to produce some new evidence, the Bill should be produced straight after."

"This will work? You are sure?"

"It will."

"Very well, but…"

"A wise decision; if you would please hand me back the Bill I will return it to you in the Chamber."

Before he had time to think too much upon the point, I snatched the document from his hand and walked quickly towards Pym, who had just entered the chamber.

"Where the hell is Digby? I'm going to kill him! I want an explanation for all of this. We've lost, and thanks to your ill-conceived advice we've lost without even producing Vane's evidence…"

"Not so. We have not lost. Our case was somewhat weak, and, worse, it was seen to be weak. If we had produced the copy of Vane's evidence it would have been held up to the same sort of ridicule as our witnesses. You and I both know that that document would never have stood up to close scrutiny."

He said nothing, so I continued.

"Have you ever thought," I asked, "about the means by which certain monarchs of yore put their opponents to death?"

He looked at me blankly.

"They used to use their parliaments as a tool for their will, did they not?" I said.

"As *our* beloved king still hopes to do."

"Indeed, and yet, what I am asking is...by what means, do you know, did kings such as Henry VII do away with their opponents when they could not altogether prove that they had specifically broken the law?"

"By...making Parliament pass a Bill....a Bill of Attainder!"

"Quite so, and if we produce the evidence from the Privy Council meeting now, then it will be much more effective than if we had done so at the trial. The defence would have torn it to pieces, and we would then have had nothing left with which to convict Strafford. He would have won, the King would have won, and together they would have destroyed us one and all!"

I left him no time to express what would doubtless have been another torrent of gratitude at my ready fount of wisdom, and instead added "But such a Bill cannot be passed without the assent of the King, so we must ensure that we place him in a position where he has no choice but to sign it."

I pretended to ponder this problem for a while, as did Pym, in earnest.

"The people are the key," I said after a few moments, "The King cannot move without the support of the Lords. If the Lords are made to fear the wrath of the people then they will support any measure that will ensure their own safety."

Pym said nothing, and indeed appeared to be waiting for my guidance, so I continued. "I believe that we should not underestimate this situation. Should we succeed in destroying Strafford, we shall be in a position to accuse the King directly concerning all his wrongdoings during his reign. He will be forced, either to accept the removal of effective power from himself to Parliament...or declare civil war."

"I agree," said Pym, "although I trust he'll have enough sense to avoid war."

"Now, here, we may produce our evidence against Strafford, and, by means of this Bill we need merely to demand that he forfeits his life for his crimes. The King's opposition to the will of the Commons will collapse under pressure from so many quarters."

Pym was clearly ashamed of his loss of faith. He said no more. With tears of gratitude welling in his eyes, we walked together, his hand upon my shoulder, to the front bench near the Speaker's chair.

Pym and I sat down with enough time before the session started for me to explain to him my reasons for not presenting the Bill of Attainder personally. As for Vane's evidence, it was easy to persuade Pym that it should come from him. The vanity of man is, after all, a most useful tool.

As the Speaker entered and prepared to begin proceedings, I hastily returned the Bill to Hazelrig then took my place again next to Pym.

"You must present the evidence immediately," I whispered to him as I sat down.

He looked at me for a moment, somewhat quizzically.

"We must make the first move...before the Lords."

He gave me a look of understanding, and stood to his feet.

The Speaker nodded, "Mr Pym."

"Honourable Members, I have here in my hand evidence, hard evidence, of Strafford's plot to invade England. These are the minutes of the meeting of the Privy Council of May fifth, taken by Sir Harry Vane. There is no ambiguity here; nothing here that is open to more than one interpretation: Strafford intended to bring an army *here* to deduce *this* Kingdom of England. Those words are, for anyone who might still doubt their authenticity, written under the heading *Lord Lieutenant of Ireland.*"

"From where did you obtain these papers?" This was Sir Harry Vane, who rose unsteadily to his feet as he spoke."

Pym answered: "Your son Harry, realising their importance, gave them to us."

"Harry, my son," he said, turning to his shifty looking son (who was sitting in the third row behind us) "how could you betray me thus?"

Young Harry Vane walked through the members to where his father was sitting; all was silent. "I knew that your sense of honour was too great to allow you to do as I have done, and I struggled myself to know which to sacrifice: my personal honour or the safety of England, whose glory you always taught me to place before my own ambition. Pater, forgive me, please!" As he said these words he fell to his knees and sobbed onto the floor.

Sir Harry Vane then made a tearful show of graciously forgiving his son, as if he somehow thought that such high drama would make us forget his pathetic performance in Westminster Hall.

"Sir Arthur Hazelrig," called the Speaker.

Hazelrig stood up and, having plunged his hands into the pockets of his coat, glared around the Chamber for a few moments.

"In the light of this new evidence I must now move that this House requires, nay *demands*, that Strafford should be taken from this place to a place of confinement, and thereafter to a place of lawful execution, and that his head should be struck from his body. This House demands also that no opposition to its demands will be tolerated! It is up to members of this House to stir the people, yea the people: that they themselves ensure that this justice is meted, and meted quickly!"

My cousin then rose to protest.

"This is incitement! That was a base threat to rouse the people against the King if he refuses to do the Commons' bidding!"

He tried to continue, but was shouted down. After a few moments Hazelrig managed to be heard again.

"How could we expect a carnal man such as *that* (he said, pointing towards Richard) to understand matters spiritual? I was saying that we should stir the people to *prayer*; that through the power of *prayer* they may move the Lord to grant a safe passage for the will of this House."

This answer was met by much in the way of raucous laughter and jeering directed at Richard Sykes and his friends, including Robert Heron who was sitting to his right.

Hazelrig said "I will now present this Bill to the House."

He then produced from his pocket the paper upon which I had so lovingly and craftily prepared Strafford's downfall.

I will confess that for a moment I felt a small twinge of jealousy as Hazelrig stood there lapping up all the emotion that, pent up in so many of the members present, manifested itself through their uproarious response to his words. But I was in the very act of reassuring myself that it had been worth my while to sacrifice this glory for the sake of personal safety, when my eyes happened to catch those of Robert Heron. The sheer hatred and anger in his face was startling, and that hatred and anger was not, as had been my purpose, directed at Hazelrig, but at me. My fear was only increased by the fact that once he had fixed me with his gaze, he placed his hand discreetly upon the hilt of his sword and pulled it about one inch from its scabbard in a manner clearly designed to demonstrate his intention to do me, at the very least, some serious bodily harm.

Now this was a threat which I could ill afford to take lightly. I looked at the Speaker to see if he had noticed Heron's gesture, but he had not. Neither, it seemed, had anyone else except for my cousin, who merely watched the whole incident and then turned his attention back to the proceedings in the House.

"The House will adjourn," said Lenthall, and I was thankful that I had elected to sit fairly near the main entrance, as I was easily able to make my way from the Chamber before Heron had a chance to get near me.

XXXI

Persuasion

M any people were gathered outside parliament on the following Monday, in the hope of personally witnessing the moment of Strafford's condemnation, as the Commons met with the Lords to discuss the Bill of Attainder.

Many of the Lords at first appeared shocked by, and vehemently opposed to the Attainder. Some of the Lords claimed that they would have to wait for Strafford's final speech before making a decision in regard to his fate. They were then almost all reduced to silence when Pym told them that there were many other Privy Councillors likely to be implicated along with Strafford if his case was not dealt with speedily.

These words plainly affected those present, some of whom appeared alarmed, and others of whom seemed to resent Pym's brazen threat of blackmail. Realising his words needed softening a little, I stood to speak.

"My Lords and Members of the Commons, whilst Morality and Justice have cried out for Strafford's condemnation, legal nuances and technicalities have enabled him to survive thus far. It was thus so when our Lord traversed the earth, seeking to bring light and love to those He met. While the common people heard Him gladly, the lawyers sought to do nought but trip him up with clever words and artful sophistry. And yet the common people – now, as much as then - cry out for justice. Hark - even as I speak I can hear them!"

The rabble outside were, fortunately, waxing loud as I spoke, and the cries of 'We want Strafford's head,' and 'Send Black Tom to the devil' had become audible to all present.

I continued. "We expected the trial to be concluded speedily and, as the crowd are demonstrating, the conviction of Strafford would have been enough both to turn the wrath of God away from the nation, and to appease the anger of the people. The Lord is both just and forgiving. Although none can speak His mind, I believe that His will, and the will of the people, would have been thus satisfied. It is only because matters are being dragged out by Strafford's counsel that it is likely that anyone else will be implicated at all!"

Now, in saying this I was relying on my knowledge of human nature. I believed that all but the most loyal of Strafford's supporters would place their own personal well-being above that of any notion of 'honour.' I could tell from the expressions of most of the peers present that I had been correct in my assumption.

Lord Arundel looked around him, turned to Pym and myself, and announced that a decision would be made as soon as the Commons had made *their* decision, as if that wasn't a foregone conclusion.

• • •

It was not just the Lords, however, whom I deemed it necessary to place under pressure. That night, putting again into practise the lesson I learned from Dr Harding, I put pen to paper:

Your Majesty,

Again, I must crave your pardon for writing to you without revealing my identity, but I pray that in your wisdom you will understand the necessity.

Strafford is a strange victim, your Majesty, for the unruly mob, for in truth he is a despiser of our faith. He did nothing to alleviate the suffering of God's Catholic servants in Ireland, and, by many accounts, is, in his heart, truly a Puritan. You must believe (may I be so bold?) that his Majesty has not gone far enough in appeasing the suffering of God's true servants in this land, and that (at the risk of invoking your Majesty's displeasure) he is intimidated by his own ignorant and spiritually blind people.

Your Majesty, it is Strafford who is responsible for the continued oppression of God's servants. You know better than all that the King will not listen to the voices of seditionists and rebels. To whom therefore, does he give ear when seeking advice on religious matters? Not enough to your Majesty I'll warrant, or the children of the True Religion would be truly free. Nay, he has given ear all this time to Strafford. It is Strafford who is responsible for preventing the King from extending the hand of true friendship to Rome.

And yet, while Laud languishes, forgotten, in the Tower, the peoples' thirst for vengeance causes them to cry out, first and foremost, for the blood of Strafford. With the blood of these two the mob's appetite for revenge will be sated - of this I am sure. By the time you read this letter the unruly mob will be baying loudly for Strafford's death, and we who love thee are most alarmed that they are making a sound hitherto unheard of: they are saying that if the King does not give them their way with Strafford, they will have their way with both Strafford and the King!

Your Majesty I must implore you, for your sake; for the sake of his Majesty; for the sake of the Royal children; above all for the sake of Holy Mother Church, urge your husband to do away with Strafford; do not let him sleep until he relents and agrees to sacrifice him for the greater cause; the cause which you, and I, hold most dear to our hearts.

Strafford's death will save all, and your actions will carry the blessing of his Holiness
I remain, as always,
Your humble servant.

I had it on good authority that she already had almost no confidence in Strafford's influence on the King, and I wasn't lying about the fact that Strafford was a puritan and knew that the Queen detested him for it, so I thought it unlikely that she wouldn't take the bait in the present circumstances. The King, under pressure from parliament and his wife, and facing the wrath of the mob, would have to betray Strafford.

XXXII

In the presence of the King

The Commons assembled the next day to vote on Strafford's fate. As I had expected, once the members had settled down the atmosphere became that of bristling expectation, fuelled as it was with a twist of intimidation. Those whom everyone knew to be Strafford's supporters were huddled together in a corner to the right of the Speaker's chair.

Digby, who had clearly been sulking to such a degree that he had decided to change sides, stood just before the votes were cast in order to say something about his conscience being clear, because he intended to vote against the taking of Strafford's life. The effect of his little speech was easy to counter anyway, for when the Speaker called for the votes to be cast I merely stood alongside Pym and shouted that *all* men present were expected to vote according to their conscience. We then watched very carefully in order to ensure that they did so.

The votes when counted were as follows: two hundred and four for the taking of Strafford's life, fifty-nine against.

To the sound of deafening cheers, Pym carried the Bill through to the Lords, and told them that the Commons would 'carry their action to its conclusion wherever and whenever their Lordships appointed.'

• • •

The Commons dispersed, and I set about quickly compiling a list of those who had voted against the Bill, which I then had posted in twenty-four places around London and Westminster, under the heading: *These are the Straffordians, enemies of justice; betrayers of their country*. This, of course, was a serious breach of parliamentary privilege, and the information as to who voted for what can only have come from someone inside the Commons, but I thought Parliament unlikely to stage any effective protest in the circumstances.

Information can have little effect without an accompanying rumour, so I also caused it to be put about that the fifty-nine members who had voted against the Bill were likely to succeed against the will of the majority of the Commons, merely because it was the will of the Lords that they should do so. Moreover, Strafford (I told John Brown to spread as far and wide as possible) intended to exact his revenge upon the people of London by means of the Irish army *with which he had formerly threatened them*, as soon as possible after he had been released. This was an easy tale to circulate, as there were already many similar reports of army plots rife throughout London and Westminster. In the atmosphere of London at that time all things gave rise to suspicion.

Inevitably therefore, by Monday, twenty sixth April, when the Lords convened to debate the Bill, the tension around the precincts of London and Westminster had caused a high sense of anxiety and confusion to descend upon the upper House. As a result of this, when the Bill was read very few of those who had formerly supported Strafford did anything other than look at the floor between their feet. And the attitude of the Lords towards Strafford in general, which had formerly been less hostile on the whole than that of the Commons, quickly became more aligned with those of his sworn enemies. The reason for this was simple: their lives were now at stake.

That evening, little expecting that one of life's unexpected but momentous events was about to occur, and before the Lords' final vote was cast, I was standing in Westminster Palace Yard with John Pym discussing the matter of the Lords' impending decision when I saw an officer of the King's Guard approaching us, and recognised him as Major Fellingham, whom I had not seen since my audience with the King in the company of Anne Hussey.

He smirked slightly upon recognising me, but addressed my companion. "Mr Pym?"

"Yes."

"I have come here directly from the Palace of Whitehall. The King commands your presence there immediately."

Pym was understandably shaken at this news, as was I. It took him several moments to respond.

"Do I have time to change? May I bring my companion?"

Major Fellingham looked at me momentarily. "You may bring Mr Sykes if you wish, I am not sure that it will avail you anything. I will announce you both, and if the King raises no objection then you may both enter. Do not worry about changing. The King is aware that he has called for you without due ceremony, but he is in a hurry and has commanded me to take you to him immediately."

My feelings, as we walked in silence towards Whitehall, were a mixture of fear and elation. This would be my first and only personal audience with the King since my humiliating encounter the previous summer, which, you will remember, ended with my being punished with a whipping. I was therefore, in more than once sense, about to find myself at the King's mercy.

The walk to Whitehall was fortunately very short, so I had little time to mull over these things before we arrived and were led to a chamber adjacent to the throne room.

Major Fellingham gestured for us to wait. From where we were standing we could hear the sounds of raised voices, or one raised voice: that of the Queen. He waited for a pause in the conversation (or argument) and then entered. Moments later he returned and signalled for us to follow him.

When we entered the Banqueting Hall all was calm again, and the King was as serene as ever he appeared in public. On his left sat the Queen and, although she had clearly managed to bring her temper under control upon the announcement of our arrival, she made no attempt to look upon us with any of the royal graciousness that the

King had contrived to muster. Pym she looked upon with undisguised revulsion. She did not even deign to glance in my direction. To their right and left stood about sixteen courtiers, some of whom I recognised from Strafford's trial.

Major Fellingham announced us, and it was only then, with a snort of derision as my name was mentioned, that the Queen made any acknowledgement of my presence at all. I might have found this disconcerting were it not for two factors: the first that I was very accustomed to people reacting to the mention of my name in this manner, and the second that I was convinced she was arguing with her husband on the basis of the advice I had given her in my recent letter. I could not be certain of this but I thought it highly likely. I decided - in the event of my reception from the King going badly - upon a strategy that would cost me nothing if it failed, but would be greatly to my advantage if it succeeded

The King looked, first at Pym, then at me, as we bowed before them. His face was void of expression.

"Mr Pym," he said, "there is little point in either of us pretending that our views on most matters do not differ greatly. Is this, would you say, a fair assessment?"

Pym bowed slightly. "Your Majesty."

"It is an error, methinks, from which many of us are suffering, that the views of those who believe otherwise than ourselves are altogether incorrect, or motivated by evil. I say 'many of us' because I have it in my mind that a spirit of intolerance has descended upon this land, and that few, or none of us, have remained entirely unaffected by it."

He stopped to look at the Queen, possibly in the hope of receiving an encouraging glance of approval. Receiving only a glare in response, he went on.

"We will not, and cannot, say that it is an error to condemn those whose views fall outside of that which is clearly acceptable to the Lord according to Holy Scripture. We have been charged with the defence of the faith in this land, and in this we will not shirk our duty."

"Your Majesty will allow," replied Pym, "that there is more than one way of falling outside of that which is acceptable to the Lord according to Holy Scripture?"

Although Pym said these words in a manner that was so respectful as to be almost grovelling, as he did so he very deliberately allowed his eyes to move from the King to the Queen, and back again. The Queen started, and looked as if she was about to reply in anger. Apparently thinking the better of it, she turned again to her husband.

"Mr Pym, I believe you are being impertinent," said the King.

"Forgive me Sir, that was not my intention. I merely wished to include both of your Majesties in the conversation."

"I will join the conversation if and when I please to do so Mr Pym," said the Queen indignantly (although she pronounced his name 'Peem'). Your views are well known on these matters."

"Somewhat impertinent, Mr Pym" repeated the King, "but this is beside the point. We have been made aware - painfully aware recently - of the frustrations of certain members of the House of Commons. These members appear to believe - mistakenly - that I do not have their interests at heart."

"It is not our interests with which we are concerned," returned Pym, "but the people who sent us hither as their representatives."

The King was visibly irritated by this by this. "Mr Pym, it was not our purpose in calling you to this place to patronise you. We would thank you to show us the same consideration."

Pym bowed. "Your Majesty."

The King's voice took on a more urgent tone, and as it did so he began to stumble over his words, and stutter a little.

"Nonetheless, I imagine you are wondering why I *have* called you here. I have always made it my first and foremost duty as your monarch to listen to the people, to hear their concerns and, where possible, alleviate their suffering. Certain people - mainly, by your leave Sir, of your own persuasion - have put it about that Parliament, but not I, care for the people's concerns. Mr Pym, I need not tell you that I love my subjects as a father loves his children. The fact that Parliament and

I have disagreed does not mean that Parliament cares more for the people, nor does it necessarily mean that Parliament knows better than I what is in the people's best interests."

Pym tried to speak but the King raised his right hand to prevent him, and returned to his former, and more regal, mode of address. "We are willing to admit however, that certain mistakes have been made, and that our government has not encompassed a broad enough scope of skill and opinion."

He paused momentarily before adding "you are aware no doubt that Cottington has resigned as Chancellor of the Exchequer."

"I am aware of this development Sir, yes."

"And that this position needs to be filled, quickly."

We both inclined our heads slightly in agreement.

"Who, in your opinion of your parliamentary colleagues, is best qualified for this position?"

"I have not had time to give much thought to the question Sir, with weightier matters pressing."

"Yes" said the King with a distinct sigh, "weightier matters."

He then paused again, this time for long enough (for me at least) to start feeling somewhat uncomfortable.

"Mr Pym," he said finally, "I will not bandy words with you. There is no one better qualified for this position than yourself. We wish you to become our Chancellor, with immediate effect."

Now, as you would doubtless expect, we were completely taken aback by this. Pym looked at me, but as long as we were there in the King's presence there was nothing whatsoever that I could say. I could only pray that he wouldn't allow his vanity to get the better of him and accept the position there and then.

"Your Majesty," he said eventually, "I am deeply flattered and humbled by your offer. May I consult my colleague before answering?"

The King turned to face me, properly, for the first time. I bowed deeply in response. At that moment he could have said something to Pym like 'I advise you strongly not to take the advice of such a fool as *this*,' or some similarly disparaging remark, and then go on to relate to him the details of the Anne Hussey incident. Thankfully he turned back to Pym and said "Of course," before gesturing towards the door through which we had entered. Major Fellingham followed us out of the room and told us to call him when we were finished speaking. He then left through the other door.

"I must say, this is something I never expected," Pym said as soon as we were alone, with ill-disguised self-satisfaction. (A bubble, clearly formed by the soap of political and worldly pride, was taking form in his soul, and I determined to burst it without delay).

"Although you must realise that the King wants to bribe you with the riches and vanity of this world in the hope that you will forget your duty to God and country?" I pointed out to him bluntly.

"Yes....I can see that" said Pym thoughtfully, although he was clearly struggling, as he went on to say "but think of the good things I will be able to do for the poor..."

"Would not the devil use words such as those when using ambition and the love of power to tempt us away from the straight path?"

Still Pym looked wistful.

"He will not let you take this position unless you agree to Strafford's release."

Now that, as I hoped it would, did the trick. Most men would never allow a single issue such as Strafford to get in the way of their worldly ambitions. And some men would willingly have taken the post of Chancellor, conveniently forgotten that Strafford *had ever been their enemy*, and started fawning over him in Privy Council meetings (having forgotten any former notion of expelling him from public office – let alone executing him) whilst treating their former friends like scum. But not Pym - as soon as I mentioned Strafford's name the dreamy expression fled from his eyes, the steely determination came back, and he said "Of course I cannot take the post, and the fact that I am unable to do all those good things as Chancellor because of Strafford, shows all the more how this country so desperately needs rid of his evil influence. I will return immediately to refuse the King's offer."

"Hold fast!" I exclaimed, taking a firm grip of his forearm to prevent his progress, "we cannot enter again into the presence of the King and Queen without our being announced....and (I added after a moment's hesitation) I would strongly advise you not to enter again into the King's presence at all."

Pym looked at me blankly.

"Think you that the King will brook such a refusal? We will end up rotting in some dungeon under this palace. That or we will wash up somewhere on the shores of the Thames! Why else do you suppose the King brought us here so suddenly and quickly? I tell you it was in the hope that no one would notice our coming. Nay, I will return to their Majesties' presence and refuse on your behalf. You must, if possible, make your escape."

"But the King will…"

"Do not fear the wrath of the King, which I believe that I, if anyone, can placate; fear the consequences for both of us if you refuse the King's offer so bluntly. We cannot afford to lose you, Brother Pym. There may come a time when duty calls some young man to place his life in jeopardy on my behalf. For now duty calls me to do so for thee."

Before he could protest I went to the door through which Major Fellingham had departed, and called loudly for his return.

"There are one or two questions that Mr Pym needs to have answered before he can accept his Majesty's gracious offer," I said to him. "For example, will their Majesties expect Mr Pym, as Chancellor, to attend frolicsome court activities?"

He looked at me, aghast. "I cannot ask that….do you have any idea at all about…"

"Tell their Majesties that this question is not asked in a spirit of criticism, but rather in order that Mr Pym can give, should it become necessary, attention to the deficiencies in his wardrobe. Now as I am sure you will agree Mr Pym has a right to ask whatsoever he wills before taking such an important position."

As I said this I led Major Fellingham by the arm (and surprised myself with the firmness with which I did so) towards the door to the Banqueting Hall. He, I think too surprised to do otherwise, entered without further question.

"Now, quickly leave" I said as I ushered Pym with equal firmness towards the other door. He made a half-hearted attempt to protest but I knew that he was dying to get out really.

"Clutch your stomach as if you are in terrible agony" I whispered after him as he started to walk quickly and purposefully down the passage.

I had just closed the door after him when the door to the Banqueting Hall opened. Major Fellingham appeared, looking vexed.

"The King demands that you...where's Mr Pym."

He has been taken with a sudden malady and has instructed me to apologise to their Majesties, as well as to speak on his behalf.

"He...just...went?"

"Suddenly – as suddenly as the illness took him."

"Well he looked alright a minute ago. The King is not altogether in the best of moods at present. I think that if he even *thinks* that you are trying to make a mockery of him, particularly in light of that ridiculous question about court frivolities, a beating is the very least you can expect *this* visit."

I had to try to maintain my self-confidence.

"Be so kind as to remember that I am here on important matters of state. Conduct me to their Majesties' presence immediately!"

He looked me levelly for a moment, his mouth twitching with the effort to prevent himself from laughing (or possibly to give himself the appearance of suffering under such an effort), and then bowed low to the floor.

"Indeed, thank you for reminding me of my true position," he said with mock gravity. "Follow me, Sir."

He opened the door and went in before me.

"Sir, Mr Pym has apparently been taken ill. Mr *He-died-for-our-sins Sykes* is here to speak on his behalf – allegedly."

It is a formidable thing (I believe the Book of Proverbs says) to stand in the presence of a wrathful King. This may have been written at a time when the people of Israel had suffered under the yoke of harsh and evil rulers such as Saul and Ahab; and the writer cannot have imagined a king such as *this* when he wrote it. Nevertheless his words were as apt in their way for Charles as they would have been for any of those ruthless, biblical kings, for when he answered Major Fellingham it was in such a way as to petrify me with the sudden reality of the situation in which I found myself. Not for the first time I was almost overwhelmed by the urge to scream with sheer terror; and I had to pinch myself painfully in the buttocks as I bowed to the King and Queen to prevent myself from doing so.

As Major Fellingham spoke, the King gripped the arms of his throne. His eyes flashed with anger.

"Allegedly, what do you mean, allegedly? Speak plainly man or I will have *you* whipped!"

"Mr Pym has *apparently*, and very suddenly, been taken ill, and according to He-died-for-our-sins here, he asked the said He-died-for-our-sins to speak on his behalf before leaving."

The King looked from Fellingham to me, and back again. When he spoke his voice was calmer. "Fellingham, you will address or speak of all of our members of Parliament as befits their station, and as befits yours."

Fellingham gave the King a small bow of acquiescence. The King then turned again to me.

"I presume that Mr Pym cannot be aware of the details of *our* last encounter Mr Sykes? We have hitherto credited him with much in the way of wisdom: it is for this that he has been invited here this day. With such wisdom we would expect him to apply great care in his choice of diplomats and representatives."

"Your Majesty," I responded, bowing lower towards the floor, and hoping as I did so that he would not expect me to actually answer the question.

After a few moments however, as he clearly *was* expecting me to answer, I decided that this would be an appropriate moment to abase myself.

"Your Majesty…." I began.

"Do not address the floor please, Mr Sykes, if you wish to be heard."

"Your Majesty," I continued (having adopted a more upright posture) "Mr Pym would, I am sure, have chosen a better qualified representative had circumstances allowed it."

"I should, if I were in your position, allow others to belittle you Mr Sykes - there are plenty who will do so in your occupation – but you were, after all, chosen for parliament; there must be some who merit your capabilities."

"Your Majesty is most gracious" I responded.

"Mr Pym has been taken ill you say."

"Most suddenly Sir, he left almost without warning – he was complaining of stomach cramps."

"One of our physicians could have assisted him."

"I believe Sir that the sense of urgency drove him, much against his will, away from your Majesty's presence; but judging by the urgency of his departure I would say that it was highly likely that he is still here, within the walls of this palace, if he has found a convenient place." The King then ordered Major Fellingham to instruct his soldiers make a search of the palace in order to ascertain whether Pym was still thereabouts, and if so to bring him medical assistance.

But I was surprised when, without explanation, he then started to dismiss me from his presence.

"Well forgive me, Mr Sykes (he said – having exchanged a momentary look of exasperation with his wife) but there seems little or no point in us continuing this interview any further. Please give our best wishes to Mr Pym - if you see him before us - for a speedy recovery. We will speak to him as soon as he is able about the matter we raised earlier."

It had taken until this moment for my confidence to gather momentum, and I was still determined to tell the King of Pym's intention to decline his offer. I therefore could not let him end the interview so suddenly. However, I also knew enough about courtroom etiquette to be aware that if I should make any attempt to force the King to listen to me against his will then nothing at all would be accomplished but further provocation of his temper.

I therefore determined to put my previously mentioned idea into action. I turned to the Queen and, bowing low to the floor, said:

"I remain, as always, your humble servant."

Now the effect of these words upon the Queen was remarkable. Her eyes took on the expression of a doe surrounded on all sides by a fire in a strange wood, and therefore in despair of any hope of survival, which is suddenly startled by the arrival of a bold and handsome stag (who, doubtless in her mind, will immediately, somehow or other, lead her to the safety of her Roman Catholic forest, and will protect her in doing so against any danger from the encroaching flames and wicked Protestant venison hunters).

I allowed the fantasy to settle into her mind for a moment. When, after a few moments, she made to speak to the King I discreetly touched the side of my nose with my forefinger in the manner of one reminding her of the need for confidence. She stopped herself, and then, barely able to contain her excitement, said "Did not Fellingham say that Mr Pym had asked Mr Sykes to speak for him?"

The King hesitated, a dark expression briefly passing his brow, and then addressed me again.

"That was an extraordinary response Mr Sykes – about 'court frivolities,' and not a little impolite. We are well aware of some of the religious sensitivities of our more…colourless subjects; but religious sensitivity is no excuse for bad manners: Charity, as St Paul instructs us, is not rude."

He pondered for a moment, then said "Mr Pym charged you to speak for him, Mr Sykes."

"He did Sir."

"Well?"

"Mr Pym - not without first taking great care to ensure that I would thank your Majesty, profusely, on his behalf - has asked me to inform your Majesty - not without first reiterating his extreme gratitude - that he regrets that he is unable to accept the position you have so kindly - and, may I add from my own point of view, wisely, offered him; and that he feels that he will best serve your Majesty by remaining apart from the government in a position where, he believes, that he is best placed to observe whether your Majesty is being faithfully advised; and that those chosen to do so are placing your interests before their own."

The King looked at me stonily, as did all the courtiers present. You may be sure that during that terrible silence I wished with all my heart that I had never thought of parliament, or of anything other than a life of peaceful farming in Northamptonshire. I even thought of Brickett, and the limitations of his career to the wall at the end of the cow shed. Yea, I even thought of that with a tinge of envy as I waited for the King's response.

He finally spoke. "Well, we appear to have misjudged his motives for his persecution of my Lord of Strafford. Please inform Mr Pym that if his sole concern is our protection from the wiles of unscrupulous ministers, then, as he regards them as unscrupulous, we will remove our Chief Minister, as well as our Archbishop of Canterbury, from office - and any hope of re-attaining office - forthwith. This has always been our intention since their persecution began in earnest. Mr Pym only needed to state his case plainly from the outset."

The Queen, who until that moment had remained silent, leaned over and whispered urgently to her husband. It was not possible to make out her words fully, but their effect was to make him look extremely downcast. I decided to take advantage of the moment.

"Your Majesty, I think that I speak for Mr Pym, as well as all of the Commons, when I say that we would give our own lives if the peace of the nation could be restored by doing so. The wrath of the people however, will not be abated thus."

"And you say that the wrath of the people will be abated by the head of the Lord Strafford, as well as that of the Archbishop," answered the King, his voice rising. "We are not accustomed, Mr Sykes, to being threatened thus. There are some who are making themselves busy at this time stirring up the people with tales of licentious behaviour at Court, as well as false rumours that the Prince of Wales is being raised in accordance with Roman Catholic doctrine. We have reason to believe that some of these stirrers are in positions of authority; people who should know better. You would never indulge in such practices, would you Mr Sykes?"

I was saved from having to answer that question directly by the Queen, who started to whisper, even more urgently, to her husband. This time I could hear her words.

"Can you not tell that he is here to help us? Do you think that he would risk the wrath of his colleagues in order to do so, were he not sincere? This is no rabble-rouser: listen to him!"

"Sir," I added tactfully and reverentially, "in speaking of 'the wrath of the nation' I was in no way attempting to threaten your Majesty, but was somewhat closer to making a confession. For I believe that it is partly our responsibility as members of Parliament to control the people. I believed that the people would be satisfied with a trial of the Lord Strafford according to the due processes of law: to a degree it appears that the people have been thus satisfied, but only if the decision goes the way they want. I fear that if the people do not get their way in this matter then they may tear this capital, nay this country, to pieces."

I was pleased to note that when I had finished speaking, the King, despite remaining silent for several moments (so I had no way of knowing the impression my answer had upon him) lost his expression of anger. His face instead took on a thoughtful, almost dreamy expression, as his eyes became fixed upon the window behind me. Everyone in the room became silent. The Queen looked at me imploringly, although I knew that she was not expecting me to speak.

After two or three minutes the King broke his self-imposed silence.

"Lord Yelvertoft."

"Your Majesty?" I replied.

"We are not unwilling to admit mistakes, Mr Sykes; over the past decade or so our subjects have been - generally speaking - a happy people; and yet it cannot be denied that there are some who, in positions of power and authority, have oppressed the very people whose poverty they had the ability to relieve through their wealth and influence. The fact that we have not kept a tight enough rein on some of our more powerful subjects has, undoubtedly, been a mistake - a grave mistake. The fact that a member of the House of Lords believes that it has become acceptable to kill children for something so common and harmless as apple-pilfering, and then speak about it openly – as if it were a virtue – is *most* alarming."

"Our people *have* suffered," he continued, "but the anger created by their suffering has been misdirected. They are frightened. I have heard of people disrupting innocent pursuits such as sports tournaments and dances; and forcing people to spend the whole of Sunday – their only day of rest - listening to dull, indoctrinating, and - in some cases - seditious sermons. Mr Sykes, none of our subjects are prohibited from working out their salvation by staring at the floor or praying at whitewashed walls; and they may spend the whole of every Sunday, and every Christmas, doing so if they wish to. But to try to force this Calvinistic version of godliness upon others: *this*, Mr Sykes, is religious oppression."

He paused momentarily. "The people's anger, as I say, has been misdirected. But they are a good people, and will willingly hear the truth, that my Lord of Strafford is not the cause of their woes. The death of Lord Yelvertoft, which is so much more deserved, will satisfy the people's thirst for justice. My Lord of Strafford shall be made to retire from public life."

"Your Majesty…" I again said.

But the King then made it clear that my audience had come to an end. "We have given the Lord Strafford our solemn promise that we will in no way consent to the taking of his life…Good day, Mr Sykes."

The King held out his hand, which I kissed. I then bowed to the Queen and the King and, walking backwards very carefully, and genuflecting repeatedly, I left the room.

• • •

The sounds of protest from outside the palace walls, which had been audible throughout the whole of my audience with the King and Queen, became distinctly louder as I walked through the passages of Whitehall. I was able to comfort myself therefore as I left the palace with the thought that the King did not really have the measure of his people at all, and that there was no way their anger was going to be appeased by the blood of Lord Yelvertoft. The King was clearly stupid to think such a suggestion would avail his cause.

'Who the hell is *Lord Yelvertoft?*' I could imagine them asking.

I was about to leave the Palace through the main door leading to the south, from which, through the courtyard, I could see the assembled masses seething, when my progress was interrupted by a gentle but firm pressure placed upon my left arm. I spun around, and beheld, looking beseechingly into mine, the doe-like eyes of the Queen.

"Mister Sykes, I must talk with you," she said as she led me into a corner of the hall where we would be safely out of anyone's hearing (the intonations of her accent I will leave, with your permission, to the imagination).

"You have, have you not Mr Sykes, written to me on one or two occasions?"

I bowed to her in a manner that indicated an affirmative answer to her question, and repeated the words "I am your Majesty's most humble servant."

"Mr Sykes, you must help us. The King will not give up Strafford, even though that rabble is on the verge of killing us."

"Your Majesty, you *must* persuade him to give up Strafford."

"But I cannot. I have been begging him to see that there is no choice left to us ever since I received your last letter. But you heard him, he has promised. He will not go back on his promise. Even now he is on his way to the House of Lords to plead for Strafford's life."

When I heard that the King had left so quickly after my recent audience I determined to do so also.

"Your Majesty," I said, "as you will have gathered from my letters, the good works I do can only be done in secret. It is not many years since that those of the true faith were openly hounded to death in this country. There are many - as you know - who would still have it so. I must move quickly to give the King what support I can at this most grave of times. There are many people in parliament willing to do all they can to undermine his good intentions."

I then bowed and kissed the Queen's hand. She wept: discreetly but imploringly.

"Your Majesty, I will no longer write to you as I have done. It is not safe to use the same means of communication too often. I will, with your permission, bring any urgent messages directly to someone appointed by you, someone you trust implicitly."

"You surely trust your cousin Elizabeth. She would be delighted to discover that your puritanism has all along been a ruse."

I smarted slightly at these words, but only slightly.

"I *do* trust my cousin Elizabeth, but I do not trust her husband, Lord Clunehaven. His allegiances are divided, and by that same token therefore *her* allegiances must be divided. I think it most gracious of your Majesty to keep Lady Clunehaven under your care and protection."

At these words she became somewhat thoughtful. After a moment however, she told me to wait. She then went through one of the doors adjacent to the hall, and returned two minutes later with quill and ink.

"This is the address of Lady Carlisle, my most trusted friend," she said as she wrote. She alone knows about you, as well as your letters. She herself has recommended that we meet at her house. So I am decided. If you need to communicate with me at any time, you must go to this house and do so through her. She will know who you are, and she will reach me. I will instruct her to be available at all times - or easily reachable from her house – until this crisis has passed."

"And you trust Lady Carlisle…entirely?"

"She is not of the True Religion, but her loyalty is beyond question."

"Your Majesty….I am forever in your debt."

"We are forever in *your* debt, Mr Sykes."

"For what though?" I could not help sniggering this question quietly to myself as, having bowed gracefully, I made my way out of the doors and across the courtyard to the crowd beyond.

XXXIII

The question of Yelvertoft

I could tell that the people crowding the gates of the palace were in a hostile frame of mind as I approached them, and I could also tell that it was only my plain, puritan attire that saved me from receiving, at the very least, a most severe beating just for the fact that I had come out of the palace. A few of them looked at me sullenly, challenging me to catch their eyes. I tried to walk through them as best as I could, but those who were nearest the gates refused to give way, making it necessary for me to jostle and shove them a little in order to pass. I managed to lose myself amongst them.

The road was just as crowded all the way to the Palace of Westminster, and I began to worry that the King would get to the House of Lords before me. After about thirty minutes, however, I arrived at the palace and managed to shake myself free of the people, who were pressing hard against the gates. I immediately made my way to the gallery of the House of Lords.

The chamber was full, and I arrived just in time to hear Black Rod, who, having entered through the eastern door, walked unceremoniously to the middle of the Chamber, struck the floor twice with his staff, and called out "My Lords, the King!" Before their Lordships could recover from their surprise the King walked in quickly and bowed, smiled benignly to the assembled peers, and sat on the throne, while most of the Lords were still rising to greet him.

Lord Bristol, who was already on his feet, addressed the King.

"Your Majesty, we are most honoured to welcome you this…"

"My Lord Bristol," interrupted the King, "it would be most unfair, having given no forewarning of our arrival, to expect you to greet us with anything other than the briefest of welcomes. We thank you for your kindness, and now, I pray you all: please be seated, for I have come to address you on a matter of the gravest importance."

The Lords sat down, and I leaned back so that my face was protected from the King's line of vision by the rail in front of me.

"My Lords, we will, without delay, alleviate your curiosity as to the purpose of our unexpected arrival. I bring before you today nothing but my conscience. I have given my solemn promise that I shall in no way consent to the taking of my Lord Strafford's life. My Lords I hope you know what a tender thing conscience is; yet I declare to you that to satisfy my people I would do much; but in regard to my conscience, no fear of consequence can make me go against it. My Lords, my people say, and rightly it appears, that they have been suffering under oppression. We have one under close confinement who has confessed, nay bragged near this place, of murder - infanticide - committed by his own hand in the guise of justice. We will publish the crimes of Lord Yelvertoft. The people shall be told of his villainy, and their anger will rightly be turned to him and away from the Lord Strafford."

This speech was greeted with considerable confusion and shuffling of feet. It was plain for all to see that the King was desperate. It was foolish in the extreme for him to expect the Lords to make any sort of decision based on the grounds that it might 'affect his conscience.' But the Lord Yelvertoft idea was not altogether bad, as the anger of a quintessential English mob could be extremely fickle, and could therefore easily change direction. It was not, however, my purpose to allow this to happen.

It was clearly not in the King's mind to partake in any sort of debate, for as soon as he had spoken these words he stood, acknowledged the reverential bows of those around him, and left the chamber. I made my way quickly to the Commons, where I found Pym, Cromwell, and Sir Harry Vane on the front bench, listening to a debate about the control of the trained bands. I sat behind them.

"Brothers," I whispered as soon as there was a suitable pause in the proceedings, "the King has just told the Lords – I have just come from there - that he will not, as a matter of conscience, consent to Strafford's death, and he has proposed that Yelvertoft should be placed before the people as a substitute."

I then told them in some detail of what the King had said, both in the Lords and in the Palace of Whitehall.

They were silent for a few moments. Pym was the first to speak.

"That thing he said about his poor kingly conscience would have ended all hope for Strafford by itself, but the thing about Yelvertoft.... by the way, did you know that Strafford tried to bribe his way out of prison with twenty thousand pounds? He offered Balfour five hundred pounds worth of gold on the spot. How the hell do you suppose he got hold of *that* sort of money in the Tower? What happened after I left Whitehall earlier?"

I was relieved that he chose to end this string of questions as he did, because the last one was the only one I had any desire to answer.

"This...this is what happened. Inviting you to become Chancellor was his last effort before resorting to this sort of desperation."

"What do you think we should do now? He might succeed: the peers aren't happy with the new paper evidence."

"Look, there's nothing we can do about this here," I answered. Whatever the Lords are thinking, the King has tried to move the burden of guilt onto them. He knows that they can't refuse to convict Yelvertoft, and he also knows that the people might be willing to forgive Strafford when they're asked to compare them."

"They should both be strung up," said Cromwell.

"Er...quite so," I replied, "but I think that the King has a slightly better understanding of the good citizens of London than I thought. I imagine the King intends to harness his people's inherent inconsistency to his advantage. He may well succeed unless we can reach the people before him."

"Right," responded Pym immediately, "It's now six of the clock. That leaves just this evening and tomorrow to galvanise the people before the lords arrive to debate the Bill on Monday. These streets must be full when they arrive, and I don't care how bloody angry the people get. In fact we'll make sure the mob are ready to erupt if need be. While the Lords are discussing Strafford we will be discussing the plot between the King and the army, the truth of which is proved by those troops still at the Tower. Sykes, it is very important for the people to know of all this. *They* are the ones who are going to make the ultimate decision. But remember - we need the people's anger steered away from this Yelvertoft business. He may be a complete shit, but no one outside his own county's even heard of him till now."

I did not intend to wait for any further instructions, and so got up to leave; but Vane suddenly caught - nay gripped - my arm as I did so, and started to speak in a manner which, in light of my previous experience of the man, I found most astonishing. "As far as I am concerned, Sykes, the King has *won*, do you hear me? I said *won*. I have been persuaded that Strafford should die, and I have been persuaded to agree to unscrupulous means to bring about his death. In fact, much against my conscience, I have been willing to say just about whatever was required of me to get to this point. My evidence is now being used to justify the Attainder. If the lords reject the Bill on the grounds that the evidence is weak, then that is *your* affair. If the lords pass the Bill despite the weakness of the evidence: then…well done. But get this: as far as I am concerned the King has *won*, because if I think for one moment that Yelvertoft is going to cheat the axe because of Strafford I will go to the House of Lords and say that most of the case against Strafford was based on lies, and that I was bullied and threatened into perjuring myself. I'll tell you this Sykes, and the rest of you, I'll demand clemency for Strafford and donate him my own estate if I have to, but the King has called your bluff and he's won."

"Calm Harry….be calm," said Pym, alarmed, then turning to me added, "he's right Sykes, if it really *does* come down to a decision between Yelvertoft and Strafford, we'll have to let Strafford go."

Oliver Cromwell nodded also.

I therefore agreed with them, outwardly, whilst inwardly seething with rage. As far as I was concerned, Pym, Vane and Cromwell could go and slaughter Yelvertoft in his cell if they felt that strongly about it, but I was not going to let them allow the King to undo our work at this stage. I knew that the crowds outside would soon start to disperse unless something happened to amuse or interest them, so I made my way as best I could to a place among them where I could not be heard by any of my colleagues, or any of the lords, but where I would be heard by as much of the crowd as possible. I waved my cane about me, not so as to hit anyone, but in order to create a space about me sufficiently large to express myself properly. I then addressed them thus:

"Make space brethren, I am a Member of Parliament, and what I have to tell you relates to a matter of great importance! You are here, are you not, to ensure that the will of the people is obeyed, and that the tyrant Black Tom Strafford receives the just reward for his treason?"

"Aye, that we are!" was the general response.

"Well the King, whatever might be the will of his people, intends to allow Strafford to return to his estates unpunished; he also thinks that you, the very people I speak of, will be content - nay pleased - to allow him to substitute the death of Strafford with the death of one Lord Yelvertoft, a Puritan baron from the county of Northamptonshire."

The general response to this was "Why?" and, "Who the hell is Lord Yelvertoft?" which, as you know, I had expected.

My answer to the question 'Why?' was that there was no very good reason why; that Lord Yelvertoft was in trouble for some local issue to do with Northamptonshire only, and that even this matter was, as I had previously stated, unproven. The important point was that the King intended to kill him, and to use his doing so as an excuse not to kill Lord Strafford.

"Now look," I shouted, for they still weren't really taking the bait, "the King has shown today that he is willing to use the army to subdue you; he intends to use the death of Yelvertoft to appease you; he intends to free Strafford the Oppressor ....but I say....Free Yelvertoft, give us Strafford's Head! Free Yelvertoft, give us Strafford's head!"

Once I was sure that they had taken up this chorus I started to make my way home on foot, visiting various taverns and ale houses on my way in order further to spread the rumours I had just created.

XXXIV

Strafford's condemnation

There was another reason why London was so over-populated at that time. The next day was a Sunday, and upon this day was a royal wedding: that of the King's eldest daughter, the Princess Mary, to William, the Prince of Orange. It was a peculiar thing to see all those people who had spent the previous day baying for the blood of Strafford - and the King and Queen if they did not get it - today drinking the health of the King, his family and *all his councillors*. The streets however, were adorned with bunting and strewn with flowers, and there was wine flowing freely from many fountains, and this it seemed, was enough to make hypocrites of everyone.

But the free wine eventually ran out, and with it the people's good humour. By ten of the clock at night reports of violent, drunken behaviour began to circulate around town. Fights started to break out in ale houses, and hostile groups started to form, seemingly, on every street corner. The trained bands were called out onto the streets to maintain order, which they largely managed to do, as the incidents that occurred that night were, despite their seriousness, mainly of the isolated kind.

There was no point whatsoever in going home that night. I therefore spent the evening enjoying the atmosphere of tense expectation, and making sure that everyone I could muster, such as Compromise-not-at-all, Flee sin and their friends, would be present at Parliament to influence the lords' decision the following morning. I then travelled to the Palace of Westminster and spent the night in the company of about six other Members who had also decided not to make the journey home, trying to sleep as best I could on one of the benches in the hall next to the Painted Chamber.

It was not possible however, despite our fatigue, to sleep any longer than a few hours, for at six of the clock we were all woken by an extraordinary series of noises. First of all we heard the distant, angry voices of many people, then a loud bang, followed by silence, a crash, a cheer, a few more bangs and, last of all, footsteps running towards us accompanied by the sound of breathless panting. Before we were fully awake and on our feet, a young nobleman ran into the lobby with blood streaming from what appeared to be a broken nose. His extremely expensive mauve doublet, as well as his shirt, was spattered with it. He stopped when he saw us, his eyes wide with terror.

"They are beside themselves! The people have gone completely insane!"

He then sprinted away towards the House of Lords.

For a moment I debated whether to follow him in order to find out what had happened, but then exactly the same thing occurred again: shouting, a loud crash, a cheer, and loud banging followed by footsteps with breathless panting. This time it was Lord Bristol, also with torn clothes, and several cuts to his head.

"Maniacs!" he exclaimed, before running off in the same direction as his predecessor.

We all ran to a north facing window on the first floor, from whence we could see events unfolding. There were, it seemed, about twenty thousand people gathered outside. Towards the front of the crowd was a carriage, and this was being rocked violently by the people surrounding it. Out of one of the windows I could see none other than Clunehaven waving his switch wildly in a desperate attempt to beat back the rioters. They stopped rocking his carriage momentarily. One of their leaders then demanded to know which way he intended to vote, there being a clear threat of instant death if he answered the question contrary to their satisfaction.

As he refused to answer at all, and refused also to desist from attempting to hit them with his switch, they started rocking his carriage again, and this time with such violence that on about the fifth movement it lost its balance and landed on its side, with a deafening crash. I realised then that among the crowd there were two carriages already in the same position; each of them being clambered upon by many people eager to use them to view the unfolding of events from the point of greatest advantage. Following the upturning of Clunehaven's coach there was a momentary silence, while the people apparently waited to see if he was dead, followed by a cheer when his head appeared through the left door of the carriage, which was now facing the sky. Clunehaven was then forced to clamber out and run, ignominiously, towards the palace, being cuffed violently and kicked as he went.

No one else attempted to get through that crowd again until a sufficient number of soldiers, both on foot and on horseback, had arrived to restore and maintain the peace. This they did by means of the foot soldiers forming a line along the front wall of the building, and the cavalry riding among the crowd batting people with their sheathed swords, until they successfully forced them into two large groups, with a sufficient gap between them for the parliamentarians to pass through.

The crowd, however, remained hostile, and although most of the Members were allowed to pass through unharmed, many of the lords suffered both physically, and in terms of their wounded pride, by being pelted with fruit and vegetables, as well as some more harmful weapons such as large stones.

Thus London, and its visitors, demonstrated its mass hangover on that Monday: the third of May 1641.

My main interest that morning was in what the Lords were doing. At about nine of the clock therefore I made my way to the gallery, from whence I beheld Lord Bristol desperately attempting to rally supporters for his campaign to prevent Strafford's execution.

"But three days since my lords," he was pleading, "this House was ready to reject this so-called evidence - which was suddenly produced after Lord Strafford's trial - on the grounds that it is manifestly tainted. It is not even original evidence; it is not even a copy: it is a copy of a copy, and while it was being copied any amount of substitutions and alterations might have been added to it. We have been through all this already."

"In the first place," answered Lord Manchester, rising to his feet, "my lord of Bristol has no right to say whether this House was ready to reject any evidence, whether 'so-called' or otherwise. Secondly, we cannot be required to make a decision, whether momentous or trivial, on the grounds that it might go contrary to such an abstract thing as a.... *conscience*.... even if the conscience in question is the King's."

"And thirdly," shouted Clunehaven (*sporting* - as fashionable speech would have us put it - a black eye) "there is a large crowd of people outside threatening to tear, limb from limb, anyone who decides to vote against the taking of Lord Strafford's life."

"Your use of the word thirdly,'" returned Lord Manchester, "implies strongly that you believe you were voicing *my* thoughts, and that I have somehow been persuaded by the mob. I have never made a decision..."

But I left them to argue amongst themselves. I still had no idea how the King intended to put his idea to the people, many of whom by now were well aware, from the rumours I had started two days previously, that some extremely unsatisfactory offer was about to be made to them. What I did know was that whatever he intended to do, he would have to do it quickly; for the violence earlier that morning had been reasonably good-natured, despite its extremity, and it would not have been possible for the soldiers to have controlled the crowd so easily had there not been at least some willingness on their part to be controlled. There could be no guarantee however, that the people would remain so compliant.

But as I left the building I discovered the answer to my question sooner than I had expected. I looked up and beheld, staring at the crowd in front of him like an eagle with his back to the parliament building, and standing on a high wooden box just behind the line of foot soldiers, a man I recognised immediately as a bishop of the Church of England, and whom I later discovered to be the Right Reverend Stephen Kerr, Bishop of Deal. It was easy to tell from his ruddy complexion that he was a *well...didn't Jesus-redeem-us-from-the-law?-come-on-break-open-that-barrel* type of Christian, although he was none the less ferocious looking for that. The crowd, used to living in awe (or fear) of high churchmen, had evidently listened to him in silence at first, but were by now becoming impatient.

"What *we* want to know," shouted a voice from the crowd, "is just *who is this* Yelvertoft person? All I have heard since the night before last is people talking about someone called Yelvertoft. We came to London for the execution of Strafford."

"It has now been explained to you more than once," replied the bishop, his voice seething with impatience, "that he is awaiting trial in the Tower of London for the murder of several children, something which he has confessed to openly and without shame; and that he is a better subject for your wrath than Strafford."

"Well why does only one of them have to be executed anyway?" asked one of the more intelligent looking members of the horde. "It's not as if, when some crime or other is committed somewhere, punishments are limited to *just one peasant*. Why, in this case, should the punishment be limited to *just one lord*?"

I could not believe that the King had failed to see this obvious flaw in his proposal.

"Because," replied the bishop, his temper still rising, "the law still states - whether it concerns a nobleman *or* a peasant - that we cannot be held responsible for the crimes of others. The case against Strafford has not been proven; and the reason that it has not been proven is that it consisted of no more than an attempt by the likes of Yelvertoft to hold him up as a scapegoat for the wretched state of the country. The real reason the country was in such a wretched state, meanwhile, was the tyranny of local magnates and landlords, such as the one we speak of."

I made my way back into the crowd a little and pulled my hat low over my brow.

"Yelvertoft is a righteous man," I shouted, "it is a lie; Yelvertoft is innocent!"

I think, in deciding whether to side with me or the bishop, the crowd made their decision based upon what was likely to lead to the most amusing outcome. But whatever their reason, they soon started to agree with me, loudly, that Yelvertoft was indeed innocent.

"Free Yelvertoft!" the people shouted, and, "Death to Strafford!"

At first these words were shouted in a good humoured sort of way, as if their purpose was merely to antagonise the bishop. But then something happened that entirely changed the whole nature of the demonstration.

You will remember that the people had been separated into two large groups, and that they were being kept in some semblance of order, both by the rows of infantry, and by two score of dragoons, who moved about the yard freely, keeping the crowd in check as well as looking for any potential sources of trouble. During the time I had been among the people several members of the Commons left the building, and whenever they did so two or three dragoons would ride up to the doors of the palace, surround them, and then escort them safely between the two main groups of demonstrators towards Tuttle Street.

About a minute or so after I had begun this latest altercation, three members of the Commons left the Palace, and were being thus escorted, when someone (who moments before had been hurling abuse at the bishop) yelled to the crowd to be silent.

He then shouted the question "What's going on in there?" to the members.

One of the three (none of whom I believe I knew personally, although my vision of them was obscured) turned his head without stopping, and replied "There is hot work, and a great fire within."

I have often since wondered whether that particular member (and I never found out who he was), said the very thing that he must have known would most inflame the people, or whether he was genuinely unaware of the effect his metaphor might have upon them. I hope to this day that the first explanation was the correct one, for I regard it as deeply preferable that our members of Parliament should hold the people under their power in the deepest contempt – detest them even – rather than be so ignorant of them. (If, good Reader, things have become so bad in society that *your* members of Parliament - whenever you chance to read this – are as badly informed and out of touch with the people as *this* member was, then I say to you: gather in your wheat, slaughter your cattle and run to the hills; look to the stars for signs of impending disaster, for the sandy foundations upon which your society is built are surely crumbling away from under your feet).

Whatever his intentions however, the effect of his words was like that of a lit match to a barn of dry hay.

"Parliament is on fire!" shouted someone.

"The Gunpowder Plot is upon us again!" shouted another.

"The papists want to blow up Parliament!" shouted yet another.

"Calm down, Parliament is not on fire…" the bishop shouted, but was then hit full on the face with a flying brick. He fell heavily onto the ground, and was dragged into the parliament building by the soldiers closest to him.

Within moments all semblance of good humour vanished as the mob started to shout accusations and counter–accusations, and to throw as many hard objects as they could find at the soldiers, particularly the ones on horseback. Many of these hard objects - which included bricks, metal pipes and clay bottles - missed their intended victims; but almost invariably as a result – due to the mass of people – hit someone at the far end of the crowd. These misdirected missiles did nothing but inflame the people even further, who then started to charge *en masse* at the soldiers, forcing them towards the palace. Before long the soldiers were compelled - as they had their backs against the palace walls - to assemble themselves as best they could for a pitched battle.

I could see immediately that I had no time whatsoever to spare in getting away from that place. The rioters made several attempts to charge at the palace, but were beaten back on each occasion by the cavalry. They in turn succeeded in forming two lines ready to charge at the protesters, and while they were doing this the infantry, who stood between them, aimed their muskets at the body of protesters, and fired.

Screams of death and terror then began to mingle with the sounds of protest. The acrid smoke from the muskets momentarily engulfed us, and the blindness added extra fuel to our fear. The soldiers spurred their horses forward through the smoke and started to slash indiscriminately at everyone in their path, knocking people down and then trampling over their prostrate bodies, as well as the bodies of several people who had already been shot. While this was happening, the infantry reloaded and then fired again into the crowd, concentrating also on the groups of people standing on the upturned carriages. As soon as the cavalry became separated they regrouped, and then charged again; and at this point the people began to run for their lives - most of them down King's Street - in the direction of Whitehall and the City of London.

While the dragoons were regrouping for about the fourth time, I made one desperate bid to break free from the crowd, and make it to what, I hoped, would be the safety of military protection. "I am a Member of Parliament – make way!" I shouted as I ran towards them, waving my arms wildly, as fast as my legs would allow me.

But instead of treating me as a refugee from the violence, two of the dragoons started charging towards me, brandishing their swords, and shouting "Mine, mine!" like two schoolboys trying to catch a ball. I turned immediately on my heels and dived back into the mass of screaming and panicking people, and with them fled as best I could, while all the time the soldiers hacked at us from behind.

It is strange when we recollect the thoughts that run through our minds at times such as this. I, as I took flight, thought that if I survived that moment I would introduce the idea of a badge or medallion hung about the necks, or pinned to the lapels, of Members of Parliament, containing a miniature portrait and signature, for the purposes of identification.

This petrifying ordeal ended sooner than I expected, for after we had been chased for about two hundred paces we were faced with at least two thousand people running towards us, yelling, screaming and shouting "Justice for Yelvertoft!," whilst brandishing a multitude of weapons and blunt heavy instruments. Whether the rioters who had been chased away from the palace had rallied, or whether they had been joined by others - or both - I did not know. I thought at first that we were going to be crushed to death, but when I looked around I saw that the dragoons had turned their horses around and were gallop-ing back towards Westminster Palace, with the mob in full pursuit. I took the opportunity to escape down a side-street, and having brushed myself down I started to make my way towards the Tower.

This journey was still fraught with danger, as the roads from Westminster and Whitehall to the City of London soon became over-run with gangs of marauding thugs, running away from Westminster in the direction of London, and other thugs coming in the other direc-tion, apparently drawn by the screams and shouts and clashes of steel, as well as the reports of gunshot. The majority of these men, realising there was a choice of direction to take, and with no particular aim or purpose in mind other than the delights and rewards of mayhem, started running in the same general direction as myself, towards the City.

I knew that it would not be long before the troops were re-gathered and reinforced, and I therefore deemed it wise to remain as far away as I could from the crowds of people, and to stay as close as possible to the river where there seemed to be less trouble; for a solitary indi-vidual, I thought, would be less likely to be killed, maimed or injured than someone in the company of others.

I walked hastily northward, and then followed the river around to the east, and arrived at the Tower without personally encountering any further violence - although the sights and sounds of it travelled with me for the whole of the journey.

The troops the King had stationed around the Tower were not hostile as I had feared, but were curious as to whether I could provide them with any information concerning the sounds of distant gunfire. I told them that I had witnessed great violence from thousands of peo-ple, who were clamouring for the death of Strafford and for the life of a certain 'Lord Yelvertoft' - who was languishing in some dungeon behind them. I then told them that this rebellion was being suppressed with appropriate authority by the militia; and that they would almost certainly be called from their post to help deal with the disturbances.

As if to confirm my words, moments later a captain of dragoons galloped across the drawbridge and spoke to the officer who had just addressed me, who in turn rallied his troops and ordered them to march immediately towards Westminster. When they had gone I knocked loudly upon the large oak door that separated me from the interior precincts of the Tower. This door was opened by a guard, who granted me access without hesitation.

I entered Strafford's cell, this time with an air of profound gravity; my forehead knitted into a frown indicative of pastoral concern. I also placed the palms of my hands together after the prayerful fashion of monks in the days before their equilibrium was disturbed by the religious innovations of Good King Hal.

He was on his knees with his back to me when I entered, muttering prayers. I stood behind him, waiting for him to turn around. But he failed to notice me, and so after about two minutes I coughed, and thereby managed to attract his attention. As soon as he had stood up I started to pace the room from one end to the other, with my palms still pressed gently, but firmly, together.

"My Lord of Strafford," I began, "- yes, pray - be seated. We have been hearing the most disturbing reports that you have been conniving your escape, and that, moreover, you have attempted to do so both with the corrupting power of money. We will leave aside from this examination the means by which you were able to make these attempts to cheat your fate; can you not see that it was this very sort of corruption that brought you to this unhappy impasse in the first place?."

"*Examination?*" was all he said in response.

I ignored him. "It was neither noble, nor Christian, of you to try to connive at your escape thus…. methinks - not that I would make any comparison between you and HIM - that had the Lord chosen such a weak path when faced with the cross the world would now be a very different and much sorrier place."

"*I* am surprised that *you* are surprised I should do something so wicked after your friends' revelations in Westminster Hall about my *true* character," answered Strafford. "You will forgive me, I hope: we should - you are correct - follow the examples set to us by the Lord whenever we possibly can. I know that you would never succumb to such a moment of weakness, but just for a moment the thought of my wife and children, whom I can never see again, interrupted my eagerness to have my head sliced away from my body in the national interest."

I hesitated involuntarily before responding, and then, turning to him, said, "Do you hear the distant sounds of conflict: the reports of musket and pistol fire; the far away, unmistakeable noise of many voices crying in anguish? This is your doing. The King has promised to save you...and you...you refuse to release him from the restrictions placed upon him by his own promise, even if it tears our country to pieces..."

"I *have* released him from his promise."

My astonishment at this answer could not easily be hidden, and must have been very satisfying for him. All I could think of to say in response was, "What?"

"I am still mystified as to why any of this is really your business, but I stated to him in a letter that he should in no way consider himself bound by the promise he made to me, as it was made at a time when he could not possibly have foreseen how difficult things would become."

"Doubtless you believe that the King will still be able to save you," I replied, "or that if he cannot do so your death will save the King. But once Parliament has had its way with you they will stop at nothing to wrest the King's power from him. The King shall only, after your death, be allowed to take advice from those appointed by Parliament. He will not tolerate this and you know it; and then? What recourse will there be for the King *or* for Parliament but civil war? The judgement of the Lord is coming swiftly to this land. The exalted shall be humbled and the humbled exalted. This country shall soon become a theocracy of the Wise and the Spiritually Blessed.

"It has never occurred to me that my death will save the King," returned Strafford, "I believe that my death will be futile, except in so far that it satisfies the malice of others. But I have misjudged you...a theocracy of the Wise and the Spiritually Blessed? I am surprised that you're so willing to cut yourself out of the picture."

"Your sarcasm avails you nothing. The monarchy is finished. The time for God's glorious republic is upon us! By the sword will this be accomplished!"

"If you will forgive me," answered Strafford, "you are speaking the language of the asylum. But so far as the abolition of the monarchy is concerned: make no mistake about it, you may wrest power from this king - but you will always have a king; the king you choose may not be a king in name, but he'll be a king nonetheless. The question you must ask is this: are hunger for power and the fulfilment of ambition better qualifications for kingship than God's anointing, and lawful entitlement?"

Not for the first time I avoided answering his question directly. I looked at him steadily and said, "In light of the fact that *this* King is now going to break a solemn promise by signing away your life in order to save his own skin, would you not agree that your loyalty has been somewhat misdirected?"

"If I believed that the King was going to sign away my life purely for the sake of saving his own skin I would agree with you completely."

"You have, perchance – you will surely agree - placed too much faith and trust in that which is transient; you have laid up treasure on earth, *where moth and rust doth corrupt,* and have neglected to lay up for yourself any heavenly reward at all."

"I cannot deny that what you say is true," he answered with his usual disconcerting frankness, "and I would, if I could, say to everyone, especially to those whose occupations involve them in matters of state: learn from the errors I have made... Put not your trust in princes, nor at all in the sons of men, for in them there is no salvation...now, unlike you, and for the very sort of reason of which you have just spoken, I still believe myself to be in need of God's mercy, so will you please leave me to my prayers?"

He then walked away and made to kneel, facing the wall at the far side of the cell. But before doing so he turned to face me again: "Forgive me, sarcasm *does* avail me nothing. I hope that we shall both find the Lord's mercy, and meet again as friends in a much better place."

He did not actually weep as he said this, but his eyes filled with tears. I was afraid for a moment that he was going to attempt to shake my hand, or, even worse, embrace me, but he turned again and knelt as he had intended, and I departed as hastily as decorum would permit.

• • •

The Lords, with a huge majority, voted for the taking of Strafford's life on Saturday the eighth of May. The King held out for another day, but so did the violence on the streets. Only on the following afternoon, when a hundred rioters broke into the Palace of Whitehall, did he finally relent and sign away Strafford's life.

"It will not be many days before my Lord of Strafford's condition is happier than mine," the King said when he had signed the warrant. He then let his quill drop to the floor, and, far too overcome with emotion to maintain any longer the façade of royal dignity, wept with abandon in front of the whole court, as well as the deputation from Parliament that had brought the Bill for his signature.

• • •

It is, as you know, the primary purpose of Parliament to maintain law and order. The day after the King signed Strafford's death warrant the House of Commons passed emergency legislation empowering the militia to deal with rioters as enemy soldiers in conflict, whether or not they were caught in arms. We also dealt most severely with all those who had been arrested during the disturbances of the preceding week. Pym stood up and said how deeply sympathetic the House was to their Majesties, but that we were pleased to inform her that sixty five of the infiltrators of Whitehall had been killed or taken up as they were forced out of the palace; and that the survivors would be held up as an example to any of the population who might have similar disorderly intentions.

"Hear, hear," the majority muttered, while nodding slowly and gravely in the manner of those who are used to hearing (but are none the less appreciative for that) words of wisdom and righteousness, both from their own mouths, and the mouths of their brethren and colleagues.

XXXV

Execution and thereafter

By the following Wednesday, the morning appointed for Strafford's beheading, all was again calm in the streets of Westminster and London. Not only had the rioting stopped, but the mood of the people had changed entirely, with everyone talking freely about the feasting and rejoicing, as well as the good lives they would enjoy, after the death of Black Tom the Tyrant. I left Westminster with Pym and a few others by barge at about eight of the clock, and upon our arrival at the Tower we were met with much in the way of cheers and slaps on the back, as well as eulogies, from the self-appointed leaders of the people. Some of these men were aldermen of the City of London, and most of them, as their attitudes made plain, were convinced that we would consider them 'co-workers' because of their resistance to the King's attempt to seize the bullion in the Tower the previous summer; and that we would therefore both desire their company and benefit from it.

This was quite frustrating at first, as they made us wait for about half-an-hour on the wharf while they recited poems and essays they had written in our praise, and in condemnation of Strafford, before we were allowed through. When we did start to make our way towards the gate it soon became apparent that there were at least sixty thousand people gathered, and that the aldermen were there to escort us, first to the place from which Strafford would leave the Tower, and then, when he had set out on his final journey, in the procession following him. They also told us, in their *fear-not-good-sirs-for-our-tongues-can provide-soothing-balm-for-your-piles* sort of voices, that they had reserved us 'the best viewing seats, on the hill just above the scaffold.'

What would have been almost as useful, but which the aldermen could not provide, was a prediction of when Strafford would appear. When we arrived at the gate it was fifteen minutes before nine, and we had to wait for a further two hours, with no protection from the toothless ejaculations of praise and thanks from the assembled swarm except for the canes of the aldermen, which they were most delighted to wield for the purpose of our comfort and protection.

We did however have the advantage of being able to see straight across the drawbridge to the main entrance of the Tower, from which Strafford was expected. I was, in fact, standing only a few yards from the place where I had my last intimate - and yet harrowing - encounter with Gwendolyn Smith. While we waited we were regaled with tales of how the aldermen had inspired so many people with their brave stance against the King.

One of them, with a strong northern accent, entertained us thus: "Nay, I said to Lord Strafford, nay. Thou shalt *not* take this money unless Parliament gives the say so, and thou shalt melt the bullion over my dead body." He then looked around the twenty or so Members of Parliament assembled, as if expecting us to applaud him. Receiving only silent glares in response, he added the words "I said to Strafford 'I know I talk blunt, but where I come from we believe in speaking our minds,'" before lapsing into a self-righteous silence.

But at about fifteen minutes past eleven the door at the far end of the drawbridge was opened, and a voice from the crowd exclaimed, "The wicked earl approacheth!" The crowd then became silent as two soldiers came out of the door and started to walk in our direction. As they were crossing the drawbridge they were followed by Strafford, dressed, as he had been throughout his trial, almost entirely in black. He was surrounded by friends and chaplains, as well as an Irish bishop.

They took a few steps in our direction, and then stopped. Strafford turned to his right, where there was a barred window just above him. He then bent one knee to the ground and bowed his head. A hand appeared through the bars and moved, shakily, over his head before disappearing again. Strafford remained on his knee for about a minute and then rose slowly to his feet. The party moved on in our direction.

"That must have been Archbishop Laud - I think that's his cell," said a voice to my left. I turned round and beheld the alderman.

So many times I had passed that cell, I thought, and I had never even realised that Laud was in there.

I remembered only too well the disappointment I had experienced at Strafford's first public appearance after his arrest, when I had furnished the expectant crowd with so much in the way of rotten fruit and vegetables, all of which were wasted as a result of their half-hearted inconsistency. I had therefore taken care not to expect too much from them this time. But even with this previous experience I could not have expected what was to follow.

The gates at our end of the drawbridge were opened against the crowd by two soldiers, who then proceeded to push the people back whilst shouting loudly for them to step to either side in order to form a pathway. At the same time, the aldermen, of whom there were about twenty, moved forward in order to help enforce the soldiers' command.

As soon as a fairly clear path had formed the soldiers walked back to Strafford's party and then led them through the gate; and the crowd, which must, at the very least in a large part, have been made up of the same people who had been rioting only a few days previously, lapsed into a respectful, nay – in some cases - a *mournful* silence, which was interrupted only by the occasional sound of *sobbing*! I, myself, on several occasions - all of which I have given an account of here - had found that the experience of being in Strafford's company was very different from anything I ever planned or envisaged beforehand. I could therefore understand, to a degree, the reaction of the crowd. But a sullen silence I might have considered reasonable, as this would have denoted a grudging respect for a fallen – but none-the-less detested - enemy… but this! At least (and had they done so it would not have surprised me) when we started to follow Strafford's party to the scaffold they did not start hurling abuse at us in his stead.

Strafford removed his hat as the procession moved towards the scaffold, and returned, with a slight inclination of his head on each occasion, the salutations and blessings of his well-wishers.

Now it would be easy for me to comment here that 'Strafford masked his fear well,' for how could anyone easily dispute such a subjective claim? But (and please forgive me for making again such a frequent reiteration) it is the purpose of these memoirs to tell the truth; the truth and no less, about my life.

So Strafford did not 'mask his fear well,' but rather looked as if he regarded his own execution with the same sort of trepidation as a forthcoming trip to the market.

But despite the lack of change in his usual calm demeanour, it was impossible not to notice something else about him. Just for a moment, and for the last time, I caught his eye as we took our places about fifteen yards from the scaffold. He recognised me of course, but there was no expression of enmity; and for the first time that disparity of power, whereby I had quelled under his gaze, was gone. I make no claim that it had shifted over to my side - merely that it was gone. It was as if the impenetrable darkness of his eyes had fled away, and that the window to his soul had been opened.

Strafford looked down at the block for a couple of seconds. He then looked around him, taking in the executioner, who was standing, silently in his mask, at the end of the scaffold nearest the Tower. With his back towards us, he then said his farewells to the people, who listened to him in silence.

When he had finished speaking, he walked about his companions, taking their hands in his. They then bowed their heads and started to pray. After a few minutes Strafford's chaplain read the following words from the Book of Psalms:

Unto thee O Lord will I lift up my soul;
My God, I have put my trust in thee: O let me not be confounded, neither let mine enemies triumph over me.
Turn thee unto me, and have mercy upon me, for I am desolate and in misery.
Look upon my adversity and misery, and forgive me all my sin.

Consider mine enemies, how many they are, and they bear a tyrannous hate against me.

Let perfectness and righteous dealing wait upon me, for my hope hath been in thee.

Deliver Israel, O God, out of all its troubles.

Strafford knelt as this was being read, and remained on his knees for about five minutes. He then got up and spoke a few words of comfort to his brother George, who was weeping extremely, before kneeling again, this time in front of the block.

His chaplain came forward and knelt with him. Taking hold of Strafford's clasped hands, they prayed together for one last time. He then stood up and stepped back. Strafford placed his head upon the block, and, after a few seconds, stretched out his arms. In one movement, and within two seconds of this signal, the executioner had lifted his axe and struck off his head.

• • •

The Demon Prince of Hypocrisy was riding aloft over London that day, showering the Capital with confetti; for it was, it seemed, only Strafford's presence that had prevented the people from displaying their joy at his imminent demise. As soon as he was dead the executioner lifted his head high into the air, and they responded with a thunderous cheer, shouting "He is dead; the Tyrant is dead!" This message was immediately carried away to the streets beyond by several riders who had been waiting at the edge of the crowd. The sounds of jubilation and mayhem could soon be heard spreading throughout the Capital.

I watched for a few minutes Strafford's friends and relations lift his body into the waiting coffin, before someone touched my arm. I looked around and beheld John Pym.

"We're going back to Westminster, now the crowd have started to disperse," he told me.

I looked once more at the people on the scaffold, and at the jubilant crowd.

"I will meet you in the Commons at about two of the clock," I replied, "I would prefer to walk today."

They nodded to me gravely as they departed, and I watched for a moment as they returned to the river. I then took one last look at Strafford's miserable relations, before moving off in a westerly direction.

It seemed as I walked through the streets of London, that a party was starting on the corner of every street, and that bonfires were being lit wherever there was space to do so. My progress was therefore slower than I had expected, and I soon began to regret my decision not to travel with my colleagues, for it was not possible to pass any of these groups of people without someone trying to drag me into some 'dance,' or force me to drink out of some spit-sodden wine skin. They also (and this was the most annoying thing) kept on shouting in my face, words like "England is free, the Tyrant is dead!" as if I needed *them* to furnish *me* with this sort of information.

I was therefore, by the time I nearly completed my walk, a little drunk; and had stopped to watch some revellers dancing in a ring around a bonfire on Fleet Street, when my attention was distracted by the sight of a woman on the other side of the road, standing apart from the revellers. I imagine that most of my readers will have experienced a sensation - when they see someone they recognise, but are not expecting to meet – of wondering for a moment whether they are beholding an apparition. Thus it was when I beheld Gwendolyn Smith. She was, as I have stated, standing apart from the crowd, watching the dancers, but taking no part in the revelry. Several men attempted to draw her in, but she spurned them all with a contemptuous flick of her head, her arms remaining folded in sullen disapproval.

I stood about ten yards in front of her, partially obscured from her sight by the dancers, and all I could do for about two minutes, not for the first time, was gaze at her; and even though she was not looking at me, her femininity, which was so potent I found it aggressive, reached out and thrust into my stomach.

"For too long," I thought to myself, "the devil has used this woman to mock me."

I watched her for a few moments longer until she walked slowly towards the entrance to an alley, which was on her right. Then, when she had got away from the main body of revellers, she suddenly disappeared.

I followed her carefully into the alley and saw her about twenty yards ahead of me. She walked on without looking round.

But I had just decided to hurry in order to catch up with her, when I realised that although she appeared still not to have seen me, she had quickened her step, and was in fact leading me northwards into a myriad of seemingly deserted lanes and alleyways, none of which I recognised. I then realised that she had not merely quickened her step once, but that she seemed to do so each time I tried to catch up with her. I was just about to make a dash for her, when I stopped abruptly in my tracks.

This encounter, I suddenly realised, was too coincidental...too contrived.

The moment that I stopped walking, Gwendolyn stopped also, and swung round to face me. She then placed her hands upon her hips in an attitude of mock defiance, although she was not laughing; and despite my confusion, the sight of her standing there; the sweat standing profusely upon her brow, causing also her shift to cling tightly to her beautiful frame, caused me momentarily to forget my panic.

But before either of us could speak, my view was entirely obscured by the figure of a tall man, who, having stepped from somewhere to my right, stood directly in front of me, facing me, with his hand upon the hilt of his sword. I looked up and beheld the face of Matthew Spencer.

"Follow me, Sykes," he ordered.

"No," I answered quickly, and, turning around, I attempted to escape in the direction I had come from.

But my way was barred by none other than Robert Heron, with his marble-throwing colleague from the Commons.

"Follow me, Sykes," Spencer repeated from behind me, prodding me sharply in the back. I turned to face him. He nodded to Gwendolyn, who, without a word, turned on her heels and started to walk further northwards.

"You are going to butcher me!" I said as I was pushed repeatedly forward. I contemplated the idea of crying out for help, but, as I could perceive neither sight nor sound of anyone but for my hostile captives, I thought it unlikely that anyone would run to my assistance.

"Be quiet, Sykes," he replied.

"That was a pretty murder, wasn't it Sykes?" Heron said as we walked, "and you had a ringside seat as well. We were not so fortunate you know. I don't suppose you noticed us behind you? There were quite a few people between us. No? Anyway, thank you for deciding to walk away by yourself, we'd have had to wait till goodness-knows-when to get you alone if you hadn't, and you were so easy to follow. Gwendolyn *told* us that she wouldn't have to do any more than stand there, and that you'd follow her. What does that *say* about you, Sykes? What does it *say* about you?"

Gwendolyn, who was walking about ten paces in front of us, led us into a stinking alley, full of fleeing rats and excrement. It was otherwise entirely deserted. Spencer grabbed the back of my collar and spun me around.

"This, Sykes, is a fitting place. I perceive, like the low-born coward that you are, that you are unarmed."

"I am entitled, as you very well know," I replied, "to carry a sword. I choose not to do so because I am a man of peace."

"A *man of peace*; he's a *man of peace*....Archie, give him your sword."

'Archie,' Heron's companion, proffered me his sword. I took it reluctantly, but let the point of the blade drop to the ground.

"Really, I have no intention of fighting you!" Having said this, I tried to run back in the direction of Fleet Street. I was grabbed again by the collar, and again dragged backwards.

"Fight, Sykes," said Spencer, "or I will simply butcher you like you said, like a pig."

"I...have...money," I pleaded, feebly.

"Don't be stupid, Sykes," said Heron.

"I can't watch this," said Gwendolyn, who had just walked over to us, "do you still need me, because I'd rather go."

"No we don't need you anymore," said Spencer, "unless you want to kiss him goodbye."

"But you swore you wouldn't kill him."

"Very well, I swear I *will* not kill him. One cut with the sword and a few kicks in the face and groin should satisfy our lust for vengeance. Now I suggest you *do* leave."

Gwendolyn glanced at me briefly, and then walked hastily away in the direction we had come from.

"Give him a moment, Matthew," said Heron as I watched Gwendolyn, morosely, as she disappeared from view.

"What for?"

"In case he wants to pray or something."

"*Do* you want to pray, Sykes?"

I could only look at him despairingly in response.

"Come on Sykes," said Archie, after a moment, "if you fight him you've at least a chance of living through this."

"Yes, come on Sykes," said Spencer. Robert and I tossed a coin to decide who fights you…I won. He then stabbed me lightly on my left forearm with the point of his sword.

"Then you *were* lying, weren't you?" I asked, unable to control my tears, "you don't intend to let me live at all."

"Yes Sykes, we *were* lying, although I promise not to kick you in the groin as well as kill you. And if I cut you before you cut me, I promise not to cut you again if my first cut doesn't kill you. That's not including this one by the way." So saying, he poked the point of his sword into my right nostril, and then flicked it out through the side, slicing my flesh in two about an inch upwards.

I screamed with the sudden pain, and involuntarily slashed at his face with the sword I'd been given.

"That's better," he said, whilst deftly parrying my sword to his right side, "try again."

I then covered my bleeding nose with my left hand, whilst with my right I jabbed and slashed repeatedly at Spenser's heart, stomach and face. But there was never any contest. He deflected each of my blows with ease, and, unlike me, did so with an air of studied calm. This went on, as I went round and round him – trying to reach him from every conceivable angle - for about ten minutes, until I started to become desperately tired. All this time Spencer had made no attempt whatsoever to take the offensive.

"Come on Matthew, stop playing with him – finish him off," said Archie, considerately.

Spencer then, and clearly with the intention of antagonising me further, started to address Archie, *whilst he continued to parry my blows without even bothering to look at me as he did so!*

"Do you think I should?"

"Yes I do. You're not a cat, and he's not a mouse."

"I suppose you're right."

He then turned back to me and casually stabbed me in the chest, so that his blade must have entered at least three inches into me.

I fell forwards onto the ground, gashing my forehead as I did so. For a few moments I felt a searing pain in my chest (my other wounds were insignificant in comparison). But then I also felt my heart start to pump the pain from my chest into every part of my body, like liquid poison; and I believed the pain was carrying death to every part of me.

I looked up and, through my blood and sweat, saw Matthew Spencer sheaf his sword. He then took a last look at me, gave a gesture of mock despair with his arms and strode away in the same direction Gwendolyn Smith had left twenty minutes previously.

"Check him Archie. See if he's still alive," I heard Heron saying, his voice becoming distant.

"I will find a physician if I can," Archie then said, his voice seeming more distant still, despite the fact that I was vaguely aware he was leaning over me. They then ran away also. As they were doing so the pain from my chest finally reached every part of me, and although I mistook it for death itself, I welcomed the feeling of my consciousness slipping away as if it was the beginning of a pleasant night's sleep.

XXXVI

Recovery

Many things, apparently, were attempted in trying to raise me out of my unconscious state: smelling salts, music, loud noises, and Goodness knows what else; but what finally awoke me was the stench of Brickett's breath, as he, with his hands under my armpits – and John Brown clasping my ankles – attempted to lift me onto a stretcher.

I moaned as my whole body racked with agony, and saw Aunt Meekness hovering behind them. I fell unconscious again.

This incident took place - I was informed later - a fortnight after Strafford's death, while they were lifting me into a carriage, within which my aunt, on the advice of a doctor, intended to return me to Northamptonshire. I had apparently woken several times before, but was delirious on each occasion.

I awoke again three days later in my Northamptonshire home, to the sight and sound of Aunt Meekness bustling about in my bedchamber. As soon as she noticed me looking at her she came straight over and started to dab my forehead with a damp cloth. I could hear her speaking to me but I could not make out her words. I remember thinking what a terrible effort it was even to attempt to understand anything going on around me, and I had a blinding headache anyway, so I gave up and fell asleep once more.

I awoke and fell unconscious again about six times in this manner before, on one such occasion, I was disturbed by the feeling of someone prizing roughly at my eyelids, and a male voice from the far side of the room saying "Shall we apply leaches, Doctor?"

"Don't be a fool," answered Dr Hair (for it was he who was peering into my eyes) the reason he's in this condition is because he's lost nearly all his blood already. Meekness, have you prepared that soup I ordered?"

"Nettle soup, Dr Hair, yes."

"Good, because if we don't get some food down him one way or another in the next day or so then he'll die, and he looks as if he's about to come round again. He is recovering from a severe trauma; and I have to say that I regard it as very unwise to have moved him here from London. Fetch the soup now please, and put a little butter in it."

"Water," I begged.

Dr Hair picked up a cup of water from the table next to my bed and placed it to my lips. He expressed no joy or emotion at the fact that I had just spoken what must have been my first words for about a month.

"You may feel as if you've been unconscious for the past few weeks," he said, "but we've managed to get you to swallow a fair deal of cabbage water in that time. You must eat now though."

As he said this, Aunt Meekness arrived. Dr Hair stood and she took his place. He instructed her to inform him immediately if she needed his assistance, and then left with his leech-recommending pupil, and I managed to swallow two mouthfuls of nettle soup.

It was a further week however, before I found the strength to sit up unassisted, and all this time the pain, which constantly racked my chest and my head, made the effort to speak unbearable.

For the whole of that summer of 1641 in fact, I did almost nothing but stare at the door in front of me. The most eventful part of each day took place in the morning and in the evening, when my aunt came to dress my wound and change my bandages. I believe that it was the sheer misery of this existence that made me so determined to recover; and recover I did - gradually.

I did not receive my first caller until the middle of September. I had been extremely disappointed not to have had any visits from my fellow Members of Parliament, and this had only served to increase my irritation at the number of requests I received for an audience from Trustworthy Fairweather, as well as many other people of purely local significance.

On the sixteenth day of September, my aunt, for about the fifth time, announced that Trustworthy Fairweather was 'awaiting in the parlour,' and I decided that I had better grant him admission, if only to curtail his continual pestering.

My aunt showed him in, nervously; and he perched himself in his usual straight-backed posture on the stool next to my bed. He acknowledged my salutation with a curt nod of his head, and then sat for about a minute in silence, his hands upon his lap, staring at the wall to the right of my bed, which was directly in front of him. This attitude was clearly contrived with a view to my discomfort, and I began after a while to become a trifle irked. I was just about to ask him to state his purpose or leave, when he spoke.

"I perceive that you find my presence – or, peradventure, my silence, somewhat infuriating. This propensity of yours for responding in a vexed manner to that which doth not please you is a sign that you have allowed your flesh to gain mastery over your spirit."

He paused, and while he did so I resisted the temptation to swear at him.

"However," he continued, "your irritation is also a sign of recovery, for which we must thank He-who-is-all-seeing-and-all-powerful, for thou hast been much in our prayers."

He paused again.

"Duelling!" he continued abruptly, "it appears that you have been duelling, and that this is the cause of the strait in which you now find yourself."

He looked at me, expecting a response. I returned his look with a silent glare.

"I hope you realise that when selecting – and not selecting – our members of Parliament, such matters as their morality and behaviour are taken very much into consideration."

For a moment I was alarmed, thinking that the King, during my illness, had yet again dissolved parliament, and that he had yet again been forced to call another one. I asked him whether this was the case.

"Nay…but…"

To my delight, my aunt entered the room at that moment and said, "Forgive my interruption. There is a gentleman here to see you by the name of William Strode. He says he is a colleague and a fellow member…"

"Show him in please, Aunt."

Having remembered, as soon as Trustworthy Fairweather made his brief admission that the King had *not* dissolved parliament, that one of our accomplishments had been to take away from the King the very power to do this, I turned to Fairweather and said, "I do not know what sort of company is kept by my fellow Members of Parliament when they are forced to reside in their constituencies, but for my part I have no desire that my colleagues should witness me consorting with one such as you. Now get out!"

"How *dare you?*"

"Just get out, Fairweather."

"If," I said loudly to William Strode as he entered my bedchamber, and while Trustworthy was still snatching up his hat and cloak, "that man would desist from his constant efforts to exert a false and non-existent authority, then I might be willing to show him a little more in the way of civility."

Trustworthy glowered at me before storming out of the room, shoving William Strode aside as he did so.

Strode, having recovered from his surprise at being assaulted thus by a stranger in high dudgeon, took the seat Trustworthy had recently vacated.

"Have you just come from London?" I asked him.

"Yesterday, I decided to do a little detour on my way north, so I stopped at the Dryden's last night, and trotted over here today."

"Well thank you for coming. I am desperate to hear what is going on, have you eaten?"

"Your aunt asked me that…no, but…"

Just at that moment my aunt came in again, this time carrying a tray with a bowl of nettle soup and a hunk of bread and butter, which she placed, with a tender smile, upon William Strode's lap. She then gave a sort of grandmother-like curtsy, and left the room.

Strode immediately placed the tray on the floor and crossed the room to the window with the bowl. He opened it and chucked the soup onto the lawn outside. He then walked back over, sat down, and started picking at the bread. "I did tell her I wasn't hungry," he said in answer to my reproachful look.

"The kitchen is just below my bedchamber, so she probably saw that; and you didn't even look. If you had you'd have seen that the washing line is out there."

"Well, your aunt's soup was a lovely shade of *Robin Hood green*, so will doubtless add a little panache to your wardrobe."

"Yes, very droll," I said, finding – to be truthful – his irritating humour a welcome contrast after the tedium of Trustworthy Fairweather's visit, and my weeks of solitude. "Please, you must tell me what is happening at Westminster."

"How long do you think it'll be before you'll be able to make it back?" he asked in reply."

"Well so far I have been unable to walk further than that chamber pot, but I am sure that I will be able to return within the month. Why do you ask?"

"Because Pym has been ranting about 'every vote being vital for every vote;' and unless you get back on your feet soon he'll probably ask some local dignitary to come and see whether you're fit to return; and if he decides that you're not then they'll declare you an invalid, and ask your constituency to elect some other reliable worthy in your place. Possibly they already have. Maybe your previous visitor came at Pym's behest to report back on your well-being...that torn nose of yours hardly adds to your beauty, by the way."

My right nostril, after it had been sliced with the blade of Matthew Spencer's sword, had been joined together in a most cumbersome fashion by the surgeon who had initially attended to my wounds in London. And now, although the stitches had succeeded in fastening together the two separated pieces of flesh, I had been left with an inflamed and somewhat repulsive scar. My nose had always been the one part of my face I had least liked to draw attention to, but in the light of Strode's comments I suddenly regarded my facial appearance as of minimal significance.

"I doubt," I said, hiding my alarm, "that if Pym had that sort of purpose in his mind he would send someone like Trustworthy Fairweather...are things very bad at Westminster?"

"Well they needn't have been so bad, but the people have always swayed easily one way or the other, and to be honest – and I did warn you - we went far too far. In the first place the only reason everyone was baying for Strafford's blood was because we suggested it to them; and once we had killed him, of course, we thought we could do anything with the King. There is also the small matter of Ireland. Strafford's 'divide and rule' method of controlling the Irish was all very well when he was alive, but now he is gone the place is ready to erupt.

"You are exaggerating, surely"

"I exaggerate nothing at all. And I also do not exaggerate when I say that a lot of people are beginning to sympathise with the King. Do you mind if I smoke?"

"Yes I do. What is causing this new-found sympathy?"

"I do not think the people altogether like the idea of their king taking orders from Parliament. What, they might ask, is the purpose of a king who is forced to obey the orders of a jumped-up bank clerk, or whoever Parliament decides to appoint in Strafford's place as his Chief-Adviser?"

I chose not to answer this question, so Strode continued. "There are three points at which I believe the dispute between the King and Parliament has become irretrievable: the first is that parliament intends to force him to sign a remonstrance, by which he would effectively cease to be king altogether in everything but name. The other points are contained in the remonstrance itself: firstly the appointment of advisers - I think the King would be willing to pay with his blood to stop Parliament usurping his authority in this way. The other point, which in my opinion has brought us to the brink of catastrophe, is the control of the militia. Neither side will trust the other at all with the power to raise troops. If Parliament insists on usurping this power then the King, I am certain, will gather in his loyal followers and declare war."

"And another point," I snapped, "is that the King is indescribably stupid, which, in my opinion, is just fine. Why do you keep on using that word 'usurping,' it is most irritating?"

"Because the raising of troops has been the King's feudal right since the Norman Conquest, whether you and I like it or not. To take that power from the King therefore is to usurp that power, unless Parliament wants to do away with it altogether – and I haven't heard anyone suggesting *that*."

"You sound as if *you* would prefer this power to remain in the hands of the King."

"Well....*better the devil you know*, and all that....look Sykes, I didn't have to come here you know. I only came to tell you that if you *are* going to get better then you'd better hurry up and do so, because a lot of the members are quite willing to vote with the mood of the people; and however much you think Pym worships the ground upon which you walk, if you're not there he'll drop you."

"Forgive me...please...I have been laid up in this bed for weeks with nothing but nettle soup and my aunt for company. What do you think the King will do next?"

"I don't know. He's in Scotland at the moment bartering his integrity for Scottish support."

"What do you mean?"

"I mean that I think he will not only say anything to anyone that they want to hear, but that he believes himself to be entirely justified in doing so. A perceived threat from the Scots for example, if he manages to get them on his side, might keep the puritan English in line; and then if the rebellious English are forced into line the Scots might be forced to come into line with the English, *etcetera, and etcetera.* I cannot prove that this is what he is about, but I strongly suspect it."

We sat in silence for a moment.

"I do have something of a confession to make, Sykes."

"Speak on," I said gravely.

"The cleaning."

"The cleaning?"

"The cleaning of the committee room; I was supposed to do the cleaning in the committee room. I said I'd do it."

He looked at me in silence, I returned his stare.

"Who *did* do it…it stank to Heaven?"

"A girl."

"What girl?"

"A certain young serving wench. She came to Digby and asked if we needed someone to do the cleaning for us. He said no. She came to me, I said yes. I really didn't want to bother with it myself, and she said that she was already employed as a cleaner in the palace."

"Black hair, blue eyes?"

"That's the one."

"And you left her alone in the committee room? You must have left her alone with all those papers?"

"Never."

"But it must have been her that stole the papers. She must have taken the papers and then brought them back with a smell of rancid meat on them."

"I think that *you* are in a better position than *me* to provide an explanation for the smell of rancid meat, and therein do I feel safe in making my confession. *I* never left my serving girl alone in the committee room, but I did, shall we say, enjoy her company there, on several occasions. The power to resist a girl with charms such as hers, even when she smells of rotten meat, is entirely beyond me, and I imagine she stole the papers on some of these occasions. She frequently gave me opium, which I had never tried before, but thoroughly enjoyed; and wine; and on more than one occasion I drifted off to sleep."

"You *bastard!* And you call yourself a Puritan!"

"No I don't, however, your response is understandable, as I am aware of your...*feelings* for this particular girl, but don't be self-righteous; and don't you dare tell anyone about what I said unless you want them also to find out about the screeching hag, and who let her pass by unchallenged into Strafford's cell a dozen times."

"Twice actually," I muttered, whilst inwardly boiling with jealousy and rage. "How did you find out?"

"I'm sorry, I just hear things sometimes. Now, I suggest we both forget all about this, seeing as we've both been made to look fools."

But I did not mind being made to look a fool half so much as I minded the fact that Gwendolyn had given herself to him, whilst she had done nought but mock me and spurn my advances for years.

But then possibly, I told myself – just possibly, she had not had sex with him at all, but had merely drugged him and stolen the papers; and after all, he had not actually *said* that they had, he had merely implied it. I did not want to ask him, and decided instead, emphatically, that he was too ashamed to tell me the whole truth so had exaggerated this tale in order to cover his embarrassment, as well as to make him appear more of a man. With these thoughts I comforted myself.

I felt the urgency, suddenly, of getting back to London.

"William," I asked, "for how long are you going to Derbyshire?"

"I hope not more than about a week, I have a little local squabble to settle - that is all."

"Could you possibly come by this way on your return if you're travelling by carriage, and give me and my manservant a lift back to London?"

"I will call by in about twelve days and see if you're well enough to travel. If you are then I will gladly take you."

And with those words he took his leave.

XXXVII

Ireland erupts

I was not ready to travel when William Strode returned, but I had enough strength to crawl into his coach, and this I did, despite the protestations of my aunt and John Brown. I climbed onto the seat opposite Strode, with his and John Brown's assistance, and told Brown to take his place next to the driver.

"Fear not, O worthy aunt of my notorious but celebrated friend," cried Strode to my Aunt Meekness, who was standing in the garden sobbing and wringing her hands as we departed on the road to Watling Street. "If he dies upon the way, I will send his corpse to you so that he may be buried among his ancestors."

The sound of her unnecessarily provoked shrieking accompanied us for about the first mile of our journey.

I did indeed nearly die on that expedition. Every jolt of the carriage seemed to shake a little of my life out of me, nor was Strode at all sympathetic, but rather sat opposite me, blowing smoke at my face and talking to me constantly. In the end I begged him to give me a small quantity of his opium, which he was smoking alternately with his tobacco. I swallowed a piece of the vile tasting substance about the size of two heads of a match. The effect, after a few minutes, was to make his chatter bearable, and even amusing.

"...I was supposed to be presiding over the trial," he said "but I couldn't help remarking upon what a very attractive young woman she was, and so I said to her, 'My dear, *you* can cast a spell on *me* anytime you like.' I don't think the mayor was very pleased with *that*...but she did have a lovely smile. I am sure she wasn't really a witch anyway – just a brewer of interesting potions, but I said..."

His voice, in the end, lulled me to sleep. This was a blessed relief, but it did not happen until the second part of our journey, when we were somewhere in the district of Dunstable. I was eventually woken by the sound of John Brown unloading my cases from the roof of the carriage, and realised that we had arrived at my home in Chelsea. I was slightly refreshed by my slumber, but still very ill. John Brown and William Strode placed my arms over their shoulders and between them half-dragged and half-carried me to my bedchamber.

This journey ended on the third day of October. I asked Strode to inform John Pym of my arrival in London as soon as he was able, and then, when I had been left in peace, set about recovering, both from my illness and the ordeal of my latest journey.

• • •

I was at first deeply offended, having received no visitors except for William Strode during my weeks of confinement, to find that there was no one willing to visit me or send me their best wishes even now, when I was back in London. This apparent dearth of friendship and Christian charity from my colleagues, however, had the effect of making me all the more desperate to regain my strength and return to Parliament.

I was fortunate that autumn, in that the weather was unusually clement; and I spent much of my first fortnight in London in my garden sitting upon a soft chair that John Brown had brought out to the lawn, firing a pistol repeatedly at various targets he placed onto the wall that separated my property from the river. I did this for two reasons: in the first place to occupy my mind, which for the past few weeks had received almost no stimulation. I was also determined to become more accomplished at fighting. I had received no training whatsoever as a child in the use of any type of weapon, and this was a considerable advantage held over me by my enemies, as I had discovered to my cost during my recent skirmish. When I found the strength to stand for a length of time, I also instructed John Brown to purchase two rapiers. With these two weapons we began to practise, as best we could, the art of fencing.

On the morning of the twentieth day of October I was waiting impatiently for John Brown in the garden (ready, in fact, to whip him, for he had been absent since I had got up from my bed). I had determined that day to return to Parliament, having woken up feeling considerably better. My annoyance therefore waxed quickly, and by the hour of ten of the clock I had decided to prepare my horse myself, and let John Brown suffer by means of his dismissal.

I was just walking round to the stable, when I heard the sound of the garden gate swinging upon its hinges. I looked around and beheld John Brown running towards me, breathless.

"Sir," he shouted, "Sir, forgive me...Sir; all is aflame with rumour and panic."

"What are you saying man? Stand still and speak plainly."

"Sir, the Catholic Irish are in revolt. They have been rampaging through the country, driving out the English and Scottish settlers. They say that the Puritan Members of Parliament in London are going to oppress their religion yet further."

"They're right there," I muttered.

"And...Sir?"

"Yes."

"They are also saying that they intend to restore to the King his sovereign rights, and...that they are acting under his royal warrant."

I stared at him for a moment, struck into silence by the significance of his words.

"Saddle my horse and bring it here...now!"

• • •

I found the House of Commons, as I had expected, in uproar.

Robert Heron was on his feet. "It was plain for all men of sense to see," he was shouting, "that the likely consequences of Strafford's mur'…forgive me – execution, were not foreseen, or even thought about, by the honourable Members present who desired it…"

This comment created understandable consternation amongst the vast majority of Members, but no one was able to come up with a retort more amusing than 'Silence, Heron!' or 'Rubbish!' The reason for this lack of wit soon became apparent: I could see that Pym, as well as all the heavyweights, was absent from the chamber.

"Where is Mr Pym," I asked an eager looking young member, who was taking advantage of Pym's absence by sitting in his customary position on the front bench.

"I believe that he is in committee," he responded in an oily sort of voice.

I decided, as I had been absent so long, to slip discreetly into the committee room in order to avoid (until the moment I deemed most appropriate) the attention of those within. This I managed to do easily, as several members, including Pym, Cromwell and Strode were all attempting to speak at once. Strode, at the time I entered the room, could be heard above the others.

"…For us, now, to act as if we believed that the King has instigated this Irish revolt would effectively be nothing short of a declaration of war."

"Exactly," Cromwell muttered.

"Oh *exactly*," returned Strode, "very brave I am sure, but you cannot have thought about the consequences. *"Do* you *really believe* that the King is behind this rebellion? And, even more important, do you really believe that the people will believe that you believe it?

"You're talking in riddles Strode, this is no time for your cryptic clattering" (this was Cromwell again).

"There is nothing cryptic or complicated about anything I have just said," replied Strode, "the people will not believe that the King has instigated the Irish revolt, they will believe that we are using the Irish revolt to destroy the King."

"There is nothing about the King's record, or behaviour up until this point, *Mr Strode*," returned Cromwell, "that gives us any reason to believe that he has *not* fomented this Irish revolt."

"Or his wife at least," muttered Pym.

"The King may or may not have fomented this Irish revolt, *Mr Cromwell*," said Strode, "but if the time really has come for us to take away all of his prerogative powers then we'd better make sure we keep the support of the people, and this isn't the way to go about it."

"Bugger the people!" retorted Cromwell, his voice rising, "we need control of the army – *then* we can worry about the opinion of the people."

A heated argument then followed, and I realised that there was no point in waiting any longer for a 'quiet' moment to speak. What was apparent from the short amount of time I'd been listening was that my colleagues, in my absence (nay *due* to my absence) had lost their sense of direction altogether.

"Gentlemen…Brethren."

They turned to face me, and the room became quiet. Pym, after a few moments, broke the silence.

"Sykes!" he exclaimed (you will have gathered by now that Pym was a somewhat emotional man, I was therefore unsurprised to see his eyes well with tears).

He stepped forward and embraced me, saying nothing at first. He then stepped back, placed his hands upon my shoulders, and, looking at me levelly (his eyes still full to weeping) said, "We have missed your wit and wisdom lad."

"And I have missed you all, good Sirs," I replied, "I understand that not a few of us have been afflicted with divers maladies; and that many of the people of London have suffered and died as a result of the plague. I therefore count myself in some way fortunate that it was merely the point of an evil man's sword that forced my absence from London."

At this jest most of the members laughed appreciatively, while some muttered words such as 'Good man,' and 'Brave fellow.'

"Brothers, with the greatest respect," I continued, "I must remind you that although we may be facing a crisis, it is our duty to manage this crisis; and in doing so we must behave in some measure as if there were no crisis at all. The Irish Catholics, it is true, have risen in revolt.

There are strong rumours abroad that the King has not only permitted this outrage, but that he has encouraged it. Gentlemen, I would suggest that it is our role neither to promote nor to discourage these rumours. The King - I believe I may now say in this company - has in many ways brought about this situation, whether he intended to or not. But Mr Strode is, I believe, correct in saying that an over-willingness on our part to blame the King for the Irish uprising will merely set the people against us. We cannot therefore accuse him openly – even now."

Unlike everyone who had spoken before me, I could not help but notice that my words were met with an appreciative silence. Cromwell and Pym - all of them in fact - (except Hampden, who was glaring at me as usual) were looking at me with an expression that can only be described as one of *awe*.

I continued. "Gentlemen, we have spoken of a remonstrance. There is no need whatsoever for us to make so controversial a step as to accuse Charles openly." (Pym and Cromwell here exchanged glances, and laughed silently at my bold impertinence in referring to the King in such an informal manner).

"We have seen that Charles is incapable of yielding to us on any point," I continued, "however much on occasions he may have pretended to do so. There is no need therefore to tempt the people to sympathise with him by making any accusations over this Irish uprising; what we need to do now is issue a set of demands that will seem at one time acceptable to the people, and yet which will, to him, seem abhorrent. The majority of the people may still love the King; and doubtless if asked who they are more ready to believe - Parliament or the King - they would side with *him*; but when certain questions are placed before them, such as: 'Do you believe that the King should be allowed to continue to rule by *Divine Right*?' Or: 'Do you believe that the King should have his way in all things?' then I am assured that they will resoundingly say 'Nay.' They will say, not only that they need a parliament, but that they will be willing to fight in order to keep the parliament they have. They are much better informed than they were in times past, and the demands, I would suggest, in this *Grand*

Remonstrance, need not be greater than the people can bear, in order for its demands to be too great for Charles Stewart to bear."

These words, as I had expected they would, were greeted with further applause by most of those present. Oliver Cromwell and John Pym, as well as several of the other members, surrounded me and slapped me on the back and shoulder.

"You see Strode," shouted Cromwell, "it's not really that difficult when you apply your wits to a problem…come on Sykes."

This was somewhat unfair, as my solution had been much more in line with Strode's words than Cromwell's. But there was no question as to which of these men truly carried the stamp of importance. I allowed Cromwell to lead me to the large oak desk.

I looked about at the members surrounding the desk for a few moments. I then spoke very slowly and deliberately. "Is there any man here present who can doubt that it has fallen to our generation to shift power away from the ungodly to the Lord's holy and elected representatives? Brothers, everything is now permissible, except for a direct attack on Charles. What I suggest we do at present is lay out the central points of the Remonstrance on the floor of the House of Commons: namely that the King should be advised, henceforth, by none other than those appointed by Parliament, and that the militia should be placed directly under our control. These are measures which will be tolerable to the people in general, whilst the King will find them impossible to accept. In the meantime, and less openly, it is reasonable that we should investigate the activities of Henrietta Maria and her Catholic courtiers, as I am sure that the encouragement for this Irish revolt, as well as some of the finance, will have come from *her.* She is not at all popular, and when the King objects to all these things he will be seen for what he truly is: a man who refuses to comply with the reasonable requests of his parliament, and who puts his Catholic wife before the interests of his own country."

Having said this I suggested that Pym should lay before the House the proposal concerning the King's advisers, and that on the following day Cromwell should move that the Trained Bands of the south should be placed under the control of Parliament. As far as the Remonstrance itself was concerned, although its contents were to be almost entirely based upon my proposals, I suggested that as their legal knowledge was vastly superior to mine, Pym, Hampden, Strode and a couple of lawyers named Denzel Holles and Oliver St John, should draft it into suitable parliamentary language, and prepare it meticulously for its presentation to the King.

"I," I said to myself quietly as I left them to their preparations, "will deal with the Queen."

XXXVIII

Lady Carlisle

The Remonstrance was presented to the Commons, and, as was inevitable (its measures being so extreme and unprecedented) it met with much in the way of opposition. It was passed, after several days of ill-tempered debate, with a majority of just eleven votes.

The ongoing battle also continued for the support of the general population, who seemed torn between sympathy for their wretched monarch (who had the sense, upon his return from Scotland on the twenty fifth day of November, to let the wine flow freely once more in the capital in celebration), and their parliament, who were taking such a brave stand against popery and the evil influences surrounding the King.

He, a week after his return, came to Parliament to answer the Remonstrance. As I expected, he objected to the Bill being printed and published before he had been given the opportunity to read it. He added that he could in no way be expected to answer it, let alone consent to it, until he had been given more time to peruse it properly, pray about it, and to seek advice as to how to respond to it in detail.

"It is reasonable, is it not" I whispered to Pym sarcastically while the King was speaking, "for Charles to expect his advisers to give an objective response to any questions concerning this remonstrance?"

"It's as likely as a child asking for the birch," Pym whispered out of the side of his mouth, "and what I object to is him expecting us to accept this. He thinks we're just testing him."

"He thinks we'll back down."

"He'll not think so for long."

"*I* think," I said after a pause, "that the person – or the people - who have the right to be confident in this situation is the person – or the people - who have the militia at their disposal. It is plain what he is doing: he is bidding for time while he hopes to ensure the loyalty of the Trained Bands."

"The Trained Bands of London will obey Parliament."

"But surely the orders of Parliament are powerless unless the King gives his consent to them. Charles will not agree to the Remonstrance until he has the trained bands safely under his command, and then he won't agree to the Remonstrance *because* he has the trained bands under his command."

Pym said nothing in response, so I waited a moment for the effect of my words to sink in, then continued.

"I would suggest that it is one thing for Mr Cromwell to raise this issue on the floor of the House. What we need is for the likes of both Cromwell and yourself to ensure that the trained bands will not waver in their support for our cause…you should address their leaders directly.

Pym's silence, it seemed, had denoted nothing but his acquiescence with my proposal, for as soon as the King departed he walked to the place Cromwell was standing, and started to converse with him quietly. I made my way discreetly through the assembled Lords and Commons, and slipped quietly out the building.

● ● ●

The house of Lady Carlisle was a place frequented only by greatest – if not the most good – of the Great and the Good. For an individual to be able to claim that he had been a guest of the most sought after and eminent Countess in England was an honour most fervently desired by the more hypocritical members of the Establishment, most of whom never received such an invitation. I could not refrain from congratulating myself in a small way therefore for the boldness with which I felt able to sound the bell at the front door. I was immediately, having given my name to the elaborately dressed footman who answered my summons, ushered in to the Countess's withdrawing room, and was told that I would be kept waiting no longer than five minutes.

But I had no time at all to enjoy my sumptuous surroundings before one of the doors was opened by the same footman. He entered and walked immediately to the centre of the room - to about five feet from where I was standing. He then looked at me haughtily and announced: "The Countess of Carlisle…" as if he were heralding her arrival to an audience of five hundred waiting devotees.

I cannot deny however, that this introduction seemed less excessive when the Countess, moments later, swept into the room. She was most striking in her appearance. Still beautiful despite the passing of her youth, her hair - with ringlets adorning her forehead - was arranged after the fashion of the time, and her blue silk dress surpassed, in sheer exquisiteness, anything I had seen since my arrival in the Capital. But despite the obvious care she had taken over her appearance, and despite her age (she was about forty-two), she had a sort of 'thrown-together' elegance that only those of true natural beauty can muster.

She stood in front of me for a moment with a smile playing on her lips, as I bowed before her. She then gestured for me to sit on an armchair next to a roaring fire. When she had arranged her dress she sat down at the opposite side of the fire. She then cocked her head slightly to one side, smiled at me mockingly, and said "Is your name really *He-died-for-our-sins Sykes?*"

"The ownership of such a name," I said gravely and carefully, "has reminded me throughout my life of the debt I owe to my Creator, and the means by which I can best pay it."

"I think – had I such a name," returned the Countess, "I would be reminded daily of the debt I owed to my *father*. Forsooth, I think I'd poison him! What a *screech*! I don't think I've heard anything so droll in all my life! He must be very, very puritan. Is that why you converted to Rome – to get your revenge?"

The Countess uttered this rapid series of comments and questions without pause, and ended it by giggling into her hand like a twelve-year-old girl. You may be sure that despite the mild humiliation of having my name mocked yet again, I was so relieved to hear her speak of my father as of one who was *still alive* (for I thought when she started to speak that she somehow knew I had poisoned him) that I found myself sniggering along with her.

"I have been instructed by the Queen," she said as soon as she had stopped laughing (which she did as soon as she saw *me* laughing) "to send for her wherever she is, whenever you request it. As your arrival here could, I imagine, betoke nothing other than such a request, I have already sent for her. She is at present at Whitehall, so I imagine she will be no longer than half an hour, unless she sends me a message to say otherwise."

"My Lady is most gracious."

"My Lady is most gracious," she repeated in a scornful tone of voice, and in a manner apparently designed to make me ill at ease. She then looked at me steadily, not removing her eyes from mine for a moment. I began to feel extremely uncomfortable.

"Would you like something to drink, Mr Sykes?"

"Thank you, no, my Lady."

"Or eat?"

"Again my Lady, no thank you."

"You are very serious, Mr Sykes (as if it were not *her* that had made me so). Peradventure, methinks, you are more in a frame of mind for prayer than food and drink. Fear not, although not of the Roman faith personally, I, like your cousin Elizabeth, am deeply sympathetic towards your beleaguered religion. The Queen is comfortable saying her prayers, with the aid of her rosary, in our presence. You are safe here to pray as your heart desires, and to converse openly about all that troubles you in the matter of the oppression of your religion."

"I thank you, Countess," I replied, whilst squirming in my seat as the perspiration gathered upon my brow.

There then followed a few moments of silence. She stared at me coldly, and after a while started to drum her fingers quietly on the table beside her.

"Well?"

"My Lady," I replied, "I have not been used to the security afforded to her Majesty. It would be a foolish person indeed who, at such a time as this, carried about his person the trappings of the True Religion without the King's protection."

"I was not necessarily suggesting that you produced your rosary. You are of course correct to be cautious. You may pray nonetheless."

I realised that I was going to have to obey her request, nay her *command*. I continued to shift uneasily on my chair for a moment, while she continued to stare at me unabated. I cleared my throat and began:

Our Father
Which art in Heaven
Hallowed be Thy...

"Not *that one*," she interrupted, "I know *that one*. I want to hear something else: something...in Latin.

This, for me, would have been one bluff too far. I could have tried, but I knew that I would be able to utter one sentence of Latin at best; and that even that sentence probably wouldn't have meant anything particularly holy. I looked at the Countess with a feeble and twisted smile, and lapsed again into silence. Not for the first time, as I sat there with streams of sweat pouring down my face, I believed myself to be facing an imminent death; this time because Lady Carlisle was almost certain to denounce me to the Queen as a fraud, and the Queen in turn was almost certain to denounce me to the King as someone who had attempted to use her as a tool against her own (and therefore his) best interests. I had already riled the King on more than one occasion, so I would not be able to expect any mercy from *that* quarter.

I decided to make one final attempt to rescue the situation by taking the offensive.

"Your Ladyship cannot expect an adherent of an already persecuted religion to pray for your amusement?"

"No - purely for our mutual edification."

But my fear and discomfort was then turned to confusion as the Countess started to laugh again. At first she tried to hide this by covering her face with her sleeve, but this effort soon became all but impossible to maintain; and, having lost the battle to preserve her severe demeanour, she threw back her head and laughed with abandon, and in a fashion that most good people would have considered unbecoming in a lady of quality. This time I was not so rash as to join in her laughter, and indeed I did not feel inclined to do so, as my feelings were a mixture of bewilderment, relief and irritation.

I therefore watched her in silence; and was forced to continue doing so for some time, as each time she made an attempt to speak she again became overcome with hilarity. My unrelieved embarrassment inevitably caused me to lose my patience, so I asked her firmly to explain herself.

"I think this is quite the funniest thing I've ever heard of," she eventually managed to say, and then added, "she really believes you, you know; how on earth did you know she's so *stupid?* I saw those letters and even I could see that they weren't genuine; especially as, for some inexplicable reason, the first one was written in Latin, and the second English, as if you had help with the first and had to do the second by yourself."

She looked at me levelly. *"Fear not your Majesty, your actions will carry the blessings of his Holiness*...do not worry *He-died-for-our-sins Sykes,* your secret is safe with me."

My instinct was to be astonished and delighted, but not a little wary of this response; my confusion was plainly visible.

"Please do not labour under a misapprehension that I like you, Mr Sykes," said the Countess, serious again, "I have no reason whatsoever to do so. I know very well that you were one of the main protagonists in the destruction of my Lord of Strafford. He was one of my very closest friends. I therefore have no reason whatsoever to like you, and plenty of reason to detest you, as well as your friend Pym."

"However," she added after another pause, "I have never been so foolish as to believe that it was anything other than a King's power that gives him his authority – or possibly that it is a King's authority that gives him his power. The one who holds the balance of power therefore is, effectively, the king, even if there is still someone else *called* the King. If Parliament, for now, has the power, then I, for now, will serve Parliament."

I was astonished at these words, and made to respond, but in truth there was not much I could think of to say, so was relieved when she stopped me with a motion of her hand. She continued speaking.

"I know little or nothing about what drives you, but I do know that there are many people of good birth and breeding who support you - or Mr Pym I should doubtless say – as you prefer to stay in the background, do you not, Mr Sykes? Mr Pym's support here in London is stronger than the King's, and I am concerned with the restoration of law and order. You may therefore know this much about me, Mr Sykes: I would rather give my support to those who had the strength to defeat Strafford than those who had not the strength to protect him; I also know that the King and Parliament are going to have to fight for the power in this country. But I cannot support a king who has lost control of his own parliament and his own capital. Believe me, Mr Sykes, a king surrounded by terrified, crying, women and children, with his fingernails chewed to the quick – completely at a loss since the death of his chief adviser as to what to do - is not a sight to inspire undying loyalty."

She then paused and, looking at me again coldly, added "You must tell me all your plans and how you intend to accomplish them. If you do not do so then I shall simply inform the Queen of what you really are. You have no idea how brutal that little woman can be. I once heard her talking about appropriate punishments for traitorous heretics and apostates. Her words were very revealing, and her views so...*Spanish*.

"The...most...important thing," I began hesitantly, "is to be sure we have control over the militia."

"There is little to concern us on *that* score. There have been so many plots - and rumours of plots – concerning Catholic uprisings, that the Trained Bands would certainly side with parliament should they be forced to make such a decision."

"Well then, your Ladyship" I said, waxing in confidence, "there is only one course open to us. We are – if I may be so bold – of the same mind. We must tell her Majesty that enough is enough; that it is time to deal with the rebellious faction within Parliament as befits the wrath of a righteous monarch. We must tell her to tell the King to take a firm grip of his country…to…even…arrest his antagonists in Parliament. We should put it into her mind that her husband's manhood can only truly be measured by the wielding of his kingly power. A truly *Catholic* monarch after all, would never allow his subjects so much room to vent their brazen impertinence."

"That's a wonderful idea," she said, her hands covering her cheeks in a motion of astonishment and excitement, "but…what is the King to do with them when he has arrested them…seriously? It would probably do no more than create another huge row and more riots…and, are you sure the King is angry enough to do this?"

"The King will do nothing with them - he will not be *able* to do anything with them - because they will not be there: they will have been warned of his intentions and so will have made their escape. The consequence, if he can be persuaded to take such a course of action, of the King not only entering the Commons to arrest some of its Members, but of failing in his attempt to do so, will cause all who have hitherto held back to rise against him.

"Which Members do you have in mind?"

"Well…not Cromwell: he'd refuse to leave. I was thinking…"

"You are very cynical, are you not, Mr Sykes? although I am aware that I might be somewhat hypocritical to criticise you for this. Did you know that Pym was in negotiation with the Scots while the King was trying to raise money from Parliament to fight against them? This, of course, is treason – *real* treason, not *constructive* treason, and it appears that Pym actually invited the Scots to invade England. I understand that the King is unaware of who – apart from Pym - is to blame for this."

But at that moment the Countess' footman again entered, and before he could say anything by way of an announcement, he was followed into the room by the Queen. We both, of course, stood and prostrated ourselves in the correct manner, according to our different stations.

The Queen smiled briefly, although it was more of a twitch really, and it was only a momentary break from her customary worried frown.

"Lucy…Mr Sykes, please be seated. Do not offer me anything. I am most fearfully worried leaving the children at Whitehall. I say to the King we must go to Oatlands or Hampton Court; but in truth I know not really whether we should stay here, for how can we know if when we leave, Parliament will incite the people to rise against us in our absence? Oh, I know not what to do…I am so frightened…and the King pretends to be brave, but in truth I know he is just as frightened as I. I know him you see…he is my husband. And how could he possibly accept Parliament's terms? I have seen him wavering, but what kind of a king could accept terms such as that from his parliament? You know that he found out while he was in Scotland that Pym and some of his colleagues encouraged the Scots to invade England? Oh but we…what can we do? But you have an idea, Mr Sykes? Yes? This is why you have called me here?"

This rant came forth from the mouth of the Queen so hastily - her only movement as she spoke being to sit down in a chair next to Lady Carlisle - that I believe she said the whole thing without pausing for breath. Both women looked at me expectantly: the one wild eyed with fear and stress, the other calm but with an expression of contrived concern.

"Your Majesty, there is, I fear, nothing left for us to – as it were – pull out of the hat. We have now seen - on far too many occasions - that the rebels in Parliament are bent upon setting the King's own people against him. His Majesty has spoken reason unto them, but these factionaries have used his words and his deeds against him, like swine trampling pearls beneath their feet."

"Or…trotters," said the Countess - unnecessarily (in my opinion) interrupting the course of my dialogue.

"Yes…trotters indeed," I continued. "The point, Ma'am, is that there is no longer any language worth speaking to these people other than the sort of language that is backed up with the point of the sword. You must now use all the means that are at your disposal to force the King to exert his authority."

I then looked from the Queen to Lady Carlisle, and back to the Queen again. I thought dark thoughts at that moment - thoughts as dark as I could conjure – in the hope that my visage would display a graveness borne of a mind filled with the gloomiest foreboding.

"I have heard rumours – I know not whether they be true, although I have reason to suspect that they are – that there are certain people about Parliament who are moving for the impeachment…of your Majesty.

"Oh Holy Mary preserve us! What is to become of us?" the Queen asked imploringly as she turned to the Countess, who clasped her hands in her own and looked compassionately into her eyes before turning to me, somewhat theatrically, for an answer.

"Your Majesty, there is no choice left but for you to persuade the King that he must take Parliament by the scruff of the neck and shake it. He must enter Parliament, personally, and arrest those who have set themselves against him - or their ringleaders at least. Your Majesty, the last hope in this country for the True Faith rests in you. They must not succeed!"

"But of which Members are you speaking?" asked the Queen, astonished. She looked at Lady Carlisle - who nodded at her slowly and gravely - and then at me again.

I thought briefly. "Pym of course, and Oliver St John; Denzel Holles…um…John Hampden, and William Strode. These people are primarily responsible for the antagonistic contents of the Remonstrance, as well as the move to impeach your Majesty." I then thought for a moment before adding, "In order to make sure that his Majesty does not seem overly partial to the Lords it would be wise for him to arrest one of their number also - one of Pym's supporters, but not too high in rank: someone like Lord Mandeville, rather than his father Lord Manchester. He can always release him later. There is no need for the King to do any of this before Christmas, as your Majesties' enemies would themselves fear the consequences of attempting to impeach you during the Season of Goodwill. But let us say in the New Year - a day or two before Twelfth Night should catch them unprepared. That would be a good time for his Majesty to strike. In the meantime you must persuade the King to show the country who is in charge. He should replace all those in a position of military authority who have opposed him openly, or who have shown themselves more loyal to Parliament than himself."

"You are right Mr Sykes. He is right, is he not, Lucy?"

"I fear that he is right Ma'am…yes."

"Your Majesty," I continued, "all the people want is for the King to be strong. It is not resentment against his Majesty that has made them restless. It is these rebels in Parliament, who have persuaded the people that *they* should be the leaders of the country rather than the King. Of a truth Ma'am: the strength of Parliament rests merely in the fact that it *seems* strong."

The Queen looked at me for a moment longer, and then stood and held out her hand, which I kissed reverently as I rose to my feet.

"There is, Mr Sykes – you are correct – nothing else to be done."

She turned to Lady Carlisle, who curtsied before they embraced.

The Queen then left the room as hastily as she had entered.

"*Impeach the Queen?*" the Countess said to me, one eyebrow raised.

"It is as easy to put such a rumour around Parliament as it is to breathe…your Ladyship has the full confidence of the Queen. I presume therefore that you envisage no difficulties in ascertaining with certainty, and therefore warning us well in time, for the Members to make their escape before the King arrives at Parliament? There is one thing of which we can be certain. If the King does make such an attempt he will most certainly arrive at Westminster from the Palace of Whitehall, as to do otherwise would spoil his perceived element of surprise. Time will therefore be short."

"Believe me, I am the only one of the Queen's ladies-in-waiting who has her total confidence. I was here when the Queen made this resolution. She will not do any of these things without keeping me informed. I, myself, will listen when bidden – and unbidden – and you will not be taken by surprise in this matter. In the meantime, Mr Sykes, I wish you well – and a merry Christmas. I shall keep you informed of all that I discover."

She did not hold out her hand for me to kiss, as was the fashion of respectable ladies when departing from gentlemen of rank, but instead gave me a casual wave before quickly leaving the room. Her footman then accompanied me to the door, and I marvelled at my fortune as I left the Countess's house. I began to think, as I made my way back to Chelsea, that if the blessings of God were to be measured by *destiny*, then my rewards in Heaven would surely be very great indeed.

XXXIX

Destiny

I awoke late upon the fourth day of January, and was deeply satisfied with the reflection I beheld before me as I burst an unwanted
boil above the scar on my nose in front of my looking-glass. Power, I
realised, was even greater and attractive possession than the skin-deep
beauty longed for by so many, owned by so few, and for which I myself
had yearned so deeply from my youth.

The atmosphere around Westminster, through all the days of
Christmas thus far, had been that of sheer tension. On the twenty
seventh day of December the streets filled once again with people, all
of them furious and terrified that the King was about give in to the
demands of his Catholic subjects – his wife in particular – by submit-
ting to papal authority in order to secure aid from the Spanish. This
rumour grew wings as soon as it was started, for all could see that the
King had become desperate to regain control, and he looked like a
man willing to try any means to do so.

A time such as this – as you will readily imagine – was perfect for
hatching a further rumour that Parliament was intending to impeach
the Queen. By now it seemed likely, nay inevitable, that things should
happen thus.

It was on the 30th day of December, as *this* rumour was gathering momentum around the Palace of Westminster, that I had spoken
quietly into the ear of John Pym while we were making ready to enter
the Commons.

"I have heard that the King may move to arrest certain members in this place on a charge of Treason."

His shock was plainly visible. At the same time I could not help but notice that his eyes contained a glint of satisfaction. "Can you be sure of this - which members are you speaking of?"

"Yourself of course, and Hampden – St John, Holles and Strode most probably, as well as Lord Mandeville. I have to say that although this news may seem alarming, it may be used much to our advantage if it comes to pass – so long as the King fails in his design; and I am certain that I will be able to furnish you with sufficient warning to make your escape. If the King does this the people will be so incensed - and the King will seem so weak as a result of his failure – that he will have no choice whatsoever to capitulate entirely to our demands – or declare war on his own parliament. Now is the time to make clear to all: parliament will brook no interference in the course it is set upon. It is well known that it is the influence of the Queen that stops the King responding to parliament reasonably. Let us make it publicly known that no rank or title will protect anyone who stands in the way of this reforming Parliament. Rumours are abounding that the Queen is to be impeached: let us give substance to these rumours: we must be bold, now, and denounce her openly!"

And so he did. It never occurred to Pym to question the fact that my information came from the most reliable of sources, as I had so far never failed to give anything but the most dependable advice in matters of intrigue. His wrath was kindled therefore, and he boldly and clearly proposed, moments after I spoke to him, that it was the intention of the House of Commons to impeach Queen Henrietta Maria.

Lady Carlisle had not failed to keep her promise, and I had already received a cryptic letter informing me that the Queen had so far not wavered in her persistent attempts to persuade the King to take the action I had recommended. I was told to be in no doubt that the King had indeed promised his wife that should he hear any direct threats against her, then he would not fail to act as a man and a husband – as well as a King.

And thus it was that I was awoken from my slumber by John Brown at half-past-eight in the morning, with a message that had been delivered moments before, and upon which Lady Carlisle had written the following words:

Today – definitely today afternoon – exactly as you advised Q. We've been up all night. K to P with mercs and any who'll help. River boat.
L.C

The meaning of this slightly enigmatic message was not hard to decipher, so I will not insult my readers' intelligence by explaining it. As soon as I had read it I called John Brown to my bedchamber. I could tell that he was expecting me to furnish him with another piece of information for the purpose of stirring up further trouble on the streets. He could not have known that this was to be no ordinary day.

"John, I am going to depart for Westminster after a hasty breakfast - I shall eat something left over from yesterday. You are to depart immediately for the Palace of Whitehall. Your purpose? Merely to loiter outside the Palace – discreetly – and to make haste to Parliament to inform me as soon as you see the King leaving. He will be making his own way to Westminster – almost certainly in the company of a sundry collection of professional soldiers, brigands and hired bullies. We must have time to prepare for his reception. I am laying this responsibility upon you, and you will be rewarded handsomely if all goes well. Go – make haste!"

And so he did, and I, having seized a leg of ham from the kitchen table, left the house. I quickly harnessed and mounted my steed, and cantered to Westminster, eating as I did so.

By the time I arrived it was half past ten of the clock. I went immediately to the back of the Palace to Westminster stairs, where there were several boatmen standing idly by. I called one of them up.

"I am hiring you, at least for the morning," I told him, "and I will pay you a whole shilling for your trouble; but be aware of this: you are to wait here until Mr John Pym, and any he brings with him – there will be six of them altogether – descends these stairs. You must then take them to the City. This is a matter of the most vital importance, which means that you must not leave your position for a moment – even to relieve yourself. I do not envisage that they will be here any later than half an hour from now. Keep on the red cap you are wearing for the purpose of identification."

He nodded and touched his cap to show his willingness. I told him that I would instruct my colleagues to pay him in addition, if he should prove worthy. I then tossed him his shilling and entered the palace through the entrance on the side facing the river, through which – all being well – my colleagues would depart shortly afterwards. I then walked straight to the Commons. As I entered Hampden was speaking. I made my way discreetly to the bench behind John Pym, and having ascertained that Strode, Holles and St John were also in the Chamber, I leant forward and whispered to him urgently.

"It is *today* – it could be any moment! The King is coming here to arrest you, as well as the other members I warned you of."

"You are *sure* it is today?"

"I am certain. Has Lord Mandeville been warned also?"

"He has."

"Then I shall get a message to him to meet you and the others at the bottom of Westminster stairs ten minutes from now. There is a boatman waiting there, wearing a red cap, who has already been paid to take you to the City."

"Were that England could be made of men like you," Pym said as, momentarily clasping my hand, he stood to his feet. As I made my way towards the door I saw him cross to where Hampden was standing. Pym did not wait for him to stop speaking, but started to tug at his sleeve, nodding to the Speaker in an apologetic manner as he did so. Hampden stopped, turned to Pym, and then listened as he whispered into his ear. They then started to walk slowly together towards where I was standing, gesturing discreetly for Strode and the others to follow them, the confused voices of the other members growing in volume as they did so. I left the Chamber and made my way hurriedly to the House of Lords, where I quickly located the Gentleman Usher of the Black Rod, and asked him humbly but urgently to inform Lord Mandeville that Mr Pym wished to see him on a vital matter at Westminster stairs. This done, I made my way to an upstairs window with a view of the river. Five minutes later I saw my colleagues, as well as Lord Mandeville, descend the stairs, enter the red-capped boatman's vessel, and make their way down river. I returned to the House of Commons. As I entered the Chamber Cromwell was speaking.

I had only been there a few moments however, when one of the palace servants entered and, having located me, informed me that there was a man named John Brown waiting for me outside the palace with an urgent message. I found him pacing the floor.

He ran over to me as soon as he saw me.

"He is coming – he is on his way here now!"

"How many?"

"Three, maybe four hundred... possibly."

"Armed?"

"All of them. The King himself is dressed in armour. He is coming by carriage. The rest are riding or walking."

"Well done John. Go out and tell as many people as you can what is happening. Go – make haste!"

So John departed back to the streets, and I returned to the Commons to wait. Cromwell was still on his feet as I entered, although he was being shouted at by Witherington.

"... The Remonstrance may well have been passed in this House, but until it is signed by the King its future is uncertain; and while its future is uncertain the measures contained within cannot be acted upon. It is therefore unlawful to take control of the Militia out of the hands of the King without the King's authority. As for this preposterous – this treasonable – notion that the Queen should be impeached: where is this all to end? Where..."

"The Honourable Member would do well to remember," interrupted Cromwell, "that since the first King was chosen for the nation of Israel the very notion of Kingship has rested upon the consent of the people. I, for one..."

But that sentence was never finished. The doors of the main entrance to the Chamber were at that moment thrown open. About a dozen officers – professional soldiers – marched into the chamber. They were followed by about eight untitled courtiers (the lords were all in the Upper House), all of whom had their swords drawn, and several of whom were carrying pistols. While the Members sat in shocked silence the soldiers took up positions in front of them and facing them; and the men following started to walk up and down the Chamber, brandishing their weapons.

Speaker Lenthall rose to his feet. "What is the meaning of this? Do you know the penalties for transgressing the privileges of this House? What is your purpose here?"

But one of the courtly brigands answered "Sit down, Sir. Be aware, all of you, that I am a good shot. Sit down Sir," he repeated, this time to Cromwell.

Cromwell did sit down – I was behind him with about two men between us – and as he did so he said that this was an unprecedented breach of privilege that would not go unpunished.

"Hear, hear," muttered some of the less terrified Members.

"That fellow's a *Catholic*," said a Member to my left, "he's one of the Queen's household!"

But the Chamber again fell silent as the sound of marching became audible for a second time from the passage outside. This time it was plain that there were a large number of people about to enter. As the tension increased several of the Members started to place their hands discreetly upon the hilts of their swords, believing, as I think they did, that the initial invasion had merely been a precursor to an all-out attack – almost certainly the Catholic uprising they had feared for so long.

I will leave to your own imagination, my most valued and treasured Reader, the expressions on the faces of the members when, moments later, in the middle of a train of about fifty men of sundry description, walked the King. It was the effect of shock - rather than respect - that gave him an entirely captive and silent audience. Had it been regard for the King that silenced the Members then they would have removed their hats. Very few of them did so.

The King made his way past his soldiers to the Speaker, his eyes discreetly roving the Chamber. His expression, which had been that of boldness and determination as he entered, soon became one of thinly disguised alarm and dismay, as he realised that Pym and the others were absent.

Maintaining his composure, however, the King nodded gravely to Cromwell, and then addressed the Speaker.

"Sir, I must make free with your chair."

Lenthall stepped aside. The King removed his hat and sat down. When everyone had again become silent the King began to speak.

"I must declare unto you here that, albeit no king that ever was in England has been more careful of your privileges than I am...you must know, as has been stated in this place on many occasions, that in cases of treason no person has a privilege...I see," he said, again scanning the Chamber, "all the birds are flown. I do expect that you will send them unto me as soon as they return here...but, I assure you on the word of a king, I never did intend any force, but shall proceed against them in a legal and fair way."

This last sentence was spoken in such a nervous fashion, and was punctuated with so much stuttering, that the Members started muttering again while the King was still speaking. As soon as he had finished his sentence, someone shouted "Privilege!"

The King, studiously ignoring the interruption (the boldness of which, like the King's entry into the Commons itself, was unprecedented) turned to Lenthall.

"There are several members of this House who appear to have absented themselves, Mr Speaker.".

Lenthall fell to his knees. "May it please your Majesty, I have neither eyes to see nor tongue to speak in this place, but as the House is pleased to direct me, whose servant I am here."

Now that was brave, and the King appeared to acknowledge this by giving Lenthall a barely perceptible nod of his head. His face was ashen, and as he stood up the sounds of the enraged people could be heard gathering outside, fired up – I doubted not – by my manservant.

"Well, well," he said with what looked like a flickering smile (if it was, it disappeared from his face in a second), "'tis no matter. I think my eyes are as good as another's."

And with those words he hastily left the Chamber, his confused followers – still waving their weapons around – following in his wake, with shouts of 'Privilege!' ringing in his ears. I caught sight of Richard Sykes and Robert Heron, sitting together, looking stunned and horrified.

I sat back, unable to control the laughter that started to convulse me. Almost all the Members except me were on their feet. I could hear Cromwell shouting among the uproar that the King had made a declaration of war. I covered my face and laughed and laughed until I thought my sides would split; then I carried on laughing until I thought I might die of it, but still I carried on laughing. Finally I laughed so much that the old wound in my eye, caused by Gwendolyn with the burning candle, reopened, and the puss started running again down my cheek. That stopped me. There is always *something* to spoil my pleasure.

The King, I was afterwards told by John Brown, had his coach rocked, and several stones thrown at him, as he and his soldiers fought their way through the crowds to the Queen and the Royal Children. He then tried to make his way to the Guildhall in the hope of finding the 'escaped birds,' but was beaten back to Whitehall by the hostile crowds. The trained bands of London refused to come to his aid, declaring instead for Parliament within a matter of two days. The King was forced to flee with his family to Hampton Court, then from London altogether in order to raise an army.

London, and the towns and villages round about, belonged to Parliament.

· · ·

As I rode home, on the same evening the Royal family fled London, I was in a joyful, contemplative mood, despite my newly reopened eye-wound. I was deeply satisfied with all I had accomplished since that sunny day upon which these memoirs began.

As I was thus musing, I chanced upon Compromise-not-at-all Jenkins and his followers giving a young Anglican curate, whom they had already beaten to the ground, a thorough and most violent kicking.

"Lads," I said to them – they spun round to face me. I dismounted. "I am going north to raise troops for the army. The time has come, brethren. Join me."

Compromise-not-at-all stepped over the prostrate – and by now unconscious – cleric, and approached me, his eyes full to weeping. He placed his hands upon my shoulders, while Flee sin and the others gathered around us.

"I doubted you," he said, the tears starting to cascade down his cheeks, "I once actually doubted you."

I allowed him to embrace me, then remounted and resumed my journey.

"We *will* follow you," cried Jenkins after me.

"Rats," I thought as I rode on... "No better than filthy, disease carrying vermin."

How calm the streets were that night, despite the sounds of distant screaming and gunfire: a combination of sound which gave rise to a tranquillity of mind so perfect for the contemplation of my destiny.

THE END.

My eyes and my writing hand are tired. I have, it seems, been writing for weeks, so determined am I to relate my tale before I make my own acquaintance with the executioner's block. I must now rest a while, however, before I continue my story. *Adieu* for now. *Perceptum ex meus errata*

Printed in Great Britain
by Amazon.co.uk, Ltd.,
Marston Gate.